TAKEDOWN

TAKEDOWN

Taming
JOHN WESLEY HARDIN

An Erotic Novel by

⇥ DALE CHASE ⇤

LETHE PRESS
MAPLE SHADE, NEW JERSEY

Published in 2013 by Lethe Press, Inc.
118 Heritage Avenue, Maple Shade, NJ 08052 USA
lethepressbooks.com / lethepress@aol.com
ISBN: 978-1-59021-516-6 / 1-59021-516-8
e-ISBN: 978-1-59021-517-3 / 1-59021-517-6

This novel is a work of historical fiction. It is not intended, and should not be read, as either history or biography. Characters, places, and incidents are products of the author's imagination or are used fictitiously. Names of certain historical figures and aspects of their biographies have been used to add verisimilitude to fictional characters in a made-up story.

Set in Caslon, Windsor, and Wanted LET.
Cover and interior design: Alex Jeffers.
Front cover: "Hands of a Prisoner" © BortN66 – Fotolia; tintype portrait of young John Wesley Hardin by an unknown photographer.
Back cover image: Duncan Walker.

LIBRARY OF CONGRESS CATALOGING-IN-PUBLICATION DATA
Chase, Dale.
Takedown : taming John Wesley Hardin / An erotic novel by Dale Chase.
    pages cm
ISBN 978-1-59021-516-6 (pbk. : alk. paper)
1. Gay men--Fiction. I. Title.
PS3603.H37933T35 2013
813'.6--dc23

2013030974

This book is dedicated to the gay and lesbian literary community which has welcomed me with open arms from the very first.

AUTHOR'S DISCLAIMER

This is a work of fiction that, for the most part, dramatizes historical fact. Liberties have been taken where facts might interfere with a good yarn.

CHAPTER ONE

I knew better than to love a desperado. That particular enterprise had landed me in the Huntsville, Texas, prison although the courts insisted it was for murder. I'd served three years when John Wesley Hardin, the notorious gunman, was captured by the Texas Rangers, convicted of murder, and sent to Huntsville. He'd killed thirty-two men, but his twenty-five-year sentence was for dispatching just one. I'd killed but one man, and suffered the same term.

You could not be a Texan and not know of John Wesley Hardin. He started killing men at fifteen and continued for ten years, all the while eluding capture mainly due to extensive family who sheltered him. His winning ways also helped. Too many sheriffs caught him only to let him go, while too many others simply turned their heads. Even Bill Hickok up in Abilene allowed Hardin to keep his guns in town, which went against local ordinance. When Hardin came into Huntsville, you'd have thought the governor was paying us a visit, such was the fuss.

We'd known of his capture for over a year, knew also that he'd sat in the Austin jail while appealing his sentence. When that was denied, he was moved under heavy guard to the prison with word of his imminent arrival preceding him. Talk ran through the shops and yard as to his reputation and manner, everyone seeming to have a handle on him. I couldn't understand the stir so I decided to try and get a look as he came in, mainly to confirm people were acting silly.

A burly guard named Duggan liked me to suck his dick on occasion which I did as I enjoyed all aspects of men, even those who had charge of me. There was also a benefit to the practice as a satisfied guard grew lax in his duties. Duggan had learned my preference one morning when he looked in and saw me and lifer Jim Scanlon fucking in our cell. From then on, Duggan couldn't wait to get it out and into my mouth, and I obliged as he was generous after letting go a load. So the day before Hardin's expected arrival, I approached him in the wheelwright shop where I worked and which he oversaw.

"I hear Hardin is expected tomorrow," I said. "I'd like to see him come in. Think you can arrange that?"

Duggan, a dark and formidable fellow looking more so in his blue uniform, reached down to adjust his privates. He said nothing, just turned to the room where were kept supplies. I followed. Once behind the closed door, he set aside his shotgun, knowing I wouldn't go for it, unbuttoned his pants, and got out his dick. He had a good one, I'll give him that, thicker than any I'd seen, and it was already coming up hard at just the notion I'd swallow his stuff. He took it in hand and pulled some, nodding his head to indicate for me to kneel, as if I didn't already know the position.

He then let go his thing, and I began to suck the knob, tasting his juice which was already dribbling. He obviously hadn't been abusing himself, which I suspect was due to his knowing I'd take him whenever he wished. As I sucked, my tongue worked down his shaft and he started to squirm which meant he wouldn't last long. Soon as I began to bob on him he began to moan, and it was but a few seconds before he cried out and spurted into my throat.

I swallowed it all down as I was used to spunk, what with taking Jim Scanlon's those times he didn't spend in my butthole. I didn't mind the taste because I liked a man coming in me in whatever hole he chose. Duggan thrust his prick into my throat, and I didn't gag as I'd learned in my trail-riding days how to open to a dick. Thus Duggan fucked my mouth and I let him do it until he went soft and pulled out. He then leaned against a shelf, breathing heavily and with no concern toward my needs. My prick was up, but no guard would stoop to pleasuring a prisoner.

"I'll hear what time Hardin is coming in tomorrow and have Nash send you to the blacksmith with a cart of wheels," Duggan said. "You can see him then."

"I appreciate that, Mr. Duggan." I knew Nash, the foreman, would do whatever Duggan said.

Duggan tugged his dick, then stuffed it back into his pants, buttoned up, and left. He allowed me some minutes so I could bring myself off if I wanted, but today I didn't want. Hardin was upon me in some way I couldn't define, and I was not about to give him any come.

Work ended at four o'clock, after which we had an hour in the yard before supper. This day you couldn't turn around without hearing Hardin's name as fellows blew hot air about besting him at poker over in Comanche or escaping his bullet down Gonzales way. Oren Glaser insisted he'd seen Hardin's capture until Ned Lally pointed out Oren had never been out of Texas and Hardin had been captured in Florida, not to mention Oren had been in prison when Hardin was taken. This got them swearing while others laughed, and I moved off as I stayed clear of any and all unrest.

My cellmate Jim stood talking with two other lifers and I didn't go over. Earl Herrick was around fifty and said to have strangled his wife when found in bed with his brother who Earl then shot in the head and the dick. Van Tolbert looked younger than Jim though I knew him five years older. He'd led a gang of bank robbers and killed seven men and one child. I think it was the child that got him life since Hardin killed far more yet got only twenty-five. I knew these lifers gave comfort to Jim as they would never move on.

While Jim had his lifer friends, I had two fellows I was close to, both having come in with me. I'd gotten to know them in the Austin jail, Lonnie Laird, a kid who said he hadn't done the crime, and Bob Tinney who said he had. Bob was a wrecked thirty-eight who'd killed a man over a horse deal gone wrong. He now came over to me. "You hear Hardin's headed our way?"

"Can't help but hear. Due tomorrow, I believe."

"They say he knows Captain McCulloch from trail riding days," Bob said. "You believe that?"

"Don't doubt it. McCulloch wasn't always running a prison. Maybe he ran an outfit to Abilene just like Hardin did."

"Might get Hardin privileges."

"I do doubt that," I countered. "More likely they'll make a show the other way and work toward breaking him."

"You think such a man can be broke?"

I couldn't help but sigh at such talk. "Look at us, Bob. We're all broke. Hardin might take longer is all."

"Said to be the best shot in Texas," Bob went on.

"Well, that's all over now."

I moved off as I wanted no more of John Wesley Hardin. He was already too much around and not even arrived so I kept moving, walking the yard's edge, guards ever watchful. They were stationed at pickets on the fifteen-foot-high brick wall and more manned the bulky tower where resided a Gatling gun. Still others were down with us, blue uniforms skirting a sea of stripes. The exercise yard was not spacious, but we didn't care. It provided time on our own and a stretch of the legs along with sun in good weather. It was October now, heat lingering into fall but absent the stifling damp that cursed the summer. Almost pleasant, save for guards, guns, and walls.

When the steam whistle blew for supper, Jim found me and we lined up as we were made to march to and from meals, each man with a hand on the shoulder of the man in front. Jim had never declared that I must eat beside him, but it became a practice for breakfast and supper. Meals were taken amid an enforced silence as some superintendent early on had decided this proper and it had stuck. If a man was in distress or needed something, he used a given hand signal to call attention. Thus Jim and I ate in quiet, the low racket of forks and spoons our sole accompaniment.

After supper we were allowed the library or chapel or we could remain in our unlocked cells. At quarter of eight, the lockdown whistle blew and at eight o'clock we were locked in. At nine candles were snuffed and the rule of silence began. Each cellblock row had a guard room down at the end and the silence rule was followed until their doors were heard to slam. Once absent guards, the men began to call out their anger and frustration. Hate and venom were liberally spewed, men going on about injustice and what they meant to do to Bob McCulloch and other officials. Sexual terms always entered into this which no doubt relieved the men of some physical tension. Occasionally there came a scream or cry. I didn't want to know what prompted these.

This particular night, with Hardin on the horizon, I found Jim especially quiet. I knew not to press as he had his moods and lifers deserved room. I had a book from the library, and commenced to lie in my upper bunk and attempt to read on whaling ships, eager to be elsewhere for a while, at least in mind. After a bit I gave up and closed my book because a man down the row was calling out he was going to fuck Bob McCulloch with an ax handle, and this got others chiming in with all manner of nasty things. Noise about sexual practices continued to such extent they caused my thoughts to wander to the bunk below.

Jim Scanlon was a sorry man, though he never said he was. Imprisoned at fifteen for murdering his sleeping father, he bore the look of a fellow long done with living yet forced to endure. It was said he offered no defense to the killing and had hoped to hang, but the jury took pity and gave him life instead. Though he wouldn't speak of his crime, he said more than once it was a jury of fools.

4

Jim was now thirty, a lean and hard man who wore tribulation on his face. I could see he'd once been handsome, though he was now creased by the lines of a man ten or even twenty years older. He looked like a cowhand too long on the range, lips thin and grim, hair gone gray. The whole of him was aging too fast except for his blue eyes which gave off a spark even he couldn't diminish. Something still burned hot within. I do believe I was placed in his cell to see firsthand what years inside did to a man.

Jim had been gruff at first, but I learned from others this was mostly due to an attachment he had formed to a former cellmate who finished his term and was released. I couldn't help but speculate on the lifer's plight as he would see many a man come and go. Jim was a good lesson on heartache, much as was Frank McGann, the bank robber who'd led me astray and the only man I ever loved.

Jim stood around six feet or so which I envied, what with me being but five foot nine. He moved somewhat slowly, but I found this more stealth than age. He'd learned care in his surroundings. He'd also earned the guards' respect. When he counseled me on how best to do my time, I knew to listen.

Our seven-by-five-foot cell was sparse with just a double high iron bunk, small table, tiny shelf, stool, water jug, wash bucket, and slop pot. This brought us close in all aspects. We dressed, undressed, slept, woke, washed, shit, and pissed together. It seemed natural we would eventually fuck.

Sometimes when Jim pissed, he'd finish and keep holding on, and I'd see his back tense as the feel of a hand on his prick, even his own, brought pleasure to his sorry life. I'd often become aroused at this, never mind his back was to me. If I was already stripped down and in bed, I'd get a hand down between my legs and sometimes come before he did.

Convicts learn silence with their sex. Some do grunt and there is the occasional strangled cry, but most accomplish things without a sound. So it was with Jim. I'd watch his backside and hear the unmistakable sound of a hand pumping a dick, and then his buttocks would seize and I knew his spunk was spurting into the pot. If he was accomplishing this in summer when it was light, I'd enjoy the sight of his body in its throes. If in winter darkness, I'd still know as I'd hear the pissing stop and not hear him get into bed. Just that dick work. Then one hot summer day when our wash bucket had just been filled, Jim stripped naked and turned to me with cock in hand. "Garland," he said, "how about we get dirty before we get clean?"

I'd bunked with him for three months and was ready, but decided to tease. "We're already filthy from our work," I replied as I undressed.

"Other kind of dirty," he countered. "Man dirty."

I pushed down my drawers to show him my stiff dick. "You want to fuck, Jim, just say so because I'm up for it, as you can see."

It was the first time I saw him smile.

Light was fading and we waited until it had gone, by which time Jim lay on his bunk. "Get in here," he said in the dark.

I did as told at which he got onto my back and shoved in. I was so pent up, I came soon as he entered, my face buried in the blanket as I couldn't hold back a cry. I hadn't taken a cock since Frank McGann so there was an edge to this one, a reminder that my time with Frank was truly ended. But then Jim was pumping in and out with a fury that I welcomed, his desire not only pleasing me, but comforting me. Nobody had needed me in a while.

When Jim came, I knew it only by his urgent thrusts and gradual slowing. He hesitated before pulling out, nipping my neck which I found endearing as horses did this when showing affection with each another. Then Jim rolled off.

I meant to get up into my own bunk, but we fell asleep. Then, just before dawn, Jim nudged me awake. "Almost sunup," he said as he reached for my dick which woke hard as usual. "Fuck me, Garland. I need a dick up there real bad."

I'd not put it to Frank McGann. He wouldn't have it which I respected even as most of the cowhands I'd known went along with whatever was asked. I didn't hesitate now. I smeared spit over my rod, climbed onto Jim, put it in, and holy God, I had me a fuck. He got a hand under to work himself and there we went at it, the bunk creaking something awful.

I stifled a moan best as I could when in a frenzy, conscious of none but my dick pounding Jim's ass. And pound I did. My juice was slow to boil first thing, so I kept on a while, hands clutching Jim's lean hips. I felt as free as a galloping horse on open range, and see now, as I set down these words, that this was the only free thing we had in prison, the only thing they couldn't fence off. No walls or bars or locks could hold off a man's come, and then I was there, spurting a gusher into Jim who was pumping his dick with equal frenzy.

At last we stilled, the bed going quiet. I pulled out and sat back, then slid a hand over Jim's bottom and ran a finger up his crack. I rubbed and played some, meaning him to know I cared, which I think he got. Nothing was said, and as light was about upon us, I got up to wash since we'd failed to do it night before.

Jim also washed in the early light, and when I caught his eye he didn't turn away like those men whose need shamed them. He let me know with his steady gaze that this was no one-time accommodation. I nodded, and soon we were clean and ready for the day. From then on we did it regular, and though I didn't feel for Jim what I had for Frank, there still was caring which, in our circumstance, went a long way.

All this thinking had wrenched my heart to the point that I now looked down to see Jim, finding him with eyes closed, enjoying the steady breathing sleep brings. His snore was soft and I wondered if this the result of his learned quiet. Slumber gave him peace, and I was glad for that. As the men down the row had now quieted, I lay back and spent the rest of the light with my whalers, wondering if they fucked on their boat.

CHAPTER TWO

Duggan kept his word. Around two o'clock next day, Nash had me take two finished wheels to the blacksmith shop where metal tires would be attached. As I loaded them onto the pull cart and set out, a couple heads turned as we usually sent over at least four. When I hit the sun I paused as I knew to mark the day, October 5, 1878. I doubted Huntsville would ever greet a more notorious man than John Wesley Hardin.

New men were always brought by wagon to the prison front entrance. Heavily shackled and chained together at the neck, they would disembark and be marched through the big iron gate. This was usually a quiet and solemn occasion, nobody much caring who we got or why. On this day, however, there came such a hullabaloo that it climbed right over the wall and spilled down upon us like some circus. For that, I suppose, is what it was. I was later told there were at least fifty reporters from newspapers far and wide, not to mention hundreds of people come to gawk. Fools to a one, I thought, though I couldn't entirely shun the excitement. This I allowed was due to us being short on occasions inside Huntsville.

I knew from experience that the new men would, once through the gate, be led immediately to the underkeeper's office where their iron collars would be removed. They would then be marched to the infirmary where they would be examined and officially received, but not before the superintendent, Captain McCulloch, stood out front and delivered a speech. This was mostly him explaining how, as convicts, they now belonged to the state and would be put to work at labor deemed most profitable to the state. He also advised them to follow the rules or suffer consequences. Knowing this routine led me to pull my cart to a spot alongside the inner fence of the wagon yard where I could appear busy while keeping near the infirmary. I had but a short wait before I heard the gate open. Shouting from the people outside rushed in, but then the gate closed and quiet descended. Life as once known to these new men was now lost.

Never had I seen a picture of John Wesley Hardin. Never had I cared to, yet I looked upon the four men being marched in under far heavier guard than usual and immediately saw which was the famed killer. All four wore iron collars, chained in twos. All four walked in leg irons and with wrists manacled, but only one was smiling. While three moved with the weight of their chains upon them, Hardin appeared amused. He looked about with curiosity, as if that circus outside had come in with him. He was a handsome fellow, I'll give him that, looking younger than his twenty-five years, with a tanned face and thick brown hair that ran amok atop his head. Still attired in his own clothes, he seemed about my size and build and why I took note of this I couldn't say, but I did. I knew he'd punched cattle like me, enjoying the life I loved, but that was no matter now. He was one of us, prisoner come to pay for wrongdoing, I don't care how much circus he caused. I kept to this idea as he moved along with the others, but it didn't hold up. Something about Hardin stood out, something I couldn't get a grip on. Never had I seen such spirit in a man about to begin a twenty-five-year sentence. He chattered to his fellow convicts and even to the guards right up until he went inside the underkeeper's office.

I found myself riveted to my spot, knowing I should get on to the black-smith, but lost to thinking back to my own arrival and how good it felt to have that iron collar removed. After two days, which was how long the trip took from the Austin jail, it roughened the skin, leaving a red welt when finally cut away. At the time, I'd thought there no worse way to rob a man of his dignity, but I'd been wrong.

My recall flew off when the men came out collar-free and headed to the infirmary. This put them in my sight line, and I noted the guards didn't attempt to quiet Hardin. Three of the keepers were stone faced, but one seemed amused by Hardin's talk. Then they reached the infirmary steps where Captain McCulloch stood ready to speechify.

The captain called them to attention and began his spiel which I didn't care to hear as I already knew it. Instead I sized up Hardin whose back was to me now. I wondered how long he could keep up his cheerful way as cells and keepers reduced all men to their base selves. I also speculated on how long it would be until Hardin was up for fucking. Popular as he was on the outside, he was sure to be sought after inside.

To keep myself from getting worked up by such thoughts, I glanced around to see other prisoners idle in their work, all eyes on Hardin. I even saw Jim, my cellmate and foreman of the saddle shop, who could wangle most anything he wanted except freedom, standing idle in the upper yard. His gaze was fixed upon Hardin who I knew he would resent as lifers tend to run that way. I also knew he'd give it to me good after lights out as the only way he ever solved upsets was by way of his prick.

McCulloch finally wound down and I realized Hardin would soon be out of sight. I kept my eyes upon him, and, as the infirmary door opened, he turned, as if taking a last look at freedom, and caught my eye. I knew my stare had drawn him, yet I didn't turn away. His look was dead-on serious, same as when he drew on a man, I'd venture, and my breath caught in those seconds, along with parts lower. Then he broke into a grin and nodded, cocking his head slightly which I took as interest. In that moment I saw how he had swayed Bill Hickok and those sheriffs and others who had helped him.

A guard said something to Hardin who turned forward and was led into the building, the door closing behind him. I should have gone on to the blacksmith, but I stood a while longer, thinking on what was to take place inside the infirmary. My own entrance three years before started playing before me which was a surprise as I hadn't thought on it since it happened.

The infirmary was where a man truly became a convict. An iron collar about the neck is an awful thing, but it doesn't compare to the pain of humiliation. Inside the infirmary, those just arrived were made to strip naked. Bad as this was, I understood the need to rid us of our clothes and put us into prison stripes. But that wasn't what happened.

We'd remained bare in a room with several guards and one doctor, a grizzled old man with foul breath. He stood beside a table on which rested a large ledger book, something more suited for a grocery or bank. As I was first in line, he began on me, measuring my height and weight, asking my name, place of origin, and date of birth. These he recorded in his ledger. He then set down his pen, took up an instrument, and held it to my heart. After this, he looked into mouth, nose, and ears and, as if this was not enough, he ran his hand over my body, poking and prodding as he descended. When he got to my privates, he handled them as well, tugging my dick, then raising it up to get his other hand onto my nuts which he squeezed and fondled. By this time I was hot with a flush of embarrassment as the guards were taking it all in. They bore a look of wicked satisfaction, not quite grinning, but I could feel their mirth. Then the doctor turned me around, parted my buttocks, and said to bend over and grab my ankles which I did with great reluctance. My humiliation was complete when he ran a finger into my bottom hole and commenced to root about, prodding my most sensitive part. I was glad I couldn't see my audience at this point.

"Stand up," said the doctor as his finger popped out. He then picked up his pen and made notes in his ledger, not bothering to wipe off the finger that had been in me. I didn't look at the guards as I waited, but rather thought on how my life was over. I was no longer in charge of myself and must suffer whatever they desired.

Once the doctor had his notes, he looked at me again, this time as if in search. When he saw the scar on my forearm, he ran his thumb over it and then made a note in his ledger. He searched his dirty finger all over me, finding but one other mark which was the bullet wound that had led me here.

"Upper thigh, gunshot," he said aloud and he duly made note in his book while my thoughts fled back to Frank McGann and the holdup gone wrong. He'd gotten away while I took a bullet. As I stood naked in the prison infirmary, suffering a terrible humiliation, it was made worse by recall of Frank's look back at me as I lay wounded on the bank floor. Our eyes had met for the last time before he took off with the money.

The doctor continued searching my body, though I could have told him I had no other marks or scars. He finally finished and said "next" and I was pushed through a door into a bathing area where I was made to wash while a guard looked on. When I was clean, I figured they would give me my striped uniform, but I was wrong. I saw they intended the humiliation to go as long as possible. Once dry from the bath, I was led to yet another room where stood a barber who shaved away my mustache and two-day beard. He was expert not only at shaving me, but in leaving my skin somewhat raw. Once my face was bare, he continued onto my head, shaving away the sandy mop that had been admired by more than one cowboy. The only good part of this ordeal was he spared the hairy patch between my legs.

At last I received my striped uniform along with well-worn underdrawers, socks, heavy brogans, and a single blanket. It surprised me to find my last name, Quick, stenciled on the shirt back. On the front was my number: 7621.

"Get moving, Quick!" I now heard, the past flying off in an instant. My head snapped around to find Mooney, a trusty, at my elbow. "Hardin is inside. Nothing more to see. Get back to work."

I did as told, but couldn't get past the idea of Hardin naked and being examined. I reached the blacksmith with a half-hard dick and paying little attention to my task which caused Mooney, who walked with me and who knew how I liked to get dirty with men, to comment. "You was thinking nasty on Hardin," he said with a leer.

"He's a handsome fellow," I replied. "Came in smiling, which I've never seen."

"Fool, if you ask me."

"Well, nobody is asking you."

I unloaded my wheels which would go on to the wagon yard once they'd had their tires affixed. After that, the finished wagons were used by state operations or sold on the outside. Once my cart was empty, I started back to the wheelwright shop, but took my time, indulging myself along the way with thoughts of the doctor's finger up Hardin's bottom. How would his smile hold up under such humiliation? Certainly there would be more than the usual number of guards attending this procedure as getting that well-traveled finger into such a notorious man was an event. I became aroused at such thoughts and toted a hard prick back to the shop, allowing that it didn't matter the butthole belonged to a notorious man. Finger up any butthole got me going.

"See him?" Duggan asked when I entered the shop.

"Yep. Only man I ever saw come in with a grin."

"We'll take care of that," Duggan boasted.

"No doubt you will." I then returned to my wood-bending machine and attempted to leave off thinking on John Wesley Hardin. I managed without him the rest of the workday, after which I stepped out into the yard for the free hour before supper.

New men were isolated until cell and work assignments could be made, so I knew not to expect Hardin in the yard though talk of him would no doubt be around. He would be at supper, though, setting heads turning once again. I'd not walked far from the shop when Jim found me. "You see Hardin come in?" he asked when he knew I had. That was Jim's way, always testing me about other men. I knew he considered me a possession, and I didn't fight the notion as it mostly worked in my favor, him scaring off fellows I wanted no part of. I knew he needed to believe I hid nothing from him, so I gave him enough truth to allow me to keep some to myself. As we walked along,

I said I had indeed seen Hardin come in. "Duggan let me run some wheels to the smith so I could get a look."

"What do you think?"

"Only man I ever saw smile coming in."

"He's a looker," Jim said, baiting me.

"He's all right, I guess. He'll look a sight different when they shave that hair."

Jim laughed and ran a hand back over the gray fuzz atop his skull. Though we were all supposed to get shorn weekly, it could be skipped with certain inducements, thus Jim had a couple week's growth while I was downright shaggy at nearly an inch. No whiskers, though. Captain McCulloch had a thing about that, every man shaved on schedule. That he bore a sizable mustache seemed a comment on the practice.

"I don't see what all the fuss is about," Jim said as we turned and started back as we'd come. The yard was small, relative to the prison itself, as most of the inside area was taken up with shops, dining hall, infirmary, chapel, library, armory, and residences for officials and guards. We enjoyed our free time in what was called the lower yard, a fenced area also housing the boilers and wood-cutting enterprise. New men were usually put to work there, splitting logs or sawing wood until getting a permanent assignment in a couple days. As we passed the spot, I thought how Hardin, in his stripes and brogans, would soon labor with an ax.

"Killing over thirty men gets you a name," I said to Jim, "as does going ten years without capture."

"No different than us now," Jim declared, putting an end to the subject. I did no more than agree.

When we formed up to march to supper, you could feel a charge in the air. Men craned and gawked as the four new convicts came out of the main building accompanied by six guards which seemed foolish as Hardin no longer had his guns. The need of Captain McCulloch to keep Hardin under such heavy guard impressed me, as I suppose was intended.

Hardin and the other three were put at the end of the line and quickly fell in with marching. Once we reached the dining hall, commands were given by the tap of a gong which was a big piece of v-shaped steel. The line was marched to about three steps of the entrance where the gong was sounded and we halted. Another ring of the gong and we marched inside. We were then directed to tables by a steward, who was a prisoner, and made to stand between bench and table until the gong sounded once more at which we all sat at once. Eating implements were on the table, but prisoners working the dining hall served the food. This had amused me early on, it being like some big but downtrodden restaurant. Like always, Jim sat beside me.

Silent it may have been in that hall, but silence has no rule over gawking of which every table had its fill. More than once an "eyes front" rang out, causing more gawking for a few seconds, then a return to eating. Hardin was apparently at a table behind me, and with Jim at my side I dared not turn.

Supper was familiar. Prison food is poor, but worse is the sameness. Fatty pork, beans, rice, cowpeas, canned tomatoes, cornbread, and coffee were staples and supper was often leftovers from lunch. On occasion we were treated to slumgullion, the stew all men liked. This night the pork was near spoiled while the cornbread bore the crust of hours. I'd not liked the food at first, having acquired a taste for chuckwagon fare on the trail. Those cooks were good at their work, and though the diet was heavy on beef and beans, there often came delicious stews, sourdough biscuits, fresh vegetables acquired from farmers along the trail, and sometimes peach cobbler or apple pie. But necessity makes a man forget such tastes, and soon enough I acquired a liking for cowpeas and cornbread. The beans and rice were tolerable, but I doubted the pork would ever have much appeal.

Cliff Chapman, who sat opposite me this night, found no cornbread on his plate so he held up a hand with fist closed to indicate he needed something. A waiter came over and took the request which he passed on to the steward. I glanced over to see the steward shake his head. Cliff would do without as the steward had final say.

Eating in the quiet, I could feel Jim's tension. Our years together, our intimacies, such as they were, had given me a strong intuition on him. I could read his mood in an instant and unrest now came on strong. He was angry at Hardin's intrusion. A lifer always found a certain ownership in his sentence, as if those condemned to live all their days behind the walls had some special claim, and I believed them right in this, given the hopelessness of their situation. They were deferred to by the prisoners and respected by guards and trusties. A man doing ten years for horse theft was often looked down upon, but a man never to know freedom again gained by way of his sentence.

When the gong declared supper ended we passed plates, forks, and spoons to the end of the table where they were piled to await collection. A waiter with a large can then gathered them, but stood fast until the gong sounded at which he hurried to get the implements into the can, the sound of this on all the tables setting up a sizable clatter. The cans were then taken to the kitchen where their dumping made another clatter. The gong then rang and we rose, formed a line, and were marched out in the same order as we came in, right hand on shoulder of the man in front. Once outside, we were allowed to break ranks.

Soon as this happened, I told Jim I was going to the library, as I often did, not only for the books, but because it was the quietest spot in the whole place. As I peeled off and headed there, Jim started for the chapel. At first I'd not seen him a man of religion, but after a while I decided he was attempting peace with God which I hoped went better than what he'd done with man.

Hardin was not about. He and the other new men would be sequestered in single cells, so I knew evening routines would progress like always. I got a book on a king of England and sat with it open, but not reading a word. Something had gotten started in me that afternoon, something Jim would need to finish, so I allowed it free rein. Sitting with my book open, I thought on fucking, but as I eased back in my chair to give my dick room to come up, no other than Hardin sprang to mind. It didn't take a minute for my hand to drop down to prod my dick, and I didn't leave off Hardin as I prodded. Instead I played along with him, picturing him in the infirmary, naked with a finger up his bottom. Only in my thoughts I got his prick up and had a guard sucking on it. This led me to once again speculate on how long before Hardin put it to one of us or dropped his pants and begged a dick up his bottom.

All men would take it in prison, I don't care their prior circumstance. Absent their women, the regular fellows were set free by their incarceration, thus I pictured Hardin, still naked, now bent over to take my prick. Best way to get a man right in prison was to fuck him. As nasty pictures ran through my mind and I prodded my swollen cock, there came Lonnie Laird in the door. When he took a seat opposite me, I left off myself and got both hands onto my book.

Lonnie was a sweet boy of sixteen when he'd been sentenced to twenty years for a murder he said his brother did. He came in frightened and with good reason as he looked about twelve, fair, slight, and not as tall as me. In our time in the Austin jail, he'd confided that he'd never known a sexual act with another person. He'd been sweet on a girl, but she turned on him.

"Who was killed?" I'd asked.

"Fellow who wanted the girl. That made it bad for me as I'd been walking out with her. My brother also wanted her so he killed the fellow, blamed me, and took the girl. I got twenty years while she married him. I hear they now have a child."

Lonnie's was the saddest case of all those related to me, but he soldiered on because that is all a man could do inside this place. Of course what I figured would happen did although I was surprised who did the doing. Doc Fletcher, the one who received us upon our arrival, the one who put his nasty finger up us all, got Lonnie to work in the infirmary which was a good job except Lonnie had to let the doctor suck his dick. For a regular such as Lonnie this was rough going, but he managed as the doc didn't do it too often.

This particular evening, Lonnie looked grim. Though now nineteen, he still looked much the boy though a tired one. Dark circles ringed his eyes while the corners of his mouth had taken a downward turn. Fair when he came in, he was now pale; thin when he came in, he now looked like he would blow away with the first breeze. Youth had been stolen from him, but I'll give him credit, he was continuing the education that had been stopped with his imprisonment. He presently studied English, but I think, like me, he sought the peace of the library more than the books.

The library was a popular place for men wanting time and thoughts to themselves. Those who came in respected the rule of silence, although talk was permitted in a whisper. There was always the hiss of conversation going, but such a thing didn't intrude when one considered the calls in the cell-block at night. The books also provided comfort, as did the roominess of the place. I'd been told it had once been the infirmary, but when they moved that to a new building, they made this over into a library which there'd not been before. Tables, benches, and shelves had been made in the carpentry shop. The books had been donated by church groups and public libraries looking to get rid of old stock, thus the new library started off with an old smell, like something come up out of your grandmother's trunk. I, for one, liked it.

The place was laid out with a reading area surrounded by of rows of shelves where resided the books, all in what was once the infirmary ward. Offices at one end remained and there sat librarian Fred Walsh, who was the oldest prisoner in the whole place, sixty-four and looking every bit of it, a lifer who could scarcely recall his crime. He loved the books and was indulged by all. Half the time he slept in his office chair. The other office was occupied by a guard name of Ian Swayne who had the easiest duty as men never gave trouble in the library. He too was known to snooze and sometimes to bring in a bottle to keep him company. At the other end of the library proper was a receiving room where donated books yet to be shelved sat in stacks as it took Fred a while to get even a few up on the shelves. I often wondered what kinds of stories were lodged in that windowless room.

This night Lonnie didn't take up his English book. He had no book. What he had was an awful look. As I was his friend, I knew I'd hear the reason and soon enough he spoke. "I can't take it no more," he said.

"Doc Fletcher?"

He nodded. "He's an old man, Gar, wrinkled and smelly. He should just lay down and be done, but he goes at me like he can suck life into his dick. Three years I've had to let him feed on me, watch him pull his shriveled worm which won't come up."

"So you've had enough of him."

"I can allow what he does because the rest of the time I have it good, only lately he's changing and I don't like it. Today he said he needed to examine me, wanted me to get naked and lay out on the table in his office. Well, this I wouldn't do and I ran out into the ward and stayed there. He means to get at me, Gar. What can I do?"

"No more than what you did. Keep away from him, keep around others."

"Can't I report him to the captain? He's not after me in a doctor way."

"You can't prove anything, and besides, a prisoner isn't listened to. Doc will say you have a sickness and he needs to get into you to fix it."

"What's he going to do with no stiff dick?"

"Put in a finger or two, or maybe some implement or his tongue. Thing is, you can't tell the captain, else you'll bring worse upon yourself."

Lonnie leaned forward. "I know you lean that way, Gar, but I don't, even when I try. It repels me, and I don't want any man up my bottom. When he sucks my dick, I tell myself it's Julia doing it. Only that saves me."

"You can ask for another job," I said.

"And get put somewhere to be got at even worse? If he'd just keep on like it has been, I could stand it, but I won't have no old man examining me. It was bad enough coming in."

"I don't know what to tell you," I said. "Just keep away from him best you can."

We fell to silence and it wasn't long before we heard the lockdown whistle.

"I won't let him get me," Lonnie declared.

"You don't have to."

We walked out together, then split up as we resided in different cellblocks. The main building housed two wings, east and west. Lonnie was in the east which had one hundred forty-four cells on two floors while I was in the west which had eighty-eight cells on two floors. In my second-floor cell, a candle burned on our little table while Jim lay naked on his bunk. "Strip off," he commanded soon as I came in and I did so, not caring if a guard might see. Nobody ever got punished for fucking as it was never reported. If the guard caught us, he usually just watched.

Once naked, I stood beside the bunk to allow Jim to play around with me, as I knew he liked to do. I spread my legs when his hand cupped my balls and when he rolled toward me, he wrapped his other hand around my cock. Thus I stood while he brought me along.

The call for lights out soon came and Jim left off long enough for me to snuff the candle. We didn't resume our play until we heard the guard door slam. As nasty calls began, I climbed onto Jim's bunk and gave up my bottom.

I expected a rough fuck and was surprised it was not. Instead it was a long one, or two actually, one before and one after a most thorough butt licking. I came three times in those long hours, once with his tongue in my butthole, the other times his cock in same.

I knew such excess was meant to claim me which Jim did again and again, though never before quite like this. I was used to pummeling and pounding, the occasional slap to the face or chewed buttock. This night I think he meant to show me he was more than just a brute. Too bad I couldn't tell him I already knew, but we didn't speak on such things. We just did them.

CHAPTER THREE

Next day there was Hardin in the lower yard splitting wood. Clad in stripes, he should have been no different that the other men working beside him, but this was not the case. He wasn't the biggest of the four, yet he stood out. As I peered out the shop door, I couldn't decide if it was his reputation that set him apart or the man himself.

The wheelwright shop was housed in a long brick building that gave onto the lower yard. We had a wide door beyond which lay a ramp down to the yard. To each side of the door was a window. There were two more windows at the back, but none did much good amid machines, boxes big and small, workbenches, tools, stores of lumber, and the debris industry leaves. Light was thin inside the shop, hampered by ever-present wood dust. Fresh air never much got in which was made worse by our sweat, spit, and a piss pot that filled too quickly.

Abram Nash, lazy lout of a foreman, was idle in conversation with Duggan this morning, back near the back where they couldn't be seen from the outside. I was thus free to linger at the door and get a look at Hardin. He swung his ax as any man, but bore a certain grace in his movements, and I thought how maybe after his year in the Austin jail, he welcomed physical exercise. He worked steadily, a most productive prisoner, and listened attentively when his foreman spoke. I wondered if this was that agreeable nature of his. Funny how a charmer could have killed so many.

Hardin split wood for three days while the men who arrived with him spent but one. I saw this as McCulloch making a show of the killer. During those three days, I looked out the shop door more than once, even as I knew it indulgence, and more than once Hardin caught me watching and nodded, attempting to charm, even at a distance.

For those three days, Hardin was not allowed free time in the yard. This I decided was more of Captain McCulloch's attempt to break his man. I also knew the other three new men had been assigned to two-man cells while Hardin remained in a single. Word was around that he took no issue with such treatment. In fact, it was told that his cell door often remained open long after others were closed, guards engaged in conversation with him and one even going in to sit.

"I hear Matt Furst is downright smitten," said John Williams on day three. "Leaves off guarding anybody else in favor of attending Hardin who makes him laugh. I don't see what's the pull."

Williams, a curly-haired blond lifer looking like some angel gone to seed, ran a wood lathe near me, and when the drone of turning ceased, he liked to talk. Duggan didn't care how much we spoke, nor did Nash as he and the guard chewed the fat until it grew lean. "Many seem to be smitten," I said as I fitted the next wood piece into my machine. "Hardin is said to be likable."

"Wonder if the men he killed found him such."

Here I let the conversation die away.

Things shifted between Jim and me around this time. From the saddlery, located in a brick building near the east wall, he could not possibly have seen me looking out my shop door at Hardin, yet he still knew I looked. Apparently I was not the only one given to intuition on the other.

"I hear Hardin is married with little kiddies," he said on the night of Hardin's third day cutting wood. "Regulars always swear upon their women, but can't get their butts high enough in here."

"I heard that too, him being married."

"What else did you hear?"

"Only that his guards find him entertaining."

We'd been locked in for the night and Jim lay naked on his bunk. "I had me a regular for a while," he said after some quiet. I hopped up to my bunk and didn't reply which led Jim to continue. "He spoke on his wife and children right up to when I stuck my dick in him and he kept on, if you can believe it. Got a hand on his cock, pulling to beat the band, and me riding him and about to come, and he's calling for dear sweet Mary, wife who he declares he loves, declares this as he takes my cock. Only way I got him to stop jawing was to put my dick in his mouth. He forgot her then, sucked me like no tomorrow. After that, every time he started talking on sweet Mary, I knew he wanted fucking. Hardin will too. They all do."

I could hear Jim working his cock. He'd paused his narrative long enough to spit in his palm and I could just make out that juicy stroke. I also knew what was next, but I made no move. I thought on Hardin's cell door now closed, guards finally leaving off their entertainment. Was the prisoner now entertaining himself the best way a man could, pants open, prick in hand? One thing made us all equals, and it grew between our legs.

"Get down here," Jim commanded, at which I left off my thoughts and climbed down. I threw off my clothes, my prick going soft soon as Hardin fled my mind. Jim lay ramrod stiff. "Crawl in here," he said.

He moved over to let me in, then put me on my stomach, raised my butt, and spread the cheeks. After viewing the target, he got down and began to run spit into my crack, and then to push gobs into my pucker. He also put more spit on his dick and once he had sufficient lubrication, he rammed his cock in to the hilt. "Best fuck is a fellow who don't want a woman," he said as he began to pump in and out. "Fellow who's never known cunt."

Here Jim left off speaking as he had a good stroke going and I had to admit, it was welcome. Why speculate on a notorious gunman when I had a man with a hard dick in the here and now? At such thoughts, I got a hand under and began to pull myself which Jim noted.

"Work that prick," he rasped, well into his throes. "Spew for me, Garland," he added as he picked up speed. There came no more words after this, just the thwack of a dick in a butthole. The squeak of the iron bed, a sound often heard up and down the cellblock rows, mingled with hoots and cries from the men, some of which, I reckoned, were from those who would like to have been doing same as us.

Jim pounded out his climax while I spewed as he wanted, the two of us then parting. He fell onto his back while I lay on my side against the wall. We reeked of sweat and sex, but this mattered little as we were used to being rank. It was two more days until we got the wash pail filled.

I knew better than to attempt a return to my bunk. Though Jim lay with eyes closed and breathing so steadily he could have slept, I knew him awake and thinking on how to get at me again. Never mattered how tired he was. If he couldn't get his cock up a second time, he put his fingers in me or used a smoothly rounded handle John Williams had made for him. He called it Little Brother and spent time working oil into it until it had become a slick and shiny brown. He often got hard when doing this oiling, and would get out his dick and let it stand next to the wooden cock. Though it was bigger than him, I doubted this mattered as a man can always outdo a piece of wood, save for it always being stiff. I didn't like Little Brother as it was roughly used, no doubt due to its owner's frustration when not able to summon the real thing.

"You hear where they're putting him?" Jim asked, eyes still closed. I noted he didn't say Hardin's name, the killer now a given.

"No, I haven't heard."

"Everybody I spoke to says it's in with them. Boyd Christy in the tailor shop swears Hardin is to start there tomorrow and says he'll put him right first thing."

"Maybe they'll assign him to you," I said. "John Wesley Hardin, bridle maker. That would be something."

"Rather not have him. Rather they put him on an outside gang."

Over one hundred convicts worked outside the prison walls each day, hired out in gangs to fell trees or work the fields. "I doubt they'll let Hardin outside the walls," I replied, "seeing how they keep extra guards on him inside."

"May be," mused Jim.

Darkness came over us and within it I felt Jim stir. Absence of light frees a man from even himself and when Jim rolled over, I knew what was next. "Lick me down there," he said. When I got around between his legs, I found he held his buttocks apart.

I attended his center first with finger, then with tongue. I then took hold of his buttocks to free him to pull his cock. "Lick me," he said again, no matter I already was.

I never put it to Jim unless asked. No matter how brutish the man, all wanted a cock up there at some time. Jim differed only in wanting a tongue first.

I'd learned tongue-fucking on the trail where I did most everything. That particular filth didn't bother me. I was riled both to do it and to have it done to me. Soon I had Jim's crack awash in spit so I stuck my tongue in. This caused a rare moan from him, and he shoved his butt back to get me deeper. I plastered my mouth to him and fucked him best as any tongue could, all the while him frantic with dick in hand. "Fuck me," he finally said so I drew back, repositioned, and stuck it to him. Soon as I began to ride his ass, I heard him choke back a cry and knew he was unloading. Driving a man to come always did me in and I grew urgent, my juice boiling up and spurting. Once again the poor bed complained, but then we were done and I fell back.

"Enough," Jim managed. "Get to your own bunk."

Weak from my satisfaction, I took my time climbing up and scarcely hit the pillow before I slept.

Next morning, I wasn't in the shop ten minutes before three guards and Assistant Superintendent Emmett Grazer marched John Wesley Hardin through the door. Having already noted him absent from the wood-cutting yard, I'd kept to my work, never thinking he might come in. I'd just finished a turn on my machine, so I let it go quiet in honor of the procession. Soon as they were inside, Hardin drew my eye but gave no nod.

I couldn't hear what Nash said to the party, just saw him puff up at being put in charge of such a notorious man. Nash nodded and played lackey to Grazer, no doubt assuring all that the prisoner would be worked hard and kept in line. Even Duggan grew a size as he stood for the occasion. And when Grazer and his cohorts had gone, the guard still held his back straight, everyone, it seemed, determined to show Hardin he had no sway in here.

Abram Nash was foreman more for time served than for any ability to govern men. He'd done seventeen of a thirty-year murder sentence, most of it in the wheel shop. I'd asked about him early on, mostly why he got thirty when twenty-five was the usual for murder.

"Grisly job," I was told. "Didn't just knife the man. Cut up his innards and strewed them about."

It was hard to see that man now for Nash had grown soft, taking on the dirty pink of a pig. He also had a drinking problem that may have come into prison with him. How he wangled whiskey was beyond me, but he often had a bottle in the shop and sometimes rendered himself senseless as a result. In my three years with him I'd learned wheel-making to such an extent that I was now left to show new men the ropes. This fact was in mind when Hardin came in.

When the shop returned to usual, it was no longer usual. Duggan began to josh with Hardin who joshed right back. Though I couldn't hear exactly what they said, I knew bullshitting when I saw it. John Williams must have caught some of it for he chuckled.

Nash showed Hardin around the shop, pointing out each job and the name of the man doing it. Duggan followed close behind for no reason but to keep up his joshing. When they got to me, Nash said how my machine bent pieces of wood to form the wheel rim which was known as the felloe. "Skill is required to operate these machines," said Nash. "You must work up to that. This here is Quick who's been with us three years and will show you your job." With this Nash and Duggan retreated to their usual sloth in the back.

"New men always start with sanding spokes," I said to Hardin who nodded. "Williams there at the lathe turns the spokes and puts them into this box. You'll take them from the box and sand them smooth, but not too much. You'll develop a feel for how to do it to specifications. Too much and you ruin the fit."

Though I gave the usual spiel, it felt like someone else saying the words, some wooden man standing decoy for the real one who had been thrown off-kilter. Unlike others, I wasn't impressed by Hardin. No joshing rose up in me, and at that moment no charm came from him. He acted as any prisoner being told his job, and I worked at treating him as such, even as I knew things were far from usual.

"You get that?" I said at the end of my spiel.

"Surely do."

"Then come over here and we'll get you working." I put him on a stool at a table, then dumped the spoke box out before him. I got a stack of sandpaper from the shelf and showed him how to use it. I gave him the specs for his work and said to use the measure rule to stay true. "The dust will play hell with you at first, but after a while you won't notice."

When Hardin took the paper from my hand, his finger brushed mine which caused me to jerk back. I glanced up to see him not offended and noted his eyes were gray. I'd never seen such eyes and turned from them.

Hardin didn't sit in the downcast way of most men. He bore a kind of defiance, like he held something on account, and this I had to admire. "You go ahead, start in and I'll watch," I said. He took up a spoke and began to work, drawing the paper up and down the shaft. "Yes, that's how it is done," I said. "You're doing fine, just keep on."

I lingered with him no longer than needed, now that I was over the initial surprise of his arrival. As he sanded his spokes, I concentrated on my work, and when the lunch whistle sounded, we lined up and marched from the shop like always.

As I'd been instructing Hardin in his work, I now rested my hand on his shoulder in the proper way, but didn't feel the least proper. We were halfway to the dining hall before it hit that he would sit beside me. Men coming from their shops at noon sat in the order of arrival. As usual the steward crowded a dozen to a bench meant to hold ten, thus Hardin and I were pressed against each other. Though I knew to sit straight, Hardin fidgeted with the arrangement, his legs wide apart which brought his left up against my right. Usually when a new man did this, he was given a push of the leg to let him know to keep to his place, but I made no such move. Instead I let Hardin's leg rest against mine, my cock stiffening as a result. When the food came and Hardin leaned forward to eat, his leg pressed me so steadily I had to think he knew what he was about.

I thought the talkative Hardin might have difficulty with meal silence, but he gave off no discomfort and ate the awful pork right down. There also came no pause at stale cornbread and he seemed to enjoy the peas. Like most of us, he swigged all the water allowed.

Marched back to the shop after lunch, Hardin went right to his table and took up his sanding while I went back to bending wood. I kept an eye on him such as I could, finding him looking around as he sanded. Men occupied in such boring occupations often let their minds wander and I figured Hardin no exception. But what would such a man run to? Was he reliving the excitement of his ten years of killing or was there maybe regret coming up in him? Then again, he could still be squirming in recall of that finger up his bottom.

When the four o'clock whistle sounded, Hardin set down his spoke and stood. Machines left off their clatter, and all of us sought the wash bucket where we cleaned up and dried faces and hands with a gunnysack towel. We then headed for the door. When I saw Hardin lagging behind, I went over. "Free time until supper," I said. "Most walk the yard."

"Sounds right good," Hardin said, and he followed me out.

"I had no idea prison was so industrious," he remarked when we'd gone a few paces. "Heard about hard labor, but always thought it cracking rocks."

"Like the captain said when you came in, labor to benefit the state. There's all manner of manufacturing here. That big building to the back is a mill where cotton and wool are spun for the tailor shop where clothes and quilts are turned out. Confederate uniforms were made here during the war. Then there's the shoe shop where they make our brogans and also shoes and boots to sell on the outside. Carpenter shop makes furniture, saddlery all manner of harnesses. Blacksmith makes hubs and tires for our wheels, plus repairs tools, and shoes horses. Things made here are used by the state or sold on the outside. That's why the prison was built near the river. Ease of bringing in materials, and ease of shipping out finished goods."

"So the wheels go out too?"

"Yes, on wagons we make, mostly freights, but some light spring numbers too. Down there is the wagon yard where it's all put together, frame, box, wheels. I tell you, you name it, we make it."

"It's like a town."

"You take down the walls and chase off the guards, you'd have just that."

"I hear you got twenty-five, like me," Hardin said.

"You're certainly steering the subject off the road."

"Just curious."

I found myself mixed on what to say, part of me wanting to tell him about my sentence and part wanting to keep it from him. As I pondered, I looked around for Jim who might be watching. When I didn't see him, I told Hardin that I'd indeed gotten twenty-five. "Though I killed but one man," I added.

"How old are you?"

"Twenty-five," I said.

"Same as me. You married?"

"I am not."

"Well, I am. Nice little wife and three kids. We hitched up when I was eighteen and her fourteen. Jane stands by me and I draw upon that to sustain me in this awful time."

I wanted to ask if she stood by his killing all those men, but held back as his reasons were none of my business. In fact, I wished he wasn't telling me what he was. I had no idea how to reply about his family, but this didn't matter as he kept on talking.

"A good woman gets a man through anything, as does all family. My father was a Methodist preacher, but he's gone now. Died just before my capture, while I was on the run in Florida. I'm named after the founder of Methodism, John Wesley. Pa hoped I'd follow him into religion, but unfortunate circumstances put an end to such plans. My brother Joe was a lawyer, but he's also gone now."

On and on he went, spilling all but the bloodthirsty part. He played the devoted family man to such extent I was somewhat put off, but I soon saw it his way of surviving his own life. I also found I liked listening to him. It was easy to forget his exploits within his friendly way and I even left off thinking on that finger up his butt.

When the supper whistle blew, I peeled away from Hardin, saying I had to get elsewhere, and I hurried a good distance to where I found Jim for the march to supper. I didn't look Hardin's way. Instead, I began to rattle about a made-up mishap in the shop, anything to keep Jim on an even keel.

CHAPTER FOUR

Jim said not a word that night which I knew was trouble. He stood fully dressed below our high barred window, leaned back against the wall, Little Brother in one hand. I'd brought in a book from the library, and held it to my chest as if the prince inside it might protect me.

"Got a good one about a prince who has adventures," I said, showing Jim the cover. "How about I read to you?" He had on occasion allowed this, and while I think he liked the stories, it pained him he couldn't make out the words on his own.

He shook his head, then reached to our little table where sat a can of grease I well knew. Used in the saddle shop, it served to soften leather. It also worked to lubricate things of a sexual nature when a man's spit or spunk was not enough. Jim took up a gob and began to smear it over Little Brother. "Get them pants down," came the command.

It was always worse when he didn't want me naked. Odd how a man has his particular way when he's angry or hurt or just crazed. I suspected Jim presently suffered all three, thus I pushed down pants and drawers. Jim had his weapon shiny with grease, but he set it aside to open his own pants and pull out his prick. If an organ could be angry red, this one was. Jim then picked up Little Brother and I saw how he wanted to work himself while he gave me what he figured I deserved, even though I'd done nothing against him.

Foolish as it was, I spoke. "I've done you no wrong."

There came no reply, but that didn't matter. His eyes bore into me, killer eyes, the same eyes that had gazed down upon his father when the deed was done. And within the threat of what was to come, I saw a knowing, like Jim could reach inside me and grab hold of my innards, knot my entrails, and lay waste to my privates. For that was where he and I lived, and who better to know me than the man who'd been inside me more than any other? Maybe he knew what I didn't. Maybe he could, from inside me, where he'd resided nearly three years, divine me like some water wizard. Maybe that dick of his pointed to a truth I didn't yet know. I didn't want John Wesley Hardin. But maybe I did.

"Bend," Jim said. As this was familiar, I took a position at the bedpost toward the back of the cell and stuck out my bottom. Jim said nothing as he rammed Little Brother into me so deep my breath caught. Pain shot through my insides, never mind the handle was greased. Nothing that size belonged in a man's passage, and yet mine accommodated. Jim started fucking me with the tool while working his prick. His way of punishment for whatever slight he imagined was to deny me the real man while still getting claimed.

I didn't know a guard was watching until I heard a low whistle. Sometimes one wouldn't retreat behind a closed door, in order to look at what men got up to. Some would get out a dick and work it while watching whatever show we gave. This time I suspected as much, for I soon heard grunting near the cell door. I didn't care about this due to the abuse of my rear. After a good long time, when I'd heard the guard come and leave, Little Brother ran dry and I begged Jim to add more grease, but he wouldn't. I'd be raw after this, but then I'd been raw before and would heal. Trouble was, Jim never left off fucking when I was in such condition.

Suddenly Jim drew close and began to spew come onto my leg. He let up on Little Brother as he spurted, but soon as he regained himself, he renewed his effort. The sweat running down my face was soon joined by tears, but even these finally ran dry. Jim only stopped when my legs gave out. I thought this the end of the ordeal as he usually left off around this point, but tonight was not the usual situation. Jim pulled me to my feet and launched a fist into my stomach and then another and another, some lower, some higher. He also hit me in the face, slapping and pummeling until blood ran from my nose. Under such an assault, I could only hold up my hands to protect myself, but this did little good. Finally he was spent and pushed me into a corner where I collapsed. He retreated to his bunk while I curled onto the floor and attempted to sleep.

Next morning, Jim said nothing, going about his business and making ready for the day. I, in turn, had great difficulty, every part of me hurting, including my butthole. My face felt puffy on one side, my eye likely blackened as I could see little from it. My side hurt most and I suspected damaged ribs, but I wouldn't seek the infirmary as this would make Jim even more angry.

All I could do was press on and hope he'd satisfied himself that I was his, even though I hadn't strayed.

"Who got you?" Hardin asked when I came into the shop that morning. He was already at his table, spoke in hand.

"Man don't talk on such things," I snapped. Soon I had my machine going and didn't so much as glance at John Wesley Hardin. And later, when Duggan came over, nothing was said before I followed him to the storeroom and sucked his dick like a madman. Even when he'd come, I kept on as I had my prick out and was in a pumping frenzy. Duggan was generous enough to let me feed on him until I shot my load, after which I spat out his limp dick and stood.

"You're right worked up today," he said as he buttoned up. "Hardin getting to you?"

"No. I just find your stuff tasty."

He looked down at my half-hard cock. "I'll accept that even as I know it a lie." And he left me alone.

Coming should have settled me, but it didn't and I knew why. When I went back out, Hardin would see me and know what I'd been doing. Didn't matter he hadn't watched. Men know when spunk is in the air and Duggan was bound to reek, maybe me too, but I had nowhere else to go. I shoved my dick into my pants and did them up, but still held back as the aches in my body that had been chased off by dicksucking now returned to make even breathing a caution.

I could feel Hardin's eyes upon me when I came out, and I avoided looking his way. Didn't matter. Condemnation heats a man like a furnace, searing all nearby, and such was Hardin as I passed him. I set to running my machine which I found welcome as it didn't care who I sucked, nor did it beat me. I thus went on to make a good many new felloes.

At the lunch whistle, I hung back to put everyone ahead of me. This worked in my favor as I was seated on a bench with men from the carpentry shop since it was next door to us and therefore put those men close in line.

"Jim do that?" asked Ned Lally when we'd marched out after the meal.

Ned, convicted of horse stealing and manslaughter, was a tall drink of water often too curious for his own good. I gave no reply, just bristled at him saying that of Jim, no matter it true. He didn't know Jim like I did and couldn't possibly understand what drove my man. Jim's life had stopped at fifteen and would never start again. He was a hollow vessel who led with his dick. I knew the beating born of desperation, and knew also I'd forgive him.

Hardin made no effort toward talking to me for the rest of the day, and after work he walked out with John Williams. They were joined by several others, and though I tried not to look, I couldn't help but note Hardin entertaining a fair crowd.

I knew how Jim would treat me that night. Though he'd never beaten me this bad, he had done some previous damage and always made up by way of his dick. And tongue. True enough, I never had such a butt licking as I got this night. Awash in soothing spit, I came into the blanket as Jim's tongue worked my passage, soothing what he had scraped raw. He also licked my pucker until it felt almost healed. and when he finally sought to fuck me, he went in easy and took it slow, twice adding more spit. Apology accepted.

I slept in his bunk, curled into his arm, and when dawn crept in, he woke me and said to suck him. I got down to find him stiff and set to feeding while his hand milked me until we both had a good come to start the day. I decided, upon leaving our cell, to start fresh with all before me. Jim was my man, no matter his faults. I'd been content for all our time together and would remain so. John Wesley Hardin would not be a problem. He could see to his work, and I to mine.

He took to his sanding with so much vigor that he soon rendered some of his spokes loose in the felloes. I didn't wish to speak to him, but had to so I kept as businesslike as possible. "Ease off some," I said one day. "You're taking off too much." I took up his measure rule and reminded him of the specs. "Keep to them."

"I'll do that. Sorry to have ruined any."

I offered no more and kept a distance in both shop and yard. I sought Jim out during free time, and we either walked in silence or talked of the saddle shop. He asked nothing on my work, which was wise.

Soon Sunday came around and we didn't work on Sunday. Though I didn't cleave to God, I appreciated his getting us a day off work. Many men attended chapel and some stayed on for Sunday school. A preacher came out from town to conduct services, while Sunday school was taught by a prisoner who had declared himself committed to God.

Cells were open all of Sunday and we were free to sleep there, all day if we chose, which some did. Or we could stay in the yard where men often got up a baseball game using a bat made in the shop and ball that had been donated.

There were some benches in the yard on which men gathered to talk. It was a day even the most grim of fellows enjoyed.

Into this John Wesley Hardin came like some striped Messiah. I doubt Jesus himself had so many men trailing him. Hardin had a gang of men following as he came from chapel out into the yard. As no baseball game had yet begun, I was lounging with Lonnie Laird and Bob Tinney when the procession came our way.

"Looka that," said Bob who then spat. "Goddamn parade."

"He charms everyone," observed Lonnie. "Said to have charmed his way out of many a scrape."

"Well, charm won't get him out of here," I countered.

"I'm going to see what he's saying," Lonnie decided, and he got up and wandered over to where Hardin was speaking to his flock. The Messiah stood leaning back against the wagon yard fence, preaching with ease. I watched Lonnie join the throng, then found myself too curious to stay put so I sauntered over.

"You boys all know how corrupt those state police were after the war," Hardin was saying. "Along with the Union soldiers, they had no regard for any private citizen and brutalized many folks. They made my preacher father's life a misery because I wouldn't submit to their riding roughshod over everyone, man, woman, and child alike. In the face of this I couldn't stand idle, so I fought against them at every turn, killing as required for the good of the people. My fight was near single-handed, but it did much to discredit and finally bring down the force."

"You were right to do it," someone called out. This prompted another to tell a story of the police beating his neighbor. "They were the worst of the worst," said still another. "Authority to beat and kill and answer to no-one."

"They answered to me," shot back Hardin which got praise from the men. "Trouble was," he went on, "bringing down the force led to the return of the Texas Rangers who, as you know, saw to my capture. But even though they put me in here, I believe what I did was right. Had the state police not been done in, we'd have no law today."

There came no applause for this show, but there might well have been. Hardin was as good as any snake-oil salesman, and the men swelled as if his enthusiasm was contagious. Hardin's color was up with the excitement. I could see how his orating heated him, and he smiled as he took in the men's gratitude for his killing.

He wasn't wrong about the state police, though they hadn't done any wrong to me or my kin. I'd been glad to see the Rangers come back and the state achieve some order, but I hadn't known details of Hardin's efforts until now. I kept listening to him, and every time he wound down, someone asked a question which wound him up again.

"How many men you killed?" asked one fellow.

"Thirty-two," Hardin answered, "but I never broke the law, never robbed anyone. I killed only those needing it. I am a man of honesty, integrity, loyalty, and fair play. All who know me will attest to this."

"I hear you shot a man for snoring," called Ned Lally. This set the men laughing and brought a grin to Hardin. He let the silliness die away before he spoke.

"Stories have sprung up about me that are not always true and that is one. I have no idea who I killed in Abilene that night in 1871, only that I'd fallen into bed alongside my cousin Gip Clements after some carousing. I wasn't yet asleep when I heard the door latch so I sought my pistol and when the intruder came in, I fired. The man stumbled back into the corridor where he died. Knowing the killing would anger Marshal Hickok, Gip and I fled out the window and made our getaway. Newspapers later gave all manner of accounts, one of which was by the *Denison Daily Herald* which said I was a very organized desperado who did not like to have my sleep disturbed so I rose in the night and slew a snorer in the next room."

Here Hardin took on a grim expression, studying faces of his audience. The men took heed and lost their humor. "The story was incorrect," Hardin declared. "Snoring does not bother me as I'm told I do some of it myself." Now his grin returned. "Snore up a storm, boys. I'll not harm you."

A good laugh was had by all, including Hardin and including me. I walked away at this point, but Lonnie stayed on. Bob Tinney asked my opinion when I rejoined him. "Entertaining fellow," I said. "He can tell a tale."

Hardin's presence in the shop changed things, no matter how much I tried to keep them the same. Work went on as usual, but the air somehow shifted. Complacent drudgery gained a certain tension with Hardin in our midst, the men stealing glances his way as he sanded his spokes. He remained earnest at his job, looking every bit the model prisoner even as he gave off an air of unmistakable unrest. It was like being caged with a bear who could revert to natural ways at any moment and kill us all.

Even my sucking Duggan took a turn due to Hardin knowing what I was up to. As cover, I started bringing supplies out with me when I was done, something I'd never bothered with before. Soon as I came through the door, I'd find his eyes upon me in a gaze flat and cold. Surely he knew what went on in prisons, and yet he continued to drill me in a manner just short of that produced by a bullet.

Two weeks went by with us all doing our work and me sucking Duggan more than usual. Then one day when I'd done just that, I came out of the storeroom to find Hardin standing by the door. He made as if waiting to get more sandpaper, thus Duggan gave him no bother. I, on the other hand, fairly ran into him, as I saw he intended. I had no wood in hand, having forgotten the cover since I'd felt a need to get myself off and was thus in a satisfied humor. It was as those gray eyes bore into me with cold condemnation that I knew him aroused. This was not unfamiliar as many a married man hated what he himself did or wanted to do, but on a man such as Hardin it seemed worse. He felt dangerous, and yet I knew his cock likely stiff in his pants.

Bill Duggan was easy when satisfied, and Hardin took note. The guard now sat kicked back for a smoke, after which he was likely to doze. The men always took advantage of this state, enjoying a welcome period of slack. Amid the lull, Hardin opened a conversation. I had hold of a wheel rim when he came up. "You fuck in there?" he asked.

I savored the moment before replying, "Nope."

"What do you do then?"

"That's between Duggan and me."

"Funny how he goes in grouchy and comes out like some calf just had his mother's tit. If he wasn't so spent, I swear he'd frolic."

I had to chuckle. "I've known Duggan almost three years. Know how to play him."

"That what you call it?"

I laid the wheel down and looked Hardin square on. His eyes were serious, but the corner of his mouth crimped up. "I suck his dick," I said. "Swallow his spunk right down."

Hardin's eyes widened. He'd obviously not expected me to admit anything. Color rushed to his cheeks and a wicked smile came over him. "What's he do for you?"

"A guard won't do anything for a convict. I do myself."

"That all you get?"

I nodded. "That and an easy guard."

As we spoke, Hardin's hand had absently slid to his crotch where it remained. "You suck other dicks?" he asked.

"That is a private matter."

"I'll take that as a yes."

From then on Hardin and I shared an unspoken knowledge that he wanted his dick sucked. He didn't act upon this, however, even as he gave off a decided heat in my company. Looks he passed were full of need, but he wouldn't allow himself indulgence. Instead he turned his energies toward something worse. Escape.

CHAPTER FIVE

"Call me Wes," Hardin said about three weeks in. "The family prefers John, but I like Wes."

"I'm Gar," I replied. "Short for Garland."

"Right nice name, Garland."

"My pa was Joe and he said Joe Quick was just that, quick, where Garland has a bit more to it."

Hardin had followed me from work at the four o'clock whistle, something he now did most days. I walked careful, due to Jim's continued use of Little Brother, and knew I'd get it this night when I saw Jim in the yard. He'd taken a position near the boilers so he could spot us coming from the shop. This made no matter as I refused to let his assaults keep me from Hardin's company. I didn't consider the new friendship a betrayal. I just had to ignore the fact that I often shit blood.

"You share a cell with a lifer, don't you?" Wes asked.

"Scanlon, yes, going on three years."

"How is that?"

"Well, lifers are a breed apart so I have to exercise care, but long as he rules his roost there's no problem."

"He doesn't seem too friendly."

"How friendly would you be if this place was all you'd ever see till the end of your days?"

"I wouldn't let that happen," declared Wes.

"What?"

"End my days here." He stopped and turned to face me. "I'm talking a breakout. It can be done."

My head snapped around to see if anyone was close enough to hear. Fortunately, for once all were some distance. When I looked back to Wes his eyes fairly sparkled and his mouth was crimped into a wicked grin. It took

36

a few seconds for me to reply as the idea of anyone escaping was outlandish. "You've been here three weeks and you're already planning an escape?"

"I can't abide this containment which is made worse by the fact that I was sentenced for murder when I killed the man in self-defense. I got twenty-five years because of who I am, not because of the killing, and I believe it illegal to imprison a man for being who he is. All are determined to keep me down, and I won't have it."

The remarkable thing about this spiel was it not being heated. It became plain at this point that Wes was a thinker. He might have killed many men, but he knew what he was about, knew his own brand of stealth. I couldn't help but admire his audacity as it came with great confidence.

"Those walls are fifteen feet high and five feet thick," I said. "Guards are everywhere."

"Right you are, but have you failed to note the armory sits not seventy-five yards from our shop?"

"I don't want to know this," I said, and I resumed walking. He made no move to follow. I found my way to Jim and initiated conversation by way of repeating a rumor I'd heard that sourdough biscuits were to be served at supper.

"Believe it when you see it," Jim said. He started walking and I kept with him though I did glance back to see Hardin talking to John Williams.

There were no biscuits at supper, but there was molasses for the cornbread. As I ate, I couldn't let go of what Hardin said about breaking out. Over and over, I thought on how it might be accomplished, but all ideas I hatched came to naught. I knew the guards who worked the outside gangs put their guns into the armory each evening when they came in, but a prisoner couldn't just go in there. Nor could he, without any weapon of his own, hold up those who carried them. It made no sense. Hardin was talking through his hat.

When night came on, Jim got naked and fucked me regular, doing it twice over the course of the night. His tongue did a good amount of work, and he sucked me to a good spurt so a fine time was had by us both. Mostly I was pleased that Little Brother remained on his table. I had no idea why Jim left off the thing. I was simply grateful he did.

Next morning, Hardin came over to me as I worked my machine. He took advantage of a friendly guard and drunken foreman to move about the shop or sometimes sit idle. Other men followed his lead and what had once been a productive place became somewhat lax. With nobody really caring how many wheels we turned out each day, there came no punishment.

"I'm going to dig a tunnel," Hardin said. He sounded like a man declaring he was going to fuck, such was his excitement. "Burrow underground to the armory, come up through the floor, and when the guards come in, take their weapons. I'll then give them to the men and we'll take the prison."

I couldn't keep to my work with such a statement hanging over me so I left off but kept the machine running. I glanced back to Duggan who lazed in a chair, shotgun propped between his legs. Nash lay prone on a stack of lumber, likely suffering the end of one drunk while looking to start the next.

"You can't dig a tunnel," I said to Hardin. "You'd be seen."

"Not if we dig from here."

"Here?"

"Come with me."

He grabbed my arm and led me to a front corner where boxes and old implements were stacked. "Behind here," he said, pulling me around the stuff. Once out of sight, he pried up a plank from the floor. "Already got a start."

"This is crazy," I said.

"Crazy like a fox."

"You really think you can do it? Tunnel all that way? There are two shops before the armory. You'd have to tunnel beneath both of them and they're brick."

"We have all the tools here that we need for digging, chisels, saw bits, you name it. I've already talked to Bill Owens and Bill Terrill and they're for it. So's John Williams. And there's others who would come in to assist. Ned Lally and my cellmate, Cliff Chapman. I've got close to a dozen men on board. How about you?"

"I told you, I don't want to know this," I said, backing away. "And I don't wish to join. You'll never make it. Do you know there's a standing offer of a shortened sentence for any man reporting on an escape attempt? It's happened before, some man nearly making it but caught because his cohort, in his own self interest, went to McCulloch and told all. The last squealer got his sentence knocked down three years and the one before that got pardoned. So it isn't that you can't dig your tunnel and maybe surprise those guards, it's odds that somebody will turn you in and it will likely be one of those helping you dig."

"I'll have to consider that," Hardin said. "I appreciate you telling me."

That night I couldn't get to Jim fast enough. I came into the cell instead of going to the library and when I found him sitting on our stool, pulling the worn insole from one of his brogans, I kneeled before him and opened my mouth. He took a moment to savor the offering, then got out his dick and guided it into me.

When I had him stiff and wet, I stripped off everything and sat on him, riding his cock while my own dribbled in anticipation. As I fucked myself, Jim took hold of my dick and began to pull at which I spurted on his shirt. Soon after this, he grabbed me at the waist and drove up into me, giving me what I craved. My passage had healed from his earlier assaults and received his stuff with ease. When he was done, I still squirmed on him before he lost his girth and slid out. I stayed put for a minute, enjoying being in his lap, but soon as intimacy took hold, he pushed me off.

It was now too cold to sleep naked, so I put my clothes back on and Jim buttoned up as well. "No book tonight," he said when I'd climbed up to my bunk.

"I don't wish to be elsewhere," I replied, to which he gave no comment.

After this, every time I saw Hardin talking to anyone, I wondered if it was about his escape. This bothered me so much that one day when nobody was doing much in the shop, Duggan sleeping after a good dick suck, I asked how the plan was going.

"Thought you didn't want to know," came the reply.

"Fair enough, but curiosity is upon me when I see you talking to the men. I start wondering if it's to make plans."

"Surely is. I have it figured out. We'll start digging in a couple days. You don't have to take part, but it would be a help if you could keep attending Duggan so he remains easy." A smile followed this spiel and I must confess, it warmed me. Much as I resisted the escape idea, I had difficulty getting past Hardin's excitement. Ever since he'd arrived, he'd given off a pleasing air that swept in around me, but now that he was planning to break out, that air was more a storm. Not a good storm that nourishes the crops, but a black funnel likely to tear us all to pieces. Still, a man who could generate such a feel was not easy to resist. More than once, after speaking to him, I'd worked my cock to a come while standing over the piss pot.

"I'll do that for you," I said.

"You can still come along."

I shook my head. "You get caught, it means time in a dark cell or even the Bat."

"What's that?"

"A whipping device, long wooden handle with heavy leather strips on the end. They flog you naked and will allow as many as thirty-nine lashes to a man."

Hardin chuckled. "I'm not a man to worry about getting caught. My past speaks for that."

"Well, I am a man to worry."

"So you'll allow them to rob you of twenty-five years? You'll let the state work you for profit and take half your life for one mistake, all because you have a worry?"

I could see he was getting worked up at the idea of me joining the escape, and I had to admit I appreciated his persuading, even as I resisted.

"You're a good man, Garland, and deserve to be set free. You could ride with me. I think we'd do well together."

Here he drilled me with those eyes, but it was not the gunman kind of drilling. His mouth crimped up at the corner and he cocked his head a little. I wondered if he knew how good he looked when he did this, and, further, if he was using this appeal to get around me. I had no idea how much he might be playing me, but that didn't keep me from his gaze. I held on, my blue eyes to his gray, and in that wonderful and awful moment, I saw I'd go in with him. I also saw he'd let me suck his dick because he was worked up in more ways than one. Sure enough, when I looked down his hand was on his privates.

"I need some sandpaper," he said.

"Let's look in the storeroom."

Nobody cared that we went in together. Nash was sucking on his bottle while Duggan was now laid out like a corpse. The men had stopped work and were engaged in idle chat, it being near lunchtime. Soon as the door closed, Wes had his dick out. It was already stiff and as he pulled it, he began to explain. "I got dick sucked on the trail, but only because I was away from my wife. In here is much the same, deprived of female company, and I'm tired of my own hand."

As I kneeled, I wondered if his Jane ever allowed him in her mouth. I suspected not, but then I drew him in and such thoughts fled. I sucked his knob which got him squirming and when I slid down to lick his shaft, I considered how I had a famous dick in my mouth. True to his ways, Wes talked as I sucked. I got my pants open so I could work myself in celebration of having not only a new man, but one so much to my liking.

"Suck my prick," Hardin said, thrusting his hips forward. "I'm gonna give it to you."

Here he took my head in hand and began to shove his cock into my throat. I opened to him while keeping tongue and lips working and it wasn't long until John Wesley Hardin came a gusher. I swallowed his sizable spurts right down, and when he slowed his thrust, I renewed my suck as I was nearing my own peak. Soon I let go a load while still feasting on his prick, thrilling not only to the climax, but to knowing Wes was watching.

Finally I was empty and sat back. Only then did I take Hardin's measure as he made no move for cover. His cock was good sized and sprang from a dark thicket that I thought I'd like to get my nose into.

"You suck a man right good," he said, looking down between my legs. He indulged but a few more seconds before tucking himself into his pants and buttoning up. "Once I'm free, I'll leave off such practice," he added. "Put it to my wife good and proper. For now, well, a man has his needs."

Before we returned to the shop, Wes put a hand to my shoulder. "You're in with me now, right?"

"I'm in with you."

Had the tunnel not been dug in our shop, I wouldn't have believed it possible but there it was, up in that front corner, out of sight behind stacks of stuff nobody ever touched. Wes managed to always have one fellow working in the tunnel while another stood guard and he did his turn too, as did I. It was crude, of course, maybe three feet high and about as wide, cramped and dusty and hot, but we chiseled away. We found the thick walls of buildings we tunneled beneath went several feet below ground, but we got through them while using a rope and bucket system to extract what we'd carved away. A cord was also stretched down the tunnel and a yank from inside meant the digger had attached a note, usually asking for a sharper or better tool. The cord would be pulled out, the request filled by another man crawling in with whatever was needed. No man did more than an hour, thus it was tolerable, and with a dozen men, it worked fine. Wes let me get by with just two of these digging sessions, saying my sucking Duggan's prick was work enough.

Hardin, it appeared, could get most anything done. How he managed to get men from other shops into the digging was beyond me. When I inquired, he just chuckled and said there were ways. I began to see he'd corrupted some guards.

The escape work excited Wes and I saw how he liked being back in charge of himself. The real man was clever and determined. He became so bold in his tunneling efforts that the digging went on during free time as nobody remained in the shop and the big door was closed but not locked. It was during these sessions that he got so excited he'd pull me into the storeroom or sometimes just into a dark place at the back and get out his dick. I'd kneel and take his come while giving up my own by hand. One time he indulged by sitting at his sanding table, pants open, and had me do him from underneath. He laughed right up until he spurted his juice. Afterward, he slapped me on the back as if we'd shared a joke.

I was careful during this period of digging to keep an even keel with Jim who I couldn't quite read. Though he'd beaten me that time over Hardin, I believed he'd now accepted the intruder as much as he ever would. Trouble was, I had only his treatment of me on which to gauge.

Tunnel work went on after supper as nobody remained in the shop. By candlelight, digging therefore progressed. It began on November first and on the evening of November nineteenth, when Jim thought me at the library, I witnessed John Williams announcing, after he'd crawled out, "We're under the armory floor."

Hardin let out a whoop, not caring who might hear, and I shook his hand and commended him for a fine idea. His grip was strong, and he held onto me looking like a kid ready to crack the candy jar. "Tomorrow we'll break through the floor. The guards come in, we'll be there to take their guns. By tomorrow night, we'll be free men."

We took some moments to congratulate ourselves, slapping each other on the back, and going on a bit about our accomplishment. I indulged in this but grew concerned at the hour. "We'd best get to our cells," I said. "It's almost eight."

Hardin agreed, but when the men left, he held me back. He then turned and unbuttoned his pants. "I'm too worked up to sleep. Need something to calm me down." Here he reached in and got his cock which wasn't stiff. Desire rose up in me as I watched him tug himself, so I dropped to my knees and sucked his softy onto my tongue. How it thrilled me to bring him along. I gave him a most ardent sucking which got him hard in no time, not to mention moaning. He didn't talk about his wife anymore, having left off that foolishness in favor of comments on what I was doing or, more often, just the grunts and moans of a man getting pleasured.

When I got out my prick, Hardin said, "You better hurry if you want to do it with me." He now began to thrust into me and I closed my mouth around him to heighten his effort. Took about ten seconds before he gave it up and about ten more before I deposited spunk on the shop floor. We thrashed in our release a few good seconds, then quieted. When I pulled off him, he laughed. "Come in here tomorrow, you'll see your stain on the floor."

I got to my feet, but didn't hurry to put away my dick. "And day after that we won't see any of it," I said. "We'll be gone."

Hardin ran a hand down onto his spent cock which drew me to look that way. I think he was getting that my interest was toward more than sucking him. He fondled himself a bit, as if to tease, then tucked away and buttoned up. Just then the lockdown whistle blew.

Back in my cell Jim lay sleeping and I was careful not to wake him. He was in drawers and they were pulled down, his hand on his sleeping cock. I could see the dried spunk where he'd brought himself off. I put out the candle and heard the lock of cells coming down the row. Hopping up into my bunk, I thought for the first time that I'd be leaving Jim. As I lay back, I considered the loss he would endure, then righted myself by thinking on what he'd done to me with Little Brother.

CHAPTER SIX

Everything I did the next day, November twentieth, I counted as the last time. I swallowed a load of Jim's morning spunk for the last time. I ran my wood-bending machine for the last time. I sucked Duggan's cock for the last time.

When the guards entered the armory before supper, six of us crouched inside the tunnel while the rest remained back in the shop. We had only to break through the plank floor to get the guns, but suddenly there came a commotion over us, like cattle stampeding. Before we could retreat, the planks were torn away and a shotgun pointed down at us. It was held by none other than Captain Bob McCulloch.

"You boys aren't going anywhere," he growled. "Now climb out of there."

Guards, who were many, pulled up Wes, then me, then Williams and the other three. "Your cohorts in the shop are already taken," said McCulloch.

We six were lined up in the armory, surrounded by a good dozen guards, while the captain worked up to a speech. "Hardin, I know this your doing. Quick, I'm surprised at you as you've been a model prisoner. You others, you are plain fools to follow so blindly. Nobody gets out of here. Nobody."

As he said this, he looked Wes straight on, but Wes, undoubtedly having faced down many a lawman, gave not a twitch and certainly no comment.

"Dark cell, fifteen days," declared McCulloch to Wes. "You planned it, you get more time. You others, ten days."

It happened so fast, it didn't seem real until we were marched through the yard, stopping only to get the men left in the wheelwright shop. My thoughts raced about, but I couldn't grasp a one. Then we were in a room I knew of but had never been inside, a cold and barren room in my cellblock where men were flogged, some nearly to death. Their cries often carried through the entire building, awful cries and pleas to be spared. Sometimes the man's friends were made to watch the whipping as a lesson toward keeping in line.

"Strip," McCulloch commanded and we shed clothes and boots to stand naked. Everyone knew what a dark cell meant: naked save for a thin gown, alone within walls painted black to make the darkness worse, living on bread and water, slop pail the sole companion unless you count insects known to visit. Far as I knew, none in the room had done such time.

As we awaited the gowns, I noted just ten of our twelve had been caught. Bill Owens and Bill Terrill were absent, which led me to conclude they had betrayed us.

Wes stood defiant. While the rest of us fidgeted in varying degrees and Ned Lally had hold of his dick like a scared little kid, Wes moved not a muscle. Even naked he gave not an inch and I had to admire this.

"He led me to it," cried Cliff Chapman, Hardin's cellmate. "I'd never do such a thing, but he persuades a man. He's a devil and I but a victim. You see a sinner before you, Captain, a sorry sinner."

"You're all sorry sinners," McCulloch declared. "Admitting it may get you good with God, but such a thing gets no truck in here. You attempted escape, you'll suffer punishment. You'll have plenty of time to speak to God."

Ned Lally began to whimper at this point, still holding himself. A guard stepped up to ram his gun barrel into Ned's gut at which Ned let out a cry and let go of his dick.

"Quiet!" roared McCulloch.

We were handed gowns and pulled them over our heads. Shapeless and thin, they came down to about mid-calf and offered little protection against the November cold. We were then marched through the yard to make plain our failure, knowing many a prisoner watched our progress. It occurred to me that I'd not endured such humiliation since I'd come in.

There were several dark cells at the end of each block, upper and lower floors. I'd heard wailing men going in, men who had to be forced. Walking toward that fate, Wes ahead of me, I determined to not give way, both to show Wes I was with him and because nothing I could do or say would do any good. My silence would be standing up for him and his plan. Had he not been betrayed, I'd no doubt the prison would have been ours.

On this final march, I sucked in all the fresh air my lungs could manage, mindful I'd soon have none. I also looked skyward to see the setting sun coloring clouds pink. Such a fanciful picture for men in our sorry state. I glanced up several times in our march, telling myself to remember the beauty as it would be my last for a while. I shivered in the evening chill, the gown already failing to keep me warm.

The dark cells where we would be housed were in my cellblock, but on the lower floor. Wes was put in first, no doubt so we could all watch and take a lesson. He was handed a pail and shoved in. He didn't take any last look over his shoulder, but stood defiant, back to us all. I was sorry he didn't look to me as it would have helped what lay ahead, but I allowed that the embarrassment of getting caught had buried all else. And if I'd figured out the Owens and Terrill betrayal, so had he as he was a sharp man.

The cell next to Hardin was to be mine, and the fact of him confined beside me made entering the dark cell not easier, I would never say that, but less painful. I took the bucket and stepped in. The cell was probably the same size as the one I shared with Jim, but it was so dark I couldn't see the back wall so I couldn't be sure. There was nothing in it, no bunk or bench, no blanket, no nothing. I turned to feast on the light, and saw Williams and Chapman looking stricken and poor Ned Lally in tears and clutching his privates through his gown. Then the heavy iron door slammed shut, beginning the punishment I suppose I deserved.

Panic immediately struck, for a darkness so complete you cannot see your hand is an unnatural state. I dropped my pail and began to shake all over. Sweat ran down the whole of me as fear unleashed a torrent from my insides. In this awful state I thrashed for some time, my breathing labored as I couldn't bear such blackness. I cried out, my pleas bouncing off the walls to taunt me, and then I just cried. Oddly, it was the crying that quieted me.

Hiccups started amid the tears which made me recall childhood and how I could never cry for long because hiccups always arrived to interfere. I now stood hiccuping inside my hellhole, and with their aid slowly regained some of myself. I sank to the floor and sat cross legged, as I often had as a boy, and, once I'd calmed, once the hiccups relented, I attempted to settle myself as I knew I couldn't let fear run me. I had to survive. No matter the torment of my confinement, no matter the inhumanity of such a cell, I had to keep my mind intact. I had to emerge as I knew Wes would, defiant and undamaged. I stood and groped along the wall until I found the back which I leaned against, wondering if maybe Wes did the same.

It didn't take long for me to realize the cell deprived me of more than light and company. It also kept sound from reaching me. And within this emptiness, time also fled as there was no way to mark its passage. I could have counted seconds, but saw this would make it worse. The thing to do was occupy myself with thought. Days and nights could be marked by meals and slops emptied. Surely things like this would be done at a regular time and could serve as markers.

The walls were cold to the touch, yet I found heat growing within me. This, I decided, was likely to my being worked up by the capture. My stomach growled as if in agreement while reminding me I'd had no supper. I knew not to dwell on this, however, or any aspect of my misfortune. After a while, I got tired, lay down on the floor, and slept.

I woke when something stung my toe, some bug I'd either brought in or maybe one already living in the dark, some crawly creature who thrived on nothingness until a poor prisoner was served. Swatting him away, I sat up and wondered what time it was, then chased off the thought. I couldn't think about time. For me it no longer existed. I sat leaned against the wall and thought instead on Wes right next door. He'd spent ten years on the run so he likely knew harsh conditions. I pictured him sleeping, strong man in gentle repose, but then I drew back his gown to find his prick up and I reached down to get at my own, finding the one comfort the authorities couldn't take away.

I wanted to indulge in the worst way. While a come wouldn't solve my predicament, it would at least give me some pleasure, but my dick didn't agree. No matter how much I pictured Wes and how nasty my thoughts became, I couldn't get myself hard. This was most distressing as doing myself had never failed. But I'd also never been in my present circumstances so I lay back down and attempted to sleep.

Next time I woke, it was to use the slops pail. Even this seemed affected by events as what my body gave up was weak and rank. Absent paper or rag, I had to use my gown to clean up which disgusted me. But in the dark, what did it matter? The other problem with this bodily function was the smell remained. Without the fresh air that blows through an open privy door, I had to live with the worst of myself. This kept me awake for some time.

Deciding I couldn't remain idle, I paced off the cell so I could walk it by counting. At first I moved like a blind man, arm outstretched as if something might get in my way, but after a while, I knew exactly when to turn and made a game of it, seeing how close I could get to the back wall without touching it. Thus I exercised and felt better, but hunger continued to gnaw my stomach.

When the iron door creaked open, I leaped to catch the light, then drew back as it hurt my eyes. This I did for just a second as I was eager to see out, even though it was just into a dank cellblock row. A guard and a prisoner stood there. "Slops," said the prisoner as he held out a pail. I handed over my rank one and took the replacement which I tossed back behind me. The guard handed me a tray bearing a piece of cornbread and a jug of water that could not have been more than two cups. "Eats," he said.

"What day is it?" I asked. This got laughs before they shut the door.

Day or time didn't matter. I was so eager for food that I ate the stale cornbread right down and drank half the water before I stopped myself. Keep some back, I thought. "Keep some back," I repeated aloud, deciding then and there it wasn't wrong for a man to talk to himself while in circumstances such as mine. "You do not know how long till the next meal."

My stomach quieted for the moment, but it wasn't long until I again became ravenous. Pacing the cell may have occupied me, but it also stirred my appetite. Was nothing going to help? I considered Wes pacing his cell, considered him eating his bread, Then I stopped pacing and began to wonder if he considered those he'd led into these dark cells. Did he care about the men he'd gotten into this fix? Did he feel guilt at drawing us into his failure? Was he sorry we suffered the dark, or did he think only on himself, larger than life by way of his fame? The more I thought on this, the more I saw how he'd drawn me to him by manly appeal. Those wicked good looks and eager dick had put asunder all reason. I was imprisoned within a dark cell because of him and his crazy idea he could get free. As I thought on this, anger began to churn where before there was only hunger. My gut began to boil, as did my thoughts, and I cried out to him, slapping the wall we shared. Didn't matter he couldn't hear me. It needed saying.

"Wes Hardin, you're a devil who led me astray. I'm paying for your crazy idea and hope you're eaten alive by bugs and suffer an internal wrath like no other. I hope your bowels are so rank you can't breathe the air around you. I hope your mind turns to mush as you suffer your guilt. You deserve thirty days, not fifteen."

Of course this didn't help anything. My rant soon lost steam as I had little energy and so I let silence return. But within it I decided to steer clear of Wes Hardin from now on. Let others bow to his fame. Let others be swayed and drawn in. I had a man and his name was Jim. I had a life before Wes

Hardin turned it upside down. I'd go back to that life and to what I knew. Far as I was concerned Wes Hardin could rot

Whatever had stung my toe continued to feast on me. I could feel various welts coming up, mostly on my legs. In running a hand over myself to see if I had other bites, I swept over my chin to find a familiar stubble, and my fingers stopped there as my mind seized upon a fact. I could measure time by the growth of my beard. I lingered on my chin which I decided bore one day's worth. I had only to examine my chin when my next meal came to see how long between feedings. The bad part was discovering I got but one meal a day. Next time the door swung open, the routine was exactly as before, and after taking the tray that bore the same meal as before, I fingered my face to find a two-day growth. My sustenance appeared to be the least possible amount to keep a man alive.

I learned to sip my water rather than gulp. I learned to nibble the cornbread and to crave it, I didn't care how stale. I learned to tolerate my own rank excrement which never gained any substance due to my pitiful meals. But I also learned a measure of self control, convincing myself darkness was now my natural state. I embraced it by declaring I was safe and secure, nobody to bother me save the bugs. I talked to myself at length, playing out bits of life already past, and making up new ones I wished to experience. I took off my filthy gown at one point and stood naked while imagining Wes bare and made to stand with hands on his ankles, offering up his butthole. This got my dick stiff and as I pulled it, I spoke all manner of nasty things, all the while picturing sticking it to Wes. This caused me to come a gusher, and I cried out as I let go, squealing like a pig. As the climax finally subsided, I spoke on how good the release and how from then on Hardin, having taken my spunk, would crave cock more than freedom. Lastly, I declared he should take Little Brother up his ass and that I would put it to him.

From this point on, I remained naked most of the time. I also abused my cock a great deal, sometimes with thoughts of Little Brother reaming Hardin's hole, other times putting myself astride the prick of a faceless man out on the prairie. I would ride to release, pleased not only by the climax, but the idea of fucking while beyond prison walls.

I got so good with time, that I knew when to dress for the guards. Though I gained a measure of self-control, it was far from constant. About five days in, the darkness suddenly overcame me and I went into a panic from which it seemed I might never emerge. It felt like I'd disappeared into the darkness, become part of it, and I ran crazy in that cell for a while, pounding on door and walls, crashing around, throwing myself against the brick. Didn't matter it was futile. Purpose was no longer a consideration. It was an outburst that couldn't be contained and it ran for some time before I exhausted myself, fell into a heap, and slept.

When I woke I was angry. My body hurt from bruises I couldn't see, my shoulders in particular as they'd slammed against the walls. I flexed my muscles and made myself pace the cell, and while this helped my body, it stirred my anger toward Wes. I'd told him early on I didn't want to know his plan and yet he'd persisted. Had he allowed me to suck his dick to get me to join him? Had he truly wanted my companionship in his freedom, or had I been used? The more I thought on it, the more cunning he became, and I paced with a fury until the idea lost steam, as did most of what I conjured in my darkness. Finally I sank to the floor, cross legged because that gave me comfort, and I spoke to myself as I thought my father would have. Wes did not make me join him. I had been free to say no, but I went ahead. I allowed myself to be swayed by base instincts and now paid the price. Wes bore a powerful guilt, but so did I.

A man cannot suffer the deprivation of a dark cell without addressing his maker, I don't care how strong or how weak his belief. I'd been raised in a Baptist household, my parents devout, but I'd never found much in God. But then, I'd never found much in any of the family ways, my father a storekeeper in Austin, my mother meek and quiet. When I'd run off to join a cattle drive at sixteen, I'd left God behind, never again setting foot inside a church. But now, in my dark cell, I contemplated His existence, and how my father had said faith was the strongest force in the world. "Faith is the evidence of things not seen," he had quoted from the Bible. I now thought on this and laughed. "Things not seen," I said aloud. "Nothing is seen in here, not a goddamn thing! Is this faith? Locked up in a darkness so complete that life itself disappears? Is this when I am to believe?"

I was naked as I uttered these words. My beard was thick upon my face, my body thin from lack of food. Weakness was my constant companion. I paced naked now, slapping the back wall, slapping the door each time I turned, my stride brisk. It wasn't faith on which I survived, it was determination. If there was a God, I was angry with him for allowing such cruelty in His world. And if there was not a God, what did it matter? I meant to come out of my cell on the eleventh day an upright man showing strength and fortitude. I would not be broken.

One day the cell door opened, but the guard had no tray. "Your time is over," he said. "Ten days have passed. Put on your gown."

I found it in a corner, stiff and rank, but I put it on. The light made my eyes sting and water, but I didn't care. I stepped from the cell and let the tears stream. It was over.

"Move along," said a guard, poking me with his shotgun.

I was taken to the infirmary where I was bathed and barbered. The doctor glanced at my spider bites, but did nothing for them and declared me fit for work. Fresh stripes awaited me, as did brogans, socks, and drawers, and I got into them eagerly. All the while, I sucked in fresh air. It might not have been outside air, but I didn't care. It was new enough.

"What time of day is it?" I asked.

"Morning," snapped a guard. "Come along. The captain wants to see you."

Captain McCulloch sat at a big desk in his office in the main building. He didn't look up when I came in, but this mattered little. I was so happy to be out of the cell, I'd stand before him forever if he chose. Finally he looked up.

"Quick, I am disappointed in you," he said. "You chose badly in following a rogue. This has cost you your job in the wheelwright shop and, until you're reassigned, you'll be cutting wood. I hope you now understand there's no escape from Huntsville. Your sentence was legal and for good reason. A man's life was taken and you must pay. If you try to escape again your punishment will be far worse than a dark cell. Do you understand?"

"Yes, sir."

"You get to your job now."

"Yes, sir."

"And leave off Hardin. He's trouble."

"Yes, sir."

I was escorted to the lower yard where I was put to work on a two-man saw cutting logs with Ned Lally. Ned was shaky. I could see he'd done badly with his confinement. "You'll be okay, Ned," I told him. We sawed slowly as he truly seemed without strength.

My arms ached with this new activity, reminding me I'd softened in the dark cell. Still, nothing mattered but fresh air. I was happy to be cutting wood as it was outdoor occupation, something I think McCulloch hadn't considered. He never would have given me pleasing work, but then he didn't catch every detail. I was still a prisoner, yet felt free. As I sawed with Ned, I wondered what job they'd give me next. And where would Wes land?

An hour or so later, I found Jim watching me. He'd again managed to leave his job and get down into the yard for a look. Seeing him made me realize he'd not been much in mind during my ten days. Now he made himself present, his gaze steady as I worked, and I thought on what lay ahead. I was up for some good fucking, would even welcome Little Brother. I just hoped I'd not be beaten for following Hardin.

When the noon whistle sounded, Ned let go of the saw and turned to line up. He held out his arm and I went around to stand in front so he could rest his hand on my shoulder. We then walked into line. The pork tasted fine, and I ate it right down, as I did rice and peas. I couldn't get enough water. My insides stopped growling for the first time in days.

CHAPTER SEVEN

Jim kept to his lifer friends that day after work, and I didn't go over. Best to let him decide when to talk and when not. I kept to myself, walking the yard as that in itself was a treat. I stretched as I went along, the day cloudy and cold. I wore no jacket as I wanted the weather. I sucked in air and was delighted to see my breath escape as steam.

Walking along, I ran a hand along the lower yard fence, happy to touch the rusty wire. I scuffed my brogan in the dirt again and again, giddy over the slightest thing. I watched the men talking in groups, some standing, some sitting, while others walked as I did, usually in twos but sometimes one alone. I saw Cliff Chapman and John Williams, but made no overture toward either. I even saw Bill Terrill and Bill Owens, who I knew had ratted on us, but as nothing could be proved, they wouldn't be called out. Unless Wes did it. Wes. Suddenly he was upon me as I thought on him still inside his dark cell. My body quickened with the image, but I fought this off as I wanted no more of him.

Jim found me when the supper whistle blew and we ate together like always. After, I said I was going to the library and he gave no comment, just walked off. I then sat with book before me until nearly eight o'clock, reading the same page over and over as I couldn't corral myself. I found comfort in just holding the book and turning a page. I looked around at the shelves, deciding I would read all the books now that I was free to do so. A world lay inside them and I needed to get my mind elsewhere, but just then Lonnie came in and he presently sat down before me.

"Missed you," he said as he settled onto the bench. He wouldn't look me in the eye, despite his declaration.

"Missed you too," I replied. "What's up?"

"I complained to the guard."

"About the doc?"

He nodded. "I won't go into his office anymore. I stay out in the ward, tending the men, so he got the guard after me for insubordination and the guard made me go in there, said he'd crack my skull if I didn't. I told him the doc wanted to do me wrong, but the guard just grinned and said, 'Can't blame him, Lonnie. You're a morsel.' He then shoved me in and stood outside, listening no doubt."

"Did he fuck you?"

"He can't get stiff enough to do that."

"Then what?"

"I can't say it, Gar."

"I understand, but I'm a man with knowledge of what men do. I'm also your friend who can hold a confidence."

He thought on this, then shook his head. "He got at me. That's all I can say. How he did is beyond words. I will tell you this, it's the last time he'll do anything to me."

"You can't hurt him," I said. "They'll add to your sentence if you do."

"I don't care. I got twenty years which is most of my life. It'll be worth the rest to be done with him."

"Don't kill him," I said.

"May have to."

The beautiful boy was now gone, in his place a ruined one. "Best not," I said, and left it at that. Lonnie said no more, just got up and left. I thought on him and his plight until I reached my cellblock which turned me toward Jim. I wasn't afraid of him, but I did feel a measure of concern at not knowing his reaction to my joining Hardin's scheme. This uncertainty was due to my not truly knowing my man. I wondered if anybody ever had.

He lay naked on his bunk, working his cock which was stiff and wet. "Don't say nothing," he said. "Just strip and get in here."

I did as told, grateful we would get back together the best way we knew. When I crawled in, Jim climbed onto my back, shoved his cock in, and started ramming with such force, I knew anger drove him. This was just fine. Let it come through his dick rather than his fist. He slapped my bottom as he went at me, and I didn't care because I wanted to be fucked raw, I deserved to be fucked raw, and because he was going to make me come. Ten days of my own hand made me eager for a dick, and Jim was the man to satisfy my wishes. Soon I was spurting a gusher into the bedding, scarcely needing assistance. Then Jim uttered a muffled cry and I knew he was there. It pleased me to satisfy him, though I knew one wouldn't be enough.

When he was done and pulled out, I rolled over and he lay down beside me. I was crowded against the wall, on my side while he was on his back. Usually I let him speak, or not, but this night I couldn't hold back. "I was foolish to get involved in the escape," I said. "I learned a hard lesson in that dark cell."

"Suck my cock," came the reply.

It didn't bother me to suck a dick that had just been up my butt as I'd some time ago acclimated to filth. And I meant to please Jim as I owed him, and also to keep him on an even keel. So far it was just his need running things. If I could keep on with his pleasure, maybe I would be spared a beating.

His prick was fully spent, but I still worked him, rolling the soft meat on my tongue. "Get around here," Jim said. I slid around so he could feed on me. My dick didn't take long to come up and when Jim put a couple fingers in me, he furthered the cause. I gave him a goodly number of spurts while attempting to fuck his mouth. This stirred his manly self and the cock in my mouth began to rise. I worked it with all my might, bobbing on it as it got hard. Finally, I had him fully up and he squirmed beneath me as his juice rose and spurted into my throat. Never had I been so happy to swallow spunk.

Again, I rolled over against the wall. Again, Jim lay on his back. We passed some quiet minutes, then he pulled me to him, getting an arm around me. This surprised me as he was usually short on embrace, and I almost chuckled when his finger worked down into my crack. He put but one up me and I saw how he meant his possession to be constant this night, if not with dick, then with finger. He probed and prodded, sometimes forcefully, sometimes gently, and he even dozed a while, finger at rest inside me. I lay against him, feeling the rise and fall of his breathing, and taking comfort that I was back where I belonged.

Every time Jim woke, he did something to me. At one point he tongue-fucked me to excess. At another, he sucked my nuts. It had to be near dawn when he said to fuck him. "Do me," were his only words as he rearranged us and raised his bottom. He'd gotten me hard with nut sucking so I parted his buttocks, found his pucker, wet my dick with spit, and pushed in. I couldn't resist speaking. "I'm home, Jim. I'm home."

The fucking went on a good while. My dick may have come up, but I doubt any spunk remained in those well-attended nuts. Still, I gave him a good one. I also found pleasure in doing him, not only from the fucking itself, but from recalling how I'd thought on just that during my confinement. I was now as free as I would be for many years, and I was fucking a man who welcomed my cock.

When my rise began, I was near exhaustion as my job had taken much of my strength. Still, I pumped and with what seemed my last, let go a modest load. I also told Jim what was happening. "I'm going to give it to you, Jim. Here it is, take it, take my stuff." This was all I managed as the climax was more than anticipated. When I was done, I fell over against the wall but not before running a hand onto Jim's bottom and giving him a squeeze. We then slept but I don't think there was much night left. I had to drag myself to breakfast and that day Ned and I sawed little wood.

I didn't want to count the five days until Wes came out of his dark cell, but found myself doing just that. Trying not to do something can make it bigger, and that is what happened. Each day when I joined Ned in the lower yard, I did my foolish best not to count, but that very act drew Wes to me so he was always present in some way. I decided this was because I'd seen him work the wood yard, and maybe some whiff of him remained amid the logs and tools and dust. I'd shake him off and concentrate on my work, only to have him get at me again.

"Why you shakin' like that?" Ned asked on day two. My efforts to resist Wes had apparently become physical, though without my knowledge. I knew Wes was on day twelve. "You look like a wet dog when you shake," continued Ned.

"Bugs at me," I said.

"Too cold for skeeters."

"Fleas maybe. I don't know. Doesn't matter. They're on me, not you."

We'd stopped sawing as we spoke and Ned studied me. "He get to you?"

"Nope."

"Not what I hear."

"What do you hear?"

"That you left off sucking Duggan to suck Hardin."

This caught me unawares and after a dumbfounded second, I pushed the saw at Ned, nearly knocking him down. "Makes no matter to me," he said. "I got sucked regular some years back, but Hardin. Well now, that is something."

A belligerent trusty named Riland stepped from the shed just then to piss in the dirt. Ned looked his way, then smiled at me. "Bet he'd welcome your mouth on him."

"Shut up, Ned. Pull your weight." He took hold of the saw and started in while I stole a look at Riland to see him tugging himself after his piss had run dry. When he caught my eye, he wagged his dick, but I turned away. I'd suck a guard, but never a trusty as those prisoners tended to be worse than the guards when it came to treating a man fair and Riland was no exception. He stood well over six feet, a dark brute who had murdered the couple living next door to him in Dallas. He got ten extra years for being caught fucking the dead woman.

It was on day four of my cutting wood that Assistant Superintendent Grazer came into the lower yard, spoke to the foreman, and then to me. "You've been assigned the carpentry shop," he said. "Come with me."

Ned's jaw dropped open and was still that way when I was marched over to the shop next door to the wheelwright. From the outside, it looked the same as that place, big door between two windows, ramp below the door. As we neared, I heard the buzz of saws and the clack of hammers and other tools. This was where Ned had worked, poor Ned who would not get his job back. Maybe I'd be doing his work. I had no idea.

Grazer followed me up the ramp and into the shop which had that same dark and dusty air as my previous one. A couple heads turned at my entrance, but most of the twenty or so men kept to their work. The foreman, who I knew to be Tom McKay, an easy sort of fellow despite his eighteen year sentence for robbery and manslaughter, stepped up to take charge of me. "Stay out of trouble," said Grazer before he left.

"I mean to do just that," I replied.

"Plenty to do in here," McKay announced. "I'm in need of a varnisher so that will be your job. Come over here and I'll get you started."

I was given a canvas apron, a can of awful-smelling varnish, and a brush. "Whatever we make, which is mostly furniture, you'll varnish. We do some repairs, but mostly manufacture for the outside, tables, chairs, dressers, the occasional wardrobe. You ever varnished before?"

"Nope."

"Well, there's a skill to it. You don't splash on the stuff, you do it with a smooth and consistent stroke, not using too much or two little. You'll get a feel for it. Jonah over there is also varnishing so you can look to him for guidance. Rule is no lollygagging in here. You keep to your work at all times, stopping only to piss or shit. You got that?"

"I certainly do."

Even with his admonishments, McKay maintained a softness that I liked. Many men were ruined by their sad state but Tom seemed to have gotten around that, how I did not know. His voice remained warm and though he was not a handsome fellow, he was a welcoming sort. I was happy to be working for him.

"Clark is the guard,"Tom went on. "He's agreeable if you don't make trouble, so don't. I like a smoothly run shop and the men get that."

"You'll get no trouble from me."

The job required me to stand at a long table upon which various pieces of furniture awaited finishing. Chairs seemed in demand as there were four on the table, all freshly made and still bearing the smell of raw wood. They were straight backed and reminded me of those in our house back in Austin. As I dipped my brush into the varnish and began to coat the first one, I thought back to my parents and meals at our table in chairs like these. This wasn't good as it brought up the shame my folks endured over their son's crime. I chased them off and tried to concentrate on my work, finding it too easy to get too much varnish on the brush.

Jonah, a skinny black man with close white hair, looked over at me on occasion, but made no comment. And I looked at him now and again, watching his brush mostly. Amid my work, I wondered what these men thought of my escape attempt and more, my alliance with Hardin.

"Carpentry shop,"I told Jim after work. "Varnisher."

"Easy work," he replied as we walked. "You plan to toe the line now?"

"That I do."

Jim had not sought Little Brother for several nights, thus we did a lot of genuine dick work. He had me fuck him which pleased me greatly. In return my ass was licked cleaner than ever. Life settled down, for which I was grateful, though in the back of my mind I kept count of another's dark cell days.

Hardin's fifteenth day got me agitated for no reason. I found it necessary to push him away several times, and once I found my varnishing brush stopped entirely as his naked image rose up to demand attention. I couldn't quite chase him off, standing in that awful bare room where we were given our gowns. So defiant and sure. I wondered how such sureness fared those two weeks. I doubted any man could remain the same after such treatment.

That night I could not suck Jim's dick enough. I read nothing in the library and soon as back in the cell I kneeled down and begged to feed. Jim unbuttoned his pants and got it out, wagging it to tease, before allowing the knob onto my tongue. He then stood with hands on hips as I brought him along while freeing my own meat which I pulled. I thought I'd get Jim's load in my mouth, but he wouldn't have it. He yanked me to my feet, shoved down my pants and drawers, and did me standing at the bedpost. And when he'd filled me with spunk, he kneeled to part my buttocks and shove in his tongue so it could fuck me. When he tired of this, he got Little Brother who he greased and shoved in. I was fucked to excess that night, but didn't care as it was what I needed. I came several times, spewing all over the place, and Jim worked himself up enough to do me twice.

Excess is not always a solution which I guess I knew, even as I attempted just that. I couldn't escape the fact of Hardin's release next day because the whole prison was waiting to see how he came out. I told myself my interest was no more than any man, even as I knew better. I'd been the one to suck his dick, after all.

I knew he was put to cutting wood not far from my shop door, but I made no move to get a look. This shop was better run than the last, thus I had to keep to my work. When the noon whistle blew, I quickly sought the bucket to wash my hands, then threw off my apron and sought the chow line. Marching from the shop, I saw Wes right off, looking like he'd never had a bad time at all. Outside of being somewhat pale, he appeared as robust as ever which surprised me as I'd lost weight during my time in the dark cell.

I couldn't keep my eyes from him. As we joined the wheelwright's line and then the wood-cutter line, Hardin caught my stare. He drilled me a hard look, then broke into a smile and gave the familiar nod. My dick stirred and I sucked in a breath, but then we were moving again and he was lost to me.

The silent lunch, which was a decent meal of beans and fresh cornbread, may have been without sound but it was not without commotion. Hardin's presence seemed to set the whole place fidgeting, Then again, maybe it was just me. Maybe the pleasurable unrest inside my pants altered my view. Maybe the crackling air came from me. All this churned my privates a good deal and once during the meal I let my hand drop to my lap where I prodded my swollen rod so as to give myself pleasure in Hardin's company. Didn't matter I couldn't see him. He was there and, much as I wanted otherwise, he had me.

I varnished slowly that afternoon as efforts to keep off Hardin had fallen away with the noon meal. He was not all that far off, out there chopping wood again, and I kept thinking on his body and how I'd seen it naked, a good body, sturdy with hair on the chest and a fine cock. I thought back to his dick on my tongue and to swallowing his spunk. I kept getting myself hard as I worked, kept having to think on other things to calm myself which was mostly futile. Then the whistle blew and work was over. I threw off my apron, sealed my varnish can, washed up, and headed outside, not intending to hunt for Hardin, but only to watch others do so.

A blustery wind had come up by late morning and blew dust around the yard. Hats flew off, debris blew high and low, men pulled jackets close, and huddled up to talk. There was not much walking. Just a few, Hardin among them.

John Williams all but clung to him, talking what seemed a mile a minute while Wes walked and nodded. No doubt Williams was complaining about the failed escape and the incarceration that followed. I wondered if Hardin offered apologies or sympathy. I started walking a good twenty yards behind him, enjoying his smooth gait. He wore no jacket and though the uniform was baggy, I could still make out his bottom which led me to thoughts of it bare.

When Wes and John turned around at the end of the yard, Wes saw me, said something to John who left him. Wes then came over to me, falling in alongside as I kept moving. "How did you do your time?" he asked.

"With some difficulty," I replied. "I've never been in a dark cell, and am determined to never be in one again. How about you?"

"It was a long spell, but I kept strong with thoughts on my wife and children. I also spoke to God a lot."

I said nothing as I didn't want to hear such things. While I'd been pulling my dick and thinking on him, he'd likely done the same while thinking on his wife. Or maybe God. Did he come while confessing to his maker?"

"Some of the guards also helped me out," he added.

"Helped you out?"

"I was given a blanket and candles and extra food. Sometimes they kept the door open a while."

Here I stopped walking. He took a couple more steps, then turned. "What?" he asked. It was then I saw that his fame had taken him over to such extent he considered nobody else. But, much as I disliked such a thing, I saw innocence in it. He'd been just a boy when his rampage began, and a boy is easy to impress, even with himself. He'd grown up with near constant fame. How could he be otherwise?

When I didn't reply to his question, he looked away and called out greetings to a couple fellows who then came over. Soon a little group of admirers had formed and I stepped away with no consequence. And that night I again could not get enough of Jim's dick.

Two days later I heard Wes had been assigned to the machine shop. This was a large and noisy place near the prison's back wall, filled with all manner of machines I didn't know. I was glad he was far from me but this, of course, made no matter. He found me after work one day and explained how he'd been put on a grinding machine to take rough edges off various parts made in the shop. "What parts?" I asked.

"Spur rowels mostly. I grind what's put before me. It's not bad work. Beats sanding spokes."

I knew he said this last to needle me. He then took hold of my arm. "I found a spot behind the boiler shed where nobody can see."

"You did, huh."

"Come on."

I meant to resist, but didn't. I let myself be led into a dirty corner where the shed was blackened and heat from the boiler raged. Soon as we were out of sight, Wes had his dick out. "Need a suck," he said, tugging himself and already halfway up.

I couldn't help but take advantage of the moment. "Thought you were fixed on your wife," I said. "She got you through your fifteen days, not me."

"She's not here and you are."

"That the only reason?"

He continued to pull his dick, bringing his fine cock to full length. I wanted nothing more than to drop down and feed, but I was determined to make him pay for what he'd cost me. He looked into my eyes. "I'm not like that," he said.

"The hell you're not."

He stopped stroking his cock and stood with it in hand. For once he appeared speechless. He then stuffed his rod into his pants, hurried with his buttoning up, and strode away, likely feeling deprived, as was my intent. I went off to find Jim.

CHAPTER EIGHT

Christmas on the way meant looking forward to a day off work and a special meal that usually included pie. I was thus in a good frame of mind when Wes said McCulloch was a fool to put him in the machine shop.

"Why's he a fool?" I asked.

"Because I can get keys made."

He'd found me in the library as he had taken to reading although he favored studying arithmetic instead of the make believe I sought. I kept to my book while thinking I didn't want to know his plan, but I didn't say that because look where that got me last time. "Keys?" I finally asked, looking up to find his face alight with excitement.

"Keys to the cells, gates, and outside doors. A guard I know got me impressions and Aaron Harper is making the keys in the shop."

"Keys alone aren't enough to get out."

"You're right. I've got a trusty bringing me a couple of six-shooters. The plan is to wait for evening, after lockdown, unlock my door and the doors of any wishing to follow me, muzzle the guard, open the gates, and we'll be free."

As reason was futile with Wes, I gave no comment.

"What do you think?" he asked. "Will you join me?"

"No, I will not. Capture this time means flogging and I don't wish that."

"Neither do I."

I let go a sigh, closed my book, and stood. "You've not been out of that dark cell a month and you're plotting again. How do you know you won't suffer another betrayal?"

"I don't, but I can't give in. I'm not suited to confinement. I mean to get free."

It crossed my mind, as he sat waiting for my reply, that containment would be easier if he'd get up to some fucking, but I kept this to myself. He'd not approached me for dick work since our last exchange which I understood, what with my challenge. Only good part of his present conversation was it let me know he was warming, although it was in the worst way.

"I want no part of your scheme," I said. "And you're a fool to try it. You can't trust the men not to tell."

"I won't be kept here."

I shook my head. "I'm not a religious man, but I will offer this. May God help you."

It mattered little that I was not part of Hardin's scheme. Knowing it afoot reeled me in without consent, and I did my varnishing while wondering when the break would come. The longer Wes waited, the more I thought he might just do it. And wouldn't that be something, the most famous prisoner doing what nobody had. Part of me wanted him to succeed while the dick-sucking part did not.

Christmas dinner was slumgullion, wheat bread, and peach pie which we gobbled right down. We were free of work on this holiday, and even with snow on the ground, spent time in the yard. There was speculation around on McCulloch's generosity with our dinner.

"I hear he finished a whole bottle of whiskey which gave him good cheer," said one fellow.

"I hear he got his dick sucked," said another.

"Whatever the reason, I'm grateful," countered the first.

"Maybe you should suck his dick to let him know."

"Maybe you should suck mine."

I moved off as the cheer was gaining an edge. When I ran into John Williams, he was all worked up. "What's got you so jumpy?" I asked.

He studied me a second, then spoke. "Guess you can be trusted, seeing how you was in on the last. We're breaking out tonight, Wes and me and whoever wants to go. Keys are in hand, as are guns."

"What time?" I asked.

"Nine."

"I wish you luck," I said, and I moved off before he could start urging me to go along.

From then on I couldn't rest. I tried both library and chapel, though sitting before God while thinking on Wes seemed blasphemy. Still, I couldn't let go of his plan as keys and pistols sounded a good way. God appeared tolerant of such thoughts as I was not struck down by an unseen hand.

Jim was near mellow when lockdown arrived. "I can't forget that pie," he said. "Once a year and it's new all over again."

"It was a fine meal," I agreed as I climbed to my bunk. We slept in our clothes as the cell never warmed, due to winter being upon us. I stretched out and thought back to the meal, recalling the taste of each thing as memory would need to serve a good while.

With Jim not getting at me, my energy remained high. I could have started him up, but didn't want to this particular night. I kept awaiting the commotion of the break, but it never came. What did come was a guard unlocking our cell later on and demanding me out.

"What for?" I asked.

"Just come out."

By the time we started down the stairs, I knew what was up, and sure enough, there were Ned Lally, Cliff Chapman, Vince Dolman and two more of Hardin's friends, all looking stricken because all knew what lay ahead. We were marched into the bare room where we had been stripped after our failed escape. We were made to stand to one side while dread came over me like some fog. I would rather have faced a dark cell than what I knew was to come. Then Captain McCulloch and Captain Grazer strode in, followed by Wes who, though captive, bore no chains. Instead he had ropes tied on hand and foot, each with a length left over. Around him were six guards and behind these the underkeeper, West, carrying the Bat.

The pie and stew that were still with me began to churn, mixing in with the dread until I thought I might bring it all up. Ned Lally began to whimper which got a slap from a guard. Wes didn't look at his friends lined up to witness his punishment. Gone was the smile that had won over so many. He was stone faced and remained so as he was made to strip naked, even his boots taken. There came no gown this time.

Captain McCulloch eyed him at length, then began his spiel which was first to us. "You men, you see what happens when a prisoner persists in attempting escape? He is caught. He will always be caught. There is no way out of here but to do your time. I want you to see what this man's foolishness has brought down upon him. I cannot know if you had planned to join him as we apprehended him before his plan got underway, but I do know you were foolish enough to follow him before and therefore likely had planned to go along now. You are fortunate to be spared the lash, but you must learn a lesson in any case."

My heart began to pound, dread giving way to fear not for myself but for Wes. I thought I might cry as they pushed him to his knees, then further, stretched out entirely, face down on the concrete floor. The rope lengths on his hands and feet were taken up by guards which got Wes spread-eagled. As he was pinned, I heard Chapman suck in a breath while Ned Lally let go a squeal. "Quiet, you men!" snapped a guard.

"John Wesley Hardin," McCulloch intoned, "for your second escape attempt I sentence you to the maximum, thirty-nine lashes. You have proven incorrigible and shall suffer the consequences. Mr. West, begin."

I'd not seen the Bat before. It looked formidable there in West's hand, wooden handle about a foot long to which were attached four straps, each about twenty inches in length and thick as harness leather. As West raised the Bat, his stern expression gave way to a smirk, and I saw he thought himself gaining fame as the man to flog John Wesley Hardin.

I flinched with the first lash, but swear Wes did not. Red welts rose as the Bat came down again and again. Blood soon appeared as a man's skin is not meant for such abuse. I kept my eyes open not to see the whipping, but to see how Wes took it. The surprise was there came not a shudder from him. The lashes were applied mostly to his back, but McCulloch soon called out, "Don't hit him in the same place so often," and West began lashing buttocks and thighs. I swallowed down my Christmas dinner that was attempting to come up while Ned Lally fainted to a heap and was dragged to a corner. I'd not counted the lashes so could only guess at the number applied, but it seemed, by both the blood on Wes and the agony of the witnesses, that it had to be a hundred.

Wes never made a sound. Throughout the ordeal he lay as if dead, and I wondered if he had the ability, by way of his violent past, to step over that line as needed, let go of life and leave his body behind while his soul traveled elsewhere.

Tears ran down my cheeks as I couldn't help but display what Wes would not. He lay so still I feared he might be dead. Only when West declared thirty-nine had been done and kicked Wes in the side, did I see signs of life. The guards let go the ropes and Wes drew in his arms, moved his feet. The bloody buttocks flexed, but not the back which was fairly ravaged. Vince Dolman turned and threw up his Christmas dinner which got the guards angry. "You'll clean that up," one declared.

While Wes still lay on the floor, McCulloch came back to us. "Take a good look, men. You want this? If I find that any of you were in with Hardin, you'll have your own thirty-nine, as you will for any further attempts at breaking out."

Rather than dismiss us, we were made to watch as Hardin was pulled to his feet. When the guards let go of his arms, he slumped but a second before regaining himself. His face was ashen, his back jellied with bloody wounds, but he made no sound. At this McCulloch began to proclaim again to Hardin.

"Because you have refused to give up details of your plot or name those in cahoots with you, you shall be confined to a dark cell without food or water until you reveal all. And if you die in that cell, it will be your choice. Men, take him over to Cell Block Six."

Wes was taken by the arms and marched out, and I admired that he didn't falter. Had I been in his place I doubt I could have stood, much less walked, but then I'm not such a man as John Wesley Hardin. Once he was gone from us, we were walked back to our cells and it was on this brief journey that I considered Wes on his way to his new cellblock which lay on the prison's other side. This meant he would be taken through the yard, going naked and barefoot through the snow before being put into a dark cell and deprived of life's essentials. By the time I got to my bunk I was a wreck, and Jim left off of me. He said nothing as I lay silently sobbing.

Next day's varnishing might well have been done by a dead man, such was my inability to regain myself. All knew I'd been made to watch the flogging, and Tom McKay didn't press at my lack of production. In the yard after work, a fool accosted me with a poor choice of words. "Hear you got to see the big man put down where he belongs," came the taunt at which I was upon him. My fist found his jaw which sent him reeling, never mind him the bigger man. Before he could recover, I'd swung again, this time to his gut, but men then got between us. "Ain't worth the punishment," one said. I shook off these efforts and stalked away.

I couldn't leave off Hardin anymore. Whatever I did, work, walking, even fucking, he remained with me as he did three days in his dark cell. Might as well have been me in there, such was my life. When I heard he was taken from the cell on the fourth day, it was said he'd revealed nothing of his plot. It was also told how, as he'd gone in, he said he meant to escape and would kill in a minute anyone standing in his way.

"They had to carry him out," said a man in the know.

"Is he in the infirmary?" I asked.

"No. They have him in a single cell in the main building. I'm told he gets medical attention for he has a high fever and can't walk. Even in that sorry state, they keep him under heavy guard."

Never had I felt more powerless. Instinct draws us to aid our fellow man, but a convict has few means toward compassionate acts. Thus I stewed for a month which is how long it took Wes to recover.

I'd always been an agreeable sort, especially toward Jim, but those thirty days wore away some of my good nature. Jim noted this though he never spoke on it directly. I caught him several times observing me as I sat grim and mute on our stool. He left off some in his fucking which I finally called him on. "I need it, Jim. Get that prick into me or if you prefer, I'll take Little Brother. I'm up for a dick and don't care it yours or his."

From then on Jim went back to regular use of me, the pain of Little Brother now welcome as a way to do in time itself. And when not carnally indulging, I sought news of Wes which came in bits from guards who liked him.

We were allowed to write two letters a month but I wrote just one, to my parents who I owed for shaming them. I spoke on my good behavior and godly ways while sparing them knowledge of my escape attempt and punishment. Now, as I penned my January letter on the twenty-second, I told about Wes as I could no longer hold back. I noted his intelligence and charm and the brutality he had endured, but left off his provoking such treatment. I fairly unwound in the writing, then tore it up when I read it back as what lay on the page were feelings that should not be put to paper. I sent no letter in January.

"Hardin is coming out and will be cutting wood," I heard on January thirtieth.

"Then he's well," I said.

"Not sure about that. Only that they say it's time. Word is he never gave up any information on his escape plan. Have to admire that."

"Quite a fellow," said someone. I found I enjoyed hearing praise of Wes.

Sure enough, first of February there stood Wes in the wood yard. Even in the baggy stripes, I knew him thinner as it showed on his face. What reassured me, as I feasted on sight of him from the shop door, was his expression which seemed unchanged by his ordeal. I did note he swung his ax with some difficulty, and once I saw him in a row with Riland, the foreman. A guard had to step between them.

I went to the library every night, but Hardin didn't show up. Likewise, he didn't walk the yard. This led me to believe he'd not entirely healed which caused me some concern. Then, one night, as I tried to make sense of a fellow called Shakespeare, Wes came into the library.

My mouth dropped open as he sat down across from me and issued a sigh. There were a hundred things for me to say, but I couldn't get a one out. Seeing my difficulty, he began. "It will take more than a whipping to beat me."

"So I see," I managed, even as I noted his edge not so sharp as before. The gray eyes still showed determination, but the mouth was grim. He also sat forward, as if his back couldn't yet relax. I thought of the playful grin he'd once borne and wondered if it might be gone forever. No man could remain unchanged by what he'd endured, even though he'd brought it on himself.

"What are you reading?" he asked.

I showed him my book and confessed to it being beyond my understanding. "I'm better with pirates and kings."

"I'll get back to my numbers," he said. "There's lots I want to learn."

As we spoke on reading, what rose up in me was not my dick. It was my heart for I felt a surge toward this man who had been changed without his consent. He fairly reeked of need, as if the fugitive, prisoner, and victim all gave way to the man who was, never mind the fame, just a man. I wanted to reach across and take his hand. I wanted to stand and offer comfort in my arms, but, of course, I did nothing but converse on books. When he finally wound down, a silence came up between us, and I welcomed this as I didn't want to talk on reading. I wanted him to know he had my support, and that I truly cared. The good part was I think he got this without my saying so for he let the silence linger, our eyes playing off each other and me having to look away finally as I feared my gaze would give away too much. He's the same man, I told myself, loyal to a wife, but I didn't listen to this. I was as bad in matters of the heart as Wes was in escape attempts.

"I'll get a book," he finally said and he went among the shelves while I tried to regain myself. He came back and showed me his choice: *Stoddard's Arithmetic*. "I started it before," he said. "Maybe now I'll finish."

He sat back down, his hand on the book, but he didn't open it. I thought he wanted to talk more so I asked about the wood yard. "I saw Riland giving you grief the other day."

"I can't do the work, but nobody will listen. The skin on my back has healed, but what lies under the scars hasn't. Riland won't allow me less production than a fit man so I told him what I think of him and we got into it. We've had to be separated more than once."

"You'd best be careful, else you'll land back in a dark cell."

Here he drew back, fixing his eyes to mine. "I can handle whatever they try," he declared which caused me a surge of admiration for he seemed as gallant as the warriors in the books. He also stirred my cock. "I've asked to be put in a shop where heavy work is not required," he continued. "There are plenty of those, tailor, shoes, something quiet. This wood chopping is just McCulloch going after me."

"No doubt."

"I think Williams gave me up," he then said, leaning forward, elbows on the table. "He was hot to join me, but I think he went cold at the last, though I have no proof."

"Not many you can trust," I noted.

Wes took this in without comment, and I saw he meant to close the subject. As I didn't know where he wanted to go, I kept still. "Not many in here tonight," he said.

"Maybe they're tired of reading the same books over and over."

"I'm not interested in reading right now."

As he said this, he stood up and let his hand fall to his crotch where, even with the loose fit, his pants revealed a bulge. "How about we try the book receiving room?"

I looked around to see if others had come in, but Wes was right. Few were present and all was quiet up front. I rose and followed him to the door. "In here," he said and we stepped inside. The room was dark and musty, but had a gaslight fixture which Wes sought. Soon we had light. He then surprised me by not just getting out his dick but by pushing down pants and drawers. His cock was stiff as a post. "I'm in need," he said, putting a hand to my shoulder.

"As am I." I got my own rod in hand, then knelt, opened my mouth, and took him.

He might not have been fit for heavy work, but he was most able with his prick, holding my head as he fucked my mouth. I had but to embrace him with tongue and lips while opening my throat to his spurts which were quick and plentiful. As I sucked and swallowed, I pumped myself and came a gusher on the floor.

I kept hold of him, even as he softened, for I gloried to feel him inside me. He allowed me to continue and I raised my eyes to find him watching me so I got a hand on him and pulled off all but my tongue which I played around his knob. He let out a moan at this attention which I took for permission. He also spread his legs and began to squirm. I continued to lick and play, then began to rub his dick around on my face, all the while with my eyes on his. He watched me like he'd never had such attention and maybe he hadn't. Maybe wives did no more than spread their legs and pray to God. I'd heard that's how it usually went.

I didn't want to let Wes go. And he didn't seem eager to leave, but then a man with his pants down and his cock in another's hand loses all purpose. I was counting on this as I slid my other hand under to his balls. He flinched at this which amused me, what with him giving no flinch to the lash. He didn't push me off, though. Instead, he thrust forward as if to tell me go ahead and so, with his spent cock still in hand, I got under to lick one nut, then the other, and finally to take one into my mouth. "Holy God," I heard him say.

Palming one nut while sucking the other, I kept my free hand playing with his cock. I was like one of the steam machines in the shop, doing several tasks at once and, come to think of it, I had a head of steam building as my cock, however spent, was stirring with such activity. And praise be, Wes started stiffening as well.

He squirmed with my attentions and I liked that as it showed not only interest but an unrest that I thought could lead to more than dicksucking. I then grew bold, what with him letting me get this far. As I sucked on a nut, I left off handling the other and slid a finger back toward his butthole. He stopped his squirm long enough for me to reach my destination, but pulled off everything. "You get out of there," he growled. "You might take it up the butt, but I don't."

His eyes were blazing now, his cock stiff again, mine too, as we'd once more gotten worked up. I pushed down my pants and drawers, deciding to chance him ready to do what I knew he wanted. He stood with hands at his side, dick pointed at me. I eyed him a good bit, then turned around, bent over, and spread my buttocks. "Fuck me," I said. "Take some real pleasure. It's what you truly want."

I didn't look back over my shoulder. There was no need. His battle came over me like a summer storm that blackens the sky in an instant, then lets go a flood. I knew he believed himself fully married to a good and loyal woman, knew he was adding it up, but I also thought his sums would come up short, what with his dick stiff and my pucker beckoning. To urge him on, I began to work my muscle as I knew that produced a wink of the hole.

"Wet your dick with spit," I told him. "Then just shove in and do it. I want you, Wes. I want you to fuck me here and now."

I felt him move in, the floor creaking as if to celebrate. I heard him spit into his hand several times. Then his cock was prodding me like some rodent. "Shove in," I urged. "I'm used to taking dick. You can't hurt me."

When his knob popped in, that did it. He grabbed me at the hips and rammed to the hilt and I wanted to shout but kept quiet as I knew it a solemn occasion. He pumped like a madman which I understood as he'd not had his wife in over a year. He was finally ready to get past his hand and even my mouth and there is nothing on God's green earth good as getting your dick into someone.

Unlike most convicts, Wes wasn't quiet in his fucking, and I enjoyed his grunts and moans. As he'd already come once, his juice was slow to rise. This I liked as I wanted his cock long as possible. When we got dry, I told him to add more spit and he pulled out to do that, then drove back in. As he pushed back inside me, his moan was not urgent but rather one of pleasure, like he was home at last. My prick remained stiff but I didn't work it, happy just to be taking the rod of John Wesley Hardin.

He was a formidable fuck, I'll say that. Never mind his wounds, he kept his cock pumping at me for a good bit, then started to boil over. "I'm going to do it," he rasped. "I'm coming in you and holy shit." He said no more as the climax overtook him. I squeezed my muscle to welcome his issue.

At last he finished and pulled out, breathing like he'd swung his ax for days. He leaned against a box of books, his prick now a spent rope but still most enticing, while I got hold of my cock and gave him a show. "You gave me your stuff," I said. "Now I'll give you mine." I proceeded to pump myself until I let go another come and him being witness was almost as good as letting go. The married man watched as the fellow he'd fucked brought himself off, and when I was done, he looked at me like he finally understood. Then he slapped me so hard I fell to the floor.

CHAPTER NINE

Had he a gun, I swear he'd have shot me. I had no doubt the look in his
eyes was that seen by men he'd killed.

It took a second for me to recover, more from the surprise than the sting
on my cheek. I rose to my feet and we stood squared off, Wes flushed red in
the face, eyes blazing. Had his pants not been at his ankles, there would be
no evidence of his satisfaction. I waited for him to speak, but for once he said
nothing, just pulled up his stripes, and stormed out.

I did up my pants and sought the table where Mr. Shakespeare waited, and
I tried to read him again but he still made no sense. Then the whistle blew,
fifteen minutes to lockdown, so I put away the book and headed to my cell.
As I walked along, I didn't think on the slap but on Hardin giving way at last.
It was only when I reached the cell that I considered what he'd left in me.

Cold as it was, Jim lay naked on his bunk. His eyes were closed as he
stroked his cock. I noted a gob of his cream at the tip and hoped it might
mask the stuff I carried. "Strip," he said.

"I'm not feeling well, Jim. Stomach out of sorts and I've got the runs. You
get into me, it's liable to make a mess."

"Don't care. I've fucked in shit before. Now strip off."

Time had worked against me as Hardin's spunk dribbled down my leg. I
wiped this away as I shed my clothes, then got in with Jim. I hoped he'd got
himself too worked up to notice but, of course, things seldom went my way.
Soon as he put his dick in me, he stopped. "You're wet," he said.

"Told you, it's the runs."

He pulled out and got his nose down to sniff. He held apart my buttocks
and ran fingers, then tongue over my pucker. "Somebody's come in you," he
declared. "You stink of it."

"Fellow got me in the library."

"What fellow."

"Don't matter."

"You tell me who did you!"

"I won't do that," I said.

"Tell me who, goddammit!"

"No, because you'll kill him."

"I should kill you right now," he growled. "Tear off your dick and shove it up your ass."

"Go ahead," I returned because I knew he wouldn't.

He gave this a few seconds, then sat back. "You let him?"

"Hell, no. I had no choice. He pinned me and did it."

"Hardin?"

"I told you, I won't say who. It's over and done. You know men get taken against their will all the time."

"Stay put," he said. He got off the bunk and I kept still. I did turn enough to see him greasing Little Brother which relieved me some as it was better taking it than a beating.

"I won't put my dick in some other man's stuff," he said when he got behind me again. "But I mean to fuck you one way or t'other." With this he shoved the wooden cock into me and reamed me until I bit the mattress to keep from crying out.

Jim brought himself off twice while Little Brother did the fucking. I felt his spurts on my bottom. Hours had to have passed when he put his spent dick in my mouth and commanded me to suck, managing, as he enjoyed this, to keep Little Brother working my butthole.

The assault fired him, but not his spent dick which I think made things worse. "Please, more grease," I begged. I knew the wet I felt inside was likely blood. "You'll ruin me in there if you keep on as you are."

"Maybe that's what you need, hole so torn up no man will do you. Blood and shit don't matter to me if I get what I want."

Here he pulled out Little Brother and held it before the candle. "Blood, but no shit," he said. He didn't wipe it off before he added more grease. Then it went back in.

He finally tired himself, but wouldn't take Little Brother out of me. "You keep him in you," Jim said. "Nobody gets in there but me or him. You sleep here with me so I can check. You take him out, there'll be hell to pay."

Exhaustion allowed me some sleep, but it was fitful. The grease on Little Brother thinned and gradually ran from me so by morning I was dry. At dawn, Jim rolled me over, pulled out Little Brother, shoved in his own stiff prick, and rode me in the most painful fuck I'd ever had. Once he was done, he allowed me up, and I felt residue run out of me. My drawers were half soaked an ugly red mix soon as I put them on. My pants covered the evidence, but it wasn't long before some soaked through.

"You stay out of that library," Jim said as we lined up to march to breakfast. Long rows of men fell in as they left their cells to descend the stairs and join the lower lines. We then marched from the block in long double rows.

I'd not replied to Jim, not only because saying anything would do no good, but also because I intended to refuse him comment on anything. He'd gone too far with his claiming me. Silence was my only weapon and I meant to use it.

After work, I didn't walk the yard. I needed to lie down as I felt awful, but I wanted to see Wes a tad more. We need not speak, I decided. I just wanted a look since he'd cost me. I leaned against the lower yard fence to watch as he regaled a bunch of men with his stories. He was so caught up in himself that he didn't catch sight of me until much of the hour had gone and even when he caught my eye he still talked. I admired how he kept on with those men while passing me a look that said, clear as all get out, that he'd fuck me then and there, were we alone. That fit right in with what everyone knew on regulars always proclaiming loyalty to wives right up until they stuck their dick up a butthole. Once satisfied, they cleaved to the woman until they came looking to fuck again.

Wes did not approach me, and I didn't care as I was out of commission. But I knew he'd be in the library that night, dick likely hard, and he'd wonder at my absence. That was exactly what happened, as he told me so three days later when he saw me walking the yard. I was feeling better each day and the bleeding had stopped.

"Haven't seen you in the library," he began. "Did Mr. Shakespeare do you in?"

"No."

I knew he wouldn't apologize for the slap, wouldn't even acknowledge there had been a slap, and I was right on that. I was also right in his being up for another fuck. "Why don't you do some reading tonight?" he suggested.

I shook my head.

"Where are you spending your time?"

"In my cell."

"With Scanlon."

"His cell too."

Wes was a smart man on all but his own self, and it took him just a couple seconds to figure things. "Did you tell him?"

He couldn't even say what it was that I would have told. This rankled me so I did what he wouldn't. "You mean your fucking me? I'm not that big a fool, but neither is Jim. He felt your stuff when he got at me. 'Course he didn't know it was you, although he did speculate."

Wes stopped in his tracks and I did too, looked him in the eye. His mouth was open and I almost laughed at his lack of words. Finally he asked if Jim had hurt me.

"Some, yes."

His eyes scoured my face.

"Not where you can see," I added.

"Punch you up?"

"I won't say how, but no more library."

"He doesn't own you."

"Well, he sorta does."

"You his wife?"

I blew out a sigh and resumed walking. "I am not his wife," I said. "Christ, Wes, you need to start looking past yourself. I'm his man."

He pondered this, then said, "There he is yonder with those other lifers. He doesn't look particularly mean."

"He's not, but where certain matters are concerned, his temper rises."

"He's the one beat you that time."

"Let's leave off Jim, okay? Any progress on you getting a new job?"

"Nope. I've asked for the shoe shop and the foreman there would welcome me, or so he says. It's McCulloch in my way. I can't keep on with the ax."

"Maybe if you stop trying to break out."

"I've decided to forgo that and toe the line from now on. I wrote that to Jane as she's concerned about my escape attempts and the punishments I've suffered."

"It's good to hear you willing to do the time. It's not so bad if you try and make the best of it."

"I'd like nothing more than to make the best of it. With you, like we did."

I chuckled. "That what you meant in that letter to your wife?"

"Damn you, Garland, you leave off Jane. That is a private matter."

"You're the one spoke on her."

"In making a point toward toeing the line, nothing more."

"You regulars, you all fight the same battle and, far as I can see, none win. Proclaim loyalty to May or Ann or Jane one minute, put your dick to a man the next."

This caused Wes to peel off and go back the way we'd come while I kept walking.

Jim settled down some after this, likely due to my evenings in the cell. I missed reading, but Jim had fashioned a set of checkers from leather scraps cut into squares and rounds and we played on a piece of board I got from the carpentry shop. I'd penciled squares onto it so we had some occupation and Jim was good at the game. Fucking resumed, but not with Little Brother. Jim remarked less and less about blood on his dick. Two weeks passed before I said I wanted to get a book.

"Nobody's going to get me there," I said. "Look at all the times nothing happened. A man can get taken most anywhere."

He couldn't argue as he'd told me the day before about just that, in his saddlery shop, a new man, or boy really, maybe fourteen, gotten by a thug who'd preyed on others. "Nothing to do but let it go on," Jim had said. "Guard just watched."

Now he considered my request. "You get a book, you bring it back here."

"Fair enough."

Wes was at a table with his *Stoddard's* and did not look up when I came in. "You caught up in your sums?" I asked.

"Garland." His face lit up with a smile that was most genuine. He had great appeal when disarmed. "How are you getting on? Feeling better? Jim okay with you?"

"I can't stay. Just get a book and go back to him. It's good to see you."

He didn't need to say what he wanted. His look was confirmation enough. I knew our last conversation still fresh, and saw him swallow as it ran by. Then he licked his lips, his tongue lingering like some cock head.

"There's a book I want to show you in the back room," he said as he stood. He didn't wait for comment, just went in there. By the time I reached him, he had his pants down.

"I can't have you in me," I said. "Jim will know."

"He can't tell if you suck me."

"No, he can't." And with that I got out my cock, kneeled, and worked myself while I fed on John Wesley Hardin.

Everything else disappeared, of course. Jim, Jane, McCulloch, the whole lineup lost its sway. With his prick in my mouth, life was Wes and me. I fairly feasted on him and his juice was plentiful on my tongue. He didn't try to fuck my mouth like usual. Instead he stood looking down while I did my best to give him pleasure. Let him try and think on Jane while I attended him.

When his moans grew frequent, I knew him on the rise and I bobbed and sucked like no tomorrow while pumping my rod to a gusher that hit just before I received his spurts in my throat. I heard him holding in a cry as he unloaded, and I thrilled to what I gave him. It felt good to do a man with no threat or coercion.

When Wes was done, he didn't pull out. I was fixed on him, sucking as he softened, letting him know I liked him in any and all ways. When I finally let go, I rubbed my cheek against his cock and the dark bush from which it sprang. He allowed this, likely missing that it was the cheek he'd slapped before.

At last I sat back, then stood. Wes blew out a long breath and did up his pants. I didn't rush for cover, and he took a good look down there. "Best you'd button up," he said, catching himself. "And get yourself a book."

I did as told and pulled a pirate book I'd read before. Wes stood close by, and when I started to leave, he stopped me. "You know you get to me," he said.

"I'm getting that idea."

"It doesn't mean I don't love my wife."

"But it does mean something, Wes. Best you stop trying to convince me and take it up with yourself." And with that, I stepped past him and left. I felt pretty good when I got back to the cell where I found Jim agreeable to my reading aloud. He liked the pirate story and fell asleep before I got halfway.

CHAPTER TEN

More than once, as spring pushed winter aside, I recalled Wes saying I got to him. I held onto this as I did my varnishing, hearing it as declaration even as I knew to him it was more a confession. I also held onto hope that he would heed my advice and consider our situation, but he buried that notion with talk on his latest letter from Jane. This, in turn, got him going about his children and his extended family. A whole clan crowded in around him which I didn't mind as they made Jane smaller.

Dicksucking continued in the library and lower yard, but all the while Wes made it known where he wanted to put his cock. I wanted the same, but held off as I didn't want Jim's fury.

"I'll pull out to come," Wes said in the library one night. "Leave no evidence."

"You'll leave your smell."

Taken aback, he went silent. After a few seconds, he asked, "Does he sniff you down there?"

"Yes, he does, among other things."

I could see this play his mind as he was a transparent fellow, especially when sexual matters cornered him. I enjoyed him stewing over something he'd not considered because it obviously aroused as much as disgusted him. To ease his distress, I said, "Men do lots of things to each other, Wes. Things no woman would ever permit."

His breathing had picked up and his hand was at his crotch. "I want you bad, Garland."

"Then get it out and let me suck it."

"I could take you by force," he said, bristling.

"I know, but I'm thinking you're too good a man to do that. Come on, let me make a meal of you."

I did him same as usual, in the room where nobody went. When I'd swallowed his load and sprayed my own onto the floor, I kept my prick in hand as I found Wes looking there. "You know, you can suck me too," I said. "It feels right good."

At this he pulled up his pants and suggested I do the same. "And get your book," he added.

"Enjoy your arithmetic," I said as I left, doubting he'd be able to concentrate, what with the idea of sucking my prick upon him.

I kept needling Wes as time went along, but he didn't suck my dick. He did keep talking about fucking which I encouraged as I thought conversation on sexual matters did him good. I was slowly breaking him down, even as I'd not let him in. Sometimes, in our library time, especially if nobody else was there, he'd ask about men doing things to each other, and I'd tell him about Jim and me.

"You mean he licks you there?"

"Nothing like it. Runs his tongue up and down my crack, licks my hole, and if he's worked up, which is most times, he puts it in."

"Tongue in you? I don't believe it."

"Christ, Wes, you were on the trail. You had to know what all went on. I got tongue-fucked many a time out there and a hell of a lot of other things. I don't see how you could miss it. Men off to themselves, be it trail ride or prison, will do things to each other. You want to lick my hole, you can."

I knew his cock was stiff under the table. He had a hand down there and it wasn't still. "Got you worked up," I said with a grin.

"You do it on purpose."

"I like getting to you."

"Then get down under the table and suck me." He unbuttoned then and there and pulled it out. "Like that time in the shop, remember? Anybody comes in, I'll be reading my *Stoddard*."

His daring surprised me, but I was not going to mention it. There were just a couple men reading down the way so I got under the table and took him into my mouth. I enjoyed his squirm as he seemed especially ripe this night. I knew him now, knew that dick and how to bring it along as I wished. He was so ready, what with having prodded himself as we spoke, that I was hardly on him before he came a gusher.

Release should have settled him, but it didn't. "I mean to fuck you," he said as I got out from under the table.

"Right now?" I asked, grinning.

"I'm not fooling, Garland. You started something in me, and you offered it up once before, so you can do so again. I can only hold out for so long."

"Don't think it's easy for me," I said, turning serious. "I go to sleep at night thinking of your dick in me."

This was maybe too much for him to handle as he went quiet and began to rummage in his book. I sought a volume and left, fearing to say more.

First of July, Wes got a job in the shoe shop. How he managed to get past McCulloch I did not know, but I suspected Riland, the wood-yard foreman, had a hand in it. Wes had continued to resist work due to his physical complaint which likely wore Riland down. One thing about Wes, once he had his mind set, he wouldn't relent. As I pondered his wearing down Riland, I considered that I too was being worn down.

Free time on his first shoe making day, Wes found me in the yard. "I hear you're a shoe maker," I said.

He slapped me on the back and laughed. "I sure as hell am though I've a lot to learn. They're making me a cutter. I operate a machine that cuts shoe soles from slabs of leather. Tricky work, but I'm told I'll work up to doing twenty or more soles in a single cut. Best of all, I'm not swinging an ax."

"How did you manage the transfer?"

"Parry, you know, guard in the wood yard, he came over to my side and leaned on Riland. That and my refusal to work did it. Parry also has sway with McCulloch."

"If anyone has sway, it's you."

"I am every man's friend until he crosses me. Agreeable to one and all, more so to some."

"That an invitation?"

"My dick won't stay quiet around you."

We were in the lower yard near the boiler and I think just being around the place where we often did things got him worked up. He pulled me into the spot, but before I could kneel, he grabbed me from behind and started humping like some dog. "Let me fuck you, Gar. I want to get it in."

He groped my cock as he rode me, pleading all the while, and I finally gave way, mostly because he had me about ready to spurt and a man in such condition will agree to most anything. I pushed down my pants and drawers while he bared himself, applied spit, bent me, and shoved in.

For a couple seconds he remained still and I hoped he was noting he was now where he belonged. Then he set to driving in and out, grunting at each thrust while I began to come with first touch. "You're driving the come out of me," I squealed. "Fuck me, Wes, fuck me."

The supper whistle blew just then, and Wes issued a cry as he came, pounding me right up until the whistle stopped. He hung on, slumped against me, arms around my chest, dick slow to lose its girth. "Holy hell," he rasped.

"That do you?" I asked, savoring his embrace as such a thing gave new intimacy.

"And then some."

He held me until his cock slipped out. "We'd best get in line," he said, "though I hate to."

"Likewise, Wes. Likewise."

A thought came to me then on how I might fare with Jim and the evidence now inside me. "Do something for me, Wes. Rough me up some on my bottom. Leave some bruises, like I was forced."

"What good will that do?"

"Probably none, but I reckon if I tell Jim up front some fellow got me, maybe he won't blame me so much. There is a conscience in him. I just have to go get it. Now dig your fingers into me. Leave some marks."

Wes did as asked, but only after I pushed him on it. "Hurt me," I said when he just squeezed. "It's for a good cause. Dig your fingers in."

My buttocks fairly throbbed when I did up my pants and left Wes. I found Jim and we marched to supper together. As I ate rice and cornbread, I enjoyed the feel of spunk dripping out of me, especially now that I had a way to avoid Jim's wrath.

I didn't go to the library as I already had a book that I'd read aloud partway, so I went with Jim to the cell where he immediately said to strip off.

"Best not tonight, Jim. A fellow got me in the yard."

"Who was it?"

"You know I won't say."

"Where'd he get you?"

"Don't matter. It's over."

He went quiet, then picked up Little Brother. "You can punish me if you have to," I said, "but you know these men can't help it. Most don't have it like us. It's just a hole, Jim. One good shit and that stuff is gone."

His grip on the wooden cock loosened. He remained quiet, back to me, while running his fingers over it. Finally he asked, "How come they're getting you lately? All this time, they've left off you which I thought because of me."

Suddenly I was cornered. He was right. I'd been taken by force many times during my first months in prison, but once Jim roughed up a few it had stopped. My mind now jumped around looking for a lie. "They haven't exactly left off me," I said, making it sound like a confession. "I was taken by a guard in the wheel shop more than once. He liked it first thing in the morning so his spunk and his smell were lost with the day. I'm sorry, Jim. I didn't tell you then for the same reason I don't tell you much now. It meant nothing, just like these latest fellows." I ventured a hand onto his shoulder and felt him slump. "I'm sorry, Jim. I remain yours. Know that, please."

He pulled back and sought his bunk, sitting on the edge. Never had I seen him give way before, shoulders rounded, head down. I knew thoughts were piling onto him so I chanced it and sat down beside him, put a hand on his knee. "Let me help you out," I offered, at which he turned to look me in the eye. He was such a wounded man that when his determination slipped, he became almost appealing. "You know what you need."

We said nothing more, just stripped naked. He got onto his bunk and raised his rump to me at which I put my cock in and gave him a good long fuck, during which he brought himself off. I did him easy rather than quick as I thought he needed me in him a while. Fucking can solve a man just as much as it can upset him. And I cared for Jim, I truly did, for he was as tragic as some of the men I'd read about, great men brought down by their own shortcomings. Finally, when my rise began, I spoke. "I'm going to come in you, Jim. I'm going to claim you with my prick, leave part if me inside you." Here I left off talk as I was spurting into this poor fellow who had none but me for comfort.

I avoided Wes for a few days so Jim would get no idea on us. I made a point to walk the yard with Lonnie and Bob. Funny part was Jim wasn't always watching. He spent time with his lifer friends, and when not with them, I went over and kept to him, even if not a word passed between us.

"Guess the library is okay," he said one day. July had turned hot and we didn't walk. Everyone in the yard lounged in the shade by the brick shop buildings, but even this didn't help. The stench of sweat overpowered all else which got me to thinking it might overpower sex smells too.

"I appreciate your trust," I said to Jim. "The library is quiet which allows me a kind of escape. You should come with me one night." I said this only to curry favor as I knew he wouldn't go. "A peaceful place," I added. "You don't have to take up a book."

"No, you go on. There's the chapel if I want quiet."

"You pray in there?" I asked.

"My father was a praying man. No, I don't talk to God. If he wants to address things, he can call on me."

"Fair enough."

My cock was stirring when I got to the library that night. As we weren't due for wash water for another day, I was rank with sweat which, for once, I welcomed. Wes looked up as I came in, like he'd been on the lookout. He closed his book as I sat down.

"I can stay," I said. "Jim has backed off some."

"Bruised bottom help?"

"Turns out I didn't need that. Things went another way, but got to the same place."

"What way?"

I saw he wanted to work himself up with sex details. We both knew we were going to go to that back room and fuck and we both also wanted to enjoy the run up. "Well," I began. "Soon as we were in the cell, I told him I'd been taken against my will which sort of broke him down."

"That all?"

I leaned forward and smiled, savoring the moment. "No, that wasn't all. I put it to him."

Wes drew back. "Fucked him?"

"Gave it to him good which settled him right down."

"I thought you were his man."

"That don't mean there are rules on who does what. A man can give and take."

He said nothing, so I went on. "Fellow on the trail, me and him did it all. Nighthawk duty, we'd stand between the horses, pants half down, and I'd fuck him, then turn and let him put it to me. Sucked each other too, one, then the other. All the way from Austin to Abilene."

"Don't you get ideas on me," Wes managed, face flushed.

"Just saying. Anyway. I do like to get my dick in sometimes."

He studied me like he wasn't convinced I stuck it to men. This amused me and I let him go on a while as I had a hand on my dick, the talk getting me stiff. Wes squirmed in his chair until I stepped up. "Don't know about you, but I am up for a fuck."

He took this in, swallowed, and blew out a breath. "I am more than up," he said, and he rose. I then followed him to the back room.

We couldn't get bare fast enough. When his pants and drawers were down, I feasted on sight of his swollen prick. He spit in his hand and began to slather it on while I stood pulling my own meat. The fact that I would not face retribution from Jim made the prospect of having Wes all the better. Then he was ready. He turned me around, pulled apart my buttocks, but instead of driving in, he ran his thumb over my pucker and prodded some. "You can put a finger in," I said. I could tell he was tempted as a finger scooted the thumb away. It then rubbed me some, but then his urge got the better of him and he said, "Ah, hell," and stuck in his cock.

I stood bent forward, hand on my dick while he pumped in and out. He took hold of my hips while he did me and I worked my prick frantically because soon as he got into me, a rise beckoned. As my juice boiled, I kept enough control of my thoughts to remind myself I had the man I wanted, he was inside me, taking pleasure, and soon to release in my passage. I listened to the slap of his flesh against mine and all too quickly hit the peak. I wasn't quite done when Wes issued a strangled cry, dug his fingers into me and rammed his cock home. "Fuck me, Wes," I said as I took his stuff. "Fuck me."

He took a while to empty which added to the power he exhibited in so many other ways. He was a forceful man and his dick was no exception. Those fat nuts that I'd had on my tongue held great stores of spunk and I was getting a good measure.

When he was finally done, he did as he had before, wrapped his arms around me and held on, breathing heavily, his head on my shoulder. This was where some men nuzzled and nipped, even kissed, but I chased off such thoughts, content just to have been done by the man I wanted. He held on until his prick softened and slid out. "It's good with you, Garland," he said.

When I squeezed the arm he had around me, he let go and stepped back. By the time I turned, he was doing up his pants. I stood bared a while longer and he did look down there. Seems he couldn't always keep himself in check, and I liked to think he was considering what it would be like with my prick on his tongue. All men sucked something. I knew married men sucked their wives' tits. I took hold of myself and raised the knob toward him and he didn't shy away. He watched, then caught himself and told me to get dressed. Nothing more was said. We went back out and took up our books, but more than once I found Wes looking not at his sums but at me.

Two days later, as I did my varnishing, a terrible commotion rose outside. I kept to my work while foreman Tom McKay went over to look out a window. All in the shop stopped in wait of news on what took place. "They've got Hardin and another in the yard. Must be thirty guards around them," McKay said. "Looks like another breakout."

I dropped my brush into the varnish pot as I wanted desperately to run to the window and see. McKay came by me, but didn't remark on my stoppage. "You'd think he'd learn," he said. "All right, men, nothing going on. Just Hardin in trouble again."

Work resumed, but with it came the buzz of conversation. Shops were meant to be silent, but foremen and guards had final say and ours were lax about the rule. Thus the men fell to speculation on Hardin's next punishment while I harked back to his saying he would toe the line. He'd even written to his wife about it. I sat for a while, then saw this as futile as the escape attempts so I picked up my brush and went back to work.

CHAPTER ELEVEN

Wes remained a presence in the yard, even when absent. Men speculated at length on his latest escape attempt, most coming out in favor of his efforts, never mind the consequences. Guards also remained sympathetic to Wes, if not his cause, and enjoyed passing along information on the latest incident. The day after the failed attempt, Clark, guard in my shop, was eager.

"You were with Hardin that first time he tried to break out," he said as he perched on the edge of my work table.

"I was."

"Learned your lesson, I suppose."

"You suppose right."

"Still his friend?"

"I am." I turned the stool in front of me and began to varnish the other side, not yet sure if I welcomed this attention.

"Know his plan this time?"

"I did not."

"A good one, till a man squealed to the captain."

A laugh escaped me at the idea of Wes betrayed a third time. Never had I seen such foolish trust.

"What was the plan?" I asked as I could see Clark wanted to tell.

"He bribed Long, a guard in the shoe shop, and Long let him out into the yard with Jim Hall, another murderer. They got onto a roof and were headed to the wall when captured. Like before, a man in the know went to McCulloch who had his men ready."

I gave no reply because I saw Clark wanted one.

"Fool, if you ask me," he went on.

"Nobody's asking."

"They flogged him though I hear it was just twenty this time. He's in a dark cell now, drew a week."

When I said no more, Clark eased off my table. "Thought you'd want to know, being his friend." He then went over to McKay where he likely repeated his gossip.

My heart did not go out to Wes this time, mostly because he'd again played the trusting fool, but also because I knew his dark cell time wasn't like that suffered by men such as me. He would have a blanket and candles, extra food, even an open door. For all I knew he had his *Stoddard* and passed the time with study.

Jim made no mention of Hardin's latest try, which I didn't know how to take. Had my actions of late settled him on that? I stayed away from talk on Wes, much as was possible during this week. When I heard his name in the yard, I passed on by, and in the shop I concentrated on my varnishing to such extent that McKay commended me on my industriousness. Nights, I couldn't get Jim's dick far enough into me. Once he'd come, I'd beg him to get in and taste his stuff. I even got Little Brother off the shelf, greased it, and made a show of shoving it up my ass while Jim stood working his cock. When Jim wore out, I went after him, licking his hole and getting my tongue in because I wanted to wallow in filth. He let me have my way and I often woke him before dawn to give him the cock that had come up in the night. I knew he took all this as a renewed bond, and I let him think that way, even as I knew otherwise.

I saw Wes in the yard after he'd done his week. He looked downright robust and, as usual, was entertaining some men. I avoided him, but knew when I went to the library he'd be there. And he was, grinning like some schoolboy who's fooled his teacher. "Missed you," he said once I'd gotten a book and sat down.

Before, I would have returned the comment. "How was your time?" I asked.

"Not bad. Guards are easy, especially Furst who I think has designs on me."

"You let him suck your dick?"

"Something eating you, Gar?"

"Nothing. Not a damn thing." I opened my book and began to read about soldiers in a great war long ago.

"I had no part of Furst," Wes declared after a bit.

"I don't care one way or the other on that."

"Then what?"

I closed my book. "For a smart man, you're awful stupid at times."

"What in hell are you getting at?" he asked.

"What about toeing the line? You wrote your wife on that and said the same to me, then you try another breakout."

He took this in, eyes fixed on mine, and in those seconds the famous man gave way to the one I favored. He blew out a sigh before he spoke. "I meant it when I wrote it to her and when I said it to you," he began. "I still mean it, but I can't leave off trying. Hours of shoe cutting weigh on me, Gar, just like your furniture work must weigh on you. I've never been penned before. Well, not for long anyway. In my whole life I've run free, and much as I try to settle with what I now have, it doesn't work. I see escape everywhere I look and this preys on me, as do the hours, so I talk on it with the men, and we go for it."

As I took in this confession, my resistance collapsed. What I'd managed to chase off all week came back with such force I wanted to bare myself body and soul. I said nothing, however, as his eyes were locked on mine, and the absence of resistance under such a gaze is a powerful thing. I had the genuine fellow sitting across from me, the wild boy grown to manhood, yet never tamed.

"I thought you a fool," I said. If he was being honest, I would be the same.

He chuckled. "I suppose I am. There's a lesson to be learned, and maybe I'm finally getting it. Somebody will always tell. I have to be careful on that."

"Then you'll try again?"

"I'm now more determined than ever."

"And the whipping?" I asked.

"Not as bad as before."

I sat back, unable to offer anything more. Wes gave it a second, then went on. "I'm not like you, Gar. I can't give in like you do. I won't be kept behind walls for twenty-five years. I won't."

"They could tire of your attempts and kill you."

"That's a possibility."

"Doesn't that concern you?"

"I've been shot nine times, my friend. When I came in the doctor said I had the most bullet wounds he'd ever seen on a living man."

"Luck must ride with you."

"Something does."

I looked over and noted a different book before him. "New book?"

"Yes. I was just brushing up on arithmetic so I'm done with *Stoddard*. This is *Davies* who teaches algebra and geometry."

"What use...?" I stopped myself too late.

"In here? None, but I won't always be in here, and I wish to continue learning. I'm not an uneducated man, Garland. I got top marks in school, even taught a few months. I also passed law courses alongside my brother who was a lawyer."

"That doesn't get much mention."

"Killing is what people want to hear about, not the man himself. Once when I was on the run, I hid out as a school teacher in Polk County. The Nash School, it was run by my aunt. I had twenty-five students, age six to sixteen. I liked the work and the children did well, but I left after three months as the state police were closing in.

"Later on, end of 1870, my brother Joe was in school at Round Rock near Austin, studying law with Professor J. C. Landrum. My father had an idea to send me there, saying he was giving up hopes of me studying for the ministry, and would settle for the law. He said Round Rock, being close to Austin, would be good cover as it was under the nose of the state police and they wouldn't look there. So I went over there and began school alongside Joe. Then I got wind the police were looking around so I hid out in some brushy woods, keeping a secret camp where Joe came late at night. He always took a different route in case the police were watching. He brought me food and lessons and we studied by the fire so I could keep up, but it was hell in between his visits. I managed to complete the work, just as Joe did, the two of us having long discussions on points of law. When time came for Joe to graduate, I slipped in one night and took the final examination on all the pre-law subjects we'd studied and I passed. Prof. Landrum graduated me same as Joe. I got the same diploma. Joe went on to practice law while I never could."

"Nobody knows this," I said, surprised by the outpouring.

Wes shrugged. "Well, now you do."

"I want to ask why you killed all those men, but won't. I think it would spoil things right now."

"I appreciate that."

Neither of us opened our books back up. We sat quiet a good while, one of the first times we weren't urgent to get at one another. It was like the latest stint in a dark cell had led Wes to settle down more than he'd admit. When the lockdown whistle blew we were downright soft.

Next day Wes came up to me in the yard. "I've written to my cousin Manning Clements to get up a petition for my release," he said as he fairly bounced with excitement.

"Petition for release? Never heard of such a thing."

"I have a great many supporters, folks who see the injustice done me and my efforts to bring down the corrupt state police. Manning says they want to help me, so I've suggested the petition which he'll present to the governor."

I couldn't help but dash such a notion. "The only thing more foolish than your trying to escape is asking to be let go, I don't care how many supporters. You've killed, Wes. You seem to overlook that more often than not."

"I'm imprisoned for one killing only and the sentence is unfair. You should be pleased I'm attempting lawful means."

"Well, I'll give you that."

I knew by his agitation he'd want to fuck. When we reached the boilers, he stopped short as two prisoners were at work on the pipes, guard close by. "I'll be damned," Wes said as we resumed our walk.

I chuckled. "You had something in mind?"

"My dick is stiff."

"You're excited over your petition."

He grabbed my arm. "I mean to fuck."

"Well, good luck on that as you're certainly not doing it here. I suggest some evening study in the library."

"You like playing with me, don't you?"

I smiled. "Some, yes. You're always ripe for it."

He reached down to adjust his swollen cock. "You'd get it good right now if we had a place."

"I don't doubt that."

One night I found Jim greasing his dick just as he'd greased Little Brother. This puzzled me until I realized it his attempt to ignore whatever spunk men left in me which, in turn, meant he was accepting, in his own way, the fact of my being taken. After he'd done me, he asked if I was still being got at and I said now and then. "Easier to give it up than not," I added.

He bristled with such an answer and got to work with Little Brother, but he still kept greasing his dick, and to tell the truth, I liked him being juicier than he had been with just spit. Of course I kept on fucking Wes. Most nights we did it in the library and, once the boilers were repaired, out there. This usually set him in good spirits, but as we walked the yard on a September day, he said, "I stopped writing to Jane."

"Why's that?"

"You of all people have to ask?"

"Well, you don't have to tell her everything."

"'Course not, but how can I profess love and devotion with what we get up to?"

"That I do not know."

He went so quiet, I had to ask. "This going put you off me?"

"No, and there lies the problem."

I said no more, and he didn't come to the library that night or the next, then on the third night he not only fucked me, but sucked my dick. After a rousing come in my passage, he dropped down to his knees, got a hand on my rod, ran his thumb over the knob, then leaned in and opened his mouth. Once he began to suck, he got a hand on himself and pumped like no tomorrow, never mind he'd just spent. I'd not let go so gave him a good load and he surprised me by swallowing it down without gagging. He also surprised me by keeping me in his mouth after I was done, rolling my softy around on his tongue. I think he was satisfying a curiosity he'd had ever since I'd first sucked him.

That night I returned to the cell most happy while I knew Wes carried fresh guilt back to his. I doubted Jim would want to get up to anything as he'd been feeling bad, having been off his feed a couple days. While he slept, I thought back to Wes kneeling before me and I drifted into a peaceful slumber, only to be rudely awakened some time later.

"Quick, get up and out here." I heard the cell lock turn after which a guard came in and pulled me from bed. As I was in just underdrawers, I reached for my stripes but he said not to bother. "Strip off those drawers." I was then dragged out naked, shoved down the stairs, and pushed to the end of the row below where guards milled about. As I approached, they took a good look. "Last one," said my captor who shoved me into the barren room where flogging was done. Inside stood about thirty naked men, Wes among them. And Lonnie.

"What's this for?" I cried out as I was made to line up with the others. Soon as I'd spoken, I knew it a mistake.

Assistant Superintendent Grazer, standing with underkeeper West, who had hold of the Bat, came over. "Since you make a demand, you'll go first. We aim to set you right. Mr. West, proceed."

West called to guards who applied ropes to my hands and feet, just as I'd seen done to Wes. I was then spread-eagled on the floor. "Ten lashes," called Grazer.

That number was rattling around in my head when the first lash hit. Pain shot through the whole of me and before it could let up, the second lash came and then the third. Some went on buttocks and thighs, but most my back, and then it was over. When I was pulled to my feet, I felt blood run on my skin. As I was pushed back into line, I looked down to see my bloody drips on the concrete floor.

I caught Lonnie's eye as the next man was whipped, a man I didn't know. Lonnie's face was a terror and I feared for his delicate skin. I didn't watch the next man's licks and when a guard caught this, he called out, "Eyes front. This is for you to see."

When Wes was laid out on the floor, I saw his scars from the earlier whippings, his back furrowed, as mine now would be. Had the circumstances been any other, I would have enjoyed his nakedness. As it was, I felt his lashes as my own.

When it came his turn, Lonnie was in tears and struggled so much the guards had to sit on his arms. He got two extra licks for his resistance and I watched that fresh young skin get laid open. After, when they pulled him up, he fell back down where he was kicked until he crawled back into line and was helped up.

While keeping my eyes on this carnage, I wondered whose idea this was. Surely Bob McCulloch wouldn't order such a thing. I decided it was Grazer feeding some need born of his being second man. As for West, he was a demented creature, the Bat having whipped away all his humanity. He and Grazer were feeding off each other and off of us. Flesh was laid open solely for their pleasure.

I glanced at Wes, lined up along the opposite wall, and found his eyes on me. We spent some time taking solace in looking at each other fully naked. I feasted on him as I heard the whip crack and men cry out. After West had flogged Nat Mackey, who'd come in with Hardin, he announced the Bat needed cleaning. "Full of blood and sweat which might affect its power. You there, come over here."

He pointed to Lonnie, the smallest and the youngest man in the room. Lonnie's mouth fell open, his jaw working as if to speak, but he gave no objection and went over.

"Kneel down, boy," said West with a leer. If he hadn't held the Bat, I'd swear he was going to get out his dick as his expression was that of a man looking to get sucked. Lonnie kneeled unsteadily, dropping a hand to the floor to regain balance. When he'd settled, West brought the Bat, red and wet, to Lonnie's mouth. "Lick it, boy. Lick it clean."

A gasp went up from several men, me included. "Quiet!" ordered Grazer.

Lonnie did as told, shuddering as he licked the four leather straps. West had the Bat in front of his privates and you couldn't mistake his arousal. He'd no doubt get a hand to his cock soon as we were dismissed. Once the Bat was clean, Lonnie was allowed to stand which he did but halfway, bending over to retch. Nothing came up, though, and he was pushed back into line.

One man pleaded to be spared. He looked about fifty, stooped and gray. He cried as he was laid out and once he'd been whipped he didn't get up. Guards carried him out.

Blood had stopped dripping off me by the time the horror finally ended. "You men, you'd best get right," declared Grazer before we were taken to our cells. No medical treatment was offered, but none was expected. I passed Wes a look as he went out. He was flushed with anger. Lonnie had tears on his face. He wouldn't look at anyone.

It was not until I was back in the cell that anger hit me. Jim sat on his bunk waiting as he'd seen me taken away naked. Had he known? Had he, in his fifteen years, seen this or maybe had it done to him?

When the lock turned, I stood at the door. Jim was no more than shadow in the dark, but he came over to look at my back. "Those wounds are going to fester," he said.

"They whipped about thirty of us for no reason," I said. "For no damn reason!"

"Grazer and West?"

"Yes. How'd you know?"

"In my years here it's been done a few times, but they left off some time back. Took to window-hanging. I think maybe McCulloch put a stop to that so they've gone back to flogging. He probably doesn't know what they're up to. Or doesn't want to."

"What's window-hanging?"

93

"Chain a man to his own cell bars up just to where his feet can't touch the floor. Leave him there all night. He'll be in agony with his own weight and later on draw up his legs which does no good, just causes leg cramps."

"That's torture."

"So is what you just got. Those two men have that kind of streak."

"Lonnie Laird got twelve licks because he resisted."

"You get ten?"

"Yes."

"Hardin there?"

"Yes, and he got ten but I don't think this was about him. Only a few of his friends were included. There were men I didn't know, and don't think he did either." Pain from my back was spreading through the whole of me. "Jim, can you please tend me some? Clean away the blood?"

He just stood there, as if he had no experience with a gentle touch. "Please," I said. "I'm in pain."

He was so hesitant that I had to tell him what to do. "Wet the cloth, apply it to my back and clean away the blood. If I'm not to fester, I need your help." At this he sat beside me and began a hesitant cleaning. "That's it, Jim, that's the way," I said and he began to lose the hesitation and clean the wounds. I found him most gentle and figured he was as surprised as I was on this.

Any touch to my back was painful, but after a while the wet cloth helped, both to soothe my back and also to let Jim discover compassion lurked within him. "I'll see if I can get something from the infirmary tomorrow," he said. "There's a salve that's supposed to help."

"Thanks, Jim. You're a good friend."

"Funny, they never took me like this."

I figured it then. "None tonight were lifers, far as I know."

"Well then, there you have it. No need to abuse those who will never leave."

I slept on my stomach that night and next morning had an awful time facing the day. The weight of my undershirt on my skin proved most painful, and I could scarcely lift my varnishing brush. Tom McKay must have heard about the whipping because he said I need not do my usual work. "Sweep the floor such as you can," he said.

I had no appetite at meals and at free time, sought the cell where I stripped and lay face down, keeping angry until I saw the futility. I was a prisoner, after all. I had no charge of myself.

That night Jim brought in some awful-smelling stuff that stung when applied to my wounds but did eventually quiet them. "Your friend Lonnie gave it to me," he said.

"How is he?"

Jim thought for a second. "Aging fast," he said.

"Has he been out in the yard?"

"Nope, but Hardin has. A more determined man I've never seen."

I gave no comment as guilt still kept me cautious with Jim.

"He says he might as well try to escape, seeing how they whip him when he doesn't."

"You talked to him?"

"Nope. Just near when he spoke to his followers. Those fellows…" Here he trailed off which was just as well.

CHAPTER TWELVE

I'd heard of men chopping off fingers to get early release, but I never knew anyone to do it until Bob Tinney gave up three to his milling machine. Everybody knew he did it on purpose, but nobody said so as it was too stupid for comment. Bob was taken to the infirmary where I heard he had it good, save for a two-fingered hand. Men began to speculate on which fingers Bob had lost.

"No doubt he kept his thumb," said Oren Glaser. "Man may be fool enough to lose three fingers, but not a thumb."

All agreed it likely the last three on the left hand, seeing Bob was right handed. "Need five to pull your dick."

The Sunday after Bob lost his fingers, I played baseball in the yard while the pious went to services. I enjoyed being active again as my back had healed enough to allow a swing of the bat and I hit a long one that went over the wagon yard fence. When I'd rounded our makeshift bases, I was made to fetch the ball, after first asking permission of the guard. It was as I got the ball that I saw men leaving the chapel, Wes in the lead. As he hit the sun he looked up, like he was still in worship, and I enjoyed the sight of him since he remained a striking fellow. Others paused to also gaze skyward, flock taking his lead. A call then came for me to stop idling and throw the ball, and I left off my Wes-gazing.

He came over and watched us play some, then moved off to stand talking to Nat Mackey and Pat Davenport, who'd come in with him, and one other man I didn't know. Fellows still sought him, some no doubt wishing to have a story later on. "Yes, child, I knew John Wesley Hardin." My gaze kept wandering his way which led me to miss a ball hit to me and suffer hoots over my lack of attention. "Get your mind right," I heard, in echo of what officials said when they issued punishment. I forced myself back to the game instead of Wes and his latest cohorts.

Jim and his lifer friends sat watching us play, which I liked. Jim knew the game and sometimes joined in. Other times, he refused. I figured baseball maybe took him back to boyhood which had not been a kind place.

The game went on until the lunch whistle at which Jim came over and we went to eat. He commented on my woolgathering during play and I agreed, it was just that. After lunch Wes continued with the three men and I watched him gesture like he was making a case on something. There were nods of agreement, but a shake of the head from Davenport. He had just five years for horse stealing so maybe wasn't interested in breaking out, while Mackey had seventeen for killing a man with a rock. Finally, the men broke off, and when Wes was alone, I went over.

"That was some discussion," I said. "You debating the Bible?"

"Could be," he returned. "Surprised to see you playing games after being whipped for no reason."

"I won't give up what I enjoy. Do that and they win."

"You play in their yard, you're theirs. I won't be owned."

"Planning another try, are you?"

"What if I am? They whipped us for no reason and I won't stand for such treatment."

"They catch you again, it'll be worse."

"Nothing is worse than counting days in here."

"You're a fool, Wes."

"Bob Tinney is a fool. I'm smart enough to get out of here with all my fingers."

"And the scars of more lashes."

"We'll see."

His attitude put me off him enough to stay away for a while. I wanted none of his nonsense, and his escape plans were just that. I avoided the library for two days and kept to others in the yard, missing both Bob and Lonnie. Ever since the whipping, Lonnie was seen only at meals and always kept his head down.

On October fifth Wes caught me in the yard, taking up as if I'd never left off. "One year today," he said. "I came in a year ago."

"You planning to celebrate?"

"Just the opposite. I find myself down in the dumps at not supporting my family."

"I'm sorry to hear you're troubled."

We were walking and got near the boilers. "Can I offer some solace?" I asked.

"My thoughts exactly, but I don't want to hurry. Come to the library tonight and I'll take your solace."

Without waiting for comment, he walked away, going over to again work his persuasion on his latest three fools. I tried to work up some annoyance, but knew it not enough to keep me off him. No point had been made in avoidance; I'd just deprived myself, so I decided to lead with my dick.

We had just under two hours before lockdown when I found Wes in the library. He had no book, and wasn't at the table. He stood at a shelf near the back like he could have been looking for a book, but when I approached he ran a hand down to his privates and said, "I'll slip away and go to the room. You hang about here a few minutes, then follow. With others around, we have to be careful." I did as suggested, even pulled down a volume to examine as I waited. Then I sauntered to the last shelf, running my fingers along book spines until I opened the door and went in. What greeted me in the gaslight was a full naked man sporting a stiff dick.

Once I'd gained my composure, fear jumped up. "You can't strip clear off," I said. "Somebody might come in and we need to be able to do up quick."

He held up a key. "Same fellow who made keys before made one for this door."

"But the guard has a key. He can unlock what you lock."

"Yes, but we'll hear him and have time to scramble into our clothes. Now lock the door and come to the back. I've made us a spot."

I did as told, thrilled with such privacy, and also that he wanted it as much as I did. The fact of him full naked led me to think he was ready to indulge more than usual. When I got to the back of the room, I found he'd moved boxes to make a barrier we could get behind. And back there his clothes were spread on the floor to make a rug of sorts. When I saw this, I shed everything, handing it to him so he could add to the bed.

Once bare, we stood opposite until he reached to wrap a hand around my dick. When I did the same with him, he didn't flinch as he might once have. Instead he issued a soft moan and pushed his hips forward to indicate welcome. We stood pulling each other a bit, eyes locked, until he said he couldn't wait. "My balls will burst if I don't get at you."

I kept my eyes on his when I said, "Fuck me, Wes."

He shuddered at the words, then took my shoulders and eased me down. I assumed the position, butt up, and he got in behind. I heard him spit into his palm and wet his cock. "Solace," he said as he pushed in.

Not having to worry about intruders sent me to the heaven of my own mind, a place where fucking was the rule and nobody said with who. No women resided in my heaven, just naked men looking to suck and fuck and do all manner of nasty things. Such was my joy at taking the Hardin cock. He didn't go easy, due to his full balls, and set up a vigorous slapping as he drove in and out. I didn't handle myself as I wanted to come for him after. I just enjoyed him taking me. Soon he was grunting, urgency upon him. His push picked up speed and he started squealing like he'd been stuck which told me I was receiving a big load. He pounded me hard for a good bit, then slowed, and eased forward, at which his dick slid out. He pulled me up to my knees and wrapped his arms around me, hugging me as he regained his breathing. I thrilled to his head on my shoulder, his breath at my ear. Then, when he'd calmed, his hand dropped to my cock which he took in hand. "You didn't come?"

"Waiting for you to help me along."

He flipped me around, pushed me onto my back, and commenced to explore, avoiding my rod to get under at my nuts. I spread my legs and raised up to assist and he began to palm one then the other. "Try sucking them," I urged.

His look was one I've seen on many a man, a descent into his base self which is the best self he has. The world was locked outside our door. In here we could use each other all we wanted, and I saw he was taken with this. He leaned down, then stretched out until his nose was in my hairy patch and began to lick me, first the hair, then around my dick, then down to my balls. I squirmed with both the feel and the idea that he was slipping ever more over to my side. Soon he was beside himself and had a nut in his mouth, sucking, while his hand was between his legs, pulling his spent cock.

Once he'd had a good nut meal, he slid up to nose around my prick, sniffing, then licking lightly which got me to begging. "Make me come, Wes. I need to come."

He rose up then, got over me, and took my dick into his mouth. He bobbed on me like he'd been dicksucking for years. Quick learner, but then he had good reason. "I'm going to do it," I told him as I hit the rise. And then I watched as I let go a load that sent waves of pleasure from dick to toe to head, heart, and every other place in my human body. Wes swallowed all I gave and didn't pull off when I softened. His hand was busy between his legs as he kept feeding. Finally, I said we didn't have to keep at it the whole time. "Take a break, Wes. Whistle won't blow for a bit."

He let go of me and sat back, but didn't let go his dick. "I want to fuck till I drop," he said.

"Well, you'll best manage that by allowing your nuts to fill back up."

"You do me in, Garland. You know that."

"I do know that, and it pleases me, Wes. You can do anything you want to me. I'll do whatever you wish."

"What else do you do with your men?" he asked.

"Lots of things. Tit sucking is pretty good as is nipping the things. And I told you about butt licking. You can play around that hole with more than your dick, and I guarantee it will drive you crazy. You don't have to take a cock to get pleasure. Finger, tongue. You want any of that, I'll do it. Just say the word."

He leaned over and ran a finger onto my tit. "Little thing on a man," he said.

"Yes, but still sensitive. Give it a try. Or I can lick yours." I could see he was comparing man tits to woman's and there was no comparison. It played across his face as much as if he'd said it right out. "Let me lick yours," I said to get him off such thoughts. "Lie back. Let me play with you some."

He frowned at this, and I respected his trying not to do it, even as we both knew he would. He had to work up to tit play as it meant giving away some of his regular manhood. His battle was plain, looking away, then coming back to me, all the while pulling his cock. Finally desire won out over nonsense. He lay back and I leaned over and gave his tit a lick. He let out a breathy moan which I took as welcome. I licked until the nub was hard, then sucked it which got him squirming. His hand was back on his cock and as I sucked and nipped one tit, I got fingers on the others to rub and pinch. He grabbed the back of my head to pull me to him all the more. No man can resist having his tit sucked.

Now he was worked up, I drew back. "Let me lick your bottom hole," I said.

"No, you're not getting at me that way."

"Better than tit play and you're liking tit play. Just let me once and if you don't like it, tell me and I'll stop."

He stroked his cock which was starting to fill. Nothing like a rising dick to draw a man into the wallow. "Coupla pigs," he said as he rolled over.

"Oink," I replied as I got between his legs and parted his buttocks.

There it was, the virgin hole of John Wesley Hardin. What I really wanted was to climb on and shove in my dick, but I remained as calm as possible, what with the prospect before me. Leaning in, I gave his pucker a lick. He flinched, but didn't put me off so I kept on licking up and down and around that hole, and when he started to squirm, I knew I had him. I poked my tongue to his pucker at which he sucked in a breath that I didn't hear him let out. Then I did it, shoved into the awful and wonderful place and gave him a good tongue fuck. He started moaning and never stopped pulling his cock. As I worked his hole, I knew I could push him to one thing more.

When I had him so worked up he was panting, I pulled out and sat back. "I need you to fuck me, Wes," I said. "Right now."

He rolled over and I was treated to his cock at full height, dripping with readiness. I lay down beside him, emboldened by our play. Then I drew my legs high, holding them so my butthole was in display. "I want you to do me front ways so I can see."

He sat up, face flushed with both need and horror as this was a challenge for a regular. Fuck a man as he fucked a woman. "Look at me as you do me," I said. "Put it in. You know you want it. Just us in here, nobody else to know, no rules on who does what. Man fucking is all it is. Now fuck me."

He had hold of himself, but made no move. He looked down at my offering and I knew he wanted to do it, but being a regular got in his way. It was plain he was thinking back to the spread legs of his wife, only now there was a filthy hole and above it cock and balls. "Fuck me," I said again, and this time he blew out a breath and did it, gritting his teeth and growling as he shoved in. Once there, he stopped as if in new territory, never mind it wasn't. He looked at me like I was the devil himself, hating me for what he needed. "Fuck me," I prompted, and this got him going. Once he started in, there was no stopping, and he gave it to me good, reaming me like some bull, all the while his eyes locked to mine. His expression told me as much as did his cock. He belonged to me for those minutes, never mind who he was or what he'd done. He was fucking me and I could, by way of his face, see exactly how he felt.

I started saying nasty things to him, telling him how good his cock felt up there, and to drive it deep, kept telling him he had a bull's dick and I wanted every inch. I pumped my cock with a fury because he was now wild eyed, and I could see his rise as his jaw tightened and his lips set. I wanted to shoot when he did, wanted him to see me spurt as I took him, and I pounded my meat as he grunted with each thrust. When his grunts choked off in his throat, I knew he was coming and I pounded my cock until it let go, sending gobs of cream up onto my chest. We were in the throes for some glorious seconds, me watching his face until his eyes again caught mine. We shared the climax in more ways than one, right down to the last second when it eased off and we relented. I squeezed out the last from myself while he gave me a grinding down there, pulling out only when he went soft. He then fell onto me and I wrapped my arms around him. We were a sweaty mess and I loved it.

"Solace," I said as I hugged him.

He gave no reply, just rolled off, panting like a horse run to lather. I lay beside him, allowing a hand onto his thigh and happy he didn't chase it off. We said nothing for a bit which got me hoping he wasn't feeling guilty. "That was powerful good," I finally said, squeezing his leg to drive off whatever he might be thinking. When he didn't answer, I kept on. "I like seeing your naked body somewhere besides that flogging room. You're finely built." I slipped onto my side and ran a hand over his chest. When I touched his tit, he reached up to pull me away. "Nothing wrong in any of what we did," I said. "We do for each other. Simple as that."

Maybe he saw my untruth. Maybe he could feel what was coming up in me. Get a man naked and now and again he'll intuit some. Wes seemed like one of the machines at that moment, wheels and gears turning inside him now his dick was asleep. Suddenly he sat up. "Whistle is going to blow before long. We'd best get dressed and out of here."

"You sorry for any of it?" I asked, regretting the question soon as it slipped out.

"No, I'm not sorry." He stood up, but didn't rush to dress. Instead he remained fixed above me and I feasted on the sight of that dick dangling like ripe fruit. He was beautiful to me. Fine body, thick thighs, good cock in a dark patch, broad chest where I'd fed on those tits, and lastly that handsome face.

"Well, then," I said. "I'm most happy."

We dressed, unlocked the door, and I slipped out among the shelves where I got a book of no consequence and sat down at a back table. Some minutes later Wes came out, but he didn't get a book. He ambled among the shelves, then walked on out of the library. He didn't come back there for a week.

It was plain he was avoiding me, so I let him have room. Goddamn married man. I should know better, I told myself. I spent time with Jim and some others, Ned and Oren mostly. I saw Wes with Mackey and Davenport and the other man who I learned was Johnson, doing twenty for beating a man to death. Why fists got less time than bullets was beyond me. Now and then Wes caught me looking at him and didn't turn away, but neither did he linger. I couldn't read his expression beyond it being grim. For a man who'd taken such pleasure, he was being way too hard on himself.

End of that week, I caught him near the boilers. "You're finally alone," I noted. "Plans all wrapped up?"

"No matter to you."

"You're right, no matter to me. But something is the matter, Wes. You down on me 'cause of what we did?"

"Leave off, Gar," he said and he stalked away.

Two days later, he found me in the library. He had his *Davies* and sat across from me, not opening the book. "What is it?" I asked.

He shut his eyes and shook his head as he spoke. "Day after our time in the room I got a letter from Jane saying she's learned I've taken up with a man. She's asking why I'm doing what I'm doing, saying she doesn't understand, and would I please explain it."

"God, no. How could she find out?"

"Beats hell out of me. Somebody had to have seen us and that somebody made it known to her. If I ever find out who it is, I'll kill him, and I won't need a gun to do it. I'll string him up by his dick, I swear I will."

"Is that why you've avoided me?"

He sighed. "I have to leave off you, Gar. There's hell to pay for what we do, and I'm paying it right now. My poor wife knows I'm putting it to a man, and if she knew what else I'm doing, she'd faint dead away. I may be a convict behind walls, but I am still married, and have no right to what we're getting up to."

I allowed this to settle as I needed time to frame a proper reply. "You mean to say you plan to honor your wife by going without satisfaction for twenty-four more years?"

"I can't address that right now. I have to write Jane a letter, and that's tearing me up, if you want to know. How can I explain?"

"I'm sorry, Wes. You're truly in a spot. I'll leave off you forever if you wish." And with that I got up, closed my book and left him to stew in his married state.

CHAPTER THIRTEEN

Dead men were put into pine boxes and buried in a cemetery outside the prison walls. There were no services. If a man had family, they were allowed to come and claim the body, but few ever did. Convicts were cast offs for the most part.

When we saw a wagon out front of the infirmary, we knew somebody had died. First thought was Bob Tinney's stumps had soured and killed him. I stood in the yard awaiting the supper whistle like everybody else, all of us now turned toward the coffin as it was carried out and put into the wagon. Just then Jim came up beside me. "It's your friend Lonnie," he said.

"No."

"Cut his throat."

"Who cut his throat?"

"He did."

"Where'd you hear that?" I demanded, voice rising. "It can't be right. He wouldn't do that. He wouldn't."

"Easy, Gar. I am just saying what's going around. They found him this morning in an examination room, lying in a pool of his own blood, scalpel still in hand."

Just then the supper whistle blew. Jim gripped my shoulder, but I shook him off. "Come on," he urged. "Supper time. You have to go in."

The coffin was in the wagon, and the driver urged his horses on. "He wouldn't do it," I declared.

"Well, maybe he wouldn't, but somebody did."

I kept my eyes on the coffin until it disappeared through the gate and Lonnie was truly gone. He'd be in the ground by nightfall, dirt thrown over him, buried before he was twenty and without ceremony to mark his passing. Jim urged me to get in line for supper, but I just stood a while, fists clenched. Never had I felt confinement as much as in those moments.

I couldn't eat my supper. Marching to the dining hall was a trial, as was the thought of food. I managed only water and when we marched out, I shook Jim off soon as we were free. "Where you going?" he asked.

"Chapel," I snapped, and he knew not to follow.

I didn't want to pray to God. I wanted to curse Him for having put a boy such as Lonnie in this awful place, an innocent boy who hadn't known the pleasure of sex, only the pain. A put-upon boy, a beautiful boy. I sat in a pew facing a cross that meant nothing to me. Might as well have been a pile of tin cans, such were my thoughts. I wanted no religion now, I just wanted to think on Lonnie and honor him for the life he led. And after a while, I wanted to know who'd killed him.

Bob Tinney still resided in the infirmary, but took meals with the rest of us. Now and again he came out into the yard at free time, but mostly he kept to his bed. His hand was still bandaged, and I knew there had been some infection that made him sick. He was better now, but taking it slow. Nobody asked if he regretted what he'd done. I decided, as I avoided the cross and looked down at my shoes, that I would ask Bob what he knew about Lonnie's death.

Jim didn't approach me that night, seeing how upset I was, and this tipped me over in some way. I slapped him hard for no good reason at which me slammed a fist to my gut and we were off, pummeling each other until we were so sweaty and worked up we had to fuck which came as rough as the fight. When Jim put his dick to me, he pounded my back with his fists. Once he'd come, which didn't take long, he got down and chewed my bottom and I came into the bedding, taking pleasure when nobody deserved any. When we were done, I said something foul and Jim got Little Brother and put him to me for half the night which I deserved because I was alive and Lonnie wasn't.

Jim finally left off abusing me, saying he was tired. We were on the floor, and he got up into his bunk while I stayed curled on the concrete, feeling like some whipped dog. Trouble was, none of what we did helped. I wanted to claw my way out of that cell, run for the wall, and let that Gatling gun shoot me full of holes.

I guess I slept because when shots came, I thought they were for me. It took a few seconds to escape my dream, and by the time I sat up, Jim was standing on our little table to look out our high window. "Men in the yard," he said. "Can't see how many."

Just then came the blast of a shotgun. It had to be Wes and his latest cohorts pulling their escape. But shots fired. That hadn't happened before. Something had gone truly wrong. "Can you see anything?" I asked Jim.

"Shadows."

There came no more shots. Instead it was shouts and what seemed an army on the run. "Yard's full of guards," Jim said before he got down.

I hopped up to look, but couldn't see any more than he had. Commands were shouted and the whole thing died down as I saw the little army move toward our cellblock. I had no doubt there would be flogging this night, Wes on the receiving end.

Jim and I got into our bunks, but I couldn't get back to sleep. I kept thinking on Wes and then on Lonnie, them together too much to bear. So I spoke out to Jim, not knowing if he was even awake. "I don't believe Lonnie took his own life," I said. "The doc killed him. I can feel it."

"Why would he do that? Why kill the dick you been sucking for three years?"

I thought back to Lonnie's tearful words about this. "The doc started demanding more from him," I explained. "Lonnie said he'd not submit, that he would kill the doc first."

"And he got killed instead."

"I'm going to ask Bob Tinney what happened in there. He should know the truth."

"Get to sleep, Gar. It's late."

"Bob will know."

"What will you do with that truth?" Jim asked.

"That I do not know."

When I saw Wes in the chow line next morning, I about buckled with relief which was followed by puzzlement at what had happened in the yard. I couldn't find Mackey, Davenport, or Johnson, but there were lots of lines so maybe I was wrong. Maybe it wasn't even them. Word wasn't yet around on what had taken place, but soon would be so I counseled myself toward patience.

As it was Sunday, and as Bob Tinney had taken to religion since his mishap, I waited for him to come out of chapel. He'd lost weight in his recovery and his hand looked like a big white mitten due to all the bandages. He said he was better and McCulloch was talking about releasing him before long as he was no use to the state anymore. "For once it's good to be no good," said Bob.

I didn't ask about prospects for a seven-fingered man. Instead I asked about Lonnie. "What really happened in there? I don't believe he'd kill himself."

"The doc has charge of me," said Bob. "I can't make trouble or I won't get out."

"You know me, Bob. I can hold a confidence. I just need to know the truth. Please. Lonnie was a good boy and my friend. He deserves the truth."

We walked some distance from the men and stood leaning against a fence, watching the ball game that was just starting up. Bob didn't look at me as he spoke. "You know what was going on," he said.

"Yes. He'd told me some of what the doc did to him, but he was upset that more was being demanded and vowed not to submit."

"The man that is saving my life when I get the infection is the most wretched creature on the face of the earth," Bob said. "I always knew when he got at Lonnie and will tell you that more than once I watched him through the keyhole in his office door. Lonnie would stand with eyes shut while Doc fed on him and worked that shriveled old cock to no end. I think that's why he wanted to do more, thinking that would get it up."

"Did he try?"

"Once I know of, he got Lonnie something awful."

"After that?"

"Lonnie would rush into the ward with a look of terror. He'd sit at the bedside of a patient because he was safe with us. The doc would be all flushed, both with his awful need and his anger. Then that day, I don't know how, I didn't see, but he got Lonnie into an examination room. I heard the commotion. Doc is old but Lonnie was small so the battle was about even. Lonnie cried out, and we men heard him. Things were thrown, there were crashes and such, and I thought Lonnie would win. Then all went quiet."

Here Bob stopped talking. His voice had gotten shaky and he sucked in some long breaths. "Tell me, Bob," I begged. "Please. I have to know. I can take it, I don't care how bad."

"I got up and went to the door which was locked so I got down to look through the keyhole. There stood the doc, pants open, dick out, and in his hand the bloody scalpel. Lonnie was half on the table with a gash at his throat. I could see him done for. Then Doc set aside the scalpel, pulled down Lonnie's pants, and started humping his bottom. Well, this disgusted me to such extent I began to pound on the door while still looking on. Doc stopped, did himself up, and shoved Lonnie to the floor. He then put the scalpel into Lonnie's hand and set about cleaning up best he could. By the time he opened the door, he had things as they were found. He came out and called to the guard that a prisoner had killed himself."

"Thank you for telling me, Bob."

"You're not going to attack the doc or something, are you?"

"I have no such plan. Lonnie just deserves the truth."

Bob walked off while I stood reeling. I saw Wes watching me so I went over. "Heard a commotion in the night," I began. "Thought it might be you making a break."

"It wasn't me."

"Who was it?"

"Mackey, Davenport, and Johnson."

"The three you've been plotting with."

Wes laughed. "That's not accurate. I was playing them. We talked on getting out and I suggested a plan but Davenport got shaky so I pulled out. Wise move, don't you think, what with them getting caught? I hear Mackey's ass is full of buckshot while the other two were flogged. All are now in dark cells while, being smarter, I'm not."

I couldn't believe what I was hearing. "You led them to it," I cried.

"It was their call," he countered. "Nobody made them go forward without me."

"Every time I saw you, you were making your case. You were like some lawyer in a courtroom, such was your persuasion. Then you desert them? You're responsible."

"The hell I am."

I shook my head. "You lead your fellow men astray to such extent they're shot and whipped, then you go to church and pray to God. I'm surprised lightning didn't strike you down."

He stretched out his arms and looked skyward. "I'm ready," he called, as if to invite his maker's wrath. When no bolt came down, he turned back to me. "Sorry. God appears to be on my side."

"For a smart man, you are blind to a great deal."

"I don't doubt that, Garland."

I left him there as I couldn't tolerate his indifference to men he'd wronged. This, on top of Lonnie's truth, ruined my Sunday until I saw my own self-interest in that notion. I went to my cell where I tried to rest, and when this didn't work, I walked the yard which also didn't help. The rest of the day crawled by, and after supper, I sought the library where I was pleased to not find Wes.

"You're not bringing books in here anymore," Jim noted that night. He was sitting on his bunk fully dressed, like he wasn't up for sex.

I didn't comment. Anger was running through me as I'd been unable to exhaust it with the day. Jim was the only person who hadn't done any wrong yet I wanted to hit him. He evidently caught this because he tripped me and while I was down, kicked me. I grabbed his leg and pulled him down and started punching him, unable to hold back. He fought me, of course, striking bruises he'd brought up before, but I didn't care. No guard came at our commotion. Prisoners called out filth at what they supposed us doing and finally we did what they said, Jim fucking me standing at the cell door. I worked my cock while he went at me and I shot a load between the bars.

When he pulled out, he bit me on the neck, but this was without any meanness and served to quiet me. "I'm sorry, Jim, I can't get past Lonnie."

He nipped me again, then said to get to bed.

"I'm not sleeping much lately."

"Try."

I'd not realized I had any enthusiasm for prison life until it left me. My varnishing work fell off so badly Tom McKay called me on it. "You have to step up," he said. "I don't care what ails you, we have quotas and you're getting us behind."

He didn't press for comment so I went back to work, but did it no faster as there seemed no fuel in me anymore. Food still had little appeal. It tasted neither bad nor good. I provoked Jim to beating me now and then which got me some rough fucking and when not doing that, I had Little Brother to excess. Lonnie was long gone now, but the doc remained which bothered me no end.

"Nothing you can do about the doc," Jim said one night as we lay in our bunks, exhausted after a long session abusing each other.

"Nothing I can do about anything. Life in here is no life at all."

Wes avoided me for about a week, then came to the library one night. "I'm sorry about your friend Lonnie," he said. When I gave no reply, he opened his *Davies* and commenced his study.

I had to admit he gave me comfort, whether or not it was wanted. Solace, I thought, which brought recall on our last attempt at that. This warmed me enough to look at my friend. He was fixed on his sums, intent, determined. I hadn't seen him talking up any new escape so maybe he was reforming, like he told his wife.

"You write that letter to Jane?" I asked.

"I did," he replied. "I spoke on attending church and assured her I embraced His word. I said I was no longer trying to escape and working hard at my job. I told how I'm studying to better myself for when I get out. And I addressed the need of guiding the children to good and godly ways."

"Did you answer her question?"

"I did not as I came to see that a good woman shouldn't discuss such matters. It was improper of her to put such a thing into a letter, but I didn't say that. I just cut off the bad path she'd fallen upon, thus saving her."

He'd leaned forward as he spoke and I saw his rationale was preface to us going to that back room and having a fuck. I almost laughed at the revelation, but held off as Wes was genuine in his self-serving delusion. He truly believed he'd done a service to his wife. Maybe he had.

"I'm pleased you cleared up the problem," I said.

"Me too."

His mouth crimped up at the corner just then which did me in. And he knew it. I forgot about his faults, I even forgot about Lonnie lying in the ground and nobody but me caring. I let my hand fall to my lap where I prodded my swelling cock. Without a word, Wes got up and went to the back, taking his book with him. I followed a few minutes later. He was again naked and while I stripped he locked the door.

Sight of him set something loose in me and I was upon him in an instant, front to front, grinding my cock against his for he was already stiff. My fingers dug into his back as I rode him, his hands upon my bottom, kneading my buttocks until I shot a load up between us. Scarcely had I finished than he pushed me down, climbed onto me from behind, and shoved in. "I need you bad, Gar."

I squirmed on his cock for I wanted it up in my gut. I wanted to choke on his juice. I wanted to be taken in the worst way, used until there was nothing left, and I started telling him this, how I needed fucking, how he should fill me with his prick. This got him so worked up he cried out and pounded a come into me, pumping until his dick finally went soft. When he pulled out,

I couldn't stand it. "Lick me," I said. "Get down there and taste your stuff. I can't get enough of you, Wes."

I reached back and pulled apart my buttocks. "There it is, the filthy hole. That's where true love resides. Not in the heart. It's in the dick and the butthole. That's the true union so taste it, lick it, fuck me with your tongue. Help me, Wes. I need it bad."

His fingers traced my pucker, gathering the wet, and then one popped in. When he began to prod I told him to add a second which he did and there we lay, him finger-fucking me, but that wasn't enough. "Eat my ass," I said, but he wouldn't do it. Finally he pulled out his fingers and flipped me over.

"I won't put my tongue in you," he said. "I'll do the rest, but I can't do that." With that, he lay down on me and began to suck my tits which I accepted.

While he attended me, I slipped a hand down between his legs and started pulling his dick. He liked this and adjusted his position so I could better get to him. He was a fine handful, even soft, and after I'd played a while, I got under to his nuts and palmed one, then the other. He allowed my finger to stray beyond, though he squirmed when I got near his butthole. He then pulled off and sat back on his haunches.

"You're a sight," I told him. "I could look upon you all night and all day."

"You're right good yourself." His hand strayed down around my cock, settling in to pet my hairy patch. I enjoyed watching him look at my privates and thrilled when he got down to lick my nuts.

We played around for some time like that, exploring, sucking, licking, pinching. He was getting comfortable with his wants, and I was basking in my accomplishments. The regular part of him was slipping away. The room was warm and stuffy so we were awash in sweat and other bodily fluids by the time we both were worked up again. I feared the lockdown whistle would blow any minute so I stepped up my efforts.

I was down between his legs, licking his crack, when I made the move. My prick was stiff, my balls full of spunk, and my man lay beneath me. All I had to do was get into him. In one quick move, I shifted position, dick replacing tongue, but as my knob popped into his hole, his arm swung back with mighty force and knocked me away.

"Goddamn you, Gar, I don't take it up there, I told you. I'm not like that."

"The hell you're not," I said and I was back upon him, wrestling with all my might as I was determined to give him a fuck he'd never forget. I wanted him to crave my cock and so I summoned all my strength, the two of us thrashing around like wrestlers trying to get a hold. At one point he had me around the neck, choking me from behind, and I felt the wet of his cock against me for the wrestling was working us up even more. I was so ready I feared I'd come on his leg, but I kept on. I had him pinned one time, but he started bucking so I couldn't get my dick in. It was as I tried my damnedest that I spurted onto him. I rode him until empty, then fell off, at which he turned and slapped me so hard it knocked me against the wall.

He gave no time to recover. He was upon me and I didn't fight. The come had taken that out of me so I let him fuck me like the animal he was, from behind, going at it hell-bent until he shot his load. Soon as he was done, he pulled out, got up, and dressed. I lay on the floor, tired for once. When I went out some minutes later, he was gone.

Back in the cell, Jim noted I reeked. "We both need a wash," I said. "To-morrow's the day so how about you dirty me tonight?"

He'd stopped adding the grease to our fucking, evidently having settled something in himself. Maybe he didn't care anymore that I was being taken, even if with consent. Maybe he was starting to like the idea of a well reamed butthole. Whatever the reason, I didn't question it. There was no point in questioning anything with Jim. I stripped off, climbed into his bunk, and sucked his dick until it was stiff. I then stuck my butt up and asked him to do me, which he did. He didn't comment that I failed to deliver. I don't think that mattered to him.

"Doc murdered Lonnie," I said later on when we lay in our bunks, sweat drying.

"How do you know?"

"Bob Tinney saw him do it, but won't say anything because the doc is treating his hand."

"You going to do something about it?" Jim asked.

"What can I do? The men need a doctor, especially Bob whose hand isn't healing like it should."

Jim had no reply, but I could feel him stir. Even in separate bunks, I could tell something was afoot. "What is it, Jim?"

He blew out a sigh. "A new boy has taken Lonnie's job. He'd been working in the mill. He's fourteen."

"Dear God."

"God appears to be looking the other way," Jim said.

Funny how one comment can change a man's whole outlook. Jim might have tossed it off, but it struck me like a knife and I saw the path ahead clearly for maybe the first time. Next day I sought Wes in the yard, and told him I wanted to escape.

He took a few moments to savor such a turn and I allowed him his satisfaction. He'd been grim at my approach, what with his sacred off-limits bottom, but once I indicated coming over to his side, that crimp of his mouth appeared. "What brought this on?" he asked.

"I can't bear the evil that resides here."

"For once I don't think you mean me. Who are you talking about?"

"Doesn't matter. I just want to get out. If I stay, I fear I'll go off the rails entirely."

"I won't plan an escape unless I know what set you off."

I walked away as I didn't wish to talk on any of it, but he followed, took me by the arm. "Garland, tell me. I can see something is at you."

"Bob Tinney saw Doc murder Lonnie, but won't say because he needs his hand tended and others are also in Doc's care. This was bad enough but I now learn Doc has taken a fourteen-year-old boy from the mill to fill Lonnie's spot. In case you don't know, Doc likes to suck boy dick. He killed Lonnie because Lonnie wouldn't submit to more, being of the regular persuasion. You know how that is, don't you?"

"Best not bring my persuasion into it if you want my help, okay?"

"Okay."

We resumed walking and said nothing for a bit. The day was cloudy and gray, fall's hold weakening. We had on our striped jackets against the chill. Finally Wes spoke.

"I've been talking to Eugene Hill who wants to get out as bad as I do. He's in the shoe shop with me and has noted that Still & Company, the contractors who run the shop, are always receiving boxes of materials by express and he thinks guns could be brought in that way. I asked if he has friends on the outside who could see to it, mark the box a certain color so we'd know it, and he's going to write to them. If we get guns, we can fight our way out."

When I didn't respond, Wes prompted. "That sound good to you?"

"Sounds too loose. I like the idea how you get the guns in, but just fighting our way out is not good planning. You have to have a route, decide whether to take the gate or climb the wall."

"Look who's planning now."

"You're right, but I'm not the same man as before."

"You're coming over to my side."

"Well, you won't come over to mine."

CHAPTER FOURTEEN

Winter slipped over us and brought a new year, 1880. Snow often dusted the yard, but we still walked there as it was the least of our confinements. On a particular Sunday I kept to Wes as he made his plan with Eugene Hill, but after a while I tired of their ideas, none of which appeared sound. Getting guns into the prison seemed easy. What to do with them was the problem. And then Hill wanted to bring in another man, Bud Bohannon, who also worked in the shoe shop. Wes wasn't sure about this. He'd been betrayed too often to not exercise caution, but he finally agreed.

Middle of January, Wes came to the library and told me he had his plan. The guns would arrive in a black box addressed to Still & Company. "We can see the express wagon come in while we await the supper whistle. Next day, we get the guns in the shop, conceal them on our persons. When the time is right, I'll take a gun and throw down on the guard on the southwest picket as that's only about ten yards from the shop door. I'll tell him if he doesn't obey I'll kill him. Then the men will go up a ladder and take that guard and his picket post. I'll follow and we'll go over the wall at that point. Once outside, we go to the stable, get horses, and leave. We may have some fighting to do, may have to kill some, but I figure we can do it so quickly not even the prisoners need know it's going on."

This surprised me because what had seemed idle talk had finally taken shape. And I was to be a part. When I said nothing, Wes grew concerned. "You're still with me, aren't you? This is going to work."

"Yes, I'm with you. It just didn't seem real until now. You and Hill have been talking for a month."

"He had some ideas that were not practical. A man wanting out as bad as he does can lose sight of things so I have to reel him in. He's agreed that this plan will work."

"And Bohannon?"

"Hill is going to tell him about it, just as I'm telling you. It will be just us four."

I chuckled and Wes asked what was so funny. "I am feeling pretty good now that getting over the wall is a possibility, riding off into a life I thought lost to me."

"You want to celebrate?"

I chuckled again. "Hell, yes. See you in a couple minutes."

Wes went to the book room and I followed. In the gaslight, I gave him all he wanted, not imposing myself upon his body, though I would have liked to go that way. Instead I let him fuck me and play with me and fuck me again. He was getting to like tit sucking and licking lots of my places, while in between the fucking, when he was spent, he allowed me to suck his cock and palm his balls. I devoured all I could of him and he of me and when the lockdown whistle blew, I called our celebration a success.

"The plan will work," Wes declared as he got up to dress.

"I don't doubt it will."

Jim was quiet when I got to the cell that night. He had the checkerboard on the little table and appeared to be playing against himself. He spoke without looking up. "I see you talking to Hardin a lot these days. You working up an escape?"

"What if I am? I can't stand this place anymore, not when a man is murdered and no action is taken against the killer. We pay a price for murder while the doctor not only goes free, he gets another boy."

"His name is Johnny Rose," Jim said.

"What?"

"The new boy working for the doc. Story is he strangled a man he caught raping his mother. Got twenty-five. I think there's more to him than Lonnie. Maybe he'll do okay over there."

I took off my shoes and climbed up to my bunk. The cell was bitter cold. I didn't take off my jacket and my blanket was about useless. Still, I curled up under it. "I don't want to know about Johnny Rose," I said. "Unless he strangles the doc."

When I next caught Wes in the yard, he was upset. "Bohannon is monkeying with the plan. Thinks we should attack the gatekeeper which is not the least bit feasible as he's outside and can get out of the way of us."

"Did you talk to Bohannon?" I asked.

"No. He's jawing at Hill and Hill is coming to me. I told Eugene it's not feasible, that it's my way or none."

"Maybe you should leave Bohannon out of it."

"We need more than three men as there are ladders required, but I won't ask around as too many get wind and one will squeal for sure."

"When are the guns due to arrive?"

"I don't know yet. Hill is waiting for word from his friends."

I blew out a breath that steamed before me. The air was sharp, the snow mushy. My feet were cold all the time now. We walked a bit and when we turned back, there came Jim. Wes kept to his stride while I lagged back some. This brought Jim and Wes face to face. "Scanlon, right?" Wes said. "You share the cell with Garland."

Jim nodded. "Done half of thirty."

"I admire that," said Wes. "Doubt I could manage what you have."

"So I hear. You planning another breakout?"

"Possibly. You interested?"

Jim shook his head. "I did my crime and will serve the time."

"Then I'll leave you to it," said Wes and he walked off, leaving me with Jim. I had no idea what to say so I stayed quiet.

"Nice enough, I guess," Jim finally said. "You like him, don't you."

"He's a friendly sort, and yes, I do like him. I liked Lonnie too, and Bob Tinney. Lots of fellows to like. You included."

The supper whistle blew just then, sparing Jim the need to address the compliment. He was never good with those the few times they came his way.

"Goddamn," Wes said next afternoon in the yard. "Bohannon let go his idea to take the gate, but he disputes climbing the wall at the southwest picket. Insists on another spot which isn't practical. He also wants to go hunting for some who've wronged him, and this I won't tolerate. I'm about ready to drop the whole plan."

I was not ready for John Wesley Hardin to back down on anything. After all the talk, his doubts hit me like one of his slaps. I stood speechless but he didn't catch my silence, so caught up was he in his problem. I half listened as he complained about Hill bringing in Bohannon and failing to corral him. He then went on to doubt the entire enterprise. "I'm starting to wonder about those men shipping in the guns as there's still no word. It's all a waste if we can't get the guns."

"I'm ready to go over that wall," I finally said.

"So am I, Gar, but without the guns and a good plan, we can't do it. There's Eugene. I'm going over to talk to him. You with me?"

"No, you go on. Let me know the outcome."

"Fair enough."

I wanted to go over the wall, but I was tired of talking about how it was to be done. This showed me I was not a planner and certainly not a leader, but then I suppose I knew that all along, what with having followed Frank McGann into a life of crime. I was now trying to follow Wes Hardin out of a life of crime. Maybe I should stop this following, but what would I have then? I liked hooking onto a man and giving myself over to him. Funny, I'd gotten involved with two criminals, but I was one of them now, forever stained.

I was down in the dumps that night and soon as I got to the cell, I stripped off. "Freeze your balls," Jim said as I stood naked before him, pulling my dick.

"Not if you heat me up."

He undid his pants and got out his cock. "Make it come up," he said and I crawled in and began a spirited suck. Soon as he was stiff and wet, he got at me and set the bed squeaking while men nearby called out the usual filth. Once Jim came, he pulled out, flipped me over, and dove onto my prick to suck out a mouthful of spunk. We then collapsed into a heap on his bunk, enjoying the warmth we'd created. I slept with him all night and in the morning he sucked me awake, and we had an early breakfast of each other.

"When are you going?" he asked as we dressed for the day.

"Going where?"

"The escape. You and Hardin. I know you're up to it."

"It may not come off," I said. "He won't try if it's not solid."

"He tried before."

"And failed because men betrayed him. He's careful on that now."

Jim did up his brogans. "No way out of here but a coffin," he said.

"You may be right."

When the chow whistle blew and we lined up to march to breakfast, Jim gripped my shoulder tighter than usual. He was telling me something and it didn't matter what exactly.

After work that day, I saw Wes and Bohannon jawing in the yard and it didn't look at all productive. Eugene Hill was with them, but he stood mute while their voices rose. I drifted over to catch what was said, but heard only "you goddamn son of a bitch" from Wes before he hauled off and slapped Bohannon. Bohannon was taller than Wes and had a good twenty pounds on him, but this made no matter. He reeled back, said Wes was a dead man, and lit into him, stopping only when restrained by friends who didn't want to see either man confined to a cell on bread and water which would be their punishment if caught fighting. Hill had hold of Wes who shook him off.

"You're a fool," Wes said and he stormed away while his adversary glowered and swore. Soon all was quiet and I went over to Wes.

"What was that about?"

"He refuses the southwest picket so I'm out of it. His way is going to get him shot."

"What about Hill? And me? I think we should go ahead with us three."

"You can go on with them," Wes said. "I have no doubt they'll make the try, but think on it before you join up as they're not likely to succeed."

I huffed a breath and kicked the dirt, then saw I was acting like a little kid. "I'm disappointed," I said.

"As am I."

That evening I found Wes in the library, still fuming at Bohannon wrecking his plan. "Never should have let him in. Goddamn Eugene talking me into it."

"You're right pent up," I noted.

"I feel like beating hell out of them both, if you want the truth."

"How about you take things out on me," I said, "though I don't mean a beating. Take solace in our disappointment."

Wes leaned in and drilled me with those gray eyes that were ablaze with frustration. "It will take some powerful fucking to set me right."

"Likewise."

He got up and we followed our usual routine. The library had a good crowd as it had steam heat so men came in just to get warm. Some read while others just sat. A few had their heads down on the table, dozing.

Soon as I stripped, Wes put it to me standing. He grunted and growled through a truly angry fuck and when he came I swear his spunk was hot with temper. When he was done, he flipped me around and sucked me while pulling his spent cock. I saw he meant to not stop but to wipe out Bohannon and Hill and the whole prison by way of his prick.

"I'm going to come," I announced as my juice boiled. I then gave up a mouthful but the climax eased me no more than had the one Wes enjoyed. He pulled off and wiped his hand over his mouth, then dove back down to get his tongue on my nuts.

"Let's lie down for this," I said and he backed off long enough for us to arrange our clothes. I then lay back, spread my legs and raised up some. Wes got down there and sucked a nut into his mouth while putting a finger in me to poke and prod.

After a while of this, he crawled onto me and set to tit work which allowed me to pull his dick and we passed a good bit this way, playing to rouse ourselves as we both needed a second go. Finally, Wes licked his way from tits to cock, sucking me until I got stiff. As he fed, he worked himself, and at last he was ready. He then surprised me by pushing my legs up around my ears before he spat in his hand to ready himself. Once wet, he shoved in and declared he would fuck until the lockdown whistle blew. And he did.

Our gaze was fixed on each other much of the time which was almost as good as his dick work. It gave me something more, and I thrilled to seeing pleasure on his face. He was easy at first, swoony-like, then gradually, as he got worked up, serious. And finally, when he was pumping like a bull, he bore the grimace of a man in his throes which is the best look there is. Out of control, dick running the show, body along for the ride. His grunts were formidable, the sweat plentiful, and as he pumped so did I, determined to come along with him. While I didn't manage this, I did let go when he was still in me. He watched the spurts I gave up for him. A second later, the whistle blew which set us to laughing.

"That feels good too," I said as he pulled out. "The laugh, I mean. Not the whistle."

"In here is the best of it," he said, which wrenched my heart so much I couldn't reply.

When we left our fuck room, I got a book to take back and read to Jim. "I've too often forgotten this," I told Wes, "and fear he might figure why."

"Good idea then. I don't want to cross him."

I chose an adventure story about a man stranded on an island far away from home. Far away always played well. Jim was dozing when I came in and woke as I climbed to my bunk. "How about I read?" I suggested.

"Go on."

As I read the adventure, I saw Wes and me on that island, running naked where it was warm and food was plentiful. Nobody around to trouble us. I kept reading even after I heard Jim's soft snore.

Two days later we saw the black box of guns come in for Still & Company. "There it is," said Wes who had spied the freight wagon. "They'll get the guns and likely go for it tomorrow."

"Who do you think will go along?"

"Just the fools."

Next day in the yard I saw Bohannon sidle up to Wes as if there had been no disagreement. They spoke briefly before Wes shook his head and walked away. Bohannon looked ready to boil over.

"What was that about?" I asked when Wes came over.

"He's got a couple guns under his coat and offered one to me. I declined."

"So he's going ahead."

"That he is, only he's again saying the gate is best."

Not twenty minutes later we saw Hill, Bohannon, Cliff Chapman, and Ned Mackey making a run for the gate. Gunfire came, but they gained no exit as, just like Wes had predicted, the gatekeeper stepped out of their way. The four then ran to the southeast picket where they fired some shots before a swarm of guards overtook them. Every man in the yard stood fixed at the sight of the four hauled away, likely toward a whipping or at least a dark cell. The whole thing had not taken five minutes.

"Taking the picket is no good anymore," Wes said. "They've ruined the plan."

"You'll have to think up something else."

He blew out a sigh. "I'm running out of ideas," he said.

"Give it time. You'll find a way."

"Only thing for sure is next time it will be you and me and nobody else."

"I like the sound of that."

I found myself excited at the prospect of escaping with just Wes. That night I went to the library, but he was absent. No matter, I told myself. He was a free man within these walls. Still, I was restless as I wanted more on his idea of the two of us breaking out. When I got back to the cell, Jim refused to let me read. "No book tonight," he declared. He lay with pants open, dick stiff. Little Brother was in his hand, shiny with grease. He got up and made me drop my pants and drawers and take position at the bedpost. As he shoved Little Brother into me, I didn't mind as I needed something to get me worked up. If I couldn't have Wes, I'd at least have a good come.

"How come you weren't in on the try?" Jim asked as Little Brother fucked me. "And Hardin. Isn't he the one who plans these things?"

"The men wouldn't do as he said so he withdrew."

"And you do what he does?"

"I saw their folly."

This got me several hard shoves of Little Brother, causing me some internal hurt. "You won't get out," Jim declared. "Neither will he."

"I agree with you," I managed as he took Little Brother still deeper. My breath then failed and I said no more until after a while I begged Jim to add more grease to the wooden prick. "Please, Jim. You'll bloody me again."

He gave no reply as he was pumping his cock and ready to shoot. My passage was aflame with pain when Jim grunted and spurted come onto my bottom. Only while in his climax did he allow Little Brother any rest, but he still kept the wooden cock in me.

Once calmed, he reached around to grab my dick which was up solely due to abuse of me. I had no desire, but the internal passage has a way of its own. As Jim milked my cock, he kept Little Brother working, and soon I issued a modest come. Though release felt good, it didn't please me as my bottom was in bad shape. Once I'd been drained of spunk, Jim pulled out Little Brother and flipped me around to face him. "You won't get out," he growled. "Not from the prison and not from this cell."

Awful as he was, I could see him anxious amid his brutality. He was afraid of my leaving him. "You're probably right," I said.

"Not probably," he countered. "It's a fact."

"Yes, Jim. I see that."

I got back into drawers and pants and by the time I lay in my bunk, I felt the wet of the bloody residue that I'd live with the next few days. I curled beneath my blanket, hoping Wes lay in his bunk thinking on how we two would escape.

"That's Johnny Rose," Jim said some days later as we lined up to march to breakfast. The kid was tall for fourteen, dark haired, not pretty like Lonnie, but not bad either. He looked like one of those fellows who has to grow into his looks. He was in a cell just two down from ours which put him at our chow table. Sitting across and down some, I saw no evidence of abuse, but then it wasn't always on the face, as I well knew. Johnny caught me looking a couple times, and I turned away too quick, like I was avoiding him which I guess I was. Interested but not, which is an entirely possible state.

Soon I realized Wes was avoiding me, and I couldn't figure why. Was he so down in the dumps at the escape plan failing that he had to leave off me?

He didn't seem the type to be hard on himself as he'd always shown such determination, but after so many failures, maybe he'd worn down. I didn't press, even though I wanted to. I went to the library most nights and brought books to read to Jim. He relaxed some at this, giving me his cock instead of Little Brother, and some nights was happy just to be read to sleep.

"I'm missing you," I said to Wes after a week or so. He'd left off talking to some men in the yard, getting off by himself which was rare, so I went over.

"There's much on my mind," he said.

"Another plan?"

"No," he snapped, and he stalked away like he'd been insulted.

The next Sunday I played baseball as the weather had warmed enough to melt the snow. We ran in mud and the ball got so dirty it slipped from my hand more than once, but we didn't care. It occupied us and gave reason to laugh and shout.

Jim watched and I knew he took pride in owning me. Herrick and Talbot, his lifer friends, stood with him and when I hit a long ball all eyes were on me. Except Wes who kept his distance.

I didn't approach him because I didn't know what was eating him. Let him come to me, I decided. But I missed him something awful and many a night scarcely saw the words in my book as I sat in the library. During this time, as winter lost her grip and spring came calling, I asked Tom McKay if I could do some other job in the shop. I pointed out I'd run machines in my previous job and he said he'd think on it which was all I could ask. Thus I kept to varnishing, the idea of escape slipping away just like winter.

Then one night as I hunted for a book I hadn't read, there stood Wes leaning against a library shelf like we hadn't ever left off. There came no crimp of his mouth to entice me, but I didn't care. "Taking up your studies again?" I asked.

He held up his hands to show he had no book, but I didn't get that he wanted to fuck. Just the opposite. I could feel an unrest on him that was not about need. When he sought a table near the back, well away from the other men, I followed. I could see he wanted to tell me something, and at the same time didn't want to.

"What is it, Wes?" I asked.

He worked his hands together, looking at them instead of me. "I had a letter from Jane recently," he said. "She accuses me of deserting her."

"That doesn't seem fair. Prison wasn't your idea."

"The life I led before this is part of it. I was on the run the whole time we were married so there wasn't a lot together. She's had the burden of the children, living with my mother mostly, and they don't get on well. It's hard for her to get by so I understand her lashing out at me, but it's still not easy to take."

"I'm sorry for your trouble," I said. "And hers."

"If I could get out I could become the man she deserves, but I'm not seeing any way ahead but to do my time."

"So you haven't any new plan for escape?"

He brought a hand to his chin to rub the stubble and my heart went out to him. "I'm seriously thinking on giving up such attempts, Gar. I hate to disappoint you, as I know you want out of here, but maybe we're meant to do the time and make the best of it. Study and better ourselves for when we go free."

"Jane is a powerful woman if she can bring you to this," I observed.

"That she is."

We sat quiet then and I didn't mind our silence as his presence alone fed me. And part of me liked him worn down, the famous gunman humbled by reality. I wanted to put an arm around him, hug him to me, and offer sanctuary the best way I knew, but I made no such move. Then he offered another bit of news.

"My cellmate, Cliff Chapman, is coming unhinged."

"How so?"

"The dark cell set him to raving and when he got out of it, he came back wild eyed, pacing all night, rambling no end. He's not himself anymore, but nobody cares. I sent a note to McCulloch asking Cliff to be sent to Cranks' Row as he belongs with the loonies, but heard nothing back. I think Cliff may try to do himself in. Either that or I'll strangle him to get some peace."

I let this sit as nothing I could say would help, and I saw Wes just needed to get it said. Some minutes had passed when I grew bold. "How about we go into the back and I distract you from your troubles?"

He chuckled. "If only I was in that frame of mind."

"How about I get you into it? You know how good it feels to get your cock into me and ride out a good fuck. And I'm aching to have you. I've been abusing my dick something awful while thinking on us, and I'm beside myself with need. Just a couple minutes, Wes. Come on, it'll relieve your tension and maybe that will help you sleep."

He squirmed on the bench, gray eyes awakening. "Tell me more," he said as his hand dropped below the table.

"My dick is stiff in my pants," I began, "and I want to get it out here and now, climb across this table and stick it in your mouth. I can feel your tongue on me, the pull of your suck." I had a hand down working myself, and told him what I was doing. "If you don't fuck me, I am going to make myself come in my pants. Why waste it? Five minutes. Your troubles can spare you five minutes."

When he stood I could see the bulge in his pants. He headed for the back and I followed a minute later. He didn't strip this time, just had his pants open and when I came in, he pushed mine down and bent me against a crate of books. He spit in his palm, slathered it onto his prick, then shoved in, and without a word rode out a good come. He didn't last even a minute. I, meanwhile, made no effort to bring myself off as I wanted him to suck it out of me. Sure enough, when he pulled out and I turned, he fell to his knees and began a noisy feeding, slurping as he licked and sucked. I wanted to last, but couldn't, such was my joy at him being upon me. As I spurted, he swallowed, and we once again enjoyed our communion.

When I softened, Wes still played around with me, then finally let my dick fall from his mouth. He leaned his head against me, his hands on my bottom, and at that moment I swear I could feel anguish come up out of him. He uttered not a sound, even though I knew a wail coursed through him. I reached down and petted his hair which was fairly long as he hadn't been shorn in a while. The urge to declare how much I cared was strong, but I knew not to speak. Actions had to suffice, lest I enter that dangerous territory where resided family obligation.

CHAPTER FIFTEEN

Summer of 1880 I was given a job running a bandsaw and was most grateful to Tom McKay for the change. This machine gave me activity where before I'd stood using a brush for hours on end. Now I fetched rough timber that I then sawed into boards and, when required, thin veneers. The saw was a big cast-iron thing with upper and lower wheels and required skill not only to run but to adjust for various sizes based on the work piece. I spent two weeks with Tom looking on before I mastered the beast, but after that I did well with it.

Wes asked to be reassigned to another shop but was not, his powers of persuasion not so strong anymore. He labored on with shoe cutting while continuing his studies, adding history to his mathematics. We also kept at each other in that library book room. At times, one or the other of us would fall to despair at the daily grind or the years ahead and the other would pick him up the best way he knew, with his cock. Fucking kept us from drying up like so many did.

That fall there came a shock for me. One day a guard found me in the yard and ordered me to accompany him. "What have I done?" I asked, but he gave no answer. Both Jim and Wes looked on as I was marched away. I wasn't taken to the captain's office, nor was I taken to the flogging room. I was taken to my cell and told to gather my personal belongings. "Why?" I asked.

"You've been assigned another cell."

I'd been with Jim five years and had no idea of life otherwise. "Why?" I asked.

"Don't know," said the guard.

I bundled my few possessions into my blanket and followed the guard downstairs to a cell looking just like the one I'd left. "Who's with me here?" I asked.

"Don't know."

The top bunk had no blanket so I knew it mine. I tossed my things up, then took a look around. All seemed familiar, the usual shelf, stool, slop, water, and wash buckets, but on the table lay my answer. There I saw water cup, paper and pencils, and two books stacked one atop the other. The first was a history of our revolution and under it *Davies' Algebra and Geometry*. "It's Hardin's cell," I said to the guard.

"Guess it is."

"Why?"

"Captain's orders."

The supper whistle blew just then and I fell in line with men who had spent their free time in the cells. I was thus not at table with either Jim or Wes, but after supper, instead of the library, I returned to the cell. I perched on the stool, still only half believing my good fortune. Then Wes strode in and removed all doubt.

"Make yourself comfortable," he said as he sat on his bunk to remove his shoes.

"How did you manage this?" I asked.

"What makes you think it my doing?"

"Because good fortune doesn't follow me."

"Maybe your luck is turning," said Wes, holding back a grin.

"Come on, Wes, how did you do it?"

He pulled a foot onto his knee and began to rub his toes. "McCulloch sought my cooperation, and after much consideration I laid out my terms which he accepted."

"What kind of cooperation?"

"He called me in a couple weeks ago and gave me a talk on shaping up. He said he believed I was behind the latest escape attempt, even if I didn't take part, and he wanted me to settle down and stop trying to get out. He said since I have sway with the men, I should be an example toward good. He encouraged me to toe the line and spoke at length on rehabilitation which is the coming thing where prisoners are concerned. Use the time to better ourselves, make it more than punishment. Oh, it was a long speech, but he was saying what I'd pretty much come around to anyway. 'Course I didn't let him know that. He said I should encourage the men to take advantage of what they were offered inside the walls. The only way to reduce a sentence would be through toeing the line."

"So you agreed?"

"Not quite. I said I had to think on it as I couldn't be seen as less of a man, and the captain understood. Then a week later we met again and I proposed a deal. I would guarantee to never again attempt escape, never encourage it of others, and would set a good example for the men. All this if I could have a new cellmate. I told him how far gone Cliff Chapman was and insisted he be put on Cranks' Row. I also told how you suffered daily assaults of Scanlon. I asked for you to live in my cell and he agreed. I am now a reformed man who will do my time."

"With me."

He nodded.

Questions crowded my mind, mostly about his married loyalties, but I held off asking as there would be time for that. Years of it. "I'm stunned," I finally said. "Nobody's ever done such a good turn for me."

"It's not all for you."

I chuckled. "We won't need the library anymore."

"Just for the books. I don't plan to stop furthering my education."

"I'm reeling, Wes. I'm standing here reeling. It feels like I could float away, such is my joy."

He smiled, absent words for once. He held out an arm and I went to sit beside him, the arm slipping around my shoulder. After a couple minutes he said, "We're good for each other." I didn't disagree.

Of course we fucked the whole night. With no wait for a whistle, we took our time, and, as it was a warm fall evening, naked was amenable. As Wes traced his hands over my every inch, he said he'd passed his two-year mark the day before. "Twenty-three to go," he said before he slid down to get his mouth on my dick.

Family loyalties slipped away that night. Maybe not for good, but for a while. Wes spent considerable time licking my nuts and running fingers up my bottom, getting himself so worked up that when he put his prick into me he lasted about two seconds before letting go. Amid calls from the other cells, he gave a roar like some beast tearing into his prey. I was so pent up I came into the bedding, my dick firing without prompting. It was a most satisfying climax.

We lay together in his bunk after that, him with arms up over his head, me nuzzled against him, sweat drying on us both. "I keep reminding myself we don't have to rush away," I said after a while.

"You think Scanlon is going to be trouble over this?"

I hadn't considered Jim and didn't appreciate Wes bringing him into bed with us. Still, it was a good question. "He'll be angry, but maybe they'll give him somebody who's right for him. Maybe another lifer."

Wes stretched his arms, then brought them down onto his chest, and after a minute one slid further down to tug his cock. "I am a reformed man," he said as he worked himself. "I'll be a good example to all, but while in this cell I need not be an example to anyone so why don't you get down between my legs and do some licking." Here he rolled over and pulled apart his buttocks. Before diving in, I paused to consider that he had come a fair piece with his desire.

Though Wes and I had been as close as two men can get, we did not easily fall to living close upon one another. The urge for sex overshadows all, but when you take away the craving for place and time there comes a surprising calm. Our initial couple days together felt a little odd in that we didn't fuck every minute. Much of the time, yes, a good go both nights, but time also to talk or sometimes, after supper, to just read our books, content with the company. In with all the book learning, came this kind of learning.

The third day after I took up in Wes Hardin's cell, Jim approached me in the yard. He'd kept his distance until then and I'd heard Earl Herrick, his lifer friend, was his new cellmate. I took this as a good sign, figuring a close friend would ease the upset of losing a valued possession.

Jim had on his jacket which was odd, it being October, but then Jim was an odd man. "Hello, Jim. I hear Herrick is with you now."

Jim didn't look angry. More he looked forlorn. "It wasn't my idea," I went on, not so much in defense as to assure him I still cared.

He kept his eyes on mine and there I saw the fire. Before I realized his intent, he opened his jacket, took a sizable club he'd concealed there, and swung it hard to my middle where I felt myself give way, pain worse than gunshot slicing through me. Before I could fall, he struck me again, this time to the head. My last recall is the club up around eye level.

It was Johnny Rose who I found tending me when I woke up a day later. My head swam like pudding and I could not see out of my left eye. Rose was applying a wet cloth to my face. "Easy now," he said. "You're in the infirmary under medical care. Lie still."

I had no thought to move as my left side throbbed in its entirety. Even drawing breath was painful. As I took stock of myself, Rose explained. "You have some rib damage and a gash stitched over your eye. You're also concussed so you'll be with us a while." His touch was gentle and the water cool on my cheek. "Your eye is fine," he said. "Just swollen shut due to the wound above. Black and blue, of course. You look a sight, but will heal."

His voice was soft as a woman's though not high pitched. My good eye took him in close up, this boy taken into the wicked doctor's care, and I saw, as I had before, a certain maturity. At fourteen he was where many a man is not at eighteen and I had to wonder if his crime had done that. Most killers used a gun and Ned Mackey had used a rock. None I knew had used his hands, but none were avenging the worst of wrongs.

"Jim got me," I croaked.

"That he did. He's on bread and water two days as a result. Confined to his cell."

It wasn't much punishment for what he'd wrought, but I hadn't the strength to complain.

"Take some water," said Rose. "You've been unconscious more than a day and need fluids."

His teeth weren't lined up proper and when not speaking, he closed his mouth as if ashamed. His lips were a robust pink, his eyes a warm brown, and he bore the tan of an outdoorsman. Overall he was plainly pleasing. He held my head up and I drank two cups of water, finding myself suddenly thirsty. Just then a man called out from another bed and only then, as Rose went to him, did I take stock of my surroundings. In all my time in prison, I'd not gone to the infirmary as I never wanted the old doc's hands upon me ever again. Most prisoners avoided it completely. If we got sick, we just kept on and got well. Looking around, I saw the room held a good twenty beds, all of which were occupied. With several hundred men imprisoned, there were many I didn't know so I made no effort to see who was with me. Moans came now and then, but most lay quiet, as if their conditions were serious. Rose moved from bed to bed, bringing water, helping one turn over, another with the piss pot. When one cried out, Rose sought Doc Fletcher from his office and there came the murderer.

I'd not seen much of him since I came in, but he looked older and more stooped. He attended the man in need, sending Rose for some medicine which was then given. Soon the man was quiet. I noted the doc and Rose all business, working together as if they had no problem with each other. As this surprised me, I made note to ask Rose about it once I got to know him.

When the doc came around to me, I couldn't help but be guarded. "You'll be with us a while," he said as he looked into my eyes. He still bore the foul odor I'd noted on my arrival. "Ribs take six weeks to heal and a concussion sometimes longer." I couldn't help but think of Lonnie, now buried outside the wall, life lost due to this awful man. I gave no reply to anything he said and soon he went on to other patients.

Though idleness was welcome, I couldn't much enjoy it due to the pain of my injuries. I sought to doze, but this was on and off, the day far from comfortable. I kept thinking on Wes, wondering how he fared in knowing Jim had attacked me. I mused on our two days sharing a cell, apart again all too quickly.

Johnny Rose, I soon saw, was an angel of mercy. Not only did he take care in helping us with the necessities, he sat holding the hand of a dying man. As this took place at the other end of the ward, I couldn't see who it was, could only hear the man's faint cry for his mother and a brief confession to God. The doctor didn't come out to see about this, Rose the only one to care. Next morning I asked Rose if the man had died.

"During the night, yes. A sad case as he brought it on himself."

"Who was it?"

"Bob Tinney. I'm told he put his fingers into his machine to try for early release. Guess he got that in a way."

"I came in with Bob," I said.

"His infection couldn't be stopped. Gangrene set in. Doc took the arm, but it was too late."

"Poor Bob. He just wanted out."

"Don't we all."

That afternoon as I attempted to doze, I heard my name. Opening my eyes, I found Wes standing over me. "Wes? Am I dreaming?"

"It's me in the flesh."

"I like the sound of that."

"How are you feeling?"

"Broken."

"I'm sorry I brought this on you," he said.

"It's Jim's doing, not yours."

"But my actions set him off."

"Don't think like that. I'm happy in your cell and mean to be back soon."

Wes sat down on the bed and took my hand. Right there for all to see, he held on to me and I to him, taking the first comfort since Jim had swung his club. For a while we said nothing.

"How's Johnny Rose?" Wes asked.

"A fine nurse. He's good with the men, sees to our needs, some of which are disgusting but he makes no matter. He sat with Bob Tinney who died last night. Poor Bob. Never should have chopped off those fingers."

Wes blew out a sigh. "May he find peace."

"Amen," I added, even though I wasn't a believer.

"I'm missing you in our cell," Wes said. "Two days and you're taken away. I'm not going to rest easy until you return."

"You'll have to step up your studies to fill the time."

"That's not how I want to fill it."

"How'd you manage to get in here to see me?"

"I worked on a guard who let me come over. Tomorrow is Sunday so I should be free to return. Want me to bring a book and read to you?"

"I'd like that. An adventure. Something far away. Sea story maybe."

"You've got it."

Just then Johnny Rose came over. "I'm sorry, Mr. Hardin, but the guard says you're to go with him."

Wes squeezed my hand. "Take good care of my friend," he told Johnny. "And call me Wes."

"I will, mister, uh, Wes. I will."

"See you tomorrow," Wes called as he went out. After that I lay thinking on my man and feeling better for it. Had I not been in such bad shape, I'd have got a hand on my dick.

Sunday there came no Wes. Who did come in was Jim though it took some time for me to learn this. All I got at first was some commotion in the hall which meant a new man admitted. Rose went to see and was gone a while, making himself useful like always. I gave little thought on the new man beyond hoping it wasn't another seven-fingered fool.

Later on, Rose came and sat beside me. "That was Scanlon they brought in."

"Jim? What happened?"

"Wes Hardin happened."

I sucked in a breath of surprise which caused my busted ribs to complain. "What'd he do?" I asked.

"Far as I can tell, Scanlon was playing baseball, happy to be out of his cell and off his bread and water, and Wes went up and took the bat from his hand and laid it across both knees. They say the legs are so bad Scanlon may not walk again."

"And Wes?"

"Two days confined to his cell on bread and water."

"Same as Jim got for hitting me."

"Fair, I guess," said Johnny Rose.

He lingered at my bedside, curiosity apparent. "Wes and I are good friends as well as cellmates," I said.

"You're fortunate to have that in such a place."

"After a while you'll have friends too."

"I suppose, but the men I meet are passing through, being sick or injured."

"Good point. Maybe one day you can get another job and work in one of the shops. Maybe go back to the cotton mill."

"It wasn't so bad over there, then I got pulled in here."

"How do you like working with the doc?"

"I know what you're asking."

"You do?"

"Bob Tinney told me a lot while in here. Told me about Lonnie Laird and how I needed to be on my guard."

"Lonnie was my friend," I said, sadness returning. "He came in with Bob and me. It hit me hard, losing Lonnie, but more that the doc did it and goes on like it never happened, like Lonnie never even was."

"I don't mean to upset you," Rose said. "Maybe we shouldn't talk on this right now."

"No, I don't want to keep it in. It just festers that way. Mostly, though, I want to warn you. Be careful of Doc. He's evil through."

"Thanks for the warning, but you don't have to be concerned. Doc already made his move and I dealt with it. He'll not approach me again."

"What did you do?"

"I don't usually speak on such things, but since you seem a man in the know, I'll tell you. He got me in an exam room, got his dick in hand, and said to bare myself as he wanted to suck me. I looked down at his wrinkled hand holding that sorry worm and told him the only thing I would do with him was tie his privates up in a knot, reminding him I was in prison for killing a man with my bare hands."

"How did he act at that?"

"I didn't think he could shrivel any more, but he did. He stood holding his sorry dick and was like that when I left the room. He's not bothered me since."

"I'm pleased to hear this."

"It won't help poor Lonnie," said Johnny, "but at least the man is stopped. He has no business doctoring anyone."

"Thanks, Johnny. You have a friend in me and I'll continue in that after I leave here."

"You may want to know they're not keeping Scanlon here. He's been taken to the hospital in town as his injuries are too serious for us to handle. Kneecaps are shattered and Doc Fletcher is unable to mend them. I doubt Scanlon will be back."

"A sorry affair," was all I could say.

CHAPTER SIXTEEN

I didn't see Wes until the following Sunday. I managed to sit in the bedside chair, clad in but a gown. Dizziness still plagued me and my ribs were a serious bother, but my spirits had lifted. Then Wes came in and I all but sparkled.

"Well, look at you," he said. "Up and about."

"Up is all," I replied. "It's good to see you."

He sat on the bed and studied me. "Your eye is better."

"I can see now the swelling is down."

"How's the rest of you?"

"Shaky, but improving."

"The cell is mighty empty without you," he said. "I'm getting tired of my algebra, if you want the truth." Here he ventured a hand to my knee which caused my poor neglected prick to wake. I sucked in a breath as he worked his hand onto my thigh. "Wes," I said and he chuckled.

"Doctor is absent," he noted. "So is Rose and the patients all lie quiet. Sight of you in that gown is getting to me, and I'll bet you can use some attention other than medically."

"I'm not going to get up to it in here," I said.

He scooted closer, his hand now at my crotch. When he palmed my dick through the gown, he nodded at its heft. I looked around as he set to working me, deciding what the hell, I was in need. I began a pleasurable squirm while Wes urged me on. "That's it," he said. "Come for me."

I couldn't reply. My balls were ready to boil over and Wes had a good stroke going through the cloth. Then I hit the rise and bit off a cry as I spurted into the gown. He pumped every last drop from me and still held on as I softened. Finally, as I sank down into myself, he let go. "Better?" he said.

"Much," I replied. Only then did I see Johnny Rose had come into the room. Wes now had a hand on his own privates, saying how he was abusing himself something awful without me. "We were just getting started," he said, his prick tenting his pants. "Now you're stuck in here."

He was reaching to bring my hand to his cock when I spoke. "They brought Jim in after you hit him. His legs are so bad they took him to the hospital in town. Shattered kneecaps."

"Got what he deserved."

"You shouldn't have done it," I returned.

Wes thought some before he spoke. "Some men have to be shown rather than told," he said. "Scanlon isn't one to listen, and I won't have him going after you."

"They say he'll likely not walk again."

"Or beat on anyone or fuck a man who doesn't want it."

I looked away, unable to reply because I'd not seen this side of Wes.

"What is it, Gar?" he asked.

"I knew you were a violent man, more violent than Jim if you consider your history, but it wasn't in front of me before."

"You think I wronged you?"

"No, I understand what you did and part of me appreciates the intent."

"But the other part?"

"Well, there's a part that dislikes brutality for whatever reason. I'm sorry, but that's how I'm built."

"He deserved it," Wes said, an edge to his voice.

"You stood as judge and jury."

"Well, goddamn, what if I did? He attacked you for no reason but leaving him, and for that he should pay. Two days bread and water are not enough."

"It's the same punishment given you."

He stood. "Then I apologize for my actions." As he stalked away, Johnny Rose came over. "You okay?" he asked.

"I'm fine, but he's not."

I had plenty of time to think over the next week as it was that long before Wes came to see me again. During that period, I attempted to see his actions as an awful endearment, but the part of me where goodness lived still balked. My only hope was Wes managing to allow a view other than his own. Of course, when I tired of this dilemma, I recalled him bringing me off there in the ward which was much a kindness.

Sunday came around again, by which time I was walking some. Rose kept close when I ambled along as dizziness still hit me sometimes, but I was doing better. I was thus engaged when Wes came in. "Hello, Wes," said Johnny.

"Hello, Johnny," replied Wes, his eyes not on the boy but on me. "You taking good care of my friend?"

"That I am," said Rose who hurried away.

"Good to see you on your feet," Wes said.

"Good to be up and around." Just then a dizzy spell struck me and I reached out to grab hold of Wes who assisted me to my bed. "My head's still not clear," I said once I'd stretched out.

I could see he had something to say, something he'd no doubt worked on all week. The notorious killer had the air of a schoolboy found with his hand in his pants, and this warmed my heart.

"I am a Godly man," he began. "Honest, loyal, and true. It is not my nature to wrong anyone, but if I see wrong, I can't help but try to set it right."

"I know that, Wes. Thirty-two men lie dead because of it."

"I won't say I was wrong to go after Scanlon, and if you think less of me for it, then so be it."

His expression was stricken and I saw him ready to be cast out of my heart, such was his loyalty to himself. I hated what he'd done but, on the other hand, I knew what he was when I took up with him. "I understand, Wes," I said. "I'm just sorry for Jim who hasn't much of a life and now will have less."

"He should have thought on consequences before he hit you."

"Let's not start up again. It's done and past."

He hung his head as he spoke the next. "We have a lot of years ahead and I don't want this between us, but I can't undo what I did."

"We're fine," I said, reaching over to give his knee a squeeze. "Just fine."

He didn't look up as he went on and I kept hold of his knee as he spoke. "Herrick came to me and said I should know something and you should too. About Jim. About his crime."

"He told Herrick?"

"Early on, it seems. Guess the lifers are closer than we thought."

"What did he tell?"

"Jim's mother ran off when he was five years old and his father then started getting after him."

"Getting after?"

"Fucking. Broke him in at five and kept on until Jim had enough and killed him. Ten years taken against his will. No wonder he's such a rough character."

"He wanted to hang for his crime."

"That so?"

"He said it was a jury of fools who let him live."

"So he's had no real life."

"None."

"That still doesn't excuse him beating you."

"No, it doesn't. I won't argue the point any longer. Jim is a sorry fellow and let's leave it at that."

"Can you?" Wes looked hard at me.

"In a while, yes."

"Fair enough."

We sat quiet for some time which I enjoyed, my hand still on his knee. Then he scooted his chair closer, looked to see if others were about. All were quiet and Johnny Rose was gone so Wes pulled my hand to his crotch where I felt his hard prick. As I prodded him he reached under my blanket, pulled up my gown, took hold of me, and set to work. And there we did it, pulling until we both shot a gusher, after which Wes sat back with a smile. I basked a bit in my release, then caught sight of Johnny Rose down the way. Once again he'd come in without notice and no doubt witnessed us doing each other. I indicated this to Wes with a nod of the head and he turned, at which Johnny busied himself with a patient. Wes chuckled. "He might as well get to know about men," he said, running a hand down to prod his spent cock. "I'm going to keep on visiting you."

Every other day the doctor examined me with the least possible effort. He asked after my dizziness and headaches, then poked my ribs. After ten days, he removed the stitches from above my eye, declaring I'd have a fine scar. Once he'd vacated the premises, Johnny Rose came over.

Ten days had gotten Johnny and me well acquainted as a man cannot help but get to know one who bathes him. Each day, Johnny brought his water bucket, soap, cloth, and towel to a couple of the men, taking great care to wash their bodies as they lay under his hand. My ribs, being tightly bandaged, were freed of such adornment on these occasions and Johnny was most careful cleaning there. The first time he bathed me, he assisted me to sit up and remove the gown and as I lay naked, he blushed like the schoolboy he was. Still, he soldiered on. Of course his attentions got my dick up. He washed his way down to a man's important parts, cleaning the hairy patch, and having me raise my legs so he could wash my nuts. He then handed me the cloth. "You'd best do the rest yourself," he said, nodding at the cock.

The unbridled lust that besets all boys was most appealing, and I could not help but offer encouragement. "I'm all right with you washing me," I said.

He looked around as if I'd suggested he suck me. Seeing those in nearby beds weren't looking, he wet his cloth and brought it to my rod. When he hardly touched me, I suggested more effort. "Cock is the dirtiest part of a man," I said. "Needs a good scrub." Here I thrust slightly which caused him to gasp before he caught my playful nature. "Go on," I said. "Doctor me."

He wrapped the cloth around my dick and began to stroke. "That's the way, Johnny. Fix me right up."

I began to thrust in time with him and soon we had a good thing going, so good he had a hand down prodding his privates. I kept my eyes on his as he was most attractive in his determination, his color high, his mouth open, tongue darting along his upper lip. Before long a climax beckoned to me and I said I was going to dirty things just before I let go some powerful spurts. Johnny, now wide eyed and breathing hard, was prodding himself and seconds after I let go, he stifled a cry which told me he'd shot a load into his striped pants. Once done, he slumped forward, one hand falling from me, his other from himself. "Now that is a bath," I remarked at which he chuckled. I was pleased he wasn't embarrassed and more so as he took care in cleaning the spunk off me, then wiping my soft dick clean. He then wet the cloth and lingered so long washing my privates that I had to get after him. "Backside too," I said at which he issued a nervous giggle.

I rolled over with some difficulty, my ribs complaining at any movement, and after Johnny washed my back and legs, I parted my buttocks. "Filthy place," I said as I held myself open. When he didn't immediately start washing, I clenched my muscle to wink my pucker. This brought a laugh. "Give it a wash," I said and he took some time in my crack before allowing his finger to escape his cloth and push into my hole. As he prodded, I realized he was experienced with men which stirred me anew.

Now, ten days and three baths past, and my stitches just removed, Johnny was most attentive. "You want to get up a while?" he said. "Doc says you need to walk more, seeing how your injuries are just ribs and noggin. I'll be here should you falter."

I knew Johnny was ripe, knew also I'd take advantage if given the chance. Wes had come to mind after that first bath-come, but with him still professing his married state, I saw no disloyalty at accepting attentions from Johnny Rose. He now got me to my feet and after I reeled some, he took my arm and we set out to walk up and down the ward.

My dick came right up to tent my gown, and I thought Johnny might have designs on it. Sure enough, after a couple turns of the ward, his hand on my elbow, he suggested we move to an exam room. "Where's the doc?" I asked.

"Went to see the captain."

Well, that was all we needed. Soon as through the door of that room, Johnny locked it and dropped his pants. His prick was stiff, bright pink, and juicy. He took a jar of salve, got onto the exam table, and stuck his bottom up. "Fuck me, Garland." Here he ran a gob of the salve into his butthole and I feasted on the sight before shedding my gown and slathering some of the stuff on my cock. I didn't much care about any complaint from my ribs at this point. I got onto that table behind him, pulled open his buttocks, and put it to him, finally getting my dick in a butthole again.

For a second I remained still, savoring my whereabouts until Johnny urged me on. "Fuck me," he said and I saw he was pulling his dick, already ahead, so I set to pumping his tight little hole. He was experienced, but not too much used, and this ignited my fire such that I fucked with a frenzy, lasting not a minute before unloading what felt a cup of come. I heard him squealing as he took it and knew he was with me, spurting out as he took in. It was a good pairing and I took great satisfaction, noting pain in my side only as I quieted.

Soon as I pulled out of Johnny and got off the table, he did likewise, still holding his dick as a fourteen year old is never without desire. Before I could comment, he was on his knees, sucking my filthy cock while pulling his own which came right back up. I had only to stand still to watch him feed and come.

From then on I fucked Johnny Rose regular. Whenever the doc was absent, Johnny managed to leave off other care to "take me walking" which became our phrase for fucking. After I'd done him and he'd come at least twice, I'd get back to bed and bask in my good fortune at having not one but two men though it was really one man and one boy.

Johnny's voice had already broken and I wondered if his early sexual activity had contributed. I got him talking on his life and he told how he and his widowed mother had a small farm. It was the hired hand who had shown him what men could do.

"Pitching hay in the barn, shirts off as it was hot, and he stops, throws aside his fork, and gets out his dick. I was already abusing mine a lot, so when he said to give his a pull I went for it. Couple hours later, I knew what all men did. He had me stick it to him which about drove me crazy, then he taught me how to take a cock up there which I liked even more. I want it all the time now, Garland. You know how it is."

"I surely do. All men have a similar story on somebody who showed them how."

He smiled at hearing this, then grew pensive. "You and Wes do it in your cell?"

"That we do."

"I hear he arranged to have you with him."

"He has some pull, being a persuasive man."

"I like him."

"So do I."

Wes visited me as often as he could manage during my three weeks incapacitation though one part of me was far from incapacitated. I fucked Johnny every chance I got while Wes brought me off most times he sat at my bedside. Finally the wretched doctor declared me fit to leave the infirmary, but I wasn't to return to work for two more weeks. "You'll remain in your cell during work hours," he said on a wave of his putrid breath. He was looking less a human man every day, as if his wickedness, without a victim, was devouring him from the inside. "You'll take meals in the dining hall as before, and you can spend time in the yard, but do not exert yourself for the two weeks."

Johnny was downcast as I dressed to leave. "I'll need the bandage changed after my weekly wash," I said. "I'll come by and we can 'take a walk' then." This perked him up a bit. "I won't leave off you," I assured him, "but you have to understand a man doesn't always get his way, especially not in here."

I could see he'd grown fond of me, maybe too much so which was a failing of mine. In my eagerness to get at him, I'd lost sight of my actions affecting parts beyond dick and butthole. I should have known better since I pretty much lived it with Wes. Still, I decided to remain attentive to Johnny as part of becoming a man is learning a dick engaged doesn't mean the heart has gone along.

I walked from the infirmary at the lunch whistle and hurried to where I knew the shoe shop would line up. Wes, busy jawing with others, didn't see me until those men looked my way. When Wes finally saw me his mouth fell open and he bolted the line to come and grab my shoulder. "You've been set free," he said.

"Free enough."

He put me in line in front of him and as we marched, he kept squeezing my shoulder. Likewise, when we crowded onto the dining hall bench, he got a hand down to give my privates a good grope before eating commenced. We ate heartily, not because the food was good, which it wasn't, but because we fueled ourselves for later.

"Will you be in the yard after work?" he asked as we lined up after lunch.

"Yep. In the cell the rest of the time."

"See you later then."

Again a tight grip on my shoulder as we marched out.

The guards seemed to know my situation and didn't question my entering the cellblock during work hours. When I stepped into the cell I drew a long breath, my ribs reminding me they weren't quite healed. While I had gained movement, they were still tender so I attempted to remain quiet. Looking around the place I'd enjoyed just two days, I found Wes everywhere: his jacket on the bed, his paper and pencils on the table alongside a stack of books. I could see how he'd passed the time. Looking at what was there, I found math, history, and theology, as well as a pirate novel. This I picked up as it was endearing that he was either reading it or just keeping company with what I liked. I stretched out on the lower bunk where lingered his scent. I dozed off thinking how happy I was to be back here and didn't wake until I heard the whistle at work's end. I sat up too fast, side seizing, then headed out to the yard.

I was greeted by friends, Oren, Ned, and Tom McKay who said I was sorely missed in the shop. "Two more weeks," I told him. Then there came Wes and the others drifted off in respect of us. He was all grins and threw an arm around me in welcome. "You've been missed," he declared. "In more ways than you know."

"I am happy to be back," I replied, running a hand onto his chest. I didn't care who saw us. Tongues undoubtedly wagged at him taking me into his cell, not to mention beating Jim. If people considered I now belonged to Wes Hardin it was fine with me though it might not be so fine with him.

But at that moment he was free of concern and set to filling me in on various events of late, none of which had much import. I enjoyed his enthusiasm as he was wound up tight. He talked until we marched to supper, again with a grip on my shoulder.

"I got you a book," he said when we'd marched from the dining hall after supper. "No need for the library."

"A pirate story," I said. "I saw it on the table. You have a good stack of books there. Why godly study?"

"Why not? I want to know everything and have only the Bible teaching of my father. There's more to belief and I mean to explore."

"I hope you don't get too godly, what with me a heathen."

"I've got a heathen part down between my legs and it remains strong."

Soon as we got to the cell, he reached down to my crotch, but not with the urgency I expected. "Remember our first night here," he said.

"I surely do," my hand now on his privates.

"I want to do all that and more."

"As do I."

CHAPTER SEVENTEEN

On the day of us taking up in the cell again, the fact of our return was as important as the prick I took. Wes insisted on undressing me and took things to the unexpected when he unwound the bandage from around my middle. He then inspected where deep bruises had gone from purple to green to yellow. He ran his fingers so gently over the colorful part that you wouldn't have thought he had a hand in his pants. Then he put his lips to my side, then his tongue, and took time soothing me.

His cock was stiff when he set it free, but he made no rush to use it. His pants down, he was a welcome sight and I drew a breath, my side pinching as if to scold. My bottom muscle clenched almost on its own in anticipation of gaining him.

Wes worked down to my stomach, licking and kissing, then rooted in my hairy patch before taking my hard cock in hand. He applied the same care as he had the rest, kissing the knob, then licking. Before he opened to suck, he looked up at me and in that moment I felt truly home. Then he set upon my rod and I became more pig than man.

His hand went under to play around with my nuts and I could see he meant not to rush. But need was upon us both and he soon pulled back and stood to throw off his clothes. "I'm in powerful need," he growled before easing me onto his bunk. He then raised my legs to see my hole, wet his dick with spit, and put my feet up on his shoulders, never once taking his eyes off his target. Once ready, he put his cock in and at that moment lost all control. "Oh hell," he cried before he began a thrust equal to that of the most prized bull. As he speared me, he made no effort toward quiet. Just the opposite, he moaned and carried on as never before which got men down the row abusing themselves and telling us what they were doing. The whole floor seemed ready to come and then Wes howled like some Indian and rammed me so hard my whole middle set to throbbing. I didn't attend myself, preferring to leave that for Wes.

When he finally finished, he slumped forward, lowering my legs so he could lie atop me where he began to grind against my stiff cock. His breath was near a gasp, but he humped me until I cried out and shot my cream up between us. As the climax rolled through me, I wrapped my arms around my man, feeling no longer damaged.

Gradually slowing, Wes chuckled. "We're slippery," he said as he moved around on the stuff coating our middles.

"And smelly," I added.

"Pigs in slop."

"Oink, oink." I nipped his neck and it was then I thought on how I wanted his kiss, how I hadn't had that since Frank whose lips had been ardent on mine. But I knew such activity could only come with time. For now the neck must suffice and I nipped and nuzzled, happy Wes didn't rush to dismount.

After a while, he slid off and I scooched over so we lay side by side on the narrow bunk, him on his side, me on my back. "Now you are truly returned," he said.

In the candle light I feasted on him, his gray eyes alight with care. I wouldn't call it love for some time, maybe never, but it was still powerful. Lying still, I traced fingers over him, finding a scar on his upper left arm. "Gunshot?" I asked.

"One of many."

"You carry your history on your body."

"Suppose so."

"Tell me how you got the wound."

"First man I shot was in November sixty-eight when he came at me. A warrant was issued and soldiers came after me so I fled and hid out. You have to understand, Gar, I could never get a fair trial from courts backed by Northern bayonets so it was with my family's consent that I ran. Then one day I saw the soldiers, two whites and one black headed toward Hickory Creek Crossing. I waylaid them where I knew they'd cross, killing the whites with my shotgun while the black fled. I chased him and demanded surrender in the name of the Southern Confederacy. He fired wild, hitting my arm, and I shot him dead. I had no mercy on a man I knew only wanted to get my body to torture and kill."

"Sixty-eight. You were fifteen."

"Yep."

"At fifteen you'd killed four men."

"All who came after me."

My finger played over the scar and I began to look for more. Wes didn't object as I skimmed along. He even assisted, bringing up a thigh and then a knee to show wounds. "Got both of these in seventy-two along with a bad one here." He ran a hand down around his navel where were a pair of wounds.

"Four wounds from one fight?"

"One fight and one hell of an aftermath."

"Tell me," I said.

"Not now. I want you to get around and lick my butthole."

I told myself to remember to ask on the four-wound fight, then forgot about wounds as we shifted around so Wes was under me, holding his buttocks apart. What a sight he was, notorious killer of four men at fifteen now begging a butt lick. My spent cock gave a twinge of recognition before I got down and set my tongue to work.

"Been missing this," Wes said as I ran up and down his crack. He was so eager for attention to his backside that I knew he'd like a dick up there if he'd only get past his loyalties as a regular. Any man holding his butt open to another man wanted fucking, I don't care how much denial.

I nipped his bottom, licked all around, and fairly had him squirming when I began on his pucker. "Yes," he moaned as my tongue poked there. "Yes," he repeated as I licked. When I stuck my tongue into him, he gave no words, just a long grunt of the kind a man utters when taking a shit. I gave him a good tongue fucking while he pulled his prick, and I savored, along with his bitter taste, the fact that a part of me was in his bottom.

This work got me heated to the point I grew bold. "I need to come, Wes. Either I put my dick to you or you get around here and suck me."

It was a good sign that he didn't throw me off. He allowed me to keep on my with my tongue, maybe while he considered taking me, but then he let go of his buttocks, pushed me back, and dove onto my cock, sucking with a fury as he palmed himself. Before I could issue a come, he spurted his juice onto my leg, at which I let go in his throat. He fed noisily, sucking my every drop until we heard the whistle for lights out. He blew out a big breath and rose to snuff the candle, after which he got water for us both and sat on the bed at my side.

"Tell me how you got shot four times," I said. "I want to know you, Wes, all of you."

He was shaking his head when he spoke. "Then you first have to understand how it was. I'm a man of fair play and God's grace. I never killed for sport, but only in self defense or for manliness or because it was the right thing to do. My mission early on was to ride forth, two guns blazing, and eliminate from the face of the earth enemies of honesty, chivalry, and the nobility of man."

He was starting to sound like men in the books I read, soldiers and kings and such, although I suspected he was repeating his preacher father's words. I didn't call him on such high ideals, though, as I wanted to hear everything.

"You get that?" he asked.

"I surely do."

"Well then, it began in the John Gates Saloon in Trinity City when a local farmer, Phil Sublett, asked me to a game of tenpins. I agreed as I enjoy all manner of bowling and we had a fine time until an argument came up on who won. He was clearly in the wrong, but got hot about things so I stopped his nonsense with a slap and close on that, sticking my bulldog in his ear."

"Bulldog?"

"Don't you know that weapon? It's a pocket gun of small caliber that I carried concealed. Only accurate up close, but in an ear will suffice. I don't know I would have shot him, though. Just wanted to set him right, but others intervened to part us. Tempers cooled and I sought the bar for a drink, but soon noted Sublett absent. This concerned me so I got my two six-shooters which were checked at the bar, stepped to the doorway, and glanced out to see Sublett coming up the street with shotgun in hand and screaming he intends to kill me. At sight of him I stepped back and just then he fired and missed. I then moved further back to conceal myself in the shadows which would have been good had a drunk not grabbed my coat to declare the two of us could whip anyone. As this fellow then stumbled back he pulled me forward so I was outlined between lanterns and the street at which Sublett fired again, hitting me in the stomach. I bled badly, but still chased him down the street where I shot him in the shoulder. He stumbled but kept running."

Here Wes stopped to sip his water, but I suspected recall was upon him in some unexpected manner. And how could it not be? Threats, shots, wounds. Such a scene would have choked my words away, but I was not John Wesley Hardin. He emptied his cup and went on.

"I thought myself dying. I was nineteen, one year married, and my life seemed at an end. My cousin Barnett Jones was with me, and I told him to take my money belt to Jane over in Gonzales County and tell her I honestly tried to avoid this trouble but when I was shot I ran my foe and made him pull freight with his life. The money was honestly earned from horse trading, horse racing, and gambling. There was around two thousand dollars in gold and about two-fifty in silver.

"Barnett helped me to a doctor who said I had two buckshot lodged between backbone and ribs. Two other were flattened against my silver belt buckle and the doc said this likely saved my life. He then rolled me onto my stomach and extracted the two slugs although I will tell you, that wound troubles me to this day. After this, I fled to Sulphur Springs, then to Sumpter where I recovered at the home of a family friend, Dr. Teagarden. A warrant was issued for attempted murder and posses rode a wide area hunting me."

"Sublett wasn't killed?"

"Nope. That time the fellow survived, but it didn't much matter. I was wanted, even though I shot in defense of my life. Well, later that month—it was August—I went to Angelina County and stayed with Dave Harrel who was a friend. Twice the state police came to his house and on their second visit I met them with a shotgun. I shot one officer, but took a bullet in the thigh. The other officer left but I didn't run as I now had a fresh leg wound on top of the stomach which hadn't healed. This compromised me some so I set to make a deal with the local sheriff, Richard Reagan, saying he could arrest me if he brought medicine for my wounds. I also said he'd need to split the four-hundred-dollar reward money."

"No," I injected as this seemed preposterous. But then other parts of his story also seemed far-fetched, such as that money belt full of gold and silver. That much metal would be too heavy for a man to wear. And surely no officer of the law would split a reward, let alone make deals with the criminal.

"It's true," Wes countered. "Lawmen are as greedy as the rest. Well anyway, Reagan came out, saying he agreed to the split. He brought medicine too which helped me, but he then asked for my guns. I lay in bed at the time, suffering awful, and pointed him to one gun in a holster on the chair. My other gun was under my pillow and as I reached for it, Reagan's deputy thought this a move on the sheriff and shot me in my knee. I now had four bullet holes in me.

"Reagan and the deputy apologized, but took me on to Rush where I was put up at a hotel under guard. Dood Reagan, the sheriff's son, played nurse and his wife cooked for me. I became most comfortable in these circumstances as people were allowed to come calling and show their care. I will say it warmed me to see such a showing of support."

Wes paused again and I thought this recall was more pleasant for him. It was easy to picture his charming side loosened to sway those who visited. "Did they ever jail you?" I asked to get him moving with the story.

"Yes, they did. September saw me to the old jail in Austin, down by the Colorado River. This was an awful place, one crude room with no windows and little good air. It reeked of the men inside who numbered at least twenty-five. Vermin scuttled about as they found such a place a delight. This gang of suffering men had stripped themselves naked due to the intolerable heat and closeness and I did too after just a couple hours.

"After some days in this hellhole, I was taken back to Gonzales County by four state policemen which was a painful ride due to my wounds. In Gonzales, where my family lived, and where I was well known, I found great sympathy among the people. The blacksmith removed my irons and I received medical attention. I then found that the local sheriff, who I knew and liked, had requested I be brought there, even as he admitted to the state police that his jail was not secure. He told me when I came in that I need only be patient. Sure enough, in November a guard slipped me a saw and with the other guards as lookouts, I cut through the bars and broke out. My cousin Manning Clements, a couple friends, and the sheriff waited with horses for the getaway."

"The lawman helped you flee?"

"That he did."

"Hard to believe," I said in all honesty.

Wes chuckled. "Many a lawful man came to my aid as I was well liked by most."

"And when not," I said, "there came gunshots."

"Sometimes, if the need arose."

"You're a remarkable man, Wes Hardin."

He didn't dispute this. Instead he suggested I suck his dick which I did for a good while. We continued in this manner much of the night, playing and prodding, and while I was in a swoon most of the time, there was now in me a thread of disbelief about some of what Wes told. Still, it was but a thread and such a thing weakens when your dick gets sucked.

Around dawn Wes fucked me, lying behind. We were rank, pure pig wallow, but I savored the kind of filth we made. As I took his cock, he worked mine and I didn't care a whit if some of his exploits were stories. He had sway with me too.

When the morning whistle blew, Wes got right up while I lay more than spent. It was not my wounds flattening me but rather a well used body begging rest. My man bore no such indisposition. Sex fueled him and he displayed a vigor that made me want to suck his dick all over again. I kept quiet on this, even when Wes carefully wound the bandage tightly around my middle. I then dressed and marched to breakfast only because I could later return to the cell and sleep away the morning.

At breakfast, Johnny Rose grinned across the table from me and I nodded as one would to a friend, even as he bore an expectant look. His prick was likely up, and sure enough, one hand dropped down. I wondered was I the only one taking note of movement there?

Eating in silence caused thoughts to rise up much as Johnny's dick and they too needed attention, else I'd be toting them around like a stiff cock. So I considered Wes, beside me, raising his hand to request more bread, which he got, and what would he think if he knew I'd been putting it to Johnny Rose. Would he see how his loyalty to his wife gave him little weight should he complain on my fucking the boy? And further, there'd been no declaration from him, no claiming. This was a solid position except that Jane was not here to be used by her man. Wes would surely point that out if we argued on it, but I would counter that his declaring his loyalty and his missing her brought the same objection in me as did his over Johnny and me. When the steward rang his gong for us to stand at meal's end, I noted Johnny reluctant to get up. Then I saw he was amid a come, hand busy below while teeth were bared. A couple seconds more and he slumped, then stood. Before we turned to march out, he reached down to adjust his prick, likely in recall of his release.

On Sunday I visited the infirmary to get a new bandage though I doubted this wrapping of my ribs did much good. I would have mentioned this had I not been fucking Johnny Rose. Soon as he saw me he left off tending a patient and led me to an exam room where he locked the door.

"Where's the doc?" I asked.

"Don't care."

"What if he comes looking?"

Johnny had his pants off and was pulling his dick. "He knows not to trouble me."

This I liked, a strong boy having it over the wretched creature. I pushed down pants and drawers, my cock already hard from the walk over. I stood slathering on spit while Johnny started to climb onto the table. "Not up there," I said.

"Then where?"

"Standing. Bent over the table."

He grinned and bent, pulling open his buttocks to invite me in. "Fuck me, Gar," he said, like always.

Every time I put it to him, I about went nuts as I truly craved my dick in a man's passage. Only fair to have it both ways, give and take, though Johnny only wanted taking. Every time I filled him with come, he set to sucking me or some such so he could get it again.

As I fucked him this Sunday, I knew a true heathen glory as fucking while standing didn't much bother my side. I thus did not hurry but rather thrust steadily while Johnny frantically worked his cock and spurted his stuff under the table. I liked to hear his squeals as I drove the spunk out of him.

Wes no longer came to mind when I did Johnny. Man and boy were separate, each getting pleased by way of me, so I gave myself over to whichever one I was fucking and had a fine time by way of such bounty. Then my juice boiled over and I unloaded into this young passage, holding his slim hips as I watched my dick do the deed. Soon as I pulled out, Johnny was on me, sucking as he worked himself.

I always managed to do him twice, so good were his efforts to work me up again. He'd suck dick, then balls, and even finger-fuck me, showing himself a good learner. Second round took longer, of course, and this Sunday there came a rattle of the door and the doc calling out, "You in there, Rose?"

I didn't pause my fuck and Johnny proved himself by calmly telling the doctor he was bandaging me and need not be disturbed, this as he pulled his cock and took mine to the root. There came no more inquiry at the door, just footsteps as the doc went away. We both chuckled before settling back to enjoy our Sunday fuck.

Once I was healed and declared fit for work, I returned to my bandsaw, heartily welcomed by the men and especially Tom McKay. I didn't mind getting back to an occupation as days in the cell had grown long without Wes. I read many books, but after the second or third time grew tired of them. Would have been different had Wes been there, but with him in the shoe shop, restlessness set in. I suppose this confirmed I was healed.

The last time I got my bandage removed, it was by the doctor who said I was now fit. Johnny stood nearby, hand at his crotch like some little kid. I knew him upset at loss of me so on the next Sunday I sought him in the yard after baseball. Wes was jawing with some men and didn't care anyways as we both had friends.

Johnny looked far too grim for his age or situation. "I need you bad, Gar," he moaned. Only then did I see the way ahead. That library book room was no longer needed by Wes and me so why not for Johnny? I told him about it, said I'd go over and get a book, but it had to be just one round. "I don't want Wes to know," I said.

"He treat you like Jim did?"

"No, not at all. I just want to spare having to explain."

That night I told Wes I wanted to turn in a book for another and I saw him think on coming along. I knew him well enough now to intuit such things, but he was tired this night, shoe cutting having worn him down. He said he'd snooze a while. "Wake me when you get back."

"Will do."

"You and Wes fuck in here?" Johnny asked as he dropped his pants in the book receiving room.

"We did," I said as I locked the door, "but let's not speak on Wes."

"Fine with me. Where'd you get the key?"

"Wes had it made. He can get most anything he wants in here."

I liked the room's soft light as opposed to the glare of the infirmary. In here felt more closed off, the books and musty library smell beckoning a man to free his dick and take up a fuck, which I did this night, turning a chapter in the sex history of the library. Johnny was happy to settle for one good go as he had feared he'd get nothing more, now I was well.

Living with Jim had been a caution and now that there was no such need, I became aware how big a caution it had been. All had gone by his moods, his anger, or his need to claim me. Wes was pretty much the opposite, the two of us equal in our five-by-seven household for that is what it became, a household where resided a pair who cared for each other and were free to express that. Nobody imposed, although the heat between us got us rough sometimes. But it was the good kind of rough, naked wrestle that one time made me come on his leg while he gripped me to him in a bear hug as he bit my neck. Other times we became gentle in rousing ourselves. In between was what I'd call everyday fucking which we did lots of, just men waking with stiff cocks and putting them to use. Of course it wasn't all pretty. Some days a man is just out of sorts, but we both worked at not inflicting too much of that. We came to know each other so well that the slightest upset was apparent, and after a spell of giving room, there would be the inquiry which resulted in either an outpouring or a pout. Wes was good at pouting which amused me, the notorious gunman still taking up a child's way.

I'd kept on asking for the history of each of his wounds and was given details, but when I asked after the last, the one that sent him to prison, when he shot Deputy Charles Webb and Webb's bullet grazed his side, I was put off. "Another time," he said and he went on to speak of an incident that day in his shop. When I asked another time, he again put me off, repeating some news gleaned in the yard. We kept up with events on the outside through men's letters from home and newspapers sent by family which eased the isolation a tad.

It was 1882 before I got the Webb story out of Wes and this was only after he got the Frank McGann story from me. When he asked, I thought it another stall, but I found myself wanting to tell about Frank because it was a story on love as much as it was on outlawry, and the idea of speaking on feelings had great appeal. Webb could wait. We weren't going anywhere.

It was one evening when we'd kept to our cell and had a fine long fuck that I asked after Webb and was turned to Frank. I'd climbed up to my bunk, tired but happy, spunk running down my leg. I no longer needed to remain in my man's arms after our coupling as we had all the time in the world. "Tell me about Frank," Wes prompted. "You know my whole history."

"All but Webb," I countered.

"You give me McGann, I'll give you Webb."

CHAPTER EIGHTEEN

"We'd been in Kansas about a year," I began. "Frank had taken me on in Abilene where I came off a cattle drive from San Antonio. Two others, Clay Gilkey and Dewey Greer, were with us and we'd hit five or six banks, but Frank liked to spend big so we always needed more money. He said Kansas was getting too hot so we came down to Texas and he decided to rob the Cattlemen's Exchange Bank in San Antonio. He said ranchers and cattle dealers kept money there so it would be fat.

"That day we went in just after noon which was always our way as most clerks will be away at lunch so the bank is easier to take. Greer held the horses while Frank, Clay, and me, went in quiet. Once inside we found few people and just one clerk so we pulled our masks down from under our hats and Frank called out for all to throw up their hands. A woman began to scream until Clay slapped her and I believe that scream was our undoing because by the time Frank had a bag full of cash and gold, in charged a deputy with gun drawn. Clay fired at him at which the deputy shot him and I in turn shot the deputy. As he fell, he got off another round which hit me in the thigh, dropping me like a sack of meal as the bullet broke the bone. I tried to stand, but couldn't. Frank, seeing Clay dead and me hobbled, looked around and I saw in that looking that he thought only of himself. Before he took a step I knew he'd leave me, but I didn't call him on it. When his gaze came to mine it lingered as if all our time together was passing before him like with a dying man except he was fine. He showed not an ounce of care and I didn't so much as raise a hand, all this in about ten seconds. Then he ran out with the money. He and Greer fled and were not seen again while I was jailed and sent here."

I'd not expected the telling to bother me as much as it did. That awful piece of the past, now five years gone, rose up like bile which maybe is what soured love tastes like. I could never figure how a man could run out on the one he professed to love, the one he had shown such care toward up until that moment. It took my whole first locked-up year to stop worrying that, but I had finally put it away, until now.

"Why'd you turn to outlawry when you had work driving cattle?" Wes asked.

I wiped my eyes before telling the hard part, the best part. "I was twenty when I met Frank, and I had no experience at love. I knew fucking and such but no more so when Frank stirred the heart as much as parts lower, he drew me in."

"You mean you loved him as I do Jane? How does that work between men?"

"Same with everybody. The party captures you unawares, and feelings take you over until you want to possess the person and have them possess you. The heart sets to driving things which can lead to poor decisions, such as following along in robbing banks."

"I never robbed anybody," said Wes. "Never was an outlaw."

"I'm not one at heart," I offered. "I knew that but I couldn't leave off Frank, no matter he was bad. Because with me he was good." Here I choked up and had to stop as I didn't want Wes to know I cried for another.

"What was he like to so impress you?"

"Big man, over six foot and solid, good looking, older, in his thirties, dark hair and the bluest eyes ever. Big laugh, big paw slapping me on the back. Big dick. We met over poker in Abilene, and when I lost a good deal and vacated the game, he did too and bought me a drink. Well, that drink led to more and he then took me to his room, as I was fairly drunk, and he stripped me and fucked me like no man ever had."

"How's that?"

"First one to take his time. First one to put his lips to mine. Told me to open my mouth and when I did in came his tongue which excited me no end. He lay atop me, kissing like that, tongue after mine, and I came a gusher against his belly where his cock lay like some log.

"Everything that night was different even though much was the same as I'd done on the trail. Maybe it felt different because he took such care. He also said things which nobody ever had, not nasty things which I'd heard a lot but sweet things, loving things I can't repeat.

"By the time I took his cock, I was gone. Hog-tied heart. He did me on my back, first time I ever got it like that, and he had the lamp turned up so

I could see him, furry chest, those blue eyes, his need upon him, yet him still showing care.

"He didn't hurry where all the men I'd known just got in and let go, me too. He used his dick different, grinding as well as shoving in and out, all the while eyes upon mine. 'Course I got hold of myself because I got hard due to all this, and I came for him while he spoke on how beautiful I was amid a come. Those words exactly, amid a come. Never called beautiful before either, not even by my folks."

When I left off talking, Wes gave no comment and I suspected he was having a hard time chewing what I'd given him. It was good we were in the dark as that helps free a man's tongue. After a bit Wes spoke. "That's sex you are talking. How did the loving work? I don't get that."

"It wasn't all robbing banks. That takes a short time, even if you include the planning and riding too and from, so we had many hours free to enjoy ourselves. As I said, Frank liked to spend and after a job and the flight to some distant town where we weren't known, he'd get us a big room at a fine hotel and at first, yes, we'd have a good long fuck as we were worked up from the job. But days to follow were a wonder. He saw to new clothes for me, good boots, haircuts and such. Entertainments every night, theater, dance halls, fine suppers, good liquor. In all this he was attentive as nobody ever was before, gestures only I would catch, small intimacies, a hand pressed to my back, a look of the eye, and sometimes a kiss not leading to fucking, just a kiss of itself. He spoke on his feelings too, said he could love only deeply and with great passion. He'd read books and learned from them, read some love stories to me, and we'd sometimes fuck after, but not always. Sometimes he'd just wrap me in his arms and tell me how much he loved me. If we did fuck then, it was in a loving way. Frank watched out for me, protected me, fussed over me, made me feel special, and I in turn followed him in his robbing because I couldn't leave off him. Nobody could leave off such care."

"But he did leave you," Wes said. "Must have been hell."

"Beyond words. I cannot tell you how bad it felt."

Wes blew out a breath and I heard him turn in his bunk. Then he asked a good question. "If you hadn't been outlaws, would you have set up house like man and woman?"

"Could have, yes, in some occupation, ranching maybe. Frank once spoke on getting a place in California when we had enough money, but he always spent it all."

"How many banks did you rob?"

"Lost count. Wichita, Dodge, Ellsworth, Salina, Emporia, and a few others. Before Kansas Frank had robbed mostly in Colorado."

"I made my money by honest means," Wes said.

"I know you did, Wes. Now. I've told you McGann, you tell me Webb."

Before Wes could reply there came a scream from down the row and then another.

"What in hell?" I said, sitting up because this was not the usual noise from the cells. This was agony.

"Grazer must be at it again," Wes replied, voice gone cold.

"Another flogging for no reason? It's louder down on this floor."

"It's just at row's end so we get it good which I think is part of it, let us know who's in charge."

"How often?" I asked.

"Every few weeks. I figure Grazer gets an urge and pulls in West. I believe their cocks are up while they go at it."

"Maybe fuck each other after."

"Hah!" cried Wes. "Now that's an awful thought."

We remained quiet as the floggings went on and we heard men scream and beg while both of us lay in recall of our own time. While we couldn't hear the Bat slice into those backs, we couldn't miss the cries from those too weak or frightened to take it in silence.

It seemed hours before quiet came and when it did, I noticed the men on the row left off their usual filthy noise. All were humbled by the cruelty, all to a man knowing next time it might be them.

In a way I was grateful for the disruption. The selfish part of me was glad to have Frank McGann chased off and with him the feelings he brought. Awful as it was, the beating returned me to the present, and the present was where I belonged. Frank McGann was long gone. Wes Hardin was now my man. I thought to climb down and take up with him but didn't as I had no idea how my telling had struck him. I liked his curiosity, but couldn't tell what he'd got from it. Was it possible, by way of example, for him to learn of love between men, or would he cling to his regular persuasion and become even more fearful he might compromise himself? I pondered this until sleep came.

Next day at lunch, as I sat with men from my shop and attempted to down putrid fare, a man one table over jumped up and declared the pork spoiled.

"I won't eat this slop when I know for a fact the guards get good meat." Here he threw his plate high in a great arc and by the time it landed, others were thrown until food and plates rained down upon us all. Men jumped up from their tables amid shouting and calls while guards, clearly outnumbered, waved shotguns and demanded order. One fired toward the roof to scare us, but the blast was ignored as most of the men were in a frenzy, jumping about, slugging guards, upturning benches and tables, the place awash in food and water. One guard opened fire, downing two men with one blast, but this made no matter. The men soon overpowered and disarmed the guards, at which one prisoner shouted, "We'll take the prison!"

"Kill the guards!" called another.

"Kill Grazer! Kill McCulloch!"

"Kill them all!"

Just then the whistle blew three times which was the riot signal. As the melee kept on, doors were thrown open and in came more guards who set to hitting the men with gun barrels. I stood fixed until I saw Wes who, as a reformed man, stood still until a guard hit old Fred Walsh, the librarian, as the elderly man stood lost in the fracas. At this injustice, Wes grabbed the guard's shotgun by the barrel, yanked it away, and swung to hit him but the guard jumped back to avoid the swipe. I rushed over and, as Wes charged forward to swing again, I grabbed him from behind. "Wes, stop it. This isn't our fight and can only lead to punishment. Drop the gun before you do serious damage to yourself. You're a reformed man."

He looked at me as if I'd called him a dirty name, then broke into a grin and dropped the gun. The guard had already fled. We then made it to the room's one end where stood those deciding not to riot, and from there we watched as order was eventually restored. But order or not, there came a full lockdown. Those not taken for punishment were ordered to our cells where we would remain as long as Bob McCulloch wished. Last riot had been my first year and we'd been locked down two days. It meant no leaving the cell for anything. Food and water were brought to us in carts just twice a day so all paid a penalty.

"Wish I had more books," Wes remarked when the cell lock had turned. He'd long finished his *Davies* and now concentrated on history and religion. "Need to get some law books."

"Law?" I said as I climbed to my bunk.

"Told you I'd studied with my brother and passed that exam. I'm interested in the process that got me here and how it turned against me so unfairly. I want to learn so I can help myself."

"Toward what?"

"Pardon."

Well, here was another dose of the preposterous, a notorious killer to be patted on the head and set free. "I see," was all I could manage, but then I thought on the supposed injustice that got him his final wound and sent him here. "Since we're locked in, how about you tell me Webb."

"Better ways to pass the time."

"You got your dick out already?"

"Thinking on it."

"Hold off on that because I won't do anything until I hear what happened."

Wes went quiet and I wondered if approaching this killing was difficult due to the poor outcome. Funny, his difficulty was on killing while mine was on loving. We were truly different, but maybe that's what gave it life. "Come on, tell it," I prompted.

He blew out a sigh to indicate giving way with reluctance, yet he spoke with force. "Deputy Sheriff Charles Webb of Comanche was out to kill me, of that there is no doubt as he knew me to be drinking and thus at a disadvantage. I'd gotten word there was a plot against me so was on the lookout. That day he wore two guns, but had his hands behind his back as I happened toward him in the square beside the saloon I'd just come from. Maybe fifteen feet stood between us when he paused and I called, 'Have you any papers for my arrest?'

"'I don't know you,' came the answer.

"'My name is John Wesley Hardin.'

"'Now I know you, but I have no papers for your arrest.'

"'I've been informed that the sheriff of Brown County has said that Sheriff Carnes of this county was no sheriff or he would not allow me to stay around Comanche with my murdering pals.'

"'I'm not responsible for what the sheriff of Brown County says. I'm only a deputy,' he replied.

"I then asked what he had behind his back at which he showed me a cigar. So I relaxed and said, 'Mr. Webb, we were just going to take a drink. Why don't you join us?'

"'Certainly,' he replied.

"As I turned to go inside, my pal Bud Dixson shouted, 'Look out!' and I spun around to see Webb drawing his gun. He fired as I tried to jump out of the way and his bullet struck my left side at which I fired, hitting him in the face. Bud then fired on him as did Jim Taylor, another friend, so Webb got several holes in him. Dead, of course."

"That when they got you?" I asked.

"Hell, no. I pulled another gun to cover the sheriff who'd come up while Jim, Bud, and I went back inside the saloon. Sheriff Carnes had a shotgun and stationed himself at the front door to both keep us in and keep a mob out. While he was occupied up front, we slipped out the back and rode away. I took a look back and saw Jane and my sister Mattie weeping in the crowd and also saw my father and Joe, shotguns in hand, rushing up from Joe's law office. The mob fired on us as we fled while the sheriff tried to protect us.

"Later on, I snuck home where my mother dressed my wound. Sheriff Carnes came and I offered to surrender, but he wouldn't have it as he couldn't guarantee protection from the mob. Once I was doctored, I hid out at Round Mountain, eight miles west of Comanche. Next day Joe, Jim, and Bud Dixson brought food and fresh horses after riding fifteen miles in the opposite direction and circling around."

"So you got away. Why was it they convicted you of that murder?"

"Beats me. Most recent maybe, but it was four more years before they got me. The thing is, Gar, and I've said it before, Webb drew on me, shot me, so I returned fire in defense of my life. It was manslaughter clear as day so an injustice was done to me."

"I see that."

"Then you should also see how I was tried in a town in which three years before, my own brother Joe and two cousins met an awful death at the hands of a lynch mob. On my jury sat six men I knew directly implicated in my brother's death. And remember, Joe practiced law, never robbed, never shot anyone. There lies more injustice."

I chose not to remind him he himself had said he was convicted because of the thirty-two men he'd killed, not the one. There may have been an injustice done him, but he failed to address his history of killing. "Thank you for telling me," I said. "We've now traded histories by way of our wounds."

As I said this, Frank McGann rose up once more because his wound was the worst. I knocked him down when I hopped from my bunk to find what I'd wanted, Wes lying with pants open, dick in hand.

"Enough talking?" he said as I reached for him. As his hand pulled away, it brushed mine, giving me rise. Small gestures loomed large inside a cell. You lock two men together with them knowing they won't be made to come out for a good while and they will start entertaining themselves which is what we did starting that day. So it seemed did the whole cellblock. The guards, knowing us secured, slammed their door and took their leisure while the men celebrated the break from work by getting nasty. "You fucking over there?" came the call. "Come put it to me as I'm naked and have a butt ready for a dick. Need me something up there. Who'll come fuck me? I've got a finger in but rather have a prick. Ah hell, gonna come."

Squeaking of bunks, grunts, calls, obscenities, the place turned wallow and my pig and I went for it. We shed our clothes as it was warm and Wes forgot about studying law or anything while he used his dick to excess. The bedding got stiff with dried come and we got rank with sweat and sex. It felt like the whole cellblock reeked, such were the goings on. I suspected the men who refused to fuck called out the most.

Meals were none but water and Johnnies which were sack lunches of sandwiches, fruit, or whatever the steward chose. They were brought around by trusties who, if they saw men up to things, stood to watch and sometimes palmed their own cocks to spray come onto the cart. They then tossed the Johnnies through the bars and if we were busy, those meals went unattended until we were done.

In this state of wallow, I thought to put it to Wes once and for all. As we had hands upon each other more than not, I meant to get him so worked up with butt-licking and tongue-fucking that he'd want a cock in him. So on the second day when we'd fucked and come in the morning, we got up to it after our first meal and Wes, on the floor where it was cool on the concrete, stuck his rump high. "Lick it," he rasped as he worked his cock. I did as asked since this was the meal I craved most. I fed heartily and when I put my tongue in, I wet him heavily in anticipation of the fucking. He was moaning with pleasure and pumping his prick when I rose up to spear him, again getting my knob in before he threw me off. But this time he came at me in a fury and threw a fist to my middle, hitting my healed ribs which then declared themselves not healed as I buckled. Wes caught me and threw a second punch to my stomach and a third up at my jaw before pushing me to the floor. As I lay in great pain, he came to stand over me, taking his now soft cock in hand to issue a long stream of piss onto me. I didn't object, nor did I roll away. I let him finish, seeing this eliminated the need of words.

He then dressed and lay on his bunk while I sought to wash. That bucket was empty as lockdown meant no attention toward cleanliness so I took a cup of drinking water and with that rinsed away the piss. I then sat naked on the stool, deciding a regular could not be changed over, no matter how much butt work he craved.

After this dustup I was happy to see the lockdown lifted the next day. At work I sawed up a storm and that night I got Johnny Rose in the book room and fucked him twice, not caring about Wes. When I'd had my fill of Johnny, I took a book and returned to the cell where I found Wes deep in study. I climbed to my bunk to read but fell asleep.

CHAPTER NINETEEN

Prison life could grind on a man which I suppose was the intent. By way of tedium and confinement, we were meant to know we had no say on anything due to our illegal actions. Of course intent and the result are often far apart, as was the case with most of the men. I seldom thought on my lawbreaking and know for a fact Wes never considered it unless asked. Even then he'd shift talk to the good life in between the killings, especially now he was a reformed man.

There were always times when the grind became intolerable. Men fought with each other over little or nothing and some went nuts and ended up on Cranks' Row which likely made it worse as fellows on that row were more confined. I succumbed to anger on occasion, thinking I could not possibly saw one more piece of wood. I'd fume so hot I'd soak with sweat on even a cold day, but I'd saw that next piece of wood and the next and the next because I was a convict and we were deprived of a normal life.

Wes had his bad moments too. Sometimes in the yard he'd refuse company and get off to himself which went against his outgoing character. Other times he'd thrash around in the cell, throw a cup against the wall, swear, and carry on how it was inhuman to lock up any man, but eventually he'd wear himself down. Not out, however. I knew these times meant rough fucking so I just got naked, climbed to my bunk, and waited for him to pull me down. The sex would take his edge off but later on, in the dark, he'd talk about running free as a boy, riding and shooting, and wishing he'd known how good he had it.

One day in late May of 1883 Wes went quiet. He made no demands upon me when we woke, said not a word as we marched to breakfast, and when I saw him in the yard after work he was avoiding everyone. I didn't go over as I respected his upsets, but I was close enough to see his expression not like usual. The heat wasn't there this time. His lips were set, but it appeared more pout than anything. He sat fixed until supper and we didn't march in together.

After we'd eaten we went back to the cell. I was trying to not overindulge with Johnny Rose for fear his attachment would become a problem, and also with concern that Wes would get wind, not that he had say over me or my dick. Anyway, when I came in there sat Wes on the stool, still in his pout.

I think he wanted me to ask after his well-being, as we usually did with each other so as to clear the air in such a small space. Had he been angry, I would have inquired but a pout was beneath a man so I let him stew until he boiled over. "I turned thirty today," he said after I was in my bunk in just drawers, book open as we still had light.

"That bothering you?"

"Hell, yes, it's bothering me. Twenty-five when I came in, now thirty. My life is slipping away and I have nothing for it but thousands of shoe soles I've cut. And were it not me at that machine, any other man could step in as it's meaningless work. And I'm now thirty."

"Well then, I won't wish you a happy birthday."

"Nothing happy about it, penned up here like animals. My children are growing up without me, probably wouldn't recognize me on the street if ever I was on a street again. Jane has to get by without a husband's support and my mother is without her son. And I cut shoes."

I knew better than to take it as insult that he professed no happiness, even as I knew our relations pleased him greatly. Though he never came out to say he cared, I knew he did.

"You thirty yet, Garland?" he asked.

"Back in February. Ninth."

"You just let it go by," he noted.

"No room for a party in here."

He chuckled, which was good. All he needed was to get outside himself a while, but with Wes Hardin this wasn't easy. "So you're older than me," he observed.

"That I am. Three months and some days."

He was quiet a bit, then went on. "I was always younger than the others. Famous at fifteen, notorious at seventeen. They called me 'Little Arkansas' which I liked, due to my killing a man by the Arkansas River. Hickok always called me that. He was around thirty-four when I knew him in Abilene and challenged him. I was young then."

"Thirty isn't old, Wes."

"You say that because you're there, but in prison thirty is old. Years are heavier in here. Might as well be forty or fifty, old by way of confinement, unable to gain with years passing."

"You have your studies."

"That's all I have, and it's not enough. A man needs to ride about on his horse, visit family, see friends, do business, let off steam in a saloon, play cards, do some bowling or horse racing, get drunk. I'd very much like to get drunk right now, but that ended like all the rest."

"I guess I don't see it as the problem you do," I said after some thought. "Age brings wisdom, like with your studies. We calm down, stop boyish ways which are often foolish. More man, less boy."

"I'll be fifty when I get out. Now that is truly old."

"Yes, it is, but think of all the knowledge you'll have."

"And a million shoes."

"You want some attention to that old body of yours?" I asked.

"I don't feel like that."

"Not yet you don't. I want to celebrate this day you were born because I wouldn't have missed you for the world. I want to show you how happy I am that you made it this far. Those gunshot wounds could have told a different story."

"I suppose."

I climbed down and for once he made no move. Desire had been run off like it'd been shot at. I went to Wes there on his stool. He sat with legs apart and I got down between them to lay my head against his crotch. My arms I draped over his legs and I nuzzled his privates a while, then slowly started to rub his legs. After a bit he ran a hand to my hair which had a good inch of length as I'd avoided shearing a while. He sort of petted me which was new and while my heart went out to his woe, it also took in the fact that he was accepting my comfort and giving some of his own.

When I pulled down my drawers to show my stiff prick, he got interested, as no man, whatever his state of woe, can resist a rod at attention. Wes leaned forward a tad to better see me handle myself, my head still in his lap, but he made no further move. He just sat watching so I decided to give him a show. I spit in my hand and got my dick good and slippery, then set to serious work only I got upright on my knees to put myself in better display. Wes sat so bland and forlorn I had to consider maybe his upset had worn him through. Still, I kept pumping my prick. It was only when I offered up good spurts that landed on his striped legs that his mouth fell open and he huffed an exhale. Soon as I was empty he said, "Let me have that thing," and I stood and guided my dick into his open mouth.

Oh, how he fed. And he didn't seek his own cock while he licked and sucked. He just feasted on me which I enjoyed, his tongue tasting me like a sweet, his suck so powerful I saw it more of that solace we'd often sought.

He went at me a good while so I grew bold and suggested we get naked in his bunk. "Don't have to do anything more," I assured him. "Just suck."

He wasn't as tired as he was worn of spirit so he did as I said and we snuffed the candle and got in together, reversed, him lying back, me over him to drop my cock into his mouth while I took his.

He didn't come up right away, but I didn't care. Having any part of him in any part of me was solace and I enjoyed his softy as much as he enjoyed my stiffy. After a while I got down to his nuts and he spread his legs in encouragement, then sought to suck my nuts too. Wasn't too long until he wet a finger and stuck it in me which got his dick up. He prodded and sucked and soon rolled me over and put it to me. He issued not a sound as he fucked while I got to moaning as I pumped my dick and came. Took him longer than usual to hit the peak, but a man will journey long to that destination. He came in silence, then pulled out and turned onto his side. I knew to get up to my bunk without a word. Next day he was fine. Thirty plus one day was apparently okay.

Wes settled down after this, becoming his old self in the yard, entertaining groups of men with tales of his exploits and entertaining me nights more like a twenty rather than thirty year old. Then one day it got him again, that awful grind which wouldn't have been so bad had I not returned to the cell after giving Johnny Rose some hard fucking in the book room. I didn't get at Johnny as often as I once did, but when the need arose, I chanced a longer time and he was expert at getting my dick up for that second go. He was now eighteen but, as he'd had his full height and was fairly mature at fourteen, he hadn't changed much, except he couldn't get enough cock. After I'd do him, he'd start talking as he played around with me, telling me how he abused his dick all the time, how it would come up when he bathed the men. "Some of those older fellows still have it, gray hair no matter. Big fat dick standing tall as I wash down there. And they can see I'm stiff in my pants and now and then one will reach over and handle me and I spurt right there.

Couple times I brought them off, I don't care we're in the ward. I think that does more toward their recovery than any doctoring."

This particular night I'd indulged something awful as I was sick of everything but fucking. I decided as I toted my hard cock to that book room that a convict has nothing else going for him, that all the books in the world matter not a whit. Man has to get his dick in to survive, and I was going to survive like hell this night. Johnny was most eager, like always, and couldn't get his rump up fast enough. Soon as we were naked, I shoved in and we set to coming right off. Then we played around like usual and I licked his bottom and such until I was hard again and gave him a long fuck during which he came twice.

Wes was standing back to me and leaned against the wall when I came in. He was looking up at the high barred window and I could see his breath heavy as his shoulders all but heaved. He was pissed at something, maybe me, but most likely the grind.

"What's up, Wes?" I asked as this was no pout.

"Tell me what you do in that library."

"I get a book and read. You know that."

Here he turned and I saw at once he knew. Jealousy has its own kind of fire and my man's face was blazing. "I can smell the sex on you. Tell me who you're fucking."

As always when cornered, my mind ran in circles. I wasn't good in tight situations, like when I shot that deputy. I needed time to gather thoughts and when there was no time, they fled and I had to run after, all the while Wes waiting. I saw his fists clench and unclench. I thought of Johnny Rose and did I need to protect him? Surely Wes wouldn't beat me as had Jim, but would he beat Johnny? These and more ideas ran through me, but nothing reached my lips.

"Tell me who you are goddamn fucking in that book room!" Wes demanded. "You think I'm a fool? You think I can't smell another man on you? You get me putting it to you all these years, you tempt me from what's right and good, and then you betray me, like what I've sacrificed for you doesn't matter."

"You think fucking me is some sacrifice? You, the man who begs me to lick his butt?"

"Don't turn away from my question. Who are you fucking?"

I didn't get much handle on my thoughts, but my heart, or whatever it is down around the middle that grabs hold in such situations and wrenches hell out of you, did so just then, and I saw, by way of that jolt, that it was more pain than jealousy that had him. His eyes were wet but I knew John Wesley Hardin would not allow a tear on his cheek. If anyone could keep them from falling, it was this notorious man. He held his jaw set, lips pressed hard together, as he waited my reply and oh, how I wanted to reach out to him, assure him I cared for no other but, of course, caring was not to be mentioned when a man had a wife.

"Garland! Tell me right now!" he shouted which set off an echo down the row as fellows repeated his demand and added their own to it. "Garland, tell me right now" we heard over and over while Wes waited.

"Johnny Rose," I said.

"The boy."

"He's eighteen now which is a man."

Now that Wes had his answer, he didn't know what to do with it. His jaw unclenched, he shook his head as disbelief came off him like a raw wind. I waited for something more, but he turned away and made a point of avoiding me while pulling off his stripes and getting into bed. He lay looking up at the underside of my bunk like there might be sky there or stars, anything but me. I went over to the stool and sat down to take off my shoes and rub my feet. As my toes all but danced in welcome of such attention, I felt sorry for us both, Wes for his pain at what he saw as betrayal, me for being in such a spot with a man I'd come to love. No tears rose in me and I don't know why. I would have liked to cry some.

I was pulling off my striped shirt when it came out of me. "I'm sorry if I've hurt you, Wes. That was not my intent."

"Your intent was fucking."

It pleased me he responded as this meant explanations could be made, not that I expected him to accept any. Still, I felt the need as once I'd said that fateful sorry word, a host of others boiled up. "That's correct," I began. "I went over there to fuck Johnny Rose, but I don't think you know why, even though it's been made plain to you."

"Nothing about it is plain to me."

"Johnny lets me put it to him. That's what I crave and I don't get that in here so when he let it be known I was welcome, I took the offer. Last time I tried it with you, you pissed on me. Johnny doesn't resist. He wants it. And so do I."

"I'm not that way," came the reply, as expected. "I told you from the first, but you keep trying to break me down. Don't you think you've gotten enough already? Married man in here fucking as God never intended, wife out there wanting her man while he's putting it to you?"

"I knew Jane would come into this conversation."

"You leave her the hell out of it!"

"You're the one brought her in. You're the one throwing her up to me every time you try to leave off what you know you want. She's your excuse, Wes, only you won't see it. Maybe if you got out you'd go back to doing her, but you're not getting out for a long time and you have a life in here with me and we do fine but you keep me from one thing I need."

"I'm nothing like you, Garland, and you're the one won't see it. You don't fuck women, I get that, and don't give a shit on it. What I do give a shit on is the here and now and how you've undone me in a way I never figured. Being locked up makes us animals and I've gone that route with you, but it doesn't mean I'll be what I'm not."

"Then I'll keep on with Johnny Rose and you'd better learn to handle it."

"I can handle any goddamned thing I want to handle," he growled. I liked him getting pissed as that meant we were down in that place where feelings gut punch you.

"Yes, the great Wes Hardin can take anything," I said. "Well then, we're going to see, aren't we."

I stood to strip down to drawers, snuffed the candle and climbed up to my bunk while he said no more. Then in the darkness it all fell away. Didn't matter who fucked who or why. Didn't matter Wes wouldn't let me do him. With the cell in shadow and scant moon outside, everything lost its sway and I didn't care about Johnny Rose or much of anything. Except Wes Hardin.

We lay in the quiet a long time, but I heard no snore from below. I heard not a move, as the old bunks tended to squeak when a man so much as shivered. Down the row went the usual nastiness and one fellow set to screaming that he wanted to die. I knew Wes heard it and wondered if he took it as I did, that we weren't dead, that we still had each other in the here and now. For maybe the first time in his life he was going to have to give himself up, one way or another. Either he offered his butthole for me to fuck, or he left off complaints about me doing Johnny Rose. Nothing else was acceptable.

I said none of this, of course. As time passed, my heart got the best of me and I said one thing more, "I'm sorry, Wes."

He gave no reply.

Next morning we went about our business as usual though Wes was quiet. I gave him room and didn't much see him until in the yard after work. He always got out there first as his foreman let him leave early, so when I stepped out and looked for him I saw him talking to Johnny Rose. It wasn't a heated conversation, but it was away from other men and Johnny was listening with great care. Wes spoke without the usual gestures that accompanied his stories. He was fixed on the boy and I didn't have to wonder why. When he finally left off Johnny and walked away, I didn't go over. I watched as Johnny scuffed along in the dirt a while, then went over to a new man I didn't know and took up talking to him like nothing had happened. Maybe nothing had. That night Wes fucked me like we'd never had cross words though he didn't ask for any butt licking. He took me on my back, thrusting steadily while drilling me with those gray eyes, and I thought he might be pretending me to be his wife to assure himself he was still a regular man. I pumped my dick and shot a load all up my front, determined to let him know otherwise. Once he'd come, he said he was tired and I went up to my bunk, hoping his climax did him more good than just release.

I caught Johnny in the yard next day, pulling him away from some other men, saying I needed to ask him something. "What did Wes say to you yesterday?" I asked.

"Nothing of note," Johnny replied.

"Did he threaten you? He knows about us and isn't pleased."

"He didn't threaten me, but it wouldn't matter if he did. I'm not his man to control. I'm nobody's man. I see to myself and won't be ordered about by a convict."

I knew this a lie but had to hand it to the kid. He said his piece with such determination that another man might have believed it. But the man putting a dick to him knows him best and I could feel that he had to weigh his actions from then on. "Meet me in the book room tonight," I said. "I need you bad."

"See you there," he agreed, giving his privates a tug.

But he wasn't there that night or any night that week and I went to the library all week, reading when I didn't want to. Wes didn't ask about my going and made no complaint at time spent there. He concentrated on his theology and I wondered if he was looking to find answers with God. Finally on Saturday night, Johnny showed up. I'd not bothered him in the yard as it would have been pitiful to chase, but I was pleased to see him that night. When I stood to go to the book room, he put a hand on my arm. "Let's talk out here," he said.

I eased back down and he sat across from me. "I've taken up with another man," he began. "New fellow in for bunco, handsome and slick. He got roughed up by the guards coming over from Austin and spent his first days in the ward where I found him eager. His second day there, we fucked in the exam room and I'll tell you, Garland, I am smitten. Keane Lattimer is his name. He's twenty-two and has a big dick so I'm not coming back to the book room anymore."

I liked that he didn't say he was sorry, because he clearly was not. And at eighteen a man is eager for more than one cock. His explanation made sense, yet I knew Wes was at the heart of it, maybe not with threats but with something. That talk had turned the kid, but I was never going to find out how. It said a lot for my man's powers of persuasion that he could not only get his way, but get the other party to act like there had been no persuasion.

"See you around the yard," Johnny said and he got up and left. I sat for some time trying to figure out just where this landed me, and when I had it figured, I went back to the cell where I knew Wes would be reading up on godly things. How wrong I was.

He lay naked on his bunk, working his cock, eyes closed like he was going to keep on and take care of himself. I knelt down to lean over and lick his knob at which his hand dropped away. When I began to bob and suck, he ran fingers through my hair which told me the upset was past. He'd forgiven me Johnny Rose and I'd forgiven him stepping in. By the time I'd stripped, stuck my rump high, and felt him spear me, I was back to enjoying what I had while again telling myself a regular couldn't be cured. Good thing I'd enjoyed Johnny Rose long as I had.

CHAPTER TWENTY

Every time we settled back down there came something to rile us back up, but in between Wes and I had a life together, two men in a cell knowing each other whether or not it was wanted. Far as I knew, it was wanted.

When, in 1884, Wes started talking escape, I was thrown. He'd been pressing Boyd Christy, foreman of the tailor shop, to get him in there, but Boyd hadn't come through despite Wes greasing him with charm. Maybe if he'd sucked Boyd's dick it might have worked as I knew Boyd got up to things.

Having had a good fuck, we were in the dark in our bunks when Wes blew out a sigh I thought born of satisfaction. "Man could escape easy from the tailor shop," he said, offering no more as he lay in wait for my response.

"Don't tell me you're back on that. Can't lay off flogging?"

"This is a good plan. I got it up with Boyd Christy who agrees a man could slip into a wagon of finished goods leaving the prison. Clothes and quilts piled high are fine cover and if a man bribed the transport guard, it would be a clean move."

"Until somebody squealed."

"No other men in on it and Boyd and the guard could be paid off to keep quiet. Boyd says the guard is a pushover."

"If it's such a good plan why doesn't Boyd make a run?"

"Foreman would be quickly missed, but a worker is a nobody and won't be noticed for some time, especially with the foreman on his side."

"You'd have to be working in that shop," I noted.

"I'm trying to get in there, but so far no luck."

"I thought you wanted the job for easier work."

"That too, and more if I can manage it."

"What job would you do in a tailor shop?" I asked. "I don't see a gunman working needle and thread."

Wes laughed. "Nor do I, but if I can get in I'll do whatever they ask. It's piecework and I hear that once you do so many pieces in a day, your time is your own. No big machines either. I'm powerful tired of cutting shoes."

"You're getting mighty tame, Wes."

"Says the man with a buttload of my spunk."

Now I had to laugh. What else was there when the conversation was nonsense? I considered going back down and sucking some dick to right things, but held off when I heard a snore.

Soon as I saw the bunco man Johnny Rose took up with, I understood why the boy was smitten. Keane Lattimer was a pretty man. No other way to say it. Not tanned like most who come in and not the least weathered, he bore fine features, arched brows, eyes dark as coal, yet fair skinned. His mouth was wide, his chin cleft, and he had a smile guaranteed to stir any cock. He and Johnny were much a pair in the yard and sought each other to march to supper, Keane making those small but telling gestures to Johnny as Wes sometimes did to me though I got them only in private. Keane didn't hesitate to throw an arm around Johnny and keep it there while telling of gambling adventures on riverboats and in saloons or anywhere money was to be had. He said his father was a bunco man who passed along his skill. Cards, horses, all kinds of betting and graft as there were always suckers around. Keane had been undone by a judge he'd skinned, a judge who got his dick sucked until he found his bank account empty. Keane had just eight years so his spirits remained high. I liked his spirit rubbing off on Johnny.

"Looks like your friend got took," Wes said from behind me. He'd crept up as I stood in the yard eyeing the two men.

"I am happy for him. Lattimer is free with his attentions."

"Well, good for him," Wes said with a sneer. "Next they'll be holding hands." Here he stalked off like I'd attempted that with him. He remained in a pout until I licked his butt that night.

One day that June we were told to remain seated after the meal. This annoyed us as the dining hall was hot from the cooking and men in so close, but we did as told. They put a box at the front, far from the kitchen, and a steward called on us to pay attention. Up onto the box stepped a man new to us, well dressed, and looking about forty. Next to him, but not on a box, stood another fellow looking much the same.

"Men," said the first in a big voice. "I am Thomas J. Goree and as of today I am superintendent of this institution. Beside me is your new assistant superintendent, J. G. Smith. My first act is to thank my predecessors, Captains Bob McCulloch and Emmett Grazer, for their service."

Here came hoots and calls and guards had to step up and quiet the men so Goree could continue. "Doctor Fletcher has chosen to retire from medical service. In his place will be two doctors and we plan to expand the infirmary into a fully equipped hospital. Other changes will be made toward your rehabilitation. You will now earn monetary compensation for your labor, a modest but honest wage. In addition to your work for the state, the state will henceforth offer you classes in English and mathematics so you may use your time here to improve yourselves. A debate society will be established, as will a church choir. Food will be improved as will certain working conditions. Certain punishment practices are presently in review and, while order and discipline must remain, this administration seeks to accomplish this through progressive means. Change is ahead, men, opportunities to improve yourselves so your return to society will find you better and not worse for your incarceration."

Murmurs ran through the hall and one was mine as I uttered an "I'll be damned" under my breath to Tom McKay who sat next to me.

"Hell must have froze over," he whispered.

The gong then sounded and we stood and when it again rang, we marched out. I doubt anybody wanted to go back to work with such news upon us, but work we did. My shop was all talk amid the whine of saws and lathes and the pounding of hammers. "Grazer gone" was said in wonderment as good fortune seldom came our way. Could the authorities have finally taken a good look at Huntsville and smelled the stink of cruelty? Whatever the reason, we passed an afternoon amid speculation and Tom McKay didn't care how much we spoke so long as the hammering and sawing kept on.

The yard was abuzz after work, groups of men hashing over the news. I saw Wes in the middle of one bunch, holding court as he tended to do, so I went over.

"As a reformed man, I'm on board with these new fellows," he proclaimed. "We need to take full advantage of all they offer to better ourselves. It is opportunity, boys. I mean to participate to the fullest."

"You'll sit in a classroom?" asked a skeptic.

"I surely will. A man can never get enough learning. I'll also join the debate society as I enjoy a good argument and maybe I'll even sing in the choir. I've been known to carry a tune."

This got a good laugh, as was intended, and I was part of it as I could resist Wes no more than the others. Bob McCulloch had been on the right track telling him to use his sway for the good. That was about to grow, it seemed. Six years Wes had been in prison and he was a changed man, a reformed man. Ready to take up needle and thread if need be or sing in a choir. A far cry from the gunman, but he was thirty-one now and all grown up. The thing was, I couldn't tell exactly how this mattered to me. He'd come in the rebel, fighting at every turn, refusing to buckle to confinement, and I'd fallen for that man, never mind his killing. But the killing was falling away with time, if such a thing can happen. Those poor thirty-two dead men were being forgotten, especially by John Wesley Hardin.

That night he was excited far more than I, but then he'd already been studying so the new opportunity suited him. Since I'd not embraced opportunities, content to flee by way of reading on adventures elsewhere, I saw little in the changes beyond getting bad men away.

"I'm going to ask the new man for law books," Wes said, pacing the cell. He all but crackled with energy and I liked seeing him wound up, suspecting he looked much the same in his killing days.

"Killer turned lawyer," I replied. "Ain't that a stretch?"

"Damn right it is, but so what? My past will have little weight once I'm released, and if I can work for a pardon, it'll come long before I'm fifty."

I took a long piss while he spoke, then climbed up to my bunk. "Nobody is going to pardon a man who took thirty-two lives," I said.

"But I am reformed."

"That don't make the bodies disappear, and surely doesn't help the families left without their menfolk. Reformed and pardoned are not the same, Wes. You know that."

He came over to the bunk and put his hands on it to lean forward. "What's eating you, Garland? You're downright cranky when we have reason to be happy."

"I'm glad to see the murdering doctor gone, but he should be hanged, not retired."

"I'll agree to that. What else?"

"Not something I can put into words."

He sighed but didn't turn away. "Boyd Christy insists they're getting rid of the Bat," he said.

"New man didn't say that," I countered.

"I doubt he told all his plans, but word is around. No more floggings."

"How will they punish escapees?"

"That what's bothering you, me telling you my plan to break out through the tailor shop?"

"I don't know, Wes. Honestly. I don't want questions right now because I have no answers, maybe never will. Sometimes it's just feelings churning up inside."

This threw him, as I expected, and he took a bit before he replied. "That a good churn or bad?"

"In between, I guess. Kind of a slop."

"I get that." Here he reached in to roll me toward him and in the light he met my eyes. "I was always a good man, Gar. The killings got in the way but never changed me. That is the man you know. Being reformed changes nothing."

"I only know you coming in here," I said. "I never saw that good man before. The only one I've known arrived hell-bent to get out, caged animal who refused to give way, the man who never flinched at the worst flogging."

"You think I'm flinching now?"

Tears came to my eyes as something rose up in me that wanted out, an ache almost too big to contain, and I saw in the next second it was my love for this man who tried to help me see his light. I cared for Wes so much it was becoming painful.

"Garland," he said softly, his fingers brushing my cheek. "We're okay, you and me. We do fine and will continue, I don't care how much educating or choir singing I do. In here is the same."

I reached over and pulled him to me to nuzzle his neck. He leaned his head to mine and we shared comfort until he pulled back. "Now you've done it," he declared and before I could ask what, he pulled me from the bed and began to undress me. "Got my dick up," he said as my stripes hit the floor. He reached into my drawers to get my cock which was as weepy as the rest of me, in soft retreat, and he began to handle me gently while I shucked my undershirt, pushed down the drawers, and began to work on my man's striped pants.

Soon we were naked and Wes pulled me to him, his log of cock between us. He began to rub and grind, his hands clutching my bottom, and all was righted. Classes and choirs and whatnot fell to nothing as I held Wes around the middle. He eased back to look me in the eye and I saw he was working toward something because his chin quivered, I swear it did. And then he put his lips to mine and I opened to admit his tongue.

It was not a hurried kiss. He continued to grind against me, his wetness down there now smeared on our stomachs, while our mouths writhed much the same. The kiss took on his passion, his breathing grew heavy, and then I felt his spurts between us, his lower part humping like a dog while his mouth remained on mine. He might not have spoken his feelings, but this night his actions told all. When he'd emptied, his kiss softened, but still his tongue remained, gentle now, like he didn't want to part. Finally he retreated. Still holding me at the buttocks, he asked, "Feeling better?"

"Some."

He chuckled and dropped to his knees where waited my cock. He'd finally gotten me up and the mouth that kissed so well now began on parts lower, playing around my nuts until I spread my legs and he ran two wet fingers up my butthole. Working me back and front, he soon had me on the rise and I thrust into his throat as I shot my load. He kept on me, swallowing spunk until I got soft, then pulled out his fingers and let go my dick. Still on his knees, he looked up and said, "*Now* you feel better?"

"That I do." I ran my fingers onto his cheek to pet him and he let me which said almost as much as the kiss.

"Still having trouble with a reformed man?"

"Not so much."

He stood then and put his hands on my shoulders. "We're good, Garland. In here we are good."

He didn't know he'd said more than he intended.

It took Wes more than six months to get his law books, but he got them. He wrote a request to Captain Goree who had indeed retired the Bat. Goree passed the request on to Col. A. T. McKinney of the Huntsville bar who replied with a list of books "that applicants for law license under the rules of the Supreme Court are examined on."

"Look at this," Wes exclaimed, handing me this letter that Goree had given him. "Captain Goree says he'll order them for the library as he wants to encourage all toward knowledge of the law. He said he's pleased I'm headed that way and complimented me on continuing to set an example for the men."

I read the list which seemed formidable:

Blackstone's Commentaries, 4 vols.

Kents, 4 vols.
Stephens on Pleading, 1 vol.
Storey's Equity, 1 vol.
Greenleaf on Evidence, 1 vol.
Parsons on Contracts, 3 vols.
Daniels on Negotiable Instruments, 2 vols.
Storey on Partnerships, 1 vol.
Storey's Equity Jurisprudence, 2 vols.
Revised Statutes of Texas, 1 vol.
Walker's Introduction to American Law, 1 vol.
Bishop's Criminal Law, 2 vols.

"Criminal and civil law," Wes said as I looked down the list. "I mean to learn it all."

That it excited him put me in a pickle. I was happy for him while at the same time concerned I was losing some part, never mind he'd been studying for years. "That's some list," I offered, handing it back.

"Well, I've got the time," he said, squeezing my shoulder which righted me for the moment.

It was small of me, I see now, to be glad the books took an age to arrive, but I didn't want Wes to be a lawyer any more than I wanted him working needle and thread. He'd been a cattle drover and I often lay in the night, when some man's screams woke me, picturing him on a horse, running a herd. I didn't even put myself in the picture. I just liked seeing him on the open range. He'd said it himself he liked that life and hadn't he spoken on loss of that occupation and on riding free and playing cards in some saloon? That was where he belonged, not in some law office.

During those months before Wes got the books, Goree's changes all came about. Two doctors arrived, Tindle and Hull, fine and knowledgeable men who kept Johnny Rose in their employ due to his great compassion with the men. Whenever I spoke to Johnny in the yard he was with Keane Lattimer and Keane fairly beamed as Johnny told how much more he now liked his work. "Good doctors," he declared. "Young and alive."

"I wonder if Bob Tinney might be with us today had they tended him instead of Fletcher," I said.

"That is possible," replied Johnny.

Keane Lattimer joined the debate society as did Wes who was immediately elected president. They met evenings and staged debates in the chapel

Sunday nights. Keane was probably the only man slick-tongued enough to give Wes a good run so they packed the house. I attended because I too liked to hear Wes orate. He spent much time preparing his arguments, as did Lattimer.

Wes also joined the choir, but I never heard him sing as I still refused religion. One time after choir practice he came in humming and was so wound up he asked would I like him to sing for me.

"Rather not," I said from my bunk where I'd been reading a war story. Goree had gotten us many new books and those lying in the receiving room had now been properly shelved. I no longer had to read the same books over and over.

"You don't like singing?" Wes asked.

"Not church singing."

"God is going to get pissed off at you one of these days."

I held my tongue as I often wondered what He thought of a man clinging to his Bible while fucking other than a woman. I'd had Sunday school as a child and attended services until I left home at sixteen so I knew what the Book said. What I couldn't figure was Wes able to pick and choose as he did and never mind the killing. A smart man is not always smart in everything.

When I said no more and went back to my book, Wes sat on the stool and began to study what I did not care. He then began to hum "Rock of Ages" and I saw compromise in order. Good thing he could carry a tune.

With debate meetings and choir practice, Wes was absent many evenings. Likewise, his Sundays were much taken as he now taught Sunday school. The more religion he took up, the more I wanted to break him down which showed me heathen through and through. But knowing him not only praying to God but teaching others the Word made my desire to address his indulgent side strong. Sunday nights, therefore, often got heated unless the damned debate society put on a show.

Sometimes when there was to be a debate, Wes would return to the cell after lunch to prepare and he'd be on the stool, hunched over papers laid out on the table. I'd strip naked and work my dick until hard, then go over and stand beside him. He'd chuckle and try to put me off but I knew, as did he, there was no resisting that particular piece of meat. He tried on occasion and it amused me to see him hunker down and attempt to write his debate while I thrust forward my dripping cock. One time, when he insisted he had to order his thoughts, I'd remained next to him, pulling my dick until I shot spunk onto his papers. He was angry for about two seconds, jumping up with a "damn you, Garland," but once on his feet I was given a fuck too rough for Sunday. "You want my prick, you'll get it," he growled as he pounded me. "I'll fuck you all the way to Monday."

"Do it," I urged, clinging to the post as he reamed my chute. "Blaze a trail up there."

Maybe it was it being God's day or maybe it was him pulled from study, but he wasn't quick and I didn't care the reason. His breath came in heaves and his sweat grew pungent but he never let up, our fuck slap heard down the row. "Fuck him!" came the call. "Fuck me!" came another.

When Wes came he called out "goddamn" which I thought appropriate. Then I managed another go and cried "holy hell" as surely the Lord was watching.

When Wes pulled out there was no nuzzle or embrace. He fell back onto the stool, pants still down, and I turned to see that fine cock slow to relax. "You're a picture," I said as he sat with legs wide.

He blew out a big breath. "Debate tonight and you just took half my energy."

"Hah! I'm sure the great John Wesley Hardin has enough left, but if you want to keep some for tonight you'd best pull up your pants as I'm getting ideas."

He shook his head, stood, and pulled up pants and drawers. "You okay now?" he asked. "Can I get back to work?"

"Guess so. For now."

Again he shook his head.

When the law books arrived, Wes was like a little kid at Christmas. Goree sent word through a guard and Wes rushed to the library that evening, as did I for I wanted to see. The books had been unboxed and stacked on a table, a good stack as it was many volumes.

"Take forever to learn all this," I said.

"Well, I have just short of that so it should work," he replied, and he picked up a book and was lost to me. From then on our sex was often me interrupting him which I think he got to like because he always gave it good. Other times, less often, he'd get fed up with studies and swear off a while and how we'd get up to it then. It was around this time he began orating while we fucked, speaking nasty and filthy things that fired us both. We thus wallowed something awful, the words working us up until we'd spew and spew and still want more. So even with all his interests, the man wanting to practice law got to orating on fucking and most of man's shameful practices which I reckon gave credit to the debating society.

CHAPTER TWENTY-ONE

It was 1885 when I finally put it to Wes Hardin. Even though we'd started kissing the year before, there came no great giving way on his part and I certainly wasn't going to try again. But one Sunday after he'd attended services and taught Sunday school, he crossed over to my heathen side for what seemed no reason beyond finally being ready. Only took seven years.

He was writing out things from a law book when I came into the cell after the ball game. Without looking up, he asked how it had gone.

"Got two hits and threw out Lattimer at home plate. Bunco men are not good at sport."

Johnny had watched the game and cheered his man, even when it was plain Keane wasn't much good. But we all liked the bunco man's effort as he had an easy way, like he was skinning us and we couldn't see it. "How goes the law?" I asked Wes. We had a full wash bucket and I quickly stripped as I'd gathered a good amount of dirt in the yard. When I picked up the wash cloth, Wes said, "Why don't you wait on that."

"What?" I chuckled. "Law got you worked up?"

"Matter of fact, it has." He got up so I could see his dick tenting his pants. "Haven't been able to concentrate the last hour what with the wash pail telling me you'd come in and get naked."

I reached down to my cock and soon as I gave a few pulls I was on the rise. Wes then began to strip. "Been at my books too long," he declared. "Other occupations can take up a Sunday afternoon."

"I'm thinking on one," I said as he shucked his drawers. His cock pointed at me like it was taking aim.

"Don't want to rush," he said as he pulled me close. "Got a couple hours till supper." He then put his lips to mine for we now kissed every time we fucked, though not any other time. I swam in pleasure at this union and the prospect of a long coupling. Wes was ardent but not urgent, and it drove me near crazy as he did me while holding back. We got onto his bunk and he began to suck me but wouldn't reverse for me to suck him. I didn't object as he had me in a swoon and nobody argues from such a state. He licked my chest, played long upon my tits, and even got over under my arms to root in the hair. He nibbled my neck, then worked back down to my crotch, fingers in the hair, petting, my prick dripping in readiness. When he had me squirming, he rose up and said, "Lick my bottom," and before I could reply he had it shoved up at me, holding himself open to display his center. "Get your tongue in," he added. "Get me sloppy in there."

I settled in to attend him while he pulled his cock but I noted no urgency down there. Despite the tongue fuck, he kept himself steady while I had a devil of a time taking it easy because butt-licking riles a man no end. Finally he began to issue little moans and I rammed my tongue deep as I could, fast as I could until he suddenly called out, "Do it, Garland, fuck me."

I pulled out my tongue and sat back, stunned as if I'd taken one of his slaps. Did I hear right? Did he want my prick in him? As if he read my thoughts, he said again, "Fuck me."

I spat in my palm and wet my rod, then got in position, my knob hovering at his pucker before I took myself in hand and shoved forward. Soon as I popped in I couldn't help but recall the two times I'd attempted this and been thrown. But no resistance came now, no throw and certainly no slap. Just that command to do it, at which set me fucking John Wesley Hardin.

Holy hell, I thought as I did him. Holy goddamned hell. He was panting and moaning, getting louder and pumping his cock while I rode him hard. I never let up, not for one second, as I wanted him to chafe some, wanted him, when he sat, to recall that he'd taken my cock. All this ran through my mind as I took my due and when a climax came calling I cried out, "I'm gonna come in you, Wes," and I began to spurt into this man I loved and it was the best ever in my whole life. A second later he issued a roar and we shared completion as I drove the come out of him. Of course men down the way carried on like usual, but were polite to not come and look, what with the cell doors open. I suspected they feared the wrath of even a reformed Hardin.

When we'd pumped ourselves dry and began to quiet, fear jumped me. Would I get that slap once Wes regained himself? He might again lay blame and say how he was not of the persuasion, might accuse me of turning him from wife and family, so I pulled out of him with some reluctance. When he didn't immediately roll over, I ran a thumb over his center and heard his soft moan which told me all was okay.

This okayness led me to bold action. I leaned in and began to lick his crack, soothing whatever damage I'd done. My hands held him open, but I let fingertips play on his bottom as I decided him giving way merited a gentle descent. Finally I sat back and he rolled over.

"You've made me happy," I said.

"Likewise."

Our eyes were upon each other and I saw reluctance in his gaze so I knew not to ask what caused him to admit me. He had, and the fact was all I needed. I kept looking at him and saw he got that I was okay not speaking on it. I lay forward and he put an arm around me and we dozed until the supper whistle.

Captain Goree's changes could not hide the fact of us being convicts, nor could they do away with the daily grind. There were still bad days when that red brick wall looked fifty, not fifteen, feet high. We might have had classes to attend, a choir to join, and better food, but guards remained on the pickets, and the Gatling gun was still ready to fire.

I better endured the tedium solely because I now had the whole of Wes Hardin. I was also determined not to ruin things by demanding entrance too often and Wes got this, all without a word on the subject. We'd been together long enough to feel our way along, and even Wes came to see past himself on occasion.

When we got up to things in his bunk, the promise of getting my dick in was always there but I didn't press. I did, however, make it plain I'd do him should he want. I'd get around to his backside to nip and play, maybe start to lick. It was when he uttered a certain kind of moan that I knew I was in. Sometimes he'd tell me to do it, other times I could feel him ready.

Of course he didn't leave off putting it to me. Maybe not every day but a good many and if we skipped one due to activities elsewhere, we'd make up for it next time. Then, about two weeks after I'd first nailed him, there came a Sunday when Wes got a letter. We were only given letters on Sunday. When Wes read it he went blank, sitting on his bunk and not responding to my inquiry on what was wrong. He just looked at the floor, letter still in hand, so I took it and read.

It was from Jane and opened as would be expected, saying she and the children send love and are getting along fine. She said Wes remained in her prayers which she knew he needed and assured him she would wait. She then told some news in town, nothing big, and at last laid him out with his mother's death.

"Your beloved mother was taken to God on June 6 after failing for the past week. Doctor Reynolds said it was a natural death, her being fifty-nine. She departed peacefully. I am sorry to bring you such sadness. May God watch over you.

"*Jane*"

His mother had never faltered in her support, sending him newspapers from home and writing several times a month. Every word she sent warmed her son and though he didn't directly share any with me, I felt him gain a measure of peace through her. Now he'd lost the woman who'd seen him through it all and worse, he'd not had opportunity to comfort her in those final days or bid her good-bye.

I sat down next to him and put a hand on his knee. He allowed about two seconds of this before batting me away and jumping up. "Get away from me," he commanded. "Get the hell away."

I knew grief compromised the best of men, so I didn't take his words to heart. When he stormed out of the cell I knew not to follow, but when he wasn't seen at supper I grew concerned. As no headcount was taken at meals, his absence might not be noted although he was probably the most noticed man in the whole place. When there came no guards hurrying around, I knew him safe.

After supper I sought the chapel and sure enough, there he sat. In the soft light he moved not a muscle and I wondered how long he'd been fixed like that, but I didn't make myself known. I was relieved to see him safe in God's hands so I went to the cell where I knew he'd return at lockdown. Except he didn't.

When the trusty doing the night count reached our cell, he stopped. "Don't see Hardin."

"In his bunk already," I said. "Wore out from the day." I'd done my best to arrange our two blankets around jackets bunched in the shape of a sleeping man, but knew the ruse thin.

"Get up, Hardin," came the trusty's call and when the bundle made no move, the trusty unlocked the door and came in. Pulling away the blankets, he saw my game and raised his billy club as if to strike me. He didn't lower it, however, being one of the trusties who'd taken up rehabilitation and left off abusing prisoners. "I should knock you around for this," he said. I didn't bite and he went out to report the absence.

Sleep failed me that night. If Wes remained in the chapel he'd be found and brought here so I knew he was on the loose within the walls. Had he been planning something there in God's house? I got out of bed more than once and spent time standing on the table to look out the window. I pissed and pissed again, paced, got angry at Wes, then scared for him. Had he gone off the rails with grief? Would he land on Crank's Row as a result and not be seen again? Every awful chance played before me, none summoned, and when I shut my eyes the awful ideas kept on. I sat on the stool, I opened and closed the law books. I had no idea the time when gunshots sounded and seconds later the whistle blew. Escape, it said. I hopped up to look out into the yard, but couldn't see movement. My view was but a portion of the place and whatever was happening was farther down. Still, I stood and pressed my face against the bars, thinking if Wes was in flight he might run by.

Two more shots fired down the way, followed by shouts and the thunder of guards' boots. I couldn't make out any of the words as they were a jumble that had no range. Fear gripped me when I thought of Wes taking a bullet, knowing he'd used up all his luck in surviving nine.

The commotion kept on a bit longer and I decided it sprang from near the southwest picket where Wes had planned his prior escape. This all but froze my heart while my gut seized as if punched. Then fell a quiet, shouts gone to talk, and I heard men moving toward the front where Captain Goree had his office and living quarters. Would he be summoned to view the carnage? And how would a man favoring rehabilitation handle Wes now?

As it all died away, it occurred to me Wes might not even be the target of those shots. Maybe he was holed up in the chapel or some dark corner and another man had made a run. I clung to this for the rest of the night and at dawn Wes was brought to the cell by four armed guards. The door was opened and he was pushed in, stumbling forward like he'd used up all his resistance. The door them slammed, was locked, and the guards left. Soon I heard that door at the end of the row that told me only prisoners remained on the floor.

I all but dissolved at having Wes returned to me. He kicked the stool in the dark so I lit the candle which was breaking the rules, but I didn't care about rules just then. I wanted to see my man. He leaned against the table and didn't object to my looking him over. He was bruised around one eye and cut above the brow, his lip was swollen, and he bore the dirt of a man shoved to the ground face first.

"You hurt other than your face?" I asked.

When he didn't answer, I wet a cloth, but he wouldn't let me tend him. He grabbed it and wiped the dirt and blood away, then tossed the cloth to the floor.

"I worried you were shot," I confessed, "so it's a great relief to have you here."

He looked at me like I should know better than to speak, and fell onto his bunk. He never said a word.

It was from others that I got the story as Wes kept a closed mouth. "Two days bread and water while confined to his cell," said Ned Lally who was always in the know.

"Did he make a run for it?" I asked.

"Came out of the shadows near the south picket, but got seen right off and the guard fired but missed. Wes ran them around, but they finally got him. Can't tell how he expected to scale the wall as no ladder was found. They say it was a run to nowhere."

"Why no dark cell?"

"Story is his mother died and he went off his head in grief. Goree took this to account in handing down punishment."

I could only nod so Ned nudged me. "He doing okay?"

"Bruised and still grieving. Quiet, which you know isn't his way."

"Hard for any man to lose his mother."

"That it is," I replied though I had no such experience. My mother's image sprang to mind, the good woman who'd brought me into the world and cared for me, but try as I might, I couldn't imagine her gone so I could capture none of what Wes was feeling. And besides, there was a difference in the two of us. I'd pretty much let go of family ties early on while he was a man whose ties wrapped tightly around him, a man whose feelings pushed him to action, with a gun early on, with his dick in my time, and now toward running crazy in his loss. "Thanks, Ned. You've always got the story."

I didn't stick around the cell much during the two days Wes was confined as he wouldn't talk. Deciding to give him room, I sought the library after work though reading didn't engage me as usual. I'd come in at lockdown and get to bed. Wes never seemed to leave his.

He drank water, but ate none of the bread given him. Bread was now pretty good as food had improved under Goree. Thick wheat bread no more than a day old was a far cry from stale cornbread. I'd often find the bread on its tin plate on the floor next to the bunk and would move it as twice I caught a rat making a meal.

It didn't worry me that Wes wasn't eating. Anybody can go two days without, and he did drink water though not much. He got up to piss, but did no study. I suppose he slept but I heard no snore.

In his absence, men in the yard speculated on him which turned me away as things tend to lose proportion when more than two men converse. Some said Wes had scaled the wall and been knocked from atop it, all with no ladder. Others put guns in his hands, pleased to learn he was not reformed after all. I didn't try to stop the talk as the men liked jawing, but I sure as hell didn't have to listen. In the shop one fellow asked after Wes and when I snapped a two-word reply, he got back to work and didn't ask again. I kept to my big saw and cut some fine veneers.

On the third day, when Wes was free of punishment, he rose, washed, dressed, and marched to breakfast like nothing had happened, except he said not a word. In the yard after work he wouldn't allow others near and he didn't march to supper with me. I kept to the library, willing to give him so much room he'd eventually come calling, but I figured wrong. It was me who finally gave way.

"I'm sorry for your loss," I said from my bunk one night. Lights were out and I figured not being in his sight would help.

"You should be," came the reply.

"What's that mean?"

"It's for you I strayed and God has taken my mother as punishment."

This hit me as would one of his slaps. I lay reeling while searching for a reply, but his statement was too far-fetched for reason. When I offered no response, he continued in a voice cold and sad. "The Bible says man is to lie only with woman, but in here men suffer a temptation beyond reason and so I succumbed. I still acted the man and saw myself forgiven the sin until I allowed you to mount me as you would a woman. This broke God's trust and he smote my mother in holy retribution, casting me down to writhe in a hell of my own making."

Of all the nonsense I'd heard from him, this was the worst, but I had to allow it as I knew grief was talking. Still, it made things no easier. The idea our fucking, no matter who did who, was a reason for death was preposterous, and Wes in his right mind would see this, surely he would. How then to reply? "I disagree," I finally said.

"That is your right."

From then on we said only the necessaries and avoided company as much as was possible for two men sharing a cell. Wes resumed his law study though I saw him less ardent. He also became short tempered in the yard, charm chased off like some dog after his own tail.

I doubt even Emmett Grazer could inflict as much punishment as Wes put to himself over the next weeks. When he attended church I wondered if he pleaded his case to the Lord, charming him instead of us. No choir, no Sunday school, no debate society, just services. I was tempted to attend just to see how he fared, but decided against the blasphemy and left it alone.

Mother Hardin had been regular in sending Wes the Gonzales newspaper once a month so when one showed up three months after her death, Wes wouldn't touch it. I was the one who looked for a return address and found it to be Manning Clements, the favored cousin. "It's from your cousin Manning," I said to Wes who slumped with relief, but wouldn't take the paper from me. I left it on the table where it remained some weeks Only when another paper arrived the following month did Wes begin to read.

Later on I took up the first paper and read of the death of Elizabeth Dixon Hardin in Ellis County on June 6, 1885. Listed among survivors was John Wesley Hardin, residing in Huntsville. I rolled up the paper and put it on a shelf, thinking one day when Wes had righted himself he'd want it.

CHAPTER TWENTY-TWO

I knew Wes had turned a corner when one night I heard the unmistakable sound of a hand working a cock. At this my own stirred so I freed it and set to doing myself which was as close to union with Wes as I was going to get. It was February 1886 and there still remained distance in the cell. Wes had given up his silence, yet might as well have kept it as what he did say was thin. Pulling our dicks, I wondered if he'd catch that I was with him and, in his determination to shun me, deny his need and unhand himself. I got a good amount of spit on myself so my work gave the same wet, slippery sound as his and I was pleased when he kept on. When I heard him pick up the pace, I did too, and when I heard him hold back what I knew a cry of pleasure, I shot a load rendered strong because I was with him. Soon as I was done, though, I saw myself pitiful in playing along as I had.

When I heard his soft snore, I took comfort as all Wes did still affected me, even as I knew he didn't want that. I suffered his moods, gave him room when I could, refused to be baited with spoken jabs, and saw to my own needs, all while knowing he'd not stopped blaming me for his mother's death. I spent hours thinking on how to scale the mountain grown up between us. Or maybe a gorge was better suited, a bottomless pit, hard and desolate with jagged rock walls impossible to navigate. Whatever it was, it remained a barrier I sought to cross, even as I had no rope for a jump. After months exhausting myself, I finally let go because even love can wear down. I got tired, and then got pissed. I found Johnny Rose and fucked him in that spot near the boilers where Wes used to do me. Johnny was always ready to take dick and Keane Lattimer didn't care what Johnny did so long as Keane got all he wanted. So I stuck it to Johnny a bunch of times and maybe it was the smell of him on me that brought Wes around.

I recall the date, April 12, 1886, not only because it brought Wes back to me, but because it began what I've come to call the second half of us. We were changed after the long impasse, but such things sometimes come out for the better.

A dusty and warm wind had swept in that day, dirtying everything, including us. Heat and grit mixed to render the cell inhospitable so I stayed in the library until lockdown. Soon as I got in the cell, I stripped to the waist, not caring that Wes sat at the table, head in hands. His stewing himself was no longer a concern. Let him boil away to nothing.

"I can't think anymore," he said.

"Then stop." I pushed off my pants and shook out the dust.

"Don't your thoughts ever run you ragged?" Wes asked.

Mine had all but run me raw, but I'd never let on since he was the cause. "On occasion," I said.

"What do you do?"

"I fuck."

Talking to him in this manner stirred me, and I didn't care if it showed. Might even be good, parade a stiff dick to let him know I didn't buy into his blaming me for God's work. I shed my shoes and socks, pushed off my drawers, and rubbed my privates which were pleased to be set free.

Wes went silent, raised his head up, but instead of turning my way he opened a law book. I knew he wasn't reading because he shifted on the stool, setting his legs wide to encourage his cock. There may have been distance between us, but I still knew my man. "You're tired, aren't you, Wes," I ventured.

"That I am."

"No wonder. You conjured up a powerful dose of God's wrath, and have no place to set it down."

His fingers ran down a page like he could feel the words. Then he turned to me. "You're a sight," he said.

"As are you."

"You gone back to Johnny Rose?" he asked.

"What makes you think that?" I was working my cock and he spoke to it, not me.

"Smell him on you which I understand, since I won't have you."

"Good then. All's right with the world."

He looked up at me and I saw the gray eyes heavy lidded. "Or maybe not so right," I said and I moved toward him. When he didn't raise a hand to stop me, I guided my dick to his mouth and he opened like a baby bird eager to feed.

He wasn't hungry upon me, but I saw this was fatigue, not lack of desire. His eyes closed as he sucked and licked, all of it slowly, like some first-timer learning what a prick tasted like. His hands went around to squeeze my buttocks and I got so hot I couldn't hold off thrusting which he opened to. "I'm gonna come," I managed just before I spurted into his throat. He kept at me, sucking and swallowing, and when I was empty and going soft he kept me in his mouth. Finally I ran a hand through his hair. "Wes," I said, and he let go and looked up.

I wanted to cry, such was his anguish, and I endured a swell of the heart while at the same instant cursing his Lord who had, by way of his teachings, sent my man to hell and back. "It's okay, Wes," I said. "We're okay. In here we're okay."

I took him by the arms and got him to his feet, then began to unbutton his shirt. He raised his arms to let me pull it and his undershirt up over his head. I undid his pants and pulled them and his drawers down. I squatted to remove his brogans and socks, then pull off pants and drawers together. When he stood naked, I raised up and ran a hand over his chest. He avoided my eyes until I reached for his soft cock at which he issued a little cry and put those gray eyes to mine. For the first time in months, I saw the spark.

"You've beat yourself up pretty bad," I said. "How about we do some healing?"

A hint of smile passed his lips. He never said yes, but he didn't say no, so I pulled him into my arms and kissed him. That he neither bit nor spat told all, and he let my tongue in, met it, and we clung to each other a while, his arms wrapping around me. His cock was soon on the rise and he reached down to pull it up between us which led him to grinding against me, kissing more ardently, then urgently. Soon he was frantic and cried out when he spewed his stuff up between us. I didn't care it wasn't inside me. I was happy to be part of his climax. He humped like mad for those seconds, then slowed, and finally slumped at which I tightened my grip around him. He rested his head on my shoulder and I whispered, "I've missed you."

I didn't need a reply, I just wanted him to know my feelings, and also it was good to say the words after the long dry spell. "How about bed?" I suggested.

He fell onto his bunk and pulled me in with him. I curled against him, my head on his chest where his breathing put me right to sleep.

Before dawn, I woke to Wes turning me onto my side which I did while half awake. He'd already wet his stiff dick and put it in as he lay pressed to my back. We thus began the day with a good fuck, the first in months, and I woke fully then, a new day truly upon us. I had my man again. I had no idea where he stood with God, but didn't much care since there was a dick working my passage.

Wes nuzzled my neck and was most loving, keeping a slow but steady thrust below. I didn't touch myself as I wanted only to receive him so my cock remained orphaned for the moment. It was a good while before Wes picked up the pace and when he did he issued a murmur that seemed one of surprise, like the rise hit him unawares. Then the old Wes kicked in and he grew frantic, flipped me onto my stomach without pulling out, raised my butt up, and set to a mighty thrusting that got me to coming. "I'm there, Wes," I cried and down the way came the echo, "I'm there, Wes." Someone else chimed in to repeat the words, adding, "Fuck me Wes, fuck me."

Wes surely didn't care about these calls as he was pounding out his own release. I need not be told when I received his spunk. I knew he was letting go and thrilled to taking him while my prick unloaded without assistance. It wouldn't be left behind.

At last Wes pulled out and sat back, but before I turned over he ran a finger up my crack as if to familiarize himself with the territory. "Most welcome," I said as he rubbed a still tingling pucker. "I am home."

He said nothing which was okay. I knew he was still troubled, but at least he'd no longer deprive himself. He rolled me over and stretched out atop me, and we lay like that as dawn came. He finally slid to one side with an arm across my chest and we lay in silence until the morning whistle. That night after supper, we fucked and fucked again, but in between we talked.

"You're not alone, Wes," I said out of nowhere when we lay sweaty and spent. "Whatever troubles you, I'll share if you'll allow me."

This didn't open him up, but then I knew it likely wouldn't. He lay silent a good while so I decided to help him along. "I can't know your pain at losing your mother," I began, "but I can understand the agony of not being with her at the end. Has to be the worst of this life we endure, worse than any beating. I want you to know, Wes, that while I can't feel your pain, I can know my own kind in not being able to comfort you. That's all I want."

"I think you are comforting me just fine."

"Can you tell me what drove you to run for the wall?"

He turned his head away. "I know they say I ran for the picket, but I had no plan there or anywhere, I just ran. Didn't think, just everything was suddenly more than I could bear because I wasn't with her when she died. A son should be with his mother in her last hours. He should see her on her way to God, but I failed her in this because I was confined. I saw life going on without me, my children growing up, my wife barely hanging on, and I couldn't stand it and ran for the wall feeling like I could climb over it, I was so angry. It honestly didn't occur to me I couldn't make it."

"I can't imagine such pain." I allowed this to land and waited some before I went on. "How full of that pain and anger are you now?" I asked.

"No idea, only that it's tired me. Maybe there's no outrunning some things. Maybe you have to stop and be trampled, then get up off the ground and start again."

"That what you're doing now?"

"Trying to."

He turned back to me and in the dark found my lips. This began the next go which was most satisfying.

I didn't expect to put it to Wes ever again. His pain may have trampled him and he may have gotten up to start again, but for some reason he stopped addressing the notion that his mother paid the price for me doing him. Whenever he spoke on the run for the wall, he always said it was driven by confinement. He left off the other part, and I didn't know if it was buried now, never to be dug up, or if it lay in wait like some rattler in a shallow hole. Much as we got back to ourselves, this remained between us so I made no attempt to gain his bottom.

I fucked Johnny Rose now and then and he came to the library one night and asked had I ever had two men at once. I let out a snort that turned heads as I'd never heard of such a thing.

"Well, I did it," he said. "Me and Keane and a new fellow who has his hand on his dick more than not. We all got into the room back here 'cause I've still got the key you gave me, and I stood to take Keane's cock while the new man, Don Ferris, kneeled and sucked my dick."

"No."

"Yes, and once Keane had come in me, Don fucked him while I sucked on Keane. We kept at it a good while, everybody doing all manner of nasty things and coming all over the place."

"Front and back at once," I mused, picturing what Johnny said.

"Getting you hot?"

"You know it. That key handy?"

He showed it to me. "Too bad Don or Keane ain't around. All you get tonight is me."

"You're enough. Now let's get in there."

If Wes smelled sex on me, he took no issue since he'd made his stand. But in the night he pulled me from my bed, bent me at the table, and gave me a hard and quick fuck, then left me there with his stuff running down my leg. As I climbed back up to bed, I had to wonder if he'd lain stewing instead of sleeping. I liked the idea of him boiling himself with jealousy.

Wes didn't go back to Sunday school until the following year, 1887, and for a while he just attended. Wasn't long, however, before he was teaching it again. Soon after this, he returned to the debate society, though he refused the presidency. When he and Keane Lattimer arranged to debate on the merits of women's rights, there came quite a stir as everyone enjoyed having a fellow who orated as well as Wes Hardin. Due to expected turnout, the debate was to be held in the dining hall. A permanent stage had been erected where Goree had stood on a box that first day.

I knew Wes would argue a woman did not need the same rights as a man and sure enough he told me just that the night before the event was to take place. I set to arguing the other side just to tease, though I did believe them equal persons who should be allowed a voice. It was fun to needle Wes as he never saw he was a pushover.

The debate took place on a Sunday evening when the men were full of good beef stew after their day of leisure. Wes had spent the afternoon studying his notes. I wondered what Jane would think of him arguing to keep women down.

Captain Goree introduced the two participants. He seemed to enjoy taking part in activities he supported and especially this one. He went on some about "our own Wes Hardin," which drew cheers, up against newcomer—two years in a man was still considered new—Keane Lattimer "who has proven himself equally articulate. I expect a fine debate on the merits of women's rights. I will ask Mr. Lattimer to begin with a two-minute opening statement after which Mr. Hardin will offer his opening. The two will then engage in debate. Judges are the Reverend Cecil Poole, who has come out from town, our own Dr. Arthur Tindle, and myself. The debate shall last no more than one hour."

Keane Lattimer grinned as he stood to begin his spiel. Though he spoke well, the bunco man remained present as he still gave off the slick demeanor that had accompanied his misdeeds. Wes sat rigid in his chair as if already the lawyer.

"Women deserve rights equal to men," Keane began. "While the man must support the family, be it store, law office, field, or the trail, he shoulders this burden as well as setting example for his children and where needed, guides his wife. But she must be seen as more than housemate as she has a mind as good and sometimes better than her husband's and therefore should have a voice in family and community decisions. It causes no hardship for a husband to allow this. He is not a king and none of us lives in a castle. And if a woman does not marry, whether by her choice or not, she should not be frowned upon as lesser. She must be free to seek education and employment, to clerk or teach and contribute to society in ways other than wife and mother. Too long we've kept women shackled."

As Keane heated up, he displayed every bit the persuasiveness of Wes who no doubt sat cringing at the idea of working beside a woman. On the other hand, I had to allow that Keane was not a married man and had likely known women only in taverns and houses of ill repute. He spoke until Goree declared his two minutes ended and the young orator took a seat amid much applause.

"Mr. Hardin, your opening statement please."

Wes was a delight to watch. As he stood I swear he grew ten inches and he might well have worn a fine suit of clothes, such was his manner. Once on his feet, he gazed over his audience, trading on his popularity, charming the men before he even spoke.

"I am a married man and know whereof I speak," he began. "My wife has a good mind, a Godly manner, and a fine heart, but she does not possess the temperament to survive in times such as these without the guidance of a man. Women have great stores of love and compassion, but lack the inner drive to succeed at life. They also have smaller brains by way of their diminutive size, thus lack capacity for deep thought. Treating them as man's equal would be a grave error for them and for us, society thrown into chaos as they make poor decisions that lead to disastrous events we men must then try to rectify. Women are to be sheltered from the harsh realities of life as their constitutions are weak in comparison to those of men. We must protect and nurture them as they protect and nurture our children. We, as the strong element of society, must decide things on their behalf, lest they be set upon the path to disaster."

As Wes continued his arrogant declarations, I couldn't help but consider the wife he used as example. Jane had no guidance but what Wes wrote her and he seldom sent her letters anymore. She had, of necessity, lived with his mother, and Wes had once let slip that it was an uneasy alliance. Now Jane hadn't even that. She was as adrift as a woman could be, nobody there to support her, forced to scrape out a living while raising three children. She of all people deserved equal rights, but self-serving Wes chose to relate only what he needed to make his case.

When Goree called time to the remarks, he threw open the debate and it surprised me that Keane hit first. "You cite your wife as example," he said, "but how does she fare when on her own due to your incarceration?"

A hum ran through the hall and Goree turned to the doctor with a raised brow. I could see Wes took the question as a personal attack and the pause before he responded was clearly required to rein his temper.

"My wife and children are living with close friends and one, being a man and clearly the head of the household, guides her in daily matters. When questions of the children arrive, she consults me by mail before taking action and she does not stray from the path I've set her on. She fully accepts this arrangement, Mr. Lattimer, and has told me so. She values the superior male intellect."

Keane grinned throughout the statement which I could see annoyed Wes who was far too serious where women were concerned. "There has been no proof shown that the larger body of a man houses a superior brain," Keane said. "I have known many a man who towered over me while possessing the intellect of a bug. Likewise, I have personally known women delicate in body who run businesses and are successful and handle money well."

"Woman was created from man," Wes countered, ignoring facts laid before him. "The first woman on earth was but a man's rib upon which was crafted a creature to help populate the earth. This is God's law and needs no further proof."

"You would have women forever as Eve?" asked Keane.

"They need no more. Man rules the world, decides on peace and war, does society's labor, be it with pen, sword, or pitchfork. He sets currency, he preaches to God, he makes business where there was none, and most often has Eve at his side, helpmate, mother of his children. It is God's way and we have no right to seek change."

There he was again, the God Wes called upon when he needed to justify himself, be it onstage in debate or offstage in life itself. His argument was ridiculous, yet I could feel those around me supporting him. And so, I suspected, could Keane who jabbed back with good points and examples, but never took the room. At the end of the hour, the judges conferred, and Wes was declared the winner. Applause broke out and went on for a good bit, Wes puffing up and taking a few bows while Keane lounged in his chair, knowing himself right. I could see he cared little about the outcome. He'd just liked poking the great Wes Hardin.

As the men filed out, Wes accepted handshakes and congratulations from the judges who all had wives at home they undoubtedly wished to keep under their thumbs. It looked like women wouldn't ever gain equality as men would never cede a inch.

I got back to the cell long before Wes. Even after the lockdown whistle, he was still absent. He made it into the cell as the trusty came along turning locks. "Been talking to Goree," he said. "A good man who says I'm setting a fine example for the men."

"Did you square things with Lattimer?" I asked from my bunk. "Shake his hand?"

"Of course. He's a fine speaker, but a bunco man has to be slick."

"Good point," I said. "On the other hand, you're a natural."

He chuckled as he saw I was playing him. I was naked in my bunk, hand on my dick because I knew he'd want to top off his success. He just needed to enjoy his puffed-up state a while longer. "Goree said they declared me the victor after observing my oratorical skills."

"With which you are well endowed. You did look right fine up there. The lawyer in you showed through."

This he warmed to. He came over to the bunk and looked at what I was up to. "You mean to entice me," he said.

"I surely do. Celebrate your victory the best way a man can."

Here I let go my dick and he took hold to start playing around.

"Why not shed those stripes?" I suggested.

"Hate to let go."

"You'll be back."

I rolled onto my side to watch him strip which he did slowly, like it really was that imaginary fine suit of clothes he was taking off. I could picture it on him and he did look fine. Then his stripes were in a pile and his dick was on the rise.

I was right that his orating would get him going. He got me down from the bunk and sucked my dick until I gave him a mouthful, then turned me around and shoved in his cock which was rampant from the get-go. Wes had a lot to say, but now let his dick do the talking. As I took him, I purposely thought of that wife he'd used as example, how she was struggling on the outside while in here her man had his cock up another man's butthole.

CHAPTER TWENTY-THREE

"**L**ook at this," said Wes one night in January of 1888, handing me a sheet of paper. "I'm writing to Smith."

Knowing he meant Assistant Superintendent Smith, I asked. "You seeking a higher authority for that tailor shop job?"

"Nope. Just read."

The note was short and to the point. "I would like to know when my time will be up if I continue my excellent conduct. I also wish to make application for pardon. From John Wesley Hardin."

I read the last part a couple times because it struck me in a way I doubt Wes intended. It was one thing to bend my ear about a pardon, but putting it before Smith opened a whole can of worms.

"What do you think?" Wes prompted as I stood feeling like I'd taken one of his slaps. When I regained myself, I asked, "You really think they'll lop years off your sentence for being the prisoner you're supposed to be? Others of us are just as good, and most haven't tried escaping."

"That's all past. They know I'm reformed. I figure that's good for at least a five-year reduction."

"And a pardon?" I could barely get the word out as saying it aloud gave it unintended weight.

"Well, that's what I'm shooting for, but I figured why not ask on a sentence reduction in case the pardon doesn't come through, even though I think it will."

I shook my head because I wanted no more of this talk.

"What?" Wes asked.

I huffed a breath and handed him back his note. "You're probably the smartest man I've every known and the craziest. Nobody is going to pardon a killer of thirty-two men. Smith is going to think you a fool for asking, and he'll show the note to Goree and they'll have a good laugh."

Wes took this in, silent for a good three seconds as surprise came over him. He always expected me to get on board with his nonsense, always missing how he made a fool of himself. "I won't believe that," he said, turning his back to me. I saw a pout coming on.

"Suit yourself," I replied.

That was all the talk we had on the subject, but I knew when Smith's answer came because Wes went quiet. Later on, when he was out of the cell, I found Smith's note lying on the table. On reading it, I realized Wes wanted me to see it, but couldn't bring himself to show it to me. Smith wrote only that Wes should continue his good behavior and would be let out at the proper time.

Wes tried to act like this didn't matter, going about his business, continuing with his studies, but I could see the wound. It was almost sad that he believed so strongly in such a lost cause. For a couple days he left off fucking, then on the third day he regained himself and was at me all night. He fucked and pummeled, roughhousing getting us stiff, and we got nasty all over the cell. I sucked him as he stood, he fucked me on the floor and against the bars, and at dawn in his bunk. We reeked of come and when the morning whistle blew were still at it, Wes gaining his last climax while cells emptied and men marched to breakfast. When he was finally spent and hopped off me to dress, I could see he didn't want to stop. The part of him unable to tolerate confinement had returned. I could only hope fucking would keep him from another run at the wall.

Around this time I secured a new job as lathe operator which was more skilled work than operating a bandsaw. Turning table and chair legs was a challenge, but this was welcome to a convict needing to occupy both mind and body. Tom McKay spent weeks teaching me the fine points of lathe work and it took many more for me to gain true skill. Three months into it, he said I was doing fine and could take pride in my work which I did. I felt a new man in this job, not only because of more skilled work, but because it was a change, and change was rare inside the walls. Then one day some months later, Tom came up and said to hold off on turning the next leg as he wanted to talk. "My release date is January first," he said.

"Well, congratulations, Tom. I don't know many that get out by way of completing the sentence."

"Thank you, Garland, but there is something more. I plan to recommend you for the foreman position."

I scarcely knew how to take such good news as a man in prison stops expecting things to fall his way. "That's right fine of you," I said.

"You've earned it," he replied. "Best man in the shop, but more importantly, you have a good temperament and that's uppermost."

I knew others would grumble when the time came as some had more years than me, but they were worn down by their time served, slow with production, and prone to poor work. When I told Wes the good news, he was most pleased. "Well deserved," he said. "When you get out you'll have no trouble finding work." He always jumped ahead to life after prison instead of looking at the here and now which annoyed me some, even though I knew it his way. Just once I would have liked him to think on us together in our cell, not out beyond. Of course I said none of this.

That fall a quilter in the tailor shop hanged himself using upholstery cording that he looped over a rafter. He tied one end to a post, the other around his neck, then stood on a chair and kicked it away. "I'm to learn quilting," Wes said in the yard the day after word had gone around about the suicide. "Boyd Christy says I get the dead man's job, and Goree called me in to confirm it. He also remarked on liking my toeing the line as a reformed man and setting a good example for the men. So it's no more cutting shoes for John Wesley Hardin."

"I don't see you with needle and thread," I remarked, unable to hold back a chuckle. "Many things, but not that."

He smiled. "I'll accept that it's woman's work, but in here that has little weight. I mean to do well."

"I have no doubt on that, and now you'll be set up for that escape you planned a while back."

"Don't need that now," he said. "Pardon is a better way to go." That put an end to the conversation as I wouldn't take up his pardon talk. Since Smith had ignored his request, I considered it a closed matter.

Word quickly got around that Wes was now a quilter which surprised everyone. When I asked Wes what exactly he did, I was treated to a lengthy story on how the tailor shop ran, how they made clothes and quilts, how cloth from the mill was stretched upon a frame where padding was then sewn in place. "Boyd Christy says my stitching is quite fine," Wes bragged. When I snickered, he asked was I thinking of my mother.

"Exactly that," I said. We were lying in our bunks, not having gotten at each other. Our new jobs seemed to have mellowed us some or maybe it was just our time together adding up. Sometimes we were content without the fucking though we did not go long in that state.

"I recall my mother making our quilts," I said. "I can see her at her frame, needle in hand. What I can't see is you doing it."

Wes laughed. "Well, neither can I, but there I am, hours of making stitches that are straight and true, yet unable to forget the hand wielding the needle was once wielding a gun."

Out in the yard, Wes was teased something awful, but he took this with a good-natured smile, finally turning it around to play up his skill with his needle, saying he could kill a man with the thing. This got a good round of laughs.

There came one fellow, though, new to prison life, who carried the teasing too far. This fool stepped into a group of men that included Wes and me, saw Wes, and began to laugh. "This the great John Wesley Hardin?" said the fool. "I hear he teaches Sunday school and quilts like a granny. Sounds like he's gone soft."

I felt Wes bristle, but before he could act I stepped in. "Last man to cross Mr. Hardin can no longer walk as his knees got smashed with a baseball bat," I said. "I suggest you keep your pissant comments to yourself."

The fellow's eyes widened and he hurried to the yard's other side.

"You're starting to remind me of me," Wes said, slapping me on the back. I fairly beamed at this, taking it as a great compliment.

Wes soon began taking a law book to work as he said he was allowed to read after completing his day's quota of stitches which he always managed an hour or two before the whistle. I doubted the hanged man had such privilege, but then nobody had such sway as Wes Hardin. So his study gained even more of his time and I had to admire his determination along with his capacity for knowledge. I doubted my humble brain could hold half as much as his, and what I did have was taken up mostly with thoughts of a sexual nature. One time I looked down from my bunk to watch him in study, not moving a muscle, not turning a page, and my heart gave a stir for I could not help but admire the gunman turned scholar. Looking on to see him finally turn a page, I wondered if, in the whole history of man, it had ever before happened, killer taking up the law. When I concluded it had not, I found myself further warmed.

This particular night Wes studied until the lights-out whistle blew and when he stood, he shook himself out and raised his arms high, then arched to stretch his back.

"Now that looks right fine," I commented as I looked over the end of my bunk. "Move like that makes an appealing display."

Wes laughed. "I'm tired, Garland. Too much reading."

"Maybe that big brain of yours has filled up."

"Feels like it."

"How's the lower part? Far as I know it's not engaged when reading law."

He laughed again. "I'm beat, Gar, but if you want to suck my dick, I won't fight you." Here he began to undress which I watched until he was naked and snuffed the candle. When he climbed into his bunk, I hopped down from mine. As I was already bare, I had only to get in with him.

"You're already stiff," he remarked as I crawled on top of him.

"Watching you study gets me going."

"How's that?"

I began to grind my cock against him. "Well, I tell myself you're not read-ing law. In my mind you are reading some book with nasty pictures."

"I wouldn't mind such a book," he replied, hands kneading my bottom.

"Could be about us."

"Now that would be truly nasty. Too bad we're not learning photography in our classes. Could set up a camera here in the cell, get some pictures, and make us a true account."

"You could write the story, what with being the scholar."

"Too filthy for words."

His cock was on the rise and he reached down to pull it up next to mine at which I began to squirm upon him. "Better than all the adventures I've read," I declared. "Here's the story of two men in a cell fucking to excess. One is a famed gunman, the other a humble cattle drover, but they find themselves well suited and most nights a cock is up a butthole."

"You're becoming downright eloquent," Wes noted.

"Your influence," I said, "although I do feel inspired by the subject. Some-times the men lie one atop the other and grind together, cocks between. And in this position they are face to face so their lips meet." Here I left off talking and descended for a lengthy kiss, putting aside story talk. As our tongues entwined, I became urgent below and while in the delicious throes of that kiss, I came a gusher. We clung to each other, still grinding, and not a minute later, Wes pulled off the kiss to cry out a "holy God" as I felt his spurts.

"Holy God," came the echo down the row amid hoots and whistles. "Suck my dick, Jesus," called one man, "and I'll come unto you." This got some laughter while others started begging to have things done or shouting what they did with their cocks. The place was all noise as Wes and I descended from our pleasure.

"The end," Wes said. "Close your nasty book. I'm ready for sleep."

I kissed his cheek, ran a hand over his chest and down to his crotch where I petted his hairy patch. Then I hopped out of his bunk and climbed up to mine, a most satisfied prisoner of love. From then on, every time I picked up a book, I thought of our nasty one.

One Sunday in November, Wes read me a letter from his cousin Manning which said support of a pardon remained strong all over Texas. Ranchers, businessmen, judges, clergy, and a host of others had not forgotten the contribution to society that Wes had made. As I listened, I wondered how all those good people could have forgotten thirty-two dead men.

"Didn't your cousin try and get up a petition for your release not long after you came in?" I asked in an attempt to derail the subject.

"He did. Manning was good on that, and it was signed by many and sent to the governor but he tossed it out as he wasn't in my favor. It was also too soon after my imprisonment, but ten years have passed. Things have calmed down and attitudes are changing."

His ten meant my thirteen. I was past the halfway point of my sentence though I never spoke to Wes on it as any mention of time served set off pardon talk. I knew he wanted me to inquire about this news of great support, but I wouldn't bite. Didn't matter. The letter wound him up and he bent my ear to excess while in the cell. At least he had enough sense to not take such talk out into the yard or to his shop. He told me this wouldn't be fair to the men as many were downtrodden and hopeless. "I don't wish to appear above them," he said, and I had to hold back a laugh as it was his nature to believe himself above everyone. So I listened to far more than I wished and at times, much as I loved Wes Hardin, I thought of other things while he rambled on. That nasty book that lived in the library of my mind grew and grew whenever I sought to remove myself from the present. I got so good at it that I tried thinking on it while at work, but this caused me to ruin a chair leg so no more of that. It came to pass that whenever Wes started his pardon ramble, I put into silent words some real nastiness.

This is pretty much how I passed the time until Tom McKay was released the first of January, 1889. Much as I hated to lose a good man, I was happy to see him set free and also to gain his job. Wes kidded me on it after my first day.

"Well, look at who we have here," he said as I joined him and some others in the yard. "Garland Quick, furniture shop foreman. Stand at attention, men. We're in the presence of authority."

The men drew up and Ned Lally saluted. "Cap'n," he added.

"Far from it," I replied, laughing. "I'm still covered in sawdust." Here I patted my pants which loosened the accumulation. "I will say, gentlemen, that running the shop is right nice as I am slave to no machine. I need only keep things organized and the men working. They seem grateful I plan to continue as had McKay, with care."

"You got a guard to keep happy," Oren noted.

"Clark is easy," I said. "I honestly don't see how such an agreeable fellow ever got into that line of work. He should be a storekeeper or maybe a parson. I'm careful to keep on his good side and if he has a suggestion toward handling a man, I take it. He also gives me some privilege on occasion, as befits a foreman."

This got some hoots and Oren bowed to me as I was seen to be taking on airs. We had a good laugh at my expense which I enjoyed, especially when I glanced at Wes who looked downright mellow. His smile was wide and when I caught his gaze on me, I saw how he got something from my attention getting. He was silently acknowledging the fact of us right there in front of others, those gray eyes saying more than he wanted. He was proud of me and of our bond and I saw this stirred him. I'd venture his dick was on the rise, both in recall of us fucking at dawn and knowing we'd get up to it again at lockdown. Despite the little crowd of men, my dick rose up in agreement.

That night Wes had me lick his crack to excess, and he wanted it as he stood naked at the bedpost, bottom thrust back and me on my knees. If I hadn't known him better, I'd have sworn he craved a cock up there, but he kept to his usual self, holding open his buttocks and urging me to put in my tongue. Funny how he suffered no holy penalty when a tongue did him.

As I gave him what he wanted, he pumped himself to a come, then turned and all but threw me on his bunk where he feasted on my prick until he got a mouthful to swallow. Once he'd sucked me dry, he rolled me over and started playing around my entire body, sniffing and snorting, poking and prodding, and finally settling down to suck my tits. He spent considerable time with the little nubs, then crawled up to get his mouth onto mine, his tongue activity a measure of his arousal. As I savored his attention, I felt his cock stiffen between us.

He put me on my back for the second go, legs high, and he ran his fingers into my hole and prodded there until I begged for a fuck. Working me, he pulled his dick until it dripped in readiness. When he guided it in, I let out a moan of welcome. Didn't matter how many years we had together, this never changed. When Wes channeled all that brain activity down between his legs, he displayed skill equal to his finest oratory. He was the best ever, better than Frank McGann and all the trail hands put together. I would happily spend hours or even days, should he manage to keep it up that long. As it was, he gave it a good run, our eyes locked much of the time. In those minutes the outside world disappeared, along with his idea toward getting free.

One Sunday in the summer, I found the law books closed and Wes sitting at our table, writing with a fury. He went on for some time, writing and crossing out what he wrote and writing still more. When he finally shook his head and stood to shake himself out like a wet dog, I asked what he wrote.

"It's a statement that will go to the governor with my pardon request," he said as if annoyed by the question. "I can't just ask to be let out, no matter how much support I have. I must make a case on how Webb was killed. I have to cite the law and such."

"You seem to be having some trouble with it."

"It's not easy to put into proper terms what is the worst injustice every done me. I get riled up every time I even think on it and have to calm myself so I present the facts well. It's also the most important thing I'll ever write in my entire life, and that weighs upon me."

"Well, at least you have time to make it come out good."

This was the wrong thing to say and as I watched his face color, I realized I'd put my foot in it. "I don't need reminding," he snapped.

"Sorry. I just meant, well, never mind that. If I say more, I'll make it worse. I'm going out and play some ball. See you later."

Men asked after Wes as we were often seen together on Sundays. "Studying" was all I said to them and they nodded and left it at that. Everybody knew Wes had turned scholar and many thought it as funny as his quilting.

I didn't play baseball well that day. The bat missed everything thrown its way and I did poorly at catching the ball while in the field. After a while, I said I was too tired to continue and the team captain gratefully accepted my resignation. I then wandered the yard and when I got over by the boilers, where Wes and I had done things, I saw Johnny Rose taking George Dunn's cock. I was distant enough to not be seen, but close enough to hear that slap of flesh that accompanies a fuck. As I looked at George, who appeared to have a fine prick, I wondered where Keane Lattimer might be. When I glanced around, he was not to be seen. Maybe he was off having his dick sucked by somebody else.

When George came he let out a groan that drew me back to watching and I noted the arch of his back as he thrust into my friend. Johnny, meanwhile, was frantic up front, arm working, his head shaking from side to side which was familiar to me as he did that when I fucked him. Then he looked skyward and I knew he was spurting which I wished I could see. Once they were done and buttoned up, they turned and couldn't help but notice me. George looked stricken and hurried away while Johnny grinned and came over.

"George looks to have a big dick," I said.

"Holy God, he does. Bigger than Keane and Keane has a fine piece of meat."

"I don't see him around?"

"He's favoring a guard down at the mill about now. Parnell Cox. You know him?"

"I do not. Don't know much about life down there."

"Cox likes to lick butt, has a real hunger for eating assholes, and Keane is partial to such attentions so it's a good fit. It also gets him privileges in the shop so it works out fine."

"Who fucks who?"

"Oh, Cox won't fuck. That's the rub. He says he's a regular so he just pulls his dick while licking ass. Won't suck cock either, but Keane doesn't care as he comes buckets which Cox tries to ignore. Once Cox has come, he pulls off, buttons up, and flees the scene, likely rushing off to rinse his mouth and wash away any recall of what he's done. These poor regulars. What a bunch."

We were walking the yard now and Johnny's talk had gotten me going. "You up for a little more?" I asked.

"I'm always up."

"How about we go get us a library book? You got your key?"

"It never leaves me."

As we walked toward the library, I couldn't shake Johnny's comment on the poor regulars, seeing how I lived with one. But Wes had strayed far from his regular self, save for that ass he kept to himself. At the library, I chased him off with thoughts of Johnny who went right to the book room while I lingered among the shelves. There were a good twenty men scattered at the various tables, some working on class assignments as many now attended the English and mathematics courses Goree had started. A bunch of scholars were being made while I, heathen convict, just wanted to fuck. After such considerations, I went into the book room where the light was lit and Johnny stood naked. He tossed me the key and I locked the door.

"All that talk on ass eating has made me hungry," I said as I undressed. "Get down and show me your butt."

On the floor, Johnny with bottom high, I forgot everything else and parted his buttocks to see his hole which he clenched to wink at me. I then dove in and had a fine lick before drilling my tongue in to the filthy place. My cock throbbed in readiness, but I held off long as I could as I wanted the bitter taste on my tongue, wanted to wallow in some nastiness, and I growled and snorfled something awful until I couldn't stand it and had to use my prick. Soon as I shoved in, Johnny squealed and started to come and this fired me as I pounded out my own release, the two of us quickly awash in spunk.

As it was Sunday, we stayed in that room a good while. In between fucking, I played with his fine body, sucking his tits as he told me what all he got up to, both on the job and off. "The new doctors have a schedule of sorts so I know their whereabouts most of the time. And, as the hospital, as it is now known, is expanded and there are two wards and treatment rooms, they're often absent when I'm bathing the patients. I get so many cocks spewing, I deserve a prize. One fellow with a broken arm said it was his dick-pulling arm and he needed to come so bad he couldn't stand it and asked would I do it for him. So I reached under his sheet and brought him off. Then the fellow in the next bed, who has a broken leg, said the same thing. 'But your arm isn't broken,' I noted. He grinned and said he wanted a hand on him other than his own. 'Unless you'll suck it.' Well, nobody was around so I sucked him which took about three seconds, he was so ready. First fellow looked on."

I pulled off my tit sucking to comment. "You are what they call insatiable," I said. "I always thought myself a heathen due to my excess, but you are beyond me, Johnny Rose."

"I'm just getting started, Garland. Now you roll over and I'll eat your butthole as I'm ready to get dirty again."

"Didn't see you playing ball," Wes said after supper that night.

"Played some, then left off as I wasn't hitting very well. You get your statement written?"

"Nope. Every time I think I have it, I read the thing and it doesn't do me justice. I'm going to have to let it lie for a while."

"Good idea. Come to it fresh later on."

"You've got a new book, I see," he said.

"Yep. Another on our revolution. I like reading how the country got started."

"So you were at the library."

"No other place to get a book."

He likely smelled Johnny on me and if not, my own excess was certainly present, but I didn't care. There passed a few moments in acknowledgement of my need to put my dick up a butthole and when Wes made no comment, I felt most justified in my actions with Johnny. I then hopped up into my bunk and began reading while Wes opened a law book.

CHAPTER TWENTY-FOUR

New men kept coming in to remind us life on the outside had not changed. Men still cheated, robbed, and killed. Men still made foolish decisions that cost them years. As new men came in, others departed, some completing their sentences but more often leaving by way of dying, sometimes by their own hand. A few even tried Bob Tinney's angle and chopped off fingers, having heard a disability would get them early release. Medical care had improved so none died, but all were disappointed to learn work would be found for seven- or even six-fingered men. Word finally got around on this and finger chopping ceased.

The hardest part of men leaving was when one who'd come in after Wes and me completed his sentence. Five or eight year men who'd robbed but not killed all but danced their way out those big iron doors while we endured a painful reminder of how long we had to go. This always set Wes on edge and he'd get short tempered, his social side disappearing as he renewed work on that infernal pardon statement. Then after a couple days he'd fuck me and I'd know he was back to himself.

In 1891 none other than Keane Lattimer was released, having done his whole eight years. "I'll miss you boys," he said on his last day in the yard. "You've kept me sharp and for that I am grateful. For some few of you, I have other, more special gratitudes I will express later on. Johnny Rose, who tended my wounds at the start and became my best friend, I will miss most of all." Here Lattimer threw an arm around Johnny who stood next to him. "A fine lad," Keane went on. He then boldly kissed Johnny's cheek which drew gasps from some men. Others slapped him on the back while Johnny beamed and blushed.

"Don't skin too many men," Wes said as he shook Keane's hand.

"Never enough suckers," responded Keane. I knew Wes respected the bunco man, maybe more than the rest of us as they were equals in so many ways. Talk continued until supper and we didn't see Lattimer later on, figuring he and Johnny were having a last go at each other. Next day, the yard seemed empty for the loss of this one man.

Though all the ins and outs, the daily grind, Wes remained as constant with me as his nature allowed. When upsets came, as they will both in and out of prison, Wes became almost tender and gave me good counsel on getting through. He'd pull me down to sit beside him on his bunk and he'd throw an arm around me, then speak in a soft and loving way in which I saw a mix of the Sunday school teacher and the aspiring lawyer. He was good with words, be they God's or his own, and he had sway with me in that regard. I couldn't stay down in the dumps with him embracing and assuring me. And in those moments, when he pulled me up out of whatever hole I'd dug myself into, I would rise up from the darkness, turn, and gaze into those gray eyes, and I would kiss him. He'd allow it, kiss back, and it wouldn't be sexual at all. I don't know if he saw this as love, but I surely did.

Later that year a parson name of Ethan Price came into our prison, but he was not hired to conduct services. He'd slain a young girl who had refused his advances, but once within our walls this slipped his mind and he set to attempting to save us sinners, never mind he wore convict stripes. Some men listened to him, but most turned away. After a couple months, he started going after those not harking unto him, which was a mistake.

It was Wes who warned him against such practice, one godly man taking another to task. "Leave off these men," Wes told the killer parson. "If they choose to speak to God, they'll do it at Sunday services. Rest of the time they don't favor preaching and if some don't follow the Lord, it's their choice which should be respected. I'm likely the most godly man within these walls, and I tell you to leave off attempts to convert anyone if they don't want it."

Price, a somber and brooding sort, even when he spoke of God's glory, nodded and faded away at which Wes received several slaps on the back from grateful men, one being me. Price had by then identified me as heathen and seemed determined to save my soul.

"You godly types can be a pain," I said to Wes the night after he'd taken care of Price. "Why does Price want us all? God himself allows us to go to hell if we choose."

"You're right on that, Gar," said Wes.

When I turned I saw he had stripped and was pulling his dick. "I wouldn't mind some hell right now," he said.

I laughed and shed my clothes and we had a grand descent with come spewing several times. I believe this was made better by the reminder it was a godly man doing the fucking.

Of course Price didn't leave me alone. "I pray for you, Brother Quick," he said one day in the yard. "I shall save you from eternal damnation. Rise up and seek God. Kneel and pray with me."

It was Sunday afternoon and he'd come up as I headed to the baseball game. Services had apparently gotten him worked up, thus he put a hand to my arm to stop me from going to play sport. When I shook him off and kept walking, he stepped in my path, and when I attempted to go around, he did it again. I then turned. "I'm not a violent man," I said, "but you're driving me toward it. My religion or lack of is not your business."

"All God's creatures are my business," he declared, throwing his arms open wide as if to embrace us all.

"I don't consider myself a creature so get out of my way," I replied.

Men had drawn near, as they always did with promise of a dustup. "My mission is to save all who stray from God's path," Price intoned like he was in some pulpit.

"What about the girl you killed? Isn't one of God's commandments against murder?"

"A poor lost creature," he said, ignoring the facts of her demise.

"You're more lost than any of us," I snapped, patience gone. I stepped to one side and when he again got in my way, I threw a punch that failed to land as someone grabbed my arm. I turned to find myself in the grip of Wes Hardin who yanked me back, stepped in, and slapped Price so hard the parson fell back onto his bottom.

"The man said to leave off, which I already told you to do. You sit there a while and consider yourself lucky I don't beat the shit out of you which I've been known to do. As it's God's day, I'll spare you my wrath, but don't preach in the yard ever again. If I see you at it, I'll render you an unholy sight."

Fear swept over Price in a most visible manner, his mouth dropping open, his eyes wide. When he squirmed as he sat there on the ground, I suspected he was shitting his pants. The crowd left him and we walked on. I don't know if Wes caught how his rescue of me looked or what it meant to me, but I didn't care on that. My man, my lover, was showing himself to all and I beamed at his display, noting how others took it in. Wes, meanwhile, rattled on at Price being a disgrace to God. He then watched me play ball and when

I got a good hit and glanced over to see him applauding, I ran like the wind to stretch a double into a triple.

"Why didn't you let me hit Price?" I asked him that night after supper. We were full of fresh pork, potatoes, beans, and bread. Sunday suppers were becoming downright fine.

"I don't see you that way," Wes said.

"What way?"

"Violent. That's more me."

"I thought you were a reformed man."

He chuckled. "To a point."

"Well, I thank you for putting Price in his place."

"I doubt he'll stay there."

There came other demonstrations from Wes, small things he likely didn't even note, but I surely did. A hand on my waist for no apparent reason, a lingering smile in the company of others, and once even asking for more bread in the dining hall when he saw I'd been missed. When he got the piece he tossed it onto my plate, and I glanced over to see Johnny Rose nodding at the gesture. Such are the generosities of circumstance.

Wes seldom wrote to Jane anymore, but he never stopped letters to others. He always took full advantage of the two per month we were allowed. I knew he wrote his children and his cousin Manning, but that summer he seemed more intent with his correspondence and so I inquired.

"I'm in touch with my attorney, W. S. Fly in Gonzales," Wes explained. "I want to see if any indictments remain active against me."

"Why?"

"An active indictment would mean re-arrest upon my release. I need to have that all cleared up before I'm pardoned."

I asked nothing more, but this didn't matter. My nosing around in his business had stirred up the issue and sure enough, there it came. "Manning is lining up judges all over east Texas in my support," the spiel began, and Wes didn't stop talking even when I quit listening. I went back to the nasty book of my mind and made a picture of me putting it to Wes who had his rump stuck up at me, buttocks held open to beg entrance. I could see my cock shove in. I took hold of the real one and worked it while I saw only fucking and heard none of pardon talk.

I didn't much care for Manning Clements, never mind I hadn't met him. That he kept Wes apprised of outside developments was enough to put me off. He continued sending the Gonzales newspapers which Wes devoured, then offered to me. I read them the first few times, but found after a while I didn't care to know about the larger world, seeing as how I couldn't live in it. Best stick to the smaller one within the walls. Then one day Wes let out a squeal as he read the latest paper. "We got ourselves a new governor," he all but whooped from the table where he sat reading. "You hear that, Gar?"

"Whole cellblock heard. Why's it such news?"

"Because the old one is gone. James S. Hogg is the new man and listen to this. 'Hogg is said to be for the underdog when the underdog has a grievance.' How about that. If there was ever an underdog with a grievance, it's me."

"I can't argue on that."

"He'll be more receptive to a pardon request. I have to get Manning working on petitions, get people in my support to set down their names on my behalf. With those and my statement, I should have a good chance."

I'd been hearing pardon talk for so long, I thought myself numb to it, but this turn, this new governor, caused a dread to rise up in me. Petitions, statement, wide support, and a more receptive governor, but what about the dead men? Their truth shouldn't be forgotten. Wes Hardin was a killer of thirty-two men and such a convict didn't deserve to be let off before his time is up. As usual, of course, I said nothing, and he rambled on about his chances and how he should be hearing from attorney Fly any day about remaining indictments. He got himself so excited he began pacing the cell while I lay in my bunk too annoyed to call up my dirty book. Even nasty thoughts couldn't stand up to the force of Wes Hardin when he got going.

"Here it is!" Wes cried one Sunday in October. "Fly's response." He opened the letter, read, then huffed out a breath.

"Good news?"

"Could be, yes. Only one indictment remains active. It's in DeWitt County for my killing James Morgan in 1873. Fly says most consider it justified, but lawmen refuse to quash it. Here's another injustice done to me. It was one bullet to the head, shot in defense of myself, but the indictment says I shot him in neck and breast which is a lie. Newspapers at the time even noted one bullet and witnesses said likewise, but the law avoids the truth where I'm concerned. Anyway, Fly says I can request to voluntarily return to De-Witt to stand trial, plead justifiable homicide, and ask that the sentence run concurrent with my twenty-five."

"Will you do it?"

"Have to study on it. Not sure justifiable homicide is the way to go as the sentence for manslaughter is less time. The good part of a guilty plea is I get to make a statement, and I know if I'm allowed to speak I can sway the jury my way. Get this matter disposed of so I can walk free one day soon."

"You think Captain Goree will let you go to DeWitt County?"

"I'll find that out when I ask."

I knew when this took place as Wes wasn't in the yard that afternoon. He came to supper but sat elsewhere so soon as we'd marched out and broke ranks, I went to him. "How'd it go?"

"Fine. Goree says he'll work with the county and arrange my transport to the courthouse at Cuero."

"You get to go outside the walls."

"I suppose I do. Hadn't thought on that. More concerned on proceedings. Maybe Jane can attend, and the children." Here he left off speaking and I saw him lost to me for the moment. Dread again came calling.

It wasn't until November that Wes learned he was to travel to Cuero and stand trial on January 1, 1892. "I'll be allowed to see Jane and the children," he said, "and cousins, aunts, uncles, and friends can attend." He trailed off, likely envisioning a packed courtroom which, given his popularity, seemed entirely possible.

"I'm happy for you, Wes," I said as I worked at enthusiasm while dread churned my gut.

"The children are nearly grown," he went on. "Let's see, Molly is…" Here he paused to calculate. "Nineteen. Good Lord. That makes John Jr. sixteen and little Jane thirteen." He blew out a sigh. "Their years add weight to mine. Thirty-eight never felt so old. They'll hardly know me."

"Then it's good you can see them and get reacquainted, however briefly."

"And Jane. Twenty years married and if you add up our time together, it's likely no more than a year. But now I can hold her and tell her I'll get a pardon and she'll be alone no longer."

The urge to rein him in with logic was strong, but I cared enough to let him enjoy his dreaming. Still, this kind of happiness pained me, as did the dread that now seemed with me more than not.

The more Wes planned for his trial, the more I wanted to fuck. As he spent time deep in thought, I considered how to break in and get him back where he belonged, with his dick out. Best part was this not being too difficult as even when he said no and pushed me off, he'd still succumb when my hand persisted between his legs. He'd then scoot back from the table, issue a great sigh, drop his pencil, and I'd find him worked up by way of his legal matters. I'd get it good then, sometimes bent over his papers. I got to thinking he liked to see me naked amid his law books, my dick pointed at his documents. He'd go at me like a wild man, but when I said I was about to come, which I did as a courtesy, he always moved us back so I'd not spurt onto his papers. But I swear, he liked fucking in their neighborhood as he wouldn't go far from the table.

Other times he welcomed the wallow and one Sunday when he'd been at his books too long, I got him away by sucking his dick beneath the table, making him come with pencil in hand which I knew he liked, after which we got naked and nearly missed supper due to feasting on dicks and my serious licking of the Hardin butthole.

Much as I tried to steer it elsewhere, that January court date loomed like a big black bear. Wes continued letters to Fly and when replies came, he was lost in thought for hours. We might fuck to excess on Saturday, but if Sunday mail brought a letter from Fly, which it usually did, Wes was gone from me until Monday.

I didn't allow myself thoughts on him seeing Jane. Kiddies didn't matter so much, just the wife. Most days and certainly all my nights, I had to push off the idea my man was a regular and as such, his wife's company, however brief, might get his dick up. Didn't matter he'd not be allowed use of it. Desire for her was betrayal of me, even if the one doing the betraying had no idea. Wes was still an innocent in that regard, a grown-up child who could not see who he truly was. Too bad he'd never look.

Baseball games went on well into fall, but finally stopped when weather went against us. Sundays took a turn as a result. Rain, wind, and finally snow rendered the yard a muddy bog so Goree increased indoor events, holding a spelling bee one time and then allowing the men to put on a play. This was so well received that a dramatic society was formed. I thought sure Wes would join as he seemed born for the stage, but he was too caught up in legal matters and had already dropped out of the debate society. I was the one who joined up, me who had never before acted. The superintendents' wives donated clothing for costumes and even a couple wigs so men could play female parts. Rehearsals were held in the evenings and we performed on the dining hall stage. What surprised me was how well I did, but then I came to see life itself is a kind of acting, the way we change our ways to suit situations or other people. I soon discovered I enjoyed becoming someone else for a time and also that I had a knack for memorizing lines which is a great help to an actor.

I was cast as a parson in a farce called *The Minster Calls* in which I succumb to the advances of a female parishioner. She was played by Oren Glaser who, being of slight build, made a fine woman when wearing dress and wig. He got such a kick out of this, he wore the getup to rehearsals. The men loved our performance and Wes even left off his legal work to attend. Afterward he threw an arm around me. "Garland here is a fine actor," he declared to all. When he didn't let go, I played along. "Acting a minister is truly acting, seeing I am heathen through."

"You'd do right good in a pulpit," Wes continued which got the men laughing.

"Except I'd preach in favor of drink and fornication."

Here Wes squeezed my shoulder and pulled me close against him. "My influence, boys," he declared. "Going to hell by way of John Wesley Hardin."

"The godly man," I countered.

"Hear, hear," he replied.

Back in our cell later on, when it was so cold our words came with steam, Wes continued in a light mood. "My friend, the actor," he said. "I liked seeing you up there on the stage although the reverend getup was far afield."

"Felt good to put on real clothes, even if a costume."

"I'd never seen you like that."

"Do you approve?"

"That I do. What say we now get naked in my bunk."

"Liable to freeze."

"Not if we keep moving."

At Christmas we put on a play called *Riverboat Holiday* which featured a bunco man trying to fleece Santa Claus on Christmas Eve only to find himself bested by the fat, white-bearded fellow. There were women on the boat and other gamblers so Oren got to dress up again. He encouraged two others to do likewise and the three men were often seen conversing like hens while wearing their costumes. I was cast as John Sharpe, bunco man, and Wes Hardin himself played Santa. Mrs. Goree, who had become our great supporter, directed the play, and got us a fine white wig and whiskers for

Wes. He got batting from his shop to pad himself which resulted in a fine Santa though this one was absent a red suit.

We got the Christmas holiday off work and had a fine turkey supper that was taken early to allow the hall cleared for the play. Then at six it was put on to a full house. Men stood three deep all around the edges and I think most every guard attended. Captains Goree and Smith brought their wives, as did both doctors. Even patients able to walk came and were given front-row seats near the officials.

The performance went off without a hitch as Wes and I had rehearsed our lines a good deal while in our cell. We'd lie in our bunks and say them out, often getting to laughing as they were sharp humor and slightly risqué. Every time we did this, Wes ended up saying Santa Claus wanted his dick sucked. I'd climb down and, cold as it was, we'd heat up while playing our parts, Santa fucking the bunco man.

"Santa's gonna come," Wes would shout as he pumped a load into me and I'd call out, "Fuck me, Santa," just to get the cellblock going. As we came we'd hear poor Santa said to be doing all manner of nastiness down the row.

After the play was over and Wes and I had received many a pat on the back, we retreated to our cell where I gave to Wes a box I'd made for him. As foreman I had time to construct, sand, and varnish it as well as carve JWH into the hinged lid. "For your papers," I said as I handed it to him.

"You made it?"

"That I did. For you. Merry Christmas, Wes."

He ran his fingers over the lettering, then along the edges. Lifting the lid, he examined the inside. He then took it to the table where his legal papers were scattered and he gathered them and slipped them into the box, then closed and held it. "I do not know when I've had a finer gift," he said. "Thank you, Garland. It means more than I can say."

"I enjoyed making it. Best part of being shop foreman is freedom to do some work of my own."

"Well, it's beautiful work and will be treasured. I'm sorry I have nothing to give you. A quilt might have been welcome."

"I need no gift beyond the one you can give," I said and I took the box, set it aside, and pulled him into my arms. The kiss that followed was most exquisite and when we paused to gaze into each other's eyes, I had to fight back the urge to declare my love. To accomplish this, I slid a hand down between his legs while I kissed him again.

It was a grand coupling, that Christmas night of 1891. "No more Santa Claus," I said as I lay atop Wes under a blanket on his bunk. "I want Wes Hardin, the real man, to give me a good Christmas fuck. There is no finer gift I might receive."

We didn't rush to it. Good food and fine entertainment led us to a mellow sort of loving in which we took a near leisurely path toward that gift I sought. Fingers explored familiar places, tongues licked all around, and mouths sucked various parts in a slow climb. Pricks rose but did not hurry us, thus I felt the coupling included the heart. When Wes finally threw off the cover to put me on my back and raise my legs, it seemed the final act of an excellent play, a fitting conclusion to a grand holiday.

Wes didn't hurry his fucking either. He went slow at first, that cock where it belonged, and mine up to acknowledge the fact. Wes took hold as he thrust, but he didn't pump me as much as just hold on, like he wanted both our dicks engaged together. So as Santa Claus retreated to his north-pole home, we concluded the celebration with a glorious climax after which we fell into a deep and blissful sleep.

Five days later, Wes departed for the courthouse at Cuero.

CHAPTER TWENTY-FIVE

A convict learns, with his years, to sleep through the near constant noise of men down the cellblock row. I'd not been troubled by the calls until Wes was gone to Cuero when I found myself unable to sleep. Listening to shouts and cries and finally to the howls of dreams and screams of assaults, I couldn't believe this onslaught had been present all my sixteen years. When I finally realized the change was in me, not the prison, it didn't matter because the noise still grated so bad I couldn't stand it. More than once I joined the screaming to plead for quiet. Unfortunately this just made things worse, men seizing upon the request. "Stop fucking my asshole," came one call and another offered, "Put your cock in my mouth and I'll quiet right down." Dawn would find me on the floor or leaned against the wall as bed became impossible. I also refused to get into my absent man's bunk as this would be as much torture as pulling my dick while thinking on him.

He was gone five days, departing on December 30, 1891, and returning January 3, 1892. Goree arranged a suit and tie for Wes to wear in court, saying no man in stripes could get a fair shake, a gesture that greatly endeared him to Wes. Guards came for Wes early on the day of departure and he gave me a long look before leaving the cell which I saw as meant to reassure me. As days wore on, however, my view changed and I decided the look was more his happiness at getting five days outside the walls.

I came to question everything during those five days, even my sanity. Not only did sleep elude me, peace of mind also fled, and in its place that awful gut-churning dread gained a foothold. I had little appetite, refused to take part in the dramatic society's new comedy, and in the furniture shop I often dozed off in my chair. What kept to me every minute of those five long days was worry.

The first day I knew Wes in transit. Six guards accompanied him by wagon which amused everyone as he was not likely to try a break. Opinion was the authorities saw a need to show force solely due to the Hardin reputation. I knew Wes would reach Cuero around noon the second day and figured a crowd would be waiting to greet him, Jane and the children among them. I could see Wes stop and wave, or maybe just nod, whatever was allowed. Then again, if he was working his charm, he'd likely get to shake everyone's hand and accept good wishes and pats on the back.

I spent time during my sleepless nights wondering exactly when Wes would meet up with Jane. Before or after the trial? The trial itself had no weight with me as all it would do was fold new years into those already set down. It was the visit I couldn't let alone.

I'd never seen the Cuero courthouse so I built it in my mind, furnished it with benches and long tables for lawyers and a fine big desk for the judge. The jury I put to one side, six men in a special section, all of them Hardin supporters. I built all this, but never went there. Instead I spent time in a room next door where Jane was brought in to see Wes.

He would be freshly scrubbed and shaved and wearing that suit that had been provided. Jane would undoubtedly wear her Sunday best, with her lips rouged, face powdered, hair fixed up in curls. A guard would remain with them, or would Wes use his sway to get time alone with his wife? I took away the guard and had Wes pull the woman into his arms and kiss her at length, pressing himself to her as his dick came up. I saw his hand slide to her breast to knead there as he began to grind against her and she, heated with the attention, rubbed back. I saw them writhe until he came in those borrowed pants, hand on his wife's tit as he spurted.

It wouldn't have been so bad had I left off at this, but knowing he could be with her on that very day led me to picture an excess I hated, even as I called it to mind. I saw Wes in that room, guard just outside, judge and jury next door, and him with his dick out and getting Jane up onto a table where she spread her legs. He'd raise her skirts, pull off her petticoats and her drawers and there would be her honey pot. He'd stand as he guided his cock into her and set to fucking while the trial waited beyond. I saw him from behind, buttocks I'd licked flexing as he did his regular brand of fucking. Then I changed things so she was full naked, him too, and he had his cock in her and was milking her tits, and then bending to suck as he kept drilling her cunt. When a scream came from down the row, I took it as Jane hating what was being done to her, but I also saw Wes unrelenting because she was his wife and thus his property.

I didn't let him come inside her. I had him pull out and work his prick to spew onto her face at which she grimaced and spat. He then left her there, naked and used, dried up for want of his fluid, and I saw him dress and go out into the court to plead his case. I didn't dispose of Jane, however. I brought her back time and again to have him fuck her, most often up her butt.

No word came on how Wes fared, even though the whole prison knew him gone to trial. I believed Goree was trying to lessen the stature of his famous prisoner who still, even as a reformed man, remained a draw among the men. When I knew Wes and party would depart Cuero for the trip back to Huntsville, I thought my torment would ease, but such was not the case as I began to fear what Jane had wrought. Could she undo all I'd gained? I had no knowledge of women and so considered it entirely possible her female sway might be as strong or stronger than what Wes enjoyed.

The fifth day should have been the best, but it became the worst. Wes would soon be with me, my torment ended, but that day in the shop I suddenly couldn't bear noise from the machines. The sawdust also began to choke me so I spent time sitting on the ramp out front, melting snow my sole companion. I enjoyed the yard bleak and bare, hard and cold. I might have been out of doors, but it seemed like I occupied a dark cell, such was the absence of life. This got me to thinking back on those ten days long ago which I found still strong when called up. I brought back all I'd felt then, the awful confinement and panic, but for all this I gained only the knowledge that the present dark was inside me more than out. The sky remained visible above, gray and ready to let go rain, the air fresh and biting.

Finally I wore myself out. Exhausted both in mind and body, I came to wonder if it all wasn't simply missing the man I'd lived with more than a decade. I lay on my bunk after supper on the fifth day, having run myself to ground, and at last slept. Then a hand shook me awake and there stood Wes, clad in stripes again, and the five days disappeared in an instant.

He lit the candle as the lockdown whistle blew, and we enjoyed some time during which we got a good look at each other. He said nothing and for this I was grateful. I wanted no news, just him, his presence alone a comfort. He fussed at the table, took a long piss, and generally occupied himself until at last I spoke. "Missed you," I said.

His reply was lost to the final whistle, at which he snuffed the candle and got into his bunk. I took no issue with his not wanting sex. He'd had a long journey and was tired. Time was again ours.

Next morning, as we made ready for the day, Wes told me the verdict. "Guilty of manslaughter, two years concurrent with my twenty-five."

"Congratulations," I said.

Just then the cell door was thrown open and we were off to breakfast.

"I'll get a new prisoner number," Wes said as we fell into line.

"Why is that?"

"No idea. New sentence does it, I suppose. Seems silly, but I no longer question authority."

Men were scarce in the yard that afternoon as the wind turned cold and blustery. Those persisting drew to Wes who announced his verdict and accepted congratulations. Then came the questions. "How was it being on the outside? Were you treated well? Were there crowds come to see you?"

"There were crowds," Wes said, warming to the topic. "Nearly one hundred people, it was said. Family and friends, supporters, and others just come to gawk at a notorious man. As for seeing the outside, I did enjoy the country, even with bad weather. When we put up the first night, word spread and next morning a crowd was in front of the hotel. I spoke with many along the way as my guards were easy."

Nobody asked about the proceedings. Verdict and sentence were enough, but I did wonder how the oratory had gone. When I asked about this that night, Wes handed me the Gonzales newspaper. "Guard passed this to me yesterday. I've been written up."

I took the paper and read how Wes had stood trial and gotten his two years. "Hardin has been reading law," it continued, "and to judge by the remarks he made to the court and jury, he has been quite a student and may yet make his mark. He was as poised as any practicing attorney, making an eloquent plea in a clear and steady voice. His presentation brought tears to the eyes of nearly everyone present and the jury took just five minutes to return their verdict."

"Five minutes?" I said. "That is impressive. I wish I could have been there to hear you."

"And see me. It's not the words alone, Gar, it's the force behind them and I am a force. That's now been proven in a court of law."

He could hardly sit still, so pleased was he. Always a man caught up with himself, he seemed to have puffed up even more, but in a cell there was no crowd to appreciate him. Just me, the one who loved him.

I didn't ask after Jane, but when night came on and Wes made no move toward me, I had my answer. He'd taken up his old regular ways which I now had to give room, just as I had when we first began. So I got up into my bunk and we settled in.

Our quiet went so long I thought Wes slept, but I heard no snore. Then he spoke. "Molly, my oldest child, has become a beautiful woman with fine olive skin, brown hair and eyes, and full lips. My son, John W. Jr., is sturdy and lean, tanned, with hands rough from ranch work. He's the age I was when I first rode the Chisholm Trail to Abilene. Molly and John had some recall of me but the baby, Jane, had none as she was just one year old when I came here. She's fair and delicate, the image of her mother when we were courting."

A long pause then came and I knew he was thinking on Jane. I clutched my blanket like some child about to get whipped. "Jane wore a blue dress and dangling earrings I always liked, but she was not the woman I knew. She looked bone tired, her hair gone gray when mine is still brown. The spirit is absent from her eyes and her cheeks are hollow. She's frail of body and slightly stooped. I was allowed to kiss and embrace her, and she felt a wisp in my arms. I'm concerned that my long absence has been too much hardship upon her. She's four years younger than me yet looks older. Never have I been more reminded of my failure as husband than when looking upon her. We had an hour together during which I assured her my love has never failed, but there was not enough time to say all I wanted. I do believe I helped her as much as I could."

I gave no comment, even as I knew I should support Wes, never mind talk of Jane sliced through me like a rusted blade. Never have I felt more heathen than in my failure to take up the family aspect of Wes Hardin.

"You awake, Garland?" he finally asked.

"I am, but you've rendered me speechless with your talk."

He took this in as I knew he would, the innocent accepting what he saw as praise. Only Wes could miss the pain such talk brought to a man who had taken his cock and wished to again.

Wes went several days without sex so I went back to the library for both books and Johnny Rose. When he ventured that Wes had returned to his regular ways, I slapped him so hard he fell back among the boxes.

"Sorry, Gar. I didn't know that a sore spot."

"How could you not? I love a man who's got a wife he's just seen and kissed. He declared his love to her and hasn't touched me since his return."

"Then you're in serious need." Here he pushed down pants and drawers, bent over a crate of books, and said, "Fuck me, Garland. Forget all but your dick up my ass."

I did just that but soon as we left the book room, I sank down into the dumps again. I got my favorite pirate book and attempted to read, but soon gave up and headed to the cell. Imagine my surprise when I found Wes naked on his bunk, pumping his cock.

His eyes were closed and I had no idea his thoughts, didn't want to know. I just kneeled and wrapped my hand around his at which he gave way. As I worked him, his eyes opened to offer a wrenching look I'd not seen before. Only Wes Hardin had the stamina to get his dick up while beset with sadness.

He was wet on his knob and I rubbed this down his shaft, adding some spit to get him juicy. When I resumed my steady stroke, he said, "Suck me, Gar," so I let go, got over him, and took him into my mouth. I didn't care his request was more resigned than eager, I just enjoyed him, all the while hoping to return him to his rightful place. Soon he bucked and I swallowed a good load that I figured had built up those five days away.

Wes made no move toward me so once I'd had my fill, I climbed up to my bunk, wet my own cock, and worked myself to a come while making some purposeful grunts and groans to make it clear I could see to myself.

It took Wes two weeks to get past the guilt Jane had laid upon him. He satisfied himself twice during this time while I left off Johnny Rose, choosing to work my cock so Wes would hear. I knew it selfish of me to want his old self back because he wasn't the man of old, thanks to the Cuero trip. New concerns saddled him, so I tried to give him room, even as I saw him often too troubled to study.

It was on a Saturday, when our wash bucket was filled, that he finally gave way. After work, I sought to bathe rather than face the cold yard. I was filthy from a week's work so I stripped naked and began to clean myself while Wes lay watching. He'd said little the two weeks and hardly studied at all, just gone to and from work. I wondered how his stitches fared on the quilts. He seemed idle in his gaze upon me and when I'd cleaned all but my privates, I decided to give him a show.

I ran the wet cloth under to my nuts where I fondled as much as washed. I then cleaned my cock until it began to fill. Glancing at Wes, I found him turned onto his side to better view so I began to attend my bottom. Wetting the cloth, I spread my legs with back turned to him and took care washing my crack. Holding one buttock apart from the other, I displayed my hole which I attended with care. I then dropped the cloth, put a finger into myself, and set to prodding. A look back at Wes found him with his hand in his pants.

I squirmed as I finger-fucked myself, my other hand on my dick, and soon I heard Wes get off his bunk. "You want something more than a finger up there?" he asked and before I could answer he speared me and began to ride.

He held me at the waist as he did me, our fuck slap a welcome sound. "I hear me a fuck," came a call from the next cell. "Do me next. I've got my pants down. How about that Hardin dick? I hear it's a whopper."

On and on down the row came the calls, each stirring the next. Soon the slap of flesh was heard in more than our cell, but we didn't care. Wes was thrusting steadily, and I did no more than receive him, my world now righted. At last he began to issue small cries, and I knew him on the rise. "Fuck me, Wes," I said over and over as he let go in me. I cried out as I took his spunk, overjoyed to have him home.

When he pulled out, I turned to find him shaken and I knew guilt was back at him. Before it could take hold, I threw my arms around him, pulled him close, and held on while he fought to be returned to me. His head lay on my shoulder, but finally I got a finger under his chin to raise him up to face me. Then I put my lips to his, banishing Jane, and he responded like a starving man. His tongue entered to go after mine and he began to grind against my hard cock which was up between us. I couldn't help but hump against him and as the kiss continued, I spurted my stuff. I was nearly in tears with the release.

As we quieted, Wes kept kissing me, but lightly now. His lips moved down to my neck, then onto my shoulder. When he leaned down to lick my tit, I suggested bed at which we got onto his bunk. Without a word, we took up where we'd left off and were at each other until the supper whistle blew.

"Never finished washing," I said as we dressed.

"Time for that later on," Wes replied. "Much later as I am far from done with you."

We slept little that night as Wes got his cock into me again and said he meant it to stay there. I was so well used, I sat careful the next day.

Wes pretty much returned to his old self which eased me a good deal. Then he ruined it by telling me he'd asked attorney Fly to lead the charge for supporters to request his pardon. "He says they are all over Texas so I've asked him to round them up, put them to use. Here's his reply."

On fine paper, W. S. Fly wrote, "I can get a thousand men in Gonzales County to sign application to the governor for full pardon. I believe you will justify my actions by living a quiet and useful life. I have faith in your integrity and manhood and I do not believe it misplaced. I will send petitions to every county in the state and am confident of potent support."

When I'd let this settle onto me, as it did like a stack of bricks, I managed only brief comment. "A thousand men," I said. "Quite a number."

Time, I saw, was going to work both for and against me. As it slipped past, so did the guilt Wes brought from Cuero, and thus we got back to being the partners we'd been before the trip. It was thus proven that Jane was no more than passing intrusion upon the true life of Wes Hardin who set to fucking like he'd never left off.

What worked against me was Fly's letters which Wes read to me. I didn't want to hear them but never asked him not to do it, so I had to endure details of growing support. "Petitions have arrived from all east Texas counties including signatures of judges, politicians, prominent business and professional men," wrote Fly. "I also obtained signatures of twenty-six sheriffs attending a lawmen's convention. I'm told by those in the governor's office that letters of support from private individuals arrive each day. Not one has been against your pardon."

Again that stack of bricks pressed down upon me. "Twenty-six sheriffs," I said. "That's something, the law itself going your way."

"Exactly," said Wes who leaned against our table while I occupied the stool. I'd been scraping dried mud from my shoes when he started in. I always liked him worked up, but preferred it not by way of W. S. Fly. I thus didn't stop my shoe work, even as Wes rambled on. "Governor Hogg is said to be a most liberal fellow. Big of body and big of heart. Do you know he's the first true Texan to hold the office? Born and raised which seems proper. Friend of the downtrodden, it is said."

It would have been good had I some consuming interest to occupy my free time but, as no pardon would ever be granted an unknown like me, and as I didn't care for study, I was somewhat adrift. I still did some playacting, but nothing drove me like the pardon did Wes. Finally I saw how things truly were. My sole and consuming interest was Wes Hardin. Nothing else could compare.

He followed the progress of Governor Hogg in newspapers Manning Clements still sent. Each issue seemed to find the politician bigger and more benevolent and Wes never failed to read out loud articles on accomplishments and kindnesses of Hogg. I had to admire the man, though I doubted my support could ever equal what Wes showed.

Then one day when Wes had bent my ear on Hogg's latest effort, he turned a page of his paper and let out a sound I'd not heard before. Half groan, half ragged breath, it was an utterance that spoke of shock. "What is it, Wes?" I asked, leaning over the edge of my bunk. When he didn't reply I hopped down to where he sat. He was blank of expression, as if he'd been struck and not yet recovered. I slipped the paper from his hand and looked up and down until I saw the small item. "Mrs. John Wesley Hardin has been ill of late, but is up and around again."

Much as I resented the woman, she didn't deserve illness. "She's up and around it says," I noted, "so she must be recovered."

Wes ignored this. "She looked so worn when I saw her," he said. "Maybe she was sick then and I didn't see. I have to...to..."

"She's better, Wes. It says so. There's nothing you can do from here but keep a good thought."

I could almost hear the machinery of his mind whirring with ideas, none good. "Come to bed," I prodded. "Whistle is going to blow shortly." It blew seconds later, reminding me how a long-term man like me doesn't need a watch to know routine. I could feel prison.

Wes wouldn't budge so I left him there sitting on the stool. He snuffed the candle as required and when the whistle blew next morning, I found him sitting on his bunk. "Did you sleep?" I asked as I hopped down.

He looked at me like I was crazy. "You expect I can sleep when Jane is ill?"

"Sorry," I said, and I pulled on my stripes and shoes, took a drink of water. When we marched to breakfast, the hand on my shoulder was light and at table Wes ate little. When we marched out after, he didn't go to work. He accosted a guard, demanding to see Captain Goree. He was taken away to plead his case.

I didn't see him again until after work when I found him pacing the yard. His look was grim and men knew to give him room in that state. I alone approached. "What happened this morning?" I asked.

"I requested a furlough to see Jane, but Goree said no, illness was no reason, and reminded me I'd just seen her in January. When I told him of the news item, he said same as you, she's recovered, but I know she's not. I know it, Gar. I can feel it. Married folks have that between them and distance can't quell it. I can see her lying in bed, children gathered round. I have to get to her, I have to."

His anguish got at my heart, even as it was on behalf of the one I most disliked. I'd not seen Wes so stricken since his mother died. I put a hand to his arm and squeezed. "They won't let you go. Best do what you can. Go to the chapel and ask God to watch over her. If ever there was a time to consult Him, it's now."

"I should be with her."

"She knows you want that and she also knows why you can't. Wives understand."

"I can't lose her, Garland."

"You won't. I'm sure the illness has passed."

I was wrong on this. Though Wes went to the chapel every day, there soon came a Sunday letter from Cousin Manning saying Jane was critically ill with consumption. Three weeks had passed since the newspaper story, three weeks during which Jane did not recover as the story had led us to believe. All the praying in the world would not help her now.

Wes sprang from the cell to again accost a guard and demand to see Goree. When he'd been taken away, I took up the letter which gave few details as Manning was not as wordy as Wes. Jane was ill, the children were at her side, all praying. There was nothing on any doctoring as all knew it futile. She had a death sentence.

I waited for Wes, hours crawling by. I went to supper and returned to an empty cell. I hardly slept as Wes was absent the whole night. When we went to breakfast next morning, I asked guards one after another for word of Wes, but none knew. The day became a trial, an awful Monday in the shop where a man new to my old bandsaw ruined several veneers. Temper rose up in me as never before, and all stepped back as I had the respect of being not only foreman, but a good and true man. Everyone knew if I was upset, there was good cause.

Not until I spied Matt Furst, the guard who'd doted on Wes since the first day, did I get an answer. Furst was crossing the upper yard when I saw him and sprinted over. "Furst! What's the word on Wes Hardin? Where is he?"

Furst came over to the fence that separated us. "He's in solitary. Three days for attacking the captain."

"Goree?"

Furst nodded. "Story is Wes asked for a furlough to see his ailing wife and was refused so he jumped Goree and beat on him. Took three men to pull him off and he struck two of them."

I knew the dark cells had been repainted white, but they were still used for hard cases. A man was now allowed a blanket and candle, though still clad in flimsy gown and fed just twice a day. "His wife is dying," I said.

"I know, as does the captain, but, as he reminded Wes, the prison makes the rules, not the convicts. There are no furloughs for any reason."

"Wes must be in agony."

"Don't doubt it," replied Furst who resumed going where he'd been headed.

I felt small as I sat on his bunk that evening. I'd offered assurance only to divert his attention back to me when the situation had warranted far more. How would Wes see that, I wondered, especially since he had three days to stew. Though I was not in solitary, I might well have been. My appetite deserted me and I slogged through those days. Then I got detail from Johnny Rose on how Goree had fared as Johnny had assisted in the doctoring.

"Stitches to close a gash to the chin, a fat lip, and bruises about the body. And one guard has a broken jaw for which he was sent to the hospital in town. The other has just painful parts."

"Good Lord," I said too loud. We were in the library and heads turned at the outburst.

"Seems the hot-headed gunman hasn't been chased off," noted Johnny. "Those were not the actions of a reformed man."

"They were the actions of one driven to his limit," I countered.

"What'll happen when the wife dies?"

"I shudder to think."

Wes wouldn't talk about the assault when he returned to the cell. He wouldn't talk on much of anything which caused me concern, him being naturally talkative. He allowed me to sit beside him on his bunk, allowed my arm around him, but when I attempted a comforting nuzzle, he jumped up. "Leave off," he commanded. "I don't want that. Not ever again."

"Just trying to soothe," I said. "Didn't mean to press, but I see you in distress and want to help."

"Then leave me alone."

I knew he wrote to his children as I stole a look over his shoulder one Sunday while filling my cup from the water bucket. "Any serious mishap to your lovable mama," he wrote, "would be to each of you, as well as to myself, a calamity irretrievable and irreparable."

I read no more as Wes looked up and caught me. "This is private," he snapped.

"Sorry."

The worst part was knowing things would not get better and middle of November confirmed this. I took the letter from my poor man's hand as he sat with tears running down his cheeks. It was from his daughter, Molly.

"Dear Papa,

"I am sorry to bring you the sad news that Mama went to God November 6 and has been laid to rest at Asher Cemetery near Coon Hollow. Fred Duderstadt says we children can stay on with him. I wish we could be with you. We vow to be good and kind as Mama wanted.

"Love, *Molly*"

I wanted to take Wes into my arms, but knew better than to approach. I was an intruder when Jane was about and she now had the whole of Wes, more so in death than in life. He shuddered as he silently cried, and when he got into his bunk and turned to the wall, I sat on the stool feeling most helpless.

Wes refused to get out of bed for two days and Goree allowed it which said a lot for the captain, especially after being beaten as he had. But he understood what death did to a man and for that I was grateful. I was even allowed to bring bread to the cell so Wes wouldn't weaken in his grief, but he refused all but water. Then, on the third day he got up and went to work which was good, although he still wasn't talking.

Men gave him room. The whole prison knew the famed man had lost his wife, and a general compassion rose up that was impressive. He wasn't made to stitch quilts but just to sweep up and do small tasks that were enough to busy but not tire him. That Sunday, two days after he'd gone back to work and five after he'd heard of Jane's death, I found him watching me play ball. He still looked hollow, but when his head turned to follow play, I was encouraged. And that night he sat on his bunk and said, "I'm so lonely, Garland. I've never known such a feeling."

I knew it invitation, but to what I had no idea. I lay in drawers, but I climbed down to sit beside him, wanting to touch, but fearing he'd put me off. So we just sat a while which I see now did help, just keeping company.

"I wanted to die with her," Wes finally said. "In that cell, I didn't eat or drink, but my body refused to go. I'm too strong. Now I don't know anymore. I feel wrapped in some hellish blanket of sorrow, or maybe one of my damned quilts, and it's smothering me instead of comforting. Jane is slipping away, even as I try to keep hold. I recall that with my mother who's now but a memory, Jane soon to be beside her in that distance. I'm empty, Garland, godawful empty." Here he turned to me and I saw more than pain his eyes. I saw need. "Fill me," he said as he slid a hand between my legs. "I'm empty and need filling." He then put his lips to mine as he prodded my waking cock.

CHAPTER TWENTY-SIX

Fill me. Could Wes possibly mean what I took him to mean? Did he prod my cock for solace or did he mean me to stick it to him? I honestly didn't know.

As we kissed, I tried not to devour him, but this wasn't easy as I was much pent up due to events of late. He wasn't urgent, which told me he sought comfort as much as satisfaction, so I followed his lead, tongue working only in response to his. We passed some tender moments which I believe addressed that spot where grief does most of its damage, the heart.

He kept on between my legs, though, and finally left off kissing to stand and shed his clothes. Only when he stood naked did I strip. His dick was soft, which I understood, given his state. He didn't reach for it, but instead took hold of mine and began to handle it easy, like he didn't know it well. When he reached under to my nuts, I spread my legs, and I saw then how he was getting reacquainted with me. This caused my heart to leap and my prick to rise.

When he lay down on his bunk, there was no pulling me in. He just rolled onto his stomach and I knew. I climbed in and began to rub his bottom, then lick, and finally to part him and attend his center. He moaned when I put my tongue in him, and I took this as encouragement. Excited as I became, I was still not sure so I pulled back to again lick and play. It was only when he said, "Fill me, Garland. I need filling," that I knew for sure.

I pulled him up to a good angle and set to spitting into my palm, lots of spit which I applied to my dick. Wes had a hand under himself now, working his cock which further encouraged me, him at the wallow's edge. I then got into position, parted his buttocks, and did not hesitate. I rammed into where I'd ached so long to return, and he cried out a "yes" which set me off on a most vigorous fuck.

As I gained the butthole of Wes Hardin, my man, my lover, as I reclaimed what I'd thought lost, I looked down to witness the event, never mind the feel of being inside him. I wanted to record it in both mind and body, make a new page for the dirty book of my mind. I wanted to get all I was due, while giving Wes what he asked. I wanted to fill him.

I managed to last only minutes, due to prior deprivation, but they were glorious minutes, and when I felt my rise I called out to let Wes know, aware of him frantic below. I think he came with me, but don't honestly care as I was gone to glory, giving him a good load of my spunk, my whole body taking pleasure in the act.

I kept pumping even when done, and didn't relent until my prick declared things ended. I then slipped out and lay on top of Wes who allowed me to nuzzle his neck while we both sought to regain our breath. At last, I slid off and he turned onto his side to face me.

"Better?" I asked.

"Well, not so empty."

"Fair enough. It was good, Wes. Powerful good."

He ran a finger onto my chest to rub a tit. "Got some left?" he asked.

"Always, for you."

He fingered a bit more, then got down to suck the tit, and I saw he meant to remain in the wallow like we used to, and fill up by way of sticking it to each other. We were one again paired and meant to continue.

I knew we weren't going to cure what ailed him, but I did believe we were treating the wound the best way we could. Wes seemed to agree, though we never spoke on it. Men together long as us knew such things and so we slept little that night. Wes had me suck his dick while I had two fingers prodding his butthole which drove a good batch of come out of him.

After that, we licked and petted, but didn't talk. No words needed, just solace. And near dawn he got me stiff by way of sucking, then hopped from bed to stand at the bedpost, bottom thrust back to invite me in. I accepted his invitation, pushed in, and did him standing for the very first time.

Our fuck slap was pure joy and once again set off men greeting the day with morning erections in hand. Wes pumped his cock as I held him at the waist and kept a steady thrust. "Fill you," I growled when my juice began to boil and Wes replied, "Fill me," just before he grunted and came. His hand was a fury up front while I was likewise at the back, shooting what felt the last of myself and savoring the knowledge he'd start his day with my spunk running down his leg. When I finally finished and pulled out, I embraced him, and he pressed back against me, his hand reaching down to squeeze my leg.

"Better?" I asked.

He chuckled. "Getting there."

He then turned and kissed me, just lips, no tongue, and I saw it a thank you. He was as righted as he could be.

Due to what Wes had endured of late, all gave him room in the yard. The sole exception was Ethan Price, killer-parson, who, despite the earlier warning, still attempted to save men's souls. His mistake was approaching Wes. The first time he did this, Wes grabbed him by the neck, just one hand in an iron grip that he held until Price's eyes fairly bugged out. Men drew near but took no action as all would have liked an end to Price, but Wes, all on his own, released the man who dropped to the ground onto all fours, panting like the dog he was.

"I said not to preach," Wes declared before he strode away. Price kept down until Wes had some distance, then stood and righted himself. I saw he'd not been swayed from his mission. Maybe set back for the moment, but still willing to court danger.

Sure enough, two days later he caught Wes coming into the yard. I don't know what sort of godly word was issued, but that matters little. Wes threw punches to gut and jaw and when the parson reeled, Wes slammed him against a wall and commenced a beating such as I'd never seen. He kept hitting and every time Price slumped, Wes pulled him up to hit him again. Face, chest, gut, even lower, until three guards ran over and pulled Wes off. This, unfortunately, didn't stop things as Wes decked one guard with a solid right and delivered a strong left uppercut to another. It was only when the third knocked a shotgun barrel to the Hardin head that the fight stopped, but even then Wes didn't fall. He staggered, put a hand to his head to find blood, almost sank to his knees, but regained his footing. Only when the shotgun pointed at him did he relent. More guards arrived as did both doctors and Johnny Rose who assisted with the stretcher to carry away what was left of Ethan Price.

Blood ran down over the ear and onto the neck of Wes Hardin as he was hauled away not to the hospital, but to the main building where he would stand before Captain Goree. I could tell by the Hardin walk that he cared little about punishment. Defiance was part of him, reformed be damned.

Wes got another three days solitary after which he was removed from quilting and put to work chopping wood. It was lowly work, but I thought

Goree smart on the change. Wes needed hard labor to get him through this latest bad patch. Get him so worn out he'd care about nothing.

"Had you a gun, would you have shot Price?" I asked when he returned to the cell after his solitary time.

"No doubt. He deserves killing more than most I've slain."

"Don't think he'll trouble you again. Johnny Rose says he's missing some teeth, can't see well, and has labored breathing due to a rib puncturing his lung. Doctors want him taken to the city hospital due to extensive injuries."

Wes huffed. "So he can preach among those unable to flee. God help the men confined to his ward."

I sat on his bunk while he stood below the window. A man just out of solitary cannot get enough air. I let silence come up, then ventured into new territory. "You know, I'm not a violent man," I began.

"That I do."

"Then tell me how it feels to beat a man as you did. Hate appears to drive you, but it also seems a kind of passion. Is it not?"

"I don't think on it, Garland, it just happens. I boil over and do something about it."

"Well, I may dislike violence," I said, "but I have to confess the look of you when you are at it has great appeal. The power behind those fists is impressive, as is the passion."

He chuckled. "Your dick come up?"

"Sure did."

"Well, mine did not, what with other parts taking me over."

"You were a sight, Wes. More man than any in the yard."

"What are you after?"

"Don't you know?"

"I'm not up for anything right now. Too much on my mind."

"Fair enough. You've been through a lot, but keep in mind I crave you."

He studied me so intently I swear I heard his gears grind, but then the lights-out whistle blew so I climbed up to my bunk and called it a night. Wes was still standing below the window as I dozed off.

Knowing he'd be chopping wood in the lower yard enticed me a great deal and, as foreman, I had liberty to stand in the shop doorway and take in the sight. There he was, swinging an ax like he could chop away his troubles which, after a while, I thought maybe he could. Then he caught me watching and stopped to meet my gaze and there we were, getting up to something at a distance, his cock maybe stirring as mine did. He held his ax in one hand and let the blade rest on the ground as he put one leg forward to thrust his lower half toward me. Then his free hand eased over to his crotch, and he took some good seconds to adjust what he had there. When my mouth fell open, he grinned and got back to work. I kept watching as Clark, my guard, didn't much care what I did since I ran an orderly shop. And he knew about me and Wes, everybody did, so he gave me room. Thus I feasted on Wes at hard labor which was a sight to behold, back and shoulder muscles at work, those strong legs, narrow hips. I couldn't help thinking how I'd had my dick between those buttocks, and I got so worked up I had to go inside and get to where I couldn't be seen, get out my dick, and give it about three pulls before letting go a gusher.

That night Wes said he ached all down his back. "Shoulders too. I'm used to wielding needle and thread," he said as he stretched and turned.

"Lie down and I'll rub your back, loosen the muscles so they don't seize on you. Take off your shirt."

I hadn't seen the corner of his mouth crimp up for some time, but it did just then, telling me he got that I had designs on him. He stripped up top, rank and sweaty, and as I took in the reek, my dick stirred. He stretched out and I climbed over his legs and began to knead his lower back, then worked my way up to his upper, and on to his shoulders. He issued welcoming groans throughout as it both hurt and helped.

"Better?" I asked after a while.

"Some," he said so I continued kneading. "You like it I'm doing man's work again," he added.

"That I do. There's no sight as stirring as that good body of yours at hard labor."

"You're getting transparent, Garland," he said with a chuckle. "I think you're looking to suck my dick."

"If we've got your back loose enough."

"Not my back you'll be addressing."

Here I climbed off and stripped while he shucked his lowers. I then got over him in reverse, and dropped my cock into his mouth while taking up his softy which quickly woke.

I liked a slow climb with Wes, and he seemed to feel the same, both of us playing around, licking, sucking like we agreed to keep from spending in throats. It was Wes who finally pulled off and rasped, "Let me fuck you."

Before I could reply, he'd flipped me around, pulled up my bottom, and shoved in. "You hold off your come so you can put it to me," he growled. This thrilled me as I saw us back in the wallow so I didn't touch my throbbing prick all the while Wes rode me.

Best part of us being older was gaining self control. At twenty-five we spewed all over the place, but at thirty-eight we could hold back, enjoy the fuck, and allow ourselves to start the climb when we chose. We did this now, Wes thrusting like there'd been no back problem. We went a good while, bed creaking, men down the row shouting their nastiness, until Wes finally said "Ah, hell" and let go into me. "Fill me," I urged as I took him, and in response he rammed harder to drive his spunk deep.

When he was done he flipped me over, then turned and stuck up his butt which I speared and we were off again, enjoying the second round of the evening, Wes all but purring as he received me.

I kept to him much as he had me, steady but not hurried, for I was where I truly belonged. I ran my hands over his buttocks as my cock worked between them, juice churning in my swollen balls. At last I could refrain no longer and stepped up my thrust. When the climax hit I cried out and kept on crying out to let my man know he was being filled. This set the cellblock off on more filth which meant many a dick spewed with me, either into a cellmate or on the floor.

When I'd spent, I pulled out and lay beside Wes, heated beyond words, sweaty, stinking, and happy. "Perfection," I finally said.

"That what it was?" he replied, hand on my chest.

"Give and take. Best there is."

"Well, we loosened up my back."

"You want to sleep alone?"

"No, stay down here. I may seek attention come dawn."

About a week after Wes began work in the wood yard, he opened his box of papers and resumed work on his pardon statement. "Have to get it done," he said. "Fly has petitions and letters coming in, so he now needs my part."

"You've worked on it a lot already," I noted.

"Much to say," he replied before losing himself to the task.

I didn't try to avoid things this time. I stayed out of the library and away from Johnny Rose as I had all I needed with Wes, but also, having him made me want good for him. I still doubted the pardon would come through, even as I couldn't deny the level of support there seemed to be. What nobody knew was how strong the law could remain when up against such an out-pouring of public opinion.

I taught myself not to dwell on things beyond my power. I indulged fully with Wes who seemed to gain with the attention. A well fucked man thrived, so I liked to say, and Wes was living proof. He even took part in another play, this one a romp called *Public House* which was most risqué as the house of the title was a brothel. Wes shined as the house owner while I played bartender. Oren and the two other men who had dressed up female for the last production played the whores and Johnny Rose played a man paying for services. At the performance, Captain Goree's big laugh could be heard throughout the hall, though I saw some wives wore frowns.

One night in June Wes sat back from the table. "It is finished, Garland. My statement is complete and I have to say it's right fine."

This was the day after we'd put on the play and we were mellow in both spirit and body, having celebrated our play acting success with a long and nasty wallow the night before. "I won't ask you to read it out to me," I said. "Not because I lack interest, but because, based on the time taken to write it, it must be a hundred pages long."

Wes laughed. "Not quite, but I do go back over a lot, all how I never plotted to kill Webb, but also further back to where mobs lynched my brother. I laid out how rangers had to protect me from a mob at my trial in Comanche and how my plea for a change of venue was refused due to that awful atmosphere. I cite chapter and verse of the law and declare myself justified in killing Webb, saying at worst it was manslaughter and for that I've served more than enough time. I also state how I'm father to three motherless children who need me to look after them. I close as follows. 'I therefore ask you to grant me a pardon. My highest hope, object, aim, and ambition is to yet lead a life of usefulness, of peace in the path of rectitude and righteousness.'"

He huffed a big breath which surprised me as I'd think someone blowing that much hot air would need to take some in. "Well?" he prompted when I didn't comment.

"Looks like you've covered it all. Do you send it to the governor or does Fly?"

"I send it to Fly who'll submit it along with all the letters and petitions. Then we wait on a decision."

"How long for that?"

"No idea, but Hogg seems fair so I don't think he'll dither."

But dither he did or maybe the man just wanted to consider the effect on his own position before he freed a killer of thirty-two men. Wes handled the delay well, especially when he was allowed back to quilting.

"I'll miss seeing you in the wood yard," I said when he told me he'd been reassigned.

"Sorry if my needlework doesn't get your dick up."

"Have to think up some other way."

"Like what?"

"Dunno. Maybe wrestle naked in the cell?"

We were in the yard on a hot July afternoon, pardon talk gone. "Sounds good to me. One who pins the other gets his dick in."

"I'm getting hard at just the talk."

In August Wes began to get fidgety due to lack of word on the pardon. He saw that whatever Hogg felt for the underdog, he remained a politician first and thus proceeded with care, or, in this case, failed to proceed. I, of course, took the delay as him putting off the difficult task of going against public opinion and refusing Wes Hardin. Wes saw the opposite, allowing Hogg time to adequately consider, but after two months of waiting his temper frayed.

Now that the pardon request was public knowledge, Manning sent several newspapers, most of which ran editorials in support of Wes. The *Cuero Star* stated that changing the criminal was the purpose of imprisonment. "After he has been transformed into a useful citizen, further punishment would be cruelty." Goree and Smith were called "men of large experience with human nature in general and the criminal class in particular. If they have pronounced Hardin a thoroughly reformed man, the *Star* accepts their decision." Wes fattened up on such comments, but took a hit in a *Gonzales Inquirer* editorial. After reading it, he jumped up and threw the paper to the floor while snarling, "Well, I'll be goddamned. I've always thought them in my support and now they publish this shit."

"Might I look?" I asked as Wes blazed. He gave a dismissive nod, so I picked up the paper and read.

"With surprise I have read sympathetic articles on behalf of John Wesley Hardin. I was astonished at the almost unanimous sympathy his speech created in the courtroom during his last trial. I was astounded by the fact that this man was once the terror of Cuero, DeWitt county, and West Texas, and large rewards were offered for his capture. But all seems to be forgotten, perhaps through his speech, gentlemanly appearance, and declaring to be a reformed man. Nothing is more detrimental to a town than these fighting characters who terrorize whole counties, where panic-stricken businessmen close their stores to avoid difficulties. Honest hard-working farmers stay away from towns and places of danger. We are well aware that a dead victim will never come to life again, no matter how much the perpetrator, after servitude perhaps, is condoned by the once terrorized and trembling citizen. I was a small schoolboy during John Wesley Hardin's best days in DeWitt county, but can remember well the deep-seated dread and fear of this once famous outlaw. Your correspondent has got nothing personally against Hardin, he only wishes to express his surprise."

It pleased me to find one man with courage to speak out. This apparently caused me to grin which Wes caught. "You think him right?" he demanded. "He was a child in those days. He knows nothing of the injustice I faced."

I let go a sigh and chose my words carefully. "You don't need every single person in your support, Wes. I'm sure you have enough."

He stood leaning against the wall, but was far from relaxed. I didn't like his look as I could see he was headed toward something. Then he said what I truly did not want to hear. "Are you in my support, Garland?"

I was on the stool and never have I felt our cell so small as I did then. Distance at such a juncture was sorely needed, but a convict lacks that luxury so I remained under what seemed a darkening storm. "I want justice for you, Wes. I would never go against you on that."

"But?"

"But, yes, there is a but. Personal interest. We've been locked together a long time and I value what we have in here, maybe too much, but I can't help it. If I can see over to your side on the pardon, surely you can see over to mine on the personal."

My heart began to pound soon as I began this spiel and when Wes didn't immediately reply, I thought I might expire then and there, such was the thump in my chest. My expression must have turned grave because, after a long silence, Wes broke into a grin and closed the subject by sucking my dick.

As I sat on the stool, pants pulled open, him on his knees, I couldn't escape the fact that I had, for the first time in all our years together, spoken on our personal side, and that Wes had chosen not to speak. I told myself, as he worked me toward bliss, that I should be happy he didn't knock my block off, and then I forgot it all and spurted.

By October, when no word had come from Hogg, Wes took to rationalizing. "I know him in my support as I am an underdog and he fights for us. He just has to be careful due to being new to his office. It's a fine line to be seen as a law-and-order man while granting pardon to one once notorious."

"Good point," I said as we walked the yard. Fall was teasing us this day, the air warm after a cold night. Had we trees, they'd be all reds and oranges, so I imagined some along the lower yard fence. I was getting good at making mind pictures. In addition to my dirty book, I made things as I wished them to be, not as they were. And when I went to the library to read made-up adventures or real history, which was often more exciting, I knew this fed me in some way. Funny how Wes had done so much writing while I just made up stuff.

Fly wrote to Wes every week, always encouraging, but after a while even he wore thin. "He's not telling me anything," Wes complained as he wadded up the latest letter. "'Support remains high, but due consideration must prevail.' Due consideration. I am goddamn to hell sick of due consideration and what is that anyway? Hogg has the facts which couldn't be more clear. Why doesn't he shit or get off the pot?"

"It's far more than taking a shit," I countered at which Wes frowned. "It's a big move," I added, affecting a grave expression when, in truth, I saw delay as an impending refusal. "Hogg has to consider his own political fortunes."

"Four goddamn months! I had no idea he'd go so slow. He has to know I'm twisting in the wind. You'd think that would carry weight."

"I'm sure it does, but I doubt much of anything weighs as heavy as political opinion."

"I wrote to the children how I'll be getting out and we can take up again as family. I wrote to Fred Duderstadt, on whose ranch they live, and he says I can stay there while I work to pass the bar examination. It's all set if Hogg would just move."

I lay in my bunk as Wes rambled on, pacing the cell while giving poor Hogg a verbal beating. After he'd worked himself up, I closed my book and pushed off my lowers, then sat up and threw my legs over the side, spread wide to display my privates. "How about you put that mouth to better use?" I suggested.

Wes had stopped below the window and turned to see me, then issued a sharp laugh which told me I had him. Blood up for any reason is always promising. He came over and stood looking at my prick while he undid his pants. Soon he was sucking me and pulling himself and it wasn't long before he got me down to stand and have him up my bottom. I knew, as he fucked like a wild stallion, that some of it was for Governor Hogg.

I will confess to taking great advantage of Hogg's dithering. Every time Wes worked himself into a state over the delay, I ventured forth with cock or bottom, one time as he sat at the table fuming. I just went over and showed my bare ass to him which caused him to jump up, get himself free, and spear me with a dick already hard. I thought how one day I should write Hogg with thanks for a delay that got me some good fucking.

Wes was now eager to take my cock. He had fully come around to where all men long to be, taking it up the butt. He now knew the pleasure of penetration and how sensitive is the shit hole. Most filthy place a man has gives such pleasure, the filth making it all the better. Wes and I never spoke on this, but words weren't needed. His presenting his bottom to me said it all.

"Maybe I'll get out for Thanksgiving," he said one night from his bunk. It was late, but the cellblock was more noisy than usual as guards had come to break up an assault inside a cell. Word was passed down the row that a man had stabbed his cellmate with a knife he'd made in the blacksmith shop. Once taken away, the row wouldn't settle and so Wes took his thoughts elsewhere.

"Thanksgiving would be right fine," I said, not believing such a thing would come to pass. "Have a grand holiday supper with your children."

"Molly says she's a good cook and little Jane helps."

"You're fortunate to have family," I said, feeding what I knew but a dream. It was easy now, the passing months piling weight onto my position to where I didn't mind indulging Wes.

"I don't believe Hogg will let the matter go into the holiday," said Wes.

"Good point."

But Hogg did let the matter hang all through November which puffed up my confidence. Then, the Sunday after Thanksgiving, when Wes sat morose on his bunk, there came another letter from Fly. "Good news," cried Wes. "Fly is in touch with an assistant to Hogg who says in confidence that the governor will soon find in my favor."

I was pissing the pot as this was said and my stream cut back to a trickle as my whole self seized. I held my dick like I was still going and said nothing.

"How about that?" Wes all but shouted. He'd been sitting on his bunk, but was now on his feet and had I not been pissing I think he'd have taken me up and swung me around. As it was, I worked to restart my stream though there was little left. Had the news dried me up? "That is something," I said as I shook off the last. Buttoning up, I meant to say more, but comment closed off as an old dread came calling.

"More than something," Wes continued. "It's the first solid news in months. It means I'll get my pardon. You were right. Hogg took time due to politics, but now he's ready to give a decision, a right and true decision. I'm to go free, Garland. Free."

"Not to throw cold water," I said, "but you should hold off excitement until Hogg issues his decision. This man could be talking out of turn."

"No, I won't believe that. It'll come to pass. I can feel it."

The supper whistle blew just then and I was grateful for the diversion, but all it did was delay things. After we ate, Wes wouldn't be contained and when we attended play rehearsal, he was useless with his lines. In defense, he announced his news and did not catch how tepid the response. Men who'd been drawn to him suddenly confronted the possibility of a killer of thirty-two men being forgiven and allowed to walk free. They offered congratulations, but not a one smiled. The rehearsal was ended earlier than usual due to the Hardin disruption, and I had to shake my head at the director giving way. Wherever Wes went, he always took center stage.

That night he could not fuck enough. He didn't want me to do him, which I understood as he was so powered up. He needed to stick it to me again and again. He gave me a good hard go soon as we got to our cell and when done he refused to leave off my butthole, sticking in fingers to prod while he put his filthy cock in my mouth.

He allowed me to lick his bottom and tongue-fuck him, but only to get himself up again which worked and he then gave me a good long one, me on my back, legs up on his shoulders. After lights out we found a stripe of moon shining across us and I was lost to the sight of my man giving me his all.

We wore ourselves out and slept some, but Wes woke me once to suck my dick and again just before the morning whistle to put to use that stiff dick all men know. At breakfast my drawers were awash in spunk.

It was the next letter from Fly that changed things. First of December, it gave the name of the man in Hogg's office and told how there were urgent matters the governor was caught up in. Hardin was to be assured all was in line for the pardon to be granted, likely in January, and asked that he continue his patience.

"Well, this is a relief," said Wes.

"Relief, yes," I replied, my voice near whisper. I was in the grip of dread and this time it meant to strangle me. I was going to be left behind. Clear as that. Wes would get out after just fifteen years and I'd be left to do seven more to finish my whole twenty-five. As this fact hardened like some newly mortared stretch of wall, I saw I was going to lose Wes Hardin. I couldn't let that happen.

CHAPTER TWENTY-SEVEN

What better escape plan than the one Wes himself had devised: bribe guards as necessary and go out in a wagon of goods. Of course it wouldn't be under quilts from the tailor shop. It would be in one of the wardrobe cabinets we manufactured and shipped every few weeks. A man could easily be concealed inside. Bribes would go to the shop guard, the trusty driving the wagon, and the transport guard who accompanied him and gave final inspection of shipped goods, sealing the doors so gate men need not bother to check. I'd saved all the pittance of wages I earned, thinking it a nest egg for when I'd done my twenty-five, but now I saw it an investment in freedom. Nights I lay working my plan and every time Wes and I fucked, I did it with new enthusiasm as we would soon be together on the outside.

Dread didn't stay around once I decided to escape. In its place came new strength and a cunning I hadn't known I possessed. As I plotted and planned, I saw in me the Hardin influence which added to my excitement. Second week of December I began to lay groundwork.

First was Ward Clark, my shop guard who I'd already befriended. "You've heard Wes Hardin will soon get pardoned," I said one day. We were sitting at my desk in the back, the shop filled with a hum and clack I now hardly noticed.

"Heard he'd applied to Governor Hogg," said Clark.

"Word is it'll be granted in January. You see what that means for me."

"You get left behind," Clark replied.

"Exactly. Wes and I have been together too many years for me to survive such a loss. I have to get out."

Clark's eyes widened. They were a handsome blue and I saw excitement in them. "Escape?" he whispered.

I nodded. "You'd have to help me. I'd go out in a finished wardrobe, bribe the trusty and transport guard, bribe you too if you'll take it."

Clark shifted in his chair. His shotgun sat propped against the desk as he often tired of having it in hand. He glanced at it while he considered what I was asking. "You bribe them. I don't want your money."

"But you'll do it?"

He blew out a breath and looked around, then stood and paced some before coming back to stand beside me. "Because I like you, Garland. Always have, and I know Wes and you are close. In that way. But there is a price."

"If not money, then what?"

Here his hand ran onto his crotch and remained there. I knew him a married man with children. He wasn't young, well past forty, but not worn by his years. He had a soft look and his easy temperament made him likable. "Tell me what you want," I said.

He rubbed his privates like he'd just found he could play down there and I knew what was upon him, knew also that he'd come in his pants if he kept on so I helped him. "You want my dick up you, I'll do it, give you a good hard fuck."

His hand got frantic below and he clamped his jaw shut to hold back a cry. Seeing him in his throes, I decided to spur him on. "I'll put my cock up your ass because I'm always looking to come in a fresh hole."

His eyelids fluttered as he was lost to his climax and when done, his hand remained at his crotch. "Where do you want it?" I asked.

"Tomorrow I'll keep you back from lunch, make up some business about production figures in case the men take note. Okay if you skip a meal?"

"I don't care about food when I'm going to get my dick in."

He shuddered at such talk. He still hadn't let go of himself. "Tomorrow," he said and he regained his composure and went outside to take some air. I wondered if he'd put it to his wife that night because he'd likely have his hand in his pants rest of the day.

Next day at lunch, Clark did as planned, making noise about Goree complaining on our production, and kept me back. He'd been pacing the shop for an hour, and I enjoyed knowing I had him. I'd get into the wardrobe on the chosen day and he'd close me in, then have the men load it onto a wagon like usual, in with some tables and chairs, maybe a dresser, whatever was ready to go. It was going to work. I could feel it.

When the men had gone, I closed the door, and by the time I got to the back of the shop, Clark had his pants and drawers off and stood holding a fine cock that was already stiff. "I put it to my wife," he said, as if I needed explanation. I saw this was more him needing to say it than me needing to hear it. "Fuck her good, have children to prove it, and I like getting into her, but I've craved men since boyhood."

"You take a cock early on?"

"How'd you know?"

"Starts early with most. Some ignore it and attempt a regular persuasion, such as yourself, while the rest of us stick to what got started and have us a time. Thing is, once you've had a dick up you, you're ruined. You'll always want it."

He issued a sigh. "You're talking about me. Ranch hand got me when I was eleven, did it two times before my pa caught him. Nearly beat him to death, me too, so I went straight after that, courted, married, but the craving never left. I'll confess only to you, Garland, because I trust you and you trust me, that on occasion, when need overtakes me, I shove a carrot or a cuke up there, fuck myself and come a gusher."

"Good to know you're broke in."

"Hell, yes. Now do it, fuck me before I come all over the floor."

He was pulling his cock and it was already drooling. As I opened pants and drawers to get at my dick, he gave a little squeal, and when he saw my cock he got wide eyed, licking his lips like that's where he'd take me. I wasn't going for any of that. I applied spit to myself and told him to bend over the desk. He not only bent, he pulled apart his buttocks. "Fuck me, Garland. Sweet Lord, fuck me."

I hadn't put my dick to anyone but Wes for a good while, but I saw what I was about to do as being for Wes so I shoved in and gave Ward Clark a good reaming. Turns out, he was a talker. Soon as I had it in, his filth began to spew, the family man so nasty it fired me and I gave it to him rough which he noted in his talk. "Shove it more, get it in, choke me with come. All I want is cock. Give me your spunk. I want to shit spunk for a week, I want spunk up inside me. Put it up there, fuck me, fuck me." On and on he went, his hand working below until his narrative cut off and he issued grunts that told me he'd gone to his glory. Seconds later I shot my load and after ramming it deep, I pulled out. He rolled onto his back, hands off to the side like he'd been flayed. "Nirvana" was all he said.

A deal was then struck. Clark would not only hide me in the wardrobe and see me out onto the wagon, he'd say I was elsewhere, should anyone inquire, and the word of a guard was not questioned. He would also carry bribe money to Sledd, the trusty, and Beam, the transport guard who inspected goods leaving the prison. All this Clark would do willingly so long as I kept putting it to him.

I knew Sledd was a brute. I didn't know his first name, suspected he had none, what with being one of Satan's own. He'd been known to ruin men in ways so awful details weren't given, the wreckage just taken away. As Goree had made little effort toward rehabilitation of the trusties, knowing them a lost cause, those not choosing the path toward rehabilitation were left to accost men as they saw fit while enjoying freedom that sometimes included going out of the prison.

I knew to tread carefully with Sledd while Beam, who would falsely certify the wardrobe empty, I knew to be a straight-up fellow which meant if paid he'd keep his word. There'd been no escape attempt for some time, thus all were ripe toward bribes.

"Sledd will assist you," Clark told me two days later. He had his pants down as before, the two of us alone in the shop at lunch. His cock was in hand. "Wants to meet and discuss details as he must be careful not to get fingered."

"Where are we to meet?"

"He'll see you in the yard tomorrow. You just follow."

"Fair enough."

I then put it to Clark who squealed like a pig and came all over the desk. Next day there came Sledd in the yard. I'd purposely held off going out until I saw Wes occupied with several men as I wanted no notice from him. The trusty spotted me and came over.

"Follow me," he said which I did, through the gate to the upper yard where stood several empty wagons. I doubted Sledd washed much as he was rank. All of us bore a stink by week's end but it was just Tuesday and he was already putrid. And even though we got fresh stripes each week, his looked dirty though I knew he did no hard labor. Seemed he preferred filthy to clean which added to his brutish way.

"Get in," he said and I climbed up into a freight that had a high canvas cover, much like a prairie schooner. It was empty, save for a couple barrels. "Let me see it," Sledd commanded, once he'd pulled the canvas cord tightly closed. I offered the money which he took, then said, "That's not what I meant. Show your dick. I know you go that way."

I pushed down pants and drawers to reveal my cock which shrank like a newborn.

"Fine morsel," he said as he kneeled and began to suck. He did this like a baby at a tit, sucking the knob like that alone would get my milk. I saw in this he had no skill for cock sucking which didn't concern me so long as he got what he wanted. But then he pulled off and pushed down his pants. I saw no drawers and a prick hard and ready. I thought he meant to fuck me, but I was wrong. "I hear you eat shit," he said.

"You heard wrong."

"Word is you lick Hardin's butthole."

"But I don't eat his shit."

"Same thing if you ask me," he countered, "but that don't matter now. You want my help, you lick my shit hole." Here he turned around, bent over, and spread himself. His crack was hairy as a bear and reeked like one, but I had to do it. No way to escape without him so I kneeled and ran a finger up between his furry buttocks.

"Tongue," he growled.

"I will. Just getting the lay of the land."

"Hole's at the center. You need me to pop a turd to show you?"

"No, thanks." I then began to lick him, poking his pucker while trying not to retch. I felt him working his cock as my poor tongue did the necessary.

I was greatly relieved when I poked his center and he showed some panic. "Don't put it in," he snapped. "Just lick. I don't want any of you in me."

So he was a regular on excursion, possibly enjoying his first ass licking as he quickly began to whimper, then cried out as he spurted while I kept to my licking. When he stopped pumping himself, his arm swung around to knock me away, and he turned, his prick with a gob of come hanging from the tip. "I should have shit in your face," he said. "I know that's what you and Hardin do." Here he squatted and issued a loud fart. He then told me to cover up as it was a disgrace to show my privates.

Once we were out of the wagon, we concluded our business arrangements. "Beam will do as I say," Sledd bragged. "I'll have him seal the wardrobe without a look and assure men at the gate all is well. We pass through enough that they go easy with us. It's a good plan you have, even if you are a shit eater. Now get back to where you belong."

"Clark will tell you when I'll be in the wardrobe."

"Fine."

Back in the lower yard, I got a cup of water and rinsed my mouth, then spat to excess which drew Wes my way. "What're you hawking up?" he asked.

"Lunch didn't set with me. Some came back up."

"That fine meal? Cornbread wasn't even a day old."

"Tell that to my stomach."

He studied me like he bought none of this, but challenged no further. To divert him, I asked if he'd heard from Fly this week.

"His inside man says January is certain. Hogg is vacationing until the New Year, but it's on his desk, top of the stack."

"Top of the stack. Can't get better than that."

Part of me longed to tell Wes I'd be with him on the outside. The only thing stronger than the desire to declare my love was the desire to let him know I'd not be left behind. I'd be out there and would hear when he was freed as it would be big news all over the state, and I'd then go to his friend's place in Comanche, Fred Duderstadt, a name not easily forgotten.

The other part of me knew to keep quiet about my plan. If Wes Hardin couldn't break out, he'd never believe Garland Quick could so I held it in which wasn't easy. Days slid by and I began to settle on a date for the escape because we were finishing up a walnut wardrobe with fine veneer work. Knowing it my way out, I stayed late in the shop one day and drilled air holes in the back, a series in a neat row so they looked a decoration. Once that was done, I was good to go.

I saw we'd have a load ready for transport three days later, on December 30, so I planned accordingly. Clark passed word to Sledd about the appointed day and he passed it on to Beam. Once all was in place I just had to do the time, three days instead of seven years. It took effort to appear my usual self both in the shop and around Wes, especially as I meant to take advantage of the last three days to fill up on fucking. I couldn't go to extreme, however, even if that was what I wanted. Still, I had my nose in the Hardin bottom so much Wes commented.

"You are getting greedy with my backside," he said when I began licking him after fucking him the first night. "I believe I'll be sitting easy a while."

"That a problem?"

"Not when you soothe me like this."

I then resumed licking him which led to getting my tongue in which in turn led, after a good while, to more fucking.

I was adding pages to the dirty book of my mind every time I fucked Wes and I took to adding certain words that pleased me more than others, words like "penetration" and "dick suck," but most of all, the best one, "fucking." When we'd finished our excess and Wes lay sleeping, whether beside me or alone, I'd think on that word which, though every man used it freely, felt very much my own. So I added it to mind pictures of Wes with his butt up, me ready to do some of it, fucking.

The day before my scheduled departure, Sledd caught me in the yard. "Captain Goree wants to see you," he said with such a leer I knew this a front for more in that wagon. Sure enough, he took me there but rather than suck my dick, he just lowered his pants and turned around. "Just had me a shit and need to you get me clean," he said.

It was plain that degrading me aroused him as much as a tongue in his crack, maybe more, but I couldn't refuse, what with depending on him. So I got down on my knees and as I pulled apart the hairy crevice, I reminded myself it was the last of any man having power over me. Then I set to licking.

As before, Sledd pulled his cock while I tended his bottom. Then he began to squirm which at first I took as him ready to come. When his grunts took on the ominous sound of a man straining his bowels, I knew he was bearing down, but I kept licking the awful pucker as my freedom depended on it. I put from mind the possibility I was to be shit upon, saying in my mind, over and over, one word: "freedom." There then came a big groan and I felt Sledd's pucker open but fortunately it let go no more than a large and smelly fart. I gagged at the stink while Sledd chuckled and said, "Clean that up, shit eater." He continued his torment until he finally cried out and came. Only when he'd quieted, did I sit back.

He turned and stood, fat cock still in hand. "Tried to get something for you to eat but all I had was perfume. Know you like it, though."

I gave no reply and he tugged his cock as if to tease before finally pulling up his pants. "Tomorrow's your big day," he said as he buttoned himself.

"I'll be in the wardrobe."

"Beam is set, as am I. Ten o'clock, like usual, right?"

"Right. No change from the normal transport schedule."

He studied me then. "Guess I'll have to find a new man to attend my shit hole."

When I didn't reply, he laughed and opened the canvas so we could part. This time I sought no water or spitting in the yard for fear Wes would see. I did slip away to the cell where I rinsed and spat and shuddered with disgust. But it was over. No more Sledd, no more cell or walls. I'd be a free man and as such take up where I belonged, with lawyer Wes Hardin.

That night Wes got deep into his study. Sure of the pardon, he was now free to pursue his next goal, passing the state bar examination. I lay on my bunk watching him, filling up on his image which occupied many pages of my mind book. For once it wasn't dirty. I recorded him hunched over his law books and writing down important things. I saw shoulders bare though stripes presently covered them. I wrote how I'd kneaded that fine back and the feel of my fingers on his muscle. It was a fine entertainment until he sat back.

"You've been watching me," he said. "I can feel your stare."

"That a problem?"

"You've not done it before."

"I've come to enjoy the sight of you as scholar."

"I'm not buying that. I think you've got your dick out."

"For once I don't," I said with a chuckle, "but since you mention it, why not?"

He stood up and stretched. "Study makes me ache nearly as much as chopping wood. How about you swing your legs over the side so I can suck some cock while upright?"

It was cold, being December, but I never hesitated to bare the necessities when promise beckoned. I stripped my lower half, then put my legs over the side of the bunk, and spread them wide. I was hard from just doing that much.

The lights-out whistle blew just as Wes started over so he stepped back to snuff the candle, then groped his way to me. No moon assisted so it was black as pitch, but this didn't matter as Wes soon found my hard rod. He got between my legs and began to feed at which I swooned. Soon he had a hand in his pants.

"I want your dick in me tonight," I said just before I gave him a mouthful. He offered no reply, due to swallowing spunk, but soon as he'd had his meal he pulled me down and fucked me standing. "Your back is going to be much improved," I said as he set up a good thrust. Soon he was grunting and pounding which set the row hooting. "Fuck me, Wes," I said, "Fill me with your spunk."

He kept on, clearly tired from the long study, but finally got his rise. His fingers dug into my hips and he let go a "yes" as he gave me what I wanted, the load I'd take with me into the outside. Once done, he collapsed onto his bunk and soon as I put back on pants and drawers, I got in with him. "Keep me warm tonight," I said and he wrapped me into his arms. I then kissed him for what I knew the last time until January, a gentle kiss that spoke of love. I could only hope he got my meaning.

Quarter of ten the next morning, I got into the wardrobe and Clark closed the door. I then felt myself carried from the shop and loaded onto the wagon after which came delay as smaller pieces were added. Finally I heard Sledd's voice call, "Ready to roll," and Beam agreeing. Then came the familiar "Hee-yah" to the horses and I was on my way.

We moved slowly, horses at a walk, and I knew every second where we were. Through the lower yard and into the upper which led to the front gate. A stop there as guards looked over the freight and passed some talk with Sledd and Beam, then the gate swinging open. Prisoners to a one know that big sound as it marks the end of their freedom on coming in and regaining it on the way out. Those iron doors had their own special moan, like some spook trying to scare us, but hearing them now made my heart leap. Then we moved through and out onto the road, the doors moaning again at loss of me. Knowing myself outside the walls for the first time in eighteen years, I sucked in a big breath, hoping for more than I got. The fresh air of freedom would have to wait until I got out of the wardrobe, which I wouldn't do for a good hour more. I settled in to wait, happy in that state for the first time.

We'd trundled along a good bit more when came the sound of horses and then the call of men. The wagon stopped and when I heard the command for the men to get down, I knew myself cooked. I next heard chairs and such thrown to the ground and then the breaking of the seal on my door. Lastly, the door swung open and I faced a shotgun inches from my nose. "Get out of there," came the order.

I stepped out and was grabbed by the arm and pulled so violently from the wagon that I fell to the ground. I was then rolled onto my stomach while my hands were cuffed behind me, after which I was roughly pulled to stand. I cared little of what was done to me at this point as I now considered my life at an end. I was no more. Nor was Wes Hardin, at least to me.

A rope was looped around my neck and I was made to walk back into the prison amid nearly a dozen guards while the freight, including the now empty walnut wardrobe, went on its way. Sledd and Beam were not detained which was good as that would have come back on me, Sledd possibly beating me if found out. It was decided I alone had done wrong and this I accepted.

Roped as I was, I knew I served as lesson on the futility of escape. I was meant to be seen as I was led back through the gates and into the yard. I doubted Wes saw me as he'd be busy with his stitching, but I didn't much care on him anymore. I considered making a run for it so I'd be shot, but found I lacked the spine for such a move. I just plodded along, eye to the ground, and soon found myself facing Captain Goree across his big desk.

"You are a disappointment, Quick," he said. He stood to receive me, his imposing size having the intended effect. Big of body, he reeked of authority, yet had a gentleman's way. When I said nothing, he sat down, then looked at some pages on his desk. "I see you attempted escape in 1878, after which you became a model prisoner. What got into you now?"

I should have told him I was done with life, but speaking would have gone against such a notion.

"I see," he said. "Not talking. That is your right and there's not much to say, is there. Attempted escape speaks for itself. You're fortunate we no longer flog escapees. You'll get solitary, however, ten days, and loss of your job as well. You'll return to the wood yard where you started and in time, if you prove yourself, you may be assigned elsewhere."

I knew this already and he knew I knew, but he still had to say it. When I remained silent, looking only at my shoes, he got up and came around to perch on the edge of his desk. He then dismissed the guard who'd stood near the door. When we were alone, Goree said, "Sit down, Garland."

No man of authority had ever addressed me by my first name so I crumpled some and sat.

"You followed Wes Hardin in your first escape attempt, and I find it telling that you now attempt to break out when his pardon is likely. Adding that you've shared a cell for over a decade carries weight so I can, I believe, see what drives you. I'm not a man without compassion, Garland, and it cannot be easy to swallow the fact that you've got seven years to go while Hardin will go free after just fifteen. You want to be with him, don't you?"

Here I looked up as, for the first time, someone was peering into me. Tears welled as I replied, "Yes, I do."

"I know you two are close. It's hard to miss such friendship, and in honor of that and your long standing as a good prisoner, I'll not add to your sentence. That is the practice now for escape attempts, no flogging, just solitary so a man can have time to contemplate the wrong of his actions, and three years added time."

"Doesn't matter," I said. "Seven years or ten. He'll be gone into a new life while I rot in here."

"You think it rotting?"

I looked him in the eye. "No, sir, you've done good things, improvements and such. The rot is inside me."

"I feel for you, Quick," he said as he stood. Going back to my last name meant his compassion had spent. "As superintendent of this prison, I can grant no favors beyond not adding to your sentence. Do your time well and it will pass quickly. Fight and the rot will get you." He then called the guard and instructed that I be taken to a solitary cell. "Ten days," he said.

Deprivation comes easy when you don't care. I lay on the floor in my thin gown hoping to freeze to death, but the grim reaper refused to call. I ate no food and drank water only when thirst was desperate. I seldom lit my candle and when an insect started in on me, I let him have a good meal.

The book of my mind was now closed. Story over, pages strewn to the wind. Nothing to see, nothing to say, life no longer existing inside the cell or out. I had no curiosity on Wes Hardin, and likewise had blame only for myself. I was a fool. I belonged locked away.

I didn't know when ten days had gone as I marked nothing. When guards opened the door and commanded me to stand, I found I couldn't so a doctor was summoned. A stretcher was then called for, and it was none other than Johnny Rose who helped carry me to the hospital.

"Dehydration and some malnutrition," pronounced Doc Tindle, "but your ordeal is now over. In here we'll feed you, get lots of fluids into you, and have you up and about in no time."

Doc Tindle appeared to be the only one not in the know about Wes and me. When I didn't reply he told me to rest and he hurried away. Johnny Rose then came over. "You're the last person I thought would try to break out, but when I look at your situation, well, I think I'd have tried it too."

"Thanks, Johnny."

"Did Goree add to your sentence?"

"No. He took pity and did not. Just solitary and loss of my job."

"You really think Wes will get pardoned?"

"My actions are your answer to that."

He nodded. "You can do the time, Garland. You've come this far."

"I know I can, but meanwhile Wes gets a new life and a man won't wait around on things, if you know what I mean."

"Hell of a fix."

"That it is."

I decided that night to starve to death. They couldn't force food into me so I'd wither away and spare myself the years. After two days not eating, Doc Tindle came and sat beside me. "You must eat to regain your strength," he said like some dunce.

As the matter was not open for discussion, I said nothing and after a little more stating the obvious, he let me alone. Then Johnny came and sat in the chair the doc had vacated. "Wes wants to see you," he said.

"I don't want to see him so keep him out of here."

"He feels bad as he believes himself the cause of your actions."

"Wes sees himself as the cause of everything. Sun don't rise without Wes Hardin's nod."

"Then you don't blame him?"

"I blame only myself. I tried to run, I failed."

"Can I tell him that?"

"Suit yourself."

Wes feeling bad should have made me feel better, but it didn't. Was that part of loving, forgiving the one who brought on foolish action? I was starting to dislike love. If only I could rid myself of it.

That Wes saw himself as cause could mean he'd finally opened his eyes to the fact of me being left behind, but I had to be careful on this. Wes was not dependable where others were concerned, and might have another idea entirely on how he was cause, might completely miss the weight his pardon put upon me. These thoughts crowded in due to Johnny talking on him so I had to work at pushing it all away. Lack of strength helped. A starving man has few resources.

Doc Tindle couldn't handle a man trying to die. He'd been schooled in saving lives, which now went against him. His attempts to encourage me toward life came out like an old granny's homilies and he gradually wound down, then stopped. It was Johnny Rose who finally got me.

Every day he'd come sit with me and not say a word. After weeks of this, and me as close to death as a living man can be, I finally couldn't stand it. "You trying to be present at the end?" I asked, mustering my worst self.

I knew I wounded him, as was my intent, but when he spoke he gave as good as he got. "You think Wes doesn't see, and maybe he doesn't, but you don't either, Garland. I sit here with feelings so strong for you it all but drowns me, yet you miss it because you seek to punish Wes. Well, you'll be punishing me too if you get your way. I love you, Garland, always have, and if you die I'll be badly hurt, but if you make yourself die, I swear I'll follow."

Nobody had declared love to me since Frank McGann which was too many years behind me to count. I looked into Johnny's eyes and saw no tears. Instead was determination which I realized born of caring. "I had no idea," I managed.

"Because you had Wes and I was okay with that. And I make no claim now, nor will I when Wes leaves because I know my love a one-way deal. I'm man enough to handle that, seeing how I have some years now, but I can't think of life without you. You're valued by many, Garland. Don't do yourself in over one man, I don't care that he's the great Wes Hardin."

Here Johnny got up and left me alone and I found myself trying not to cry. Then I slept and when Johnny brought me toast and coffee next morning, I ate and drank and we said no more on it.

I dreaded returning to the cell and will confess to some malingering to avoid it. Johnny saw through this but played along, as a good friend will. Doc Tindle gave me room, but at last declared me well and fit for work. "Get up and dressed. You are released from care as of now."

"What day is it?" I asked Johnny who stood nearby.

"February fifth."

"Has the pardon come through?"

"Granted three days ago."

"Is he gone?"

"Nope. The decision came down, but there's paperwork in Austin that may take time."

"Have you talked to Wes?"

"Every day when he asks after you."

I sat on my bed, fully dressed, putting on shoes. "I'm resigned now," I said which was a lie. I was as adrift as the shipwrecked sailor I liked to read about. I envied him his island.

CHAPTER TWENTY-EIGHT

"**S**ledd gave you up," Wes said after some silence. He'd come into the cell after work and found me sitting on the stool. When I didn't reply, he went on. "Whole month to think up what to say and that's all I've got."

I felt the same. Much to say and no way to say it. "I'm tired, Wes. More than you can know."

"Fair enough."

I climbed up to my bunk while he sat at the table and opened a law book, and we stayed that way until the supper whistle, me not resting and him not turning a page. I thought the dining hall crowd would ease things, but it all seemed changed. It was like some grizzly had followed us in, sat down, taken a meal, and was going back to the cell with us where it would tear us apart.

"No library?" Wes said when we broke ranks after supper. "Warm in there."

"Enough stories." I heard my voice flimsy. I lacked interest in life now, even as I decided to keep on with it. "Get me some sleep."

Wes didn't follow me to the cell and I cared not a whit where he went. He came in after the lockdown whistle and lit the candle. He said nothing and I didn't look his way as I wanted him to get my being done with us. The only way to survive the situation was to embrace emptiness so it wouldn't blindside me when he left. I heard him open a book and close it, heard him take a piss. I felt him stand below the window though it was now the coldest spot, what with winter upon us. As he moved about the cell, I knew his every inch of travel due more to our familiarity than the small space. Then came lights out and he snuffed the candle. We lay in the dark, no more than two prisoners sharing a cell. Convicts. Killers. What we'd known together was gone, at least to me. It had to be.

"You asleep?" came the question some time later.

He knew I wasn't, just like I knew he wasn't. Such was our damnable bond. "No," I said.

"Thought I'd do better with you back. I haven't slept much in your absence."

"Sorry to hear that."

After a long pause, he ventured further. "I don't know what you want of me, Garland. Try as I might, I find myself ignorant on that, and I am sorry."

"I don't want anything of you."

"I get why you tried to break out."

"Go to sleep, Wes."

I'd been truthful in saying I was tired, but tired doesn't always mean sleep. I'd done fine in solitary and the hospital, snoozed away whole days, but in all fairness I'd taken no nourishment back then. Maybe I'd have to starve to get through this last with Wes.

My eyes wouldn't stay closed. I doubted his would either. We used to have an easy solution to the problem back before it all came apart, fuck, but that was over. He was getting out maybe tomorrow, maybe day after or one after that. It couldn't come soon enough. End the torment.

We said nothing the entire next day, a Tuesday. Got up and went to work, took our meals, and when the supper whistle sounded we didn't meet up. I spent the evening at the library which was crowded as more men took refuge in the steam heat while those taking classes studied their lessons. The librarian, old Fred Walsh, had died some months before and in his place we had a new man, Dean Hawley, who was energetic and sought to form a discussion group on books he recommended, most of which I'd read.

"You should get in on that," said Oren Glaser who liked a good yarn as much as I did.

"Maybe," I replied, but the adventures didn't work for me anymore. All they did was remind me I'd never sail on that boat or fight that battle. I'd just grind away my days.

When I came into the cell at lockdown that night, Wes was deep in his law and didn't turn. I got into bed and when lights went out, he lay down and gave off such quiet you'd have thought him dead, yet I could feel him about to speak. Again and again the orator's urge drifted up my way like candle smoke, but he held off which I knew not easy. For that I respected him, his silence respect of me.

Nobody mentioned Wes staying on. Nobody felt free to venture an opinion on why he remained imprisoned if a pardon had been granted. He went about his work, jawed in the yard, and read his law. I likewise kept to myself, expecting with each new dawn to see him leave.

By Friday his presence was wearing on us both. Distancing myself in our confines was hard labor, plus I was annoyed at him remaining, never mind it not his fault. How long could I keep myself steeled for his departure when he wouldn't depart? Finally I cracked.

"What do you think is the delay?" I asked when once again nobody came for him.

"You looking to have me gone?"

"I'm looking to have your wait ended," I said.

"And therefore yours."

I couldn't reply which likely conveyed as much as words. Wes apparently got this and left off pressing further, for which I was grateful. Maybe he was starting to understand the wreck he'd leave behind. Maybe not the love part, but at least the pain part. I stood at the cell door, back to him until we were let out for breakfast. In line, I stepped back to allow another man to put a hand to the Hardin shoulder.

My appetite didn't come back as it should have, likely due to the awful state in which I now resided. Chopping wood after losing twenty pounds was a trial and I had a foreman who took no excuses. I was thus well worn when work ended that Friday. Instead of walking the yard I sat, and when others came over they didn't stay as I wasn't up for any jawing. When the supper whistle blew, I got up and started for a line, but Sledd stepped into my path.

"You still here?" he asked with a wicked grin. He then feigned squatting to shit. I went around him and continued on, hearing his laugh behind me.

When the cell was unlocked Saturday morning, Wes demanded to see Captain Goree. The guard went along with this, what with Wes technically being a free man. I went to breakfast and then to work, chopping wood in bitter cold which got no easier. Still, I kept on as I had no other occupation. I didn't see Wes at lunch and feared he'd throttled Goree again. Much as I didn't want to lean his way, curiosity got the better of me so instead of walking the yard after work, I went to the cell as I thought he might go there, which he did.

He came in like he'd been knocked around and maybe he had been, at least verbally. I wondered how his quilting stitches had fared with him in such a state. Though asking what had happened went against my effort at distance, I decided it might work in my favor as news of the pardon could release me from torment. "You see Goree?"

"That I did." He stood below the window, back to me.

"Learn anything?"

"Only that Hogg is the problem. Goree says he can't release me until he has the pardon in hand and there's some holdup in Austin. He's written to Hogg asking about the delay, but hasn't gotten a reply so he tells me to be patient, assures me it's any day now. Well, it's been seven days and didn't the Lord make a whole goddamn world in that time?"

Here he turned from the window and I saw he sought no comment. He was ablaze with an anger not to be ignored. He ran his hands down onto his legs, rubbing the sides, breathing like he'd been the one chopping wood. Then he began to undo his pants.

I was on the stool not three feet from him and made no move to flee because where can a man go inside a cell? Under the bed where a foot can be caught to drag him out? Into a corner from which he'll be pulled? Onto the upper bunk where he'll be yanked down? So I sat while Wes got out his cock and began to pull. "I'm tired of going around you," he said. "I've done without over a month and that's going to end here and now. Drop 'em."

I did as asked, shed pants and drawers, but made no sign of interest. Didn't matter, of course. He just wanted a place to put his dick. He spit into his palm and applied it to his rod, all the while his eyes drilling me with need and hate of that need. When he had himself ready, he stood me at the bedpost and shoved in, issuing what sounded the roar of that grizzly as he set to giving me a rough fuck. I just took it, denying myself interest in a man looking to leave me. My prick played dead even as my passage quivered at the vigorous occupation. Wes didn't last, of course. All too quickly he uttered grunts that told me he was coming while resenting doing it in me. Soon as he finished, he pulled out, and when I turned, he slapped me so hard I reeled but didn't fall. I hit the wall, my head banging back which jarred me, but not enough to damp the rage he'd ignited. There was no thought to my actions. I just went at him, hands around his neck, squeezing as he tried to push me off.

My eyes were upon his, both of us blazing now, his face red due to lack of air, mine likely the same shade as I was hot beyond reason. Finally, he gave up trying to pull my hands free and laid a punch to my gut which forced my air out in a great huff and kept any new from coming in. I let go and fell to the floor gasping. As I managed a breath, Wes hauled off and kicked me in the back at which I sprang to my feet and swung at him.

I don't know where my power came from. Maybe a man at the end of himself discovers a store he didn't know he had. Whatever the source, I felt myself iron and I laid into Wes with punches to his middle and face which he returned until guards came in to separate us. Blood was in my mouth, I knew not exactly from where, and an eye was fast closing. As we were taken from behind, I got a look at Wes who had blood coming from nose and the corner of his mouth. He also had a bruise coming up below one eye. I figured I looked much the same.

"Pull up your pants," the guard commanded. This I did before being roughly marched from the cell. I heard the same command behind me, Wes made to get his pants up and get moving. We were taken to the hospital where we were seen in separate examination rooms, Johnny Rose passing me a startled look as we came in. Doc Tindle cleaned my wounds and applied stinging ointments where necessary, then admonished me some. I knew Wes, in the room next door, got much the same. Once cleaned up and doctored, we were taken to Captain Goree where we stood side by side before his desk.

"I won't have this," he growled. "You want a single cell, Hardin, you've got it. That what you want?"

"Can I talk to Garland?" Wes asked. I'd never seen him contrite before.

Goree frowned and I had to consider the great Wes Hardin's sway might have thinned. But then the captain blew out a sigh and said, "All right. I'll step out of the room for a few minutes. When I come back, this will be ended."

In his absence seconds ticked by, or maybe minutes, I didn't know, didn't care. It was over, it just wouldn't lay down and die. I sank into a chair as Wes finally spoke. "You're shunning me," he declared.

"You're leaving me."

"I got a pardon. You can't expect me to turn it down. What would you have me do?"

"Nothing. That's the problem. Nothing to be done, nothing for anyone to do. No fixing, no nothing."

"Except you won't have me."

"Doesn't seem to matter since you take what you want."

"But that's it, don't you see? I want you. Don't get us split up now. Can't we pass these last days together?"

I was so tired I felt about to dissolve into a puddle on the floor. To make matters worse, Hardin spunk was dripping from my butthole. "How do you want me?" I asked.

"Like before. It's always been good. You can't deny that."

"It has been good, but that's over now."

"Not yet, Garland. Please. Not yet."

He'd never get it. He couldn't see past his own version of events, but then I already knew that. "Okay. Stay in the cell together."

He kneeled beside me, put a hand on my thigh, but I looked away and we were like that when Goree came back in. "Settled?" he asked.

"We are," said Wes, getting to his feet. "I'll stay with Garland in the same cell."

"No more fighting?"

"No more."

"Quick?"

"No more," I said.

Just then the supper whistle blew. "You men go on to supper," Goree said, and we were escorted to the dining hall where we sat together and I got some food down.

All I wanted after supper was to lie down. I'd eaten a little stew and a biscuit, had coffee, but nothing sat well. My stomach still objected to the situation. In the cell, before I could get to my bunk, Wes suggested I take his.

"You looking to fuck me again?"

"No, I just want you down near me."

"How about your studies?"

"I'm taking the night off."

Our impasse churned my gut. "You take the stool for now," I said.

"Fair enough."

He pulled it to the bedside while I lay down. I did appreciate not having to climb up. "Lower is nice," I said as I closed my eyes. Stretched out felt good and I relaxed some in the quiet, but after a while I could feel the orator at my bedside holding back a spiel. "What?" I asked.

"How come you put trust in Sledd when you're the one who kept telling me convicts will always betray you?"

"Sometimes a man is too driven to listen," I replied. "Remember how that is?"

"Guess I do."

He went quiet and I felt him fidget on the stool. "What?" I asked again.

"Sledd's been saying nasty things about you."

"Don't go breaking his legs on my account."

"He says you ate his shit."

"You believe that?"

"'Course not."

"Then let it be."

He got up then, took a long piss, fussed with his papers, stood below the window, then came back to the bunk, but didn't sit. I kept my eyes closed, fearing if opened them I'd see a stiff dick.

"Whatever has gotten between us," he said but stopped, words a problem for maybe the first time ever. Then he tried again. "Whatever that is, it doesn't have to stay like this. At the rate things are going, hell may freeze over before they let me out. I don't mean to impose upon you, Gar, as you've been through a lot, but can't we mend this?"

"Mend it only to tear it apart."

"Dammit all, Garland, you've got me in a hole and won't let me dig my way out. Take the pardon, but pay hell for it. Why are you so determined to make us miserable for the time we have left together? Is that it? You're unhappy, so I should be too?"

I tried to muster something sharp, but found no resources. I was tired of pushing. "Getting cold," I said. "How about you get in here and keep me warm? Not do anything, just some warmth."

He slid away the stool, then got my blanket from up top, and when he crawled in beside me, he pulled the two blankets over us. "Bundle up," he said.

He made no move until I got up against him. Then we did like always, him wrapping an arm around me. Once secure, I fell right to sleep. We didn't move until the morning whistle blew.

"Well, how about that," said Wes. "Slept like a baby."

"Me too. Maybe getting warm helped."

"Maybe."

I pissed, he shit, and we made ready for the day, going around each other as much as possible in our small space which felt bigger now, the air cleared some. I marched to breakfast with his hand on my shoulder and when his leg rested against mine as we ate, I allowed it as I saw how he was trying to win me back.

Cornbread, molasses, and coffee perked us up and when the line broke and men went all directions to work, Wes put a hand to my shoulder. "Don't work too hard," he said with a squeeze. I had no reply.

Chopping wood in cold weather heats a man, but plays hell with his extremities. My hands were gloved, my jacket buttoned, and on my head I wore a cap, but my nose felt ready to crack and fall like an icicle and I feared my dick might do the same. After work I sought the library to get warm. I got a favored book, more to visit an old friend than to read, and had it open when Wes came in.

It was as he stood looking at me from across the room that the last of my resolve fell away. He wore a half-stricken expression, appearing far from a pardoned man, and I saw how I'd ruined what should be his time of joy, all because I wasn't man enough to face the loss of him. He came over and when the fellow next to me saw who it was, he got up and gave his place on the bench, not in fear, but in recognition of the situation which was known to all.

"You warmed up yet?" Wes asked.

"Will be about the time we face a cold cell."

He chuckled. "You've got that same book I've seen you with a hundred times."

"*The Life and Strange Surprising Adventures of Robinson Crusoe*. My favorite. About a shipwrecked man alone on an island. You should read it. Take a break from all that study."

"Might be good."

I slid the book over to him. Far as I knew, he'd never read for entertainment. "You read it, then we'll talk about it."

"Fair enough."

I knew, as we walked to the cell, that we'd get up to something. I was done for, resistance gone. It would all but kill me when he left, but we had the night, and if his God had any heart at all, he'd allow a few more. We lit the candle, pissed the pot, then stood looking at each other. "We mended?" Wes asked.

"Enough," I replied at which he took me into his arms and kissed me.

I will not say he ignited great passion. Something in me remained compromised by the situation, our fucking of a bittersweet nature. He put his cock to me soon as we'd snuffed the candle, shed pants and drawers, and got under the covers. After taking his satisfaction, he attended me most gently and most thoroughly, getting us past all that had happened though not past what lay ahead. At last he had me stiff and he kept on until I took my first pleasure in weeks. Once satisfied, we lay entwined, his leg over mine so our soft pricks touched. When he ran a hand up under my shirt to play around my tit, he asked, "Better?"

"Better," I purred.

We dozed on and off all night and at one point I wished they'd come take him away right then, while I was woozy with satisfaction. But nobody came then or in the morning, Saturday, so we went to work. As we left the cell, I told Wes I wanted to sleep the whole of Sunday.

"You sleep. It's mail day so I expect a letter from Fly."

He'd been writing to his attorney as much as was allowed, pleading for assistance in resolving whatever problem held up the pardon papers. "Maybe get some answers," he added.

That night I fell onto the bottom bunk which made Wes smile. "You lie down there, you'd best take off your pants." When I began to do just that, he let out a laugh and I joined in.

Sunday we divided our time, spending some in the library to warm ourselves, and some in the cell to fuck. We slept some as well, naked in our wallow, spunk all up us as we'd had a come while grinding upon each other. Then the mail arrived at two o'clock and Wes got up and dressed. "Three letters," he said. "Molly, Manning, and Fly." He sat on the bunk's edge to read Fly first while I remained under the covers.

"I don't believe it," he said. "I do not goddamn believe it. Fly says there may be a problem. Political, he says, which means Hogg might go back on his word."

Here he stood up as there was no containing a man getting bad news. Good thing the cell door stood open so he could go out and walk the yard, stomp around and carry on if need be. I felt his anger rising and in with it disappointment, which can be far worse. "They can't take it back," he said, trying to convince himself. "Hogg said it. He said it was granted. People were told."

What could I say? That I wanted it turned back so he'd finish his twenty-five with me? Part of me glowed with hopes I'd get my way, but a bigger part felt shame at such selfish joy.

"February twelfth tomorrow," he said. "Ten days."

I seldom kept track of the date as it did little good for a long term man, even one with just seven to go. My birthday had come on the ninth. Turned forty-one.

"How can Hogg be for the underdog, then do this?" Wes asked. "Sacrifice me for political purposes."

"Politics seldom considers those outside it," I offered.

"Have I been a fool, Garland? Has all the effort been foolish?"

"No, Wes, and I don't believe the pardon is gone. Stalled maybe, but not gone. Why don't you read Molly's letter. She'll cheer you."

She tried, as did Cousin Manning, but neither undid what Fly had set upon Wes. And that night when we got into his bunk together, he made no move upon my body. As I lay wrapped in his arms, I started to have mixed feelings about James S. Hogg.

CHAPTER TWENTY-NINE

I kept wishing for something to happen. If not the parting, then some event to take us up for a while, man killing another man or somebody setting fire to something. Maybe a fool running for the wall and that Gatling gun put to use. I wanted its fire to tear up the night. I wanted something loud and mean to break the grind, but nothing did because that's what a grind is, life trod under rather than lived. Wes didn't read *The Life and Strange Surprising Adventures of Robinson Crusoe* and I didn't join the library discussion. I also did no playacting. We worked, ate, and fucked. That was the only good we had, fucking, and we did it to excess as, when going at each other, we almost forgot the grizzly that now lived with us. It ate on us some each day, gnawing away good nature and patience. Wes and I got to scrapping way too easily, a look or a word causing that awful bear to rise up and growl. More than once we bruised each other just short of guards coming to stop us, but more than that we just plain fucked.

I didn't go to the library. I didn't care how cold I got. Lose a toe or a nose, what did it matter? All I needed were dick and butthole. Let the rest go. Wes left off his studies entirely, and once got so angry at the waiting that he threw his books against the wall. One by one, he gave them a pitch that would have been fine on the baseball field, then turned to me with such fire in his eyes that I stripped off my clothes, and bent over to offer my bottom. He gave me a good one then, his book toss having gotten him up. Anger roused him and kept rousing him. My butthole had never had so much cock.

He tried to see Goree again to plead for assistance, but the captain turned him away, likely not wishing to face a man he couldn't help. Wes wore his disappointment now, scowl nearly permanent. Only time it fled was when he had my dick in his mouth, but even then frustration filled his eyes. There was not enough sex to set things right.

Then, on Friday of the second week of waiting, when we'd had lunch and broke the line to go back to work, Wes ran over to me. "Goree called me in this morning, showed me the papers. It's here, Garland. The pardon. I go free tomorrow morning."

I allowed a couple seconds for my heart to restart as I swear it had stopped. I then needed a bit more to find words as my throat had gone dry. At last I managed to squeak congratulations at which Wes grabbed me up in a great hug and whirled me around like some damsel, then put me down and shouted for all to hear, "The pardon has come! I go free tomorrow!"

A shout went up from the men, but the guards put that right down and got us to work, no matter the excitement. Even Wes, which seemed silly, but authority was not to be questioned. I doubted he'd do much stitching. How can a man to be set free even sit? I chopped wood in a brisk wind, finding myself happy for him. Hard labor righted a man, as was the intent. I would survive. What that might entail was up to me.

After work I hurried out into the yard, expecting Wes to be holding court, and sure enough, there he was, accepting pats on the back from most everyone. He was lit up like a drunk, smile wide, laugh big, and I think the men were now past jealousy. It was easy to forgive Wes Hardin for being special enough to beat the law. I didn't go over to the crowd, but stood back and he finally saw me and gave a nod. I went to the cell and after a while he came in. "Look at it," he said, taking the paper from his pocket and handing it to me. It had the seal of the governor and was most official, granting pardon to John Wesley Hardin on February 17, 1894.

"Well, this is surely it. Did Goree have any detail on why so long?"

"I didn't even ask," Wes said with a laugh. "Who cares anymore, it's over. I go free first thing tomorrow."

"I'm happy for you, Wes. You worked hard for this and I know you'll continue to work hard when you're a lawyer."

He then begin to speak on his plans and I encouraged this for I had to be man enough to not deter his happiness. He said he'd go to Gonzales by train where his son would meet him at the station and take him to Fred Duderstadt's ranch where they had a room all ready. "Can't take the law books with me," he said, as if just realizing this.

"Surely you've learned it all by now," I replied.

"Never learn it all, but I have enough. I think I can pass the bar."

"That will be right fine."

When the supper whistle blew, I realized it was the last for him and he did too, pausing to listen as if he'd not heard it before. He then put a hand to my shoulder and we went out to join the others.

Everyone took note of Wes as we marched along and when we came into the dining hall, heads turned and whispers got so loud a call for silence was shouted out which got some laughs. Then, after supper, when we marched out and broke ranks, men started coming over to shake the hand of Wes Hardin, most to express good wishes, but some, I knew, just to say they'd shook the hand of the notorious man. Finally Wes broke away and we went to our cell.

"It's all the last time now," I noted as we went in. I lit the candle while he stood looking around. "Been home how many years?" he asked. "Twelve, thirteen?"

"Not quite fourteen," I said, having added it up that day while chopping wood. "September 1880 you got me in here. That makes it thirteen and not quite a half."

"And we're still friends."

"Good friends," I said, "the best."

I didn't wait for him to take me into his arms. For once I made the move, opening mine and stepping forward to embrace him. We held on for a bit, then pulled back to look at each other, studying faces that would soon be absent, and, in my case, making a picture for the book of my mind. Then Wes put his lips to mine and I forgot about all that. We had a whole night to ourselves.

Nature was in our favor and I liked to think Wes Hardin had charmed her. Whatever the reason, she let up on the cold and, if that wasn't enough, hung out a full moon. We didn't light the candle. We did strip naked and stand together for some time, my arms around him, his hands on my bottom. When our cocks rose, we stood rubbing almost gently, enjoying a slow rise in the soft gray light. Our lips met on and off, as did our tongues. There came nibbling and licking of neck, shoulders and further. Wes sucked my tit for a while, then eased down to his knees and took my cock in hand, pulling some before getting it into his mouth. He didn't suck long until I gave him my all.

"I want my dick in you the whole damned night," he said when he stood up and wiped a hand across his mouth. We then got onto his bunk with our two blankets which we soon threw off as we were well heated on this last night.

Wes put me onto my back and drew my legs up, then put a finger into me to play and prod, his hard cock enduring the tease. Finally he guided it into me and set up an easy thrust, the scowl of late chased off not only by his pardon, but by having his dick where it belonged.

"Just like in our twenties," he said.

"Just the same. A good fit."

Conversation slipped away as he suffered what I'd call a swoon, the joy of having his cock in a hole overtaking all else. From then on it was just bodies and he took my feet in hand to better get into me, increasing his effort as his juice stirred. Once on the boil, he picked up speed, and I was grateful for the generous light that allowed me to see him grimace with his climax. His thrust became urgent and as he bore down into me, his grunts announced I was taking his spunk. He kept at me, pumping when he couldn't have a drop left, holding onto the pleasure until at last it faded. Only then did he let go of my feet and ease down my legs. When he slid out, he crawled over to lie atop my body, and when he'd regained his breath he kissed me. "Not bad for a man of forty," he said.

"Not bad at all," I replied, squeezing him.

He kissed me a bit more, little kisses which were a joy all their own, then he pulled back like he'd just thought of something. "Your birthday is February. Has it come yet?"

"And gone. Forty-one on the ninth."

"You should have said."

"Why announce getting older in this place?"

He chuckled. "Happy birthday anyway. Should have got you a present."

"You just did."

I had no idea how to part well as I had no experience at such a thing. Frank McGann had run out on me and nobody else much mattered. It seemed I should say more in honor of all we'd been, but I hesitated to go the direction my heart dictated for fear love would scare Wes. Didn't matter I'd once explained two men could share that affliction. I wasn't sure he'd gotten it then, and I sure as hell couldn't count on it now. There was also no way to gauge how much of his regular persuasion remained after the death of his wife. I suspected a good deal, what with his Bible favoring men lying with women. All this rose up in me, as present as the man who now rolled off and lay with an arm across me. All I could do, I realized, was convey what I thought he could handle.

"You know I have feelings for you," I said.

"And I you."

"Strong feelings."

Here he went silent, the orator who'd convinced the law to turn on itself done in by what he had to know was love. "It's been good," he finally managed. "Good as it can be inside the walls."

I held back a torrent. "Best I've known," I said. "Best man I've known."

"Likewise."

I knew him well enough to see I'd not get what I craved most. There'd be no last minute declaration so I'd best adjust my attitude and enjoy the here and now. I ran a hand over his chest, petting him.

"You've made this awful place tolerable," he said and I realized silence was working against him, like he feared I'd say too much or maybe he would so he had to keep saying little things.

"Tolerable is pretty good for prison," I replied as I ran a finger onto his tit to play around the nub. Finally I asked how things would work next day.

"They'll come at dawn, give me a suit of clothes to wear, then I'll be taken out. Simple as that."

"Simple as that," I repeated. "Funny word, simple, after all the time and effort to get there. Far from simple."

"You're right on that."

I got up to get us water and we sat in the moonlight, sipping. "Last time," Wes said. "Everything is the last time now. Feels strange."

"Once in a lifetime, a man freed from prison."

"Suppose it is." He put a hand to my thigh and squeezed. "You'll do fine," he added.

I waited for more, but saw him choked up so I came to his aid. "Dean Hawley in the library has gotten up a book discussion group which I'll join, and a new man is trying to write a play. If he succeeds, I'll get in on that, maybe try for the lead."

"When you get out you can go on the stage."

"When I get out, first thing I'll do is look you up."

"Call on Fred Duderstadt in Comanche. He's well known and can tell you my whereabouts."

"You can write and tell me yourself."

"Of course, yes, I'll do that once I'm settled. I surely will."

"Lawyer Hardin."

"Best not count chickens until I pass the bar."

"I have no doubts in that regard."

His hand remained on my leg and now drew up to my crotch. "We're wasting time," he said, setting aside his water cup. Mine dropped to the floor when his hand got hold of my dick. As he played around, he put his lips to mine and I received a most inquiring tongue while spreading my legs to encourage him below.

Soon we eased back to lie together, my prick awake to the attention. "I want you to fuck me," Wes whispered at my ear. "I want to take a load of your spunk with me tomorrow. Fill me one more time."

He continued to pull my rod and when it began to dribble with anticipation, he smeared this down the shaft, then spat in his hand and added that to ready me. "Make it easy," he said. When I was awash, he lay back and raised his legs, holding them high. "Stick me, Garland."

I feasted on the sight of him in such a position, my mind book opened up again, pages filling rapidly. No other man got what I did, the notorious and now free Wes Hardin offering his butthole. I scooted up and pushed in at which he issued a welcoming groan. I noticed then, for what seemed the first time, the cellblock quiet. Were the men listening for our fuck sounds, poised to call out their filth, or did they mean to restrain themselves and allow Wes a quiet night? They had to know we'd be at it.

"Quiet," I said when I was inside Wes.

"So I hear."

I began to thrust and the bunk began its usual creak, to which I added my own murmur of pleasure. "This I will remember," I said. "Long as I live, this I will remember."

"As will I."

I felt like the twenty-five year old I used to be, such was the hardness below. Gun barrel stiff and making good use while Wes did not address his cock, even as it had come up. "Never mind we're forty," I said.

"You're forty-one," he reminded. I rammed him in reply. "Forty," he amended. "Thirty-nine if you want."

"Twenty-five," I said as the urge was hot upon me. "I mean to do serious damage."

Here I began to go at him as my juice was stirring. I set up a serious thrust which Wes encouraged with loud breathing and some good moans. His hand drew to his cock, but just held on and I took pleasure in the fact of us, this final fuck. I cried out when the climax hit, fairly screamed, such was my passion. As I thrashed in pleasure, I managed to lock eyes with Wes who drilled me a look I'll never forget. Pure joy at receiving me, pure joy.

Spent, I slipped out of him, then ran my fingers over his hole, feeling the wet of us. I pushed in a finger to feel around at which he moaned so I withdrew, put his legs down, and took his cock into my mouth. Soon as I had him, he bucked, and I kept to him as he let go some spurts which I gobbled right down. When done, I all but fell off him and we lay quiet, then slept.

When I woke in the night, it was with a start, but I found I alone had jarred myself. Wes lay sleeping, his soft snore evidence of good slumber. I watched him in the moonlight, adding pages to my mind book which was getting fat. I enjoyed him being content, yet hated to waste time, what with him naked, so I got down and took his soft prick into my mouth. This woke him and he was soon clawing at my bottom so I switched around to get over him and dropped my softy into his mouth.

This too was the last. There'd be no time for anything in the morning. They'd come get him so we had only the present. I knew he got this too as he kneaded my buttocks while sucking my dick. Due to earlier excess, we didn't spring right up, but due to persistence we did rise. I didn't care if I swallowed his spunk or not, I just wanted to have him once more so I kept to him, licking like a sweet at times, taking him into my throat others, and sucking his knob still others. He came before me, modest issue, but still the moan of satisfaction. I spent a few minutes later, happy to spurt onto the orator's tongue one last time. I then climbed off, happy to let sleep again overtake us. We didn't stir until a clanking came against the bars at dawn.

The jolt this time was unwelcome as the cell was unlocked and a guard came in with a suit of clothes. "Here's your duds, Hardin," he said.

Wes was still rousing himself. As the guard waited, the naked Wes stood to snort and wheeze like a horse, which tickled me. He then reached down to absently tug his cock before taking the clothes. "Be ready to go in twenty minutes," said the guard as he went out. "Captain Goree will come to escort you."

Wes set the clothes on the table, took a long piss, then sought the wash pail. "I'm still half asleep," he said as he slapped his wet face to fully wake. "You about did me in, Garland."

"I should get up and dress," I said, trying to encourage myself. "Goree doesn't want to see a naked prisoner."

As we dressed, I couldn't resist comment. "A fine night," I said.

"Some good sendoff," Wes replied.

Soon he was all spiffed up and I must say he was a sight in black suit, white shirt, black tie, new black shoes, even new drawers and socks. I enjoyed the transformation, but could not get past time ticking away. Thirteen years down to twenty minutes. Wes came over and took me by the arms. "It's been good, Garland," to which I agreed. "Right good." He then kissed me in that rare non-sex way, the kind of kiss that speaks what a man will not say. When he pulled back and let me go, he said, "You'll do fine. I know you will."

"I'll do my best," I replied. "You certainly look the lawyer," I added and he stepped back, took hold of his lapels to play the man he sought to be. His hair hadn't been cut during his wait so he had a bit of length which made him all the more handsome. He'd also been allowed to start a mustache as no man could venture into society without one. "Think I can pass muster?" he asked.

"On looks alone."

"Hah!" he laughed. "Only you would say that."

"Because nobody sees you like I do."

Footsteps were heard coming down the row, also voices. Men began to call out to Goree, pleading their cases as he came by. It hit Wes then that our time was up and he looked at me with that stricken expression. I bit my lip as tears pooled in my eyes.

"I will miss you, Garland," he said, voice cracking. "Every day."

I smiled best I could. "Miss you too, every minute."

Then Goree was in the cell, shaking hands with Wes. "You're a free man, John Wesley Hardin," he pronounced. "Let's get you on your way."

Wes didn't jump right to it but stood to savor the moment. Then he took up his wooden box of papers and a sack of other belongings and started out. As he went he glanced back, bars now between us. I saw him look me up and down, taking in the man much as I'd done with him in the night. Then he nodded and was gone. In his honor, I didn't collapse. I listened to footsteps fade, then set to picturing Goree escorting him to the gate. Would reporters be on the outside as they'd been when he came in? Was he still news? I had no idea, but what did it matter? I was his past now and he had a future to embrace. He'd make a new life, likely accomplish more than I ever would, and I had to admire that. I also took heart that he'd left a good part of himself in the book of my mind.

CHAPTER THIRTY

"That doesn't make sense," said Johnny Rose. "You can't lose something you never had."

"The hell you can't."

We were walking the yard on a Sunday three weeks after Wes left. Johnny had pried me from the cell where I'd taken to lying prone and letting life pass by. It amused me that my new theory had him puzzled. He was a sharp fellow, and, having reached manhood inside the walls, he had a good take on men, or maybe I should say on convicts. His compassion was great, no doubt due to years of hospital work, but also, I believed, due to a good nature. I had to keep remembering he'd said he loved me. How I wished that mattered more than it did.

"Long as Wes was with me," I explained, "there remained the promise of him declaring his love. When he left he took that promise with him, so I lost what I never had."

"How does that feel?"

"Better now that I have it figured, but still a weight."

"You know what you need."

"Don't start on that," I snapped.

"You gonna save it the whole seven years?"

I stopped in my tracks. "How can you say such a thing?" I demanded.

"I'm sorry. I didn't think."

"No, you certainly did not. Get away from me. Go on. Right now. I want no sight of you."

He tossed back another "Sorry" as he scurried away, leaving me boiling mad as he'd not only insulted my manhood, he'd defiled the fact of Wes and me, and everybody, to a man, knew not to do that.

Nine days after Wes had left, when I'd hardly regained my footing, I'd come upon some men in the yard, all fairly new, and one running his mouth to excess. Unfortunately he spoke on Wes. "Hear his wife dried up and died because he wouldn't put it to her, what with him wanting it the other way. Hear he spreads 'em like a woman to take a dick up the butt."

The fellow said nothing more for I was upon him from behind, arm around his throat as I choked off both his spiel and his air. "You don't know Wes Hardin so you damn well better leave off your talk," I growled into his ear as he gasped and kicked in an effort to free himself. When I released him, he took a swing at me, but I dodged this and felled him with a punch to the jaw. I then put a foot on his chest to hold him down. "Hardin is well thought of in here," I continued, "without exception. If you differ, you keep it to yourself. I'd best hear no more slanderous talk from you or anyone. You get that?"

"Yes," he said as blood trickled from his mouth.

I then offered a hand to pull him up and he took it somewhat reluctantly. "There are better ways to entertain," I advised. "We have a fine theater company. I suggest you join."

He was young, maybe twenty, and full of the fire I recalled. He nodded and I did too and walked away. Johnny then came up. "Wes would be proud," he said.

"I won't have him slandered," I declared and we left it at that. Mindful of that incident, Johnny should have known not to idly call up Wes, even without specific mention, especially when addressing sexual matters he should not have been addressing in the first place.

He was partly right, though, which was another reason I didn't take his comment well. I wanted no sex, wasn't even doing myself. My poor prick lay unattended, my balls full to bursting which likely contributed to my short temper on matters concerning Wes. I did need a good fuck, which Johnny would have welcomed, but knowing his feelings put me off.

One month after Wes left, I was assigned to the wheelwright shop. "Of all the goddamn places," I railed to Johnny in the library that night. "Must be fifty shops inside these walls, whole goddamn cotton mill, and I am put where Wes and me started."

"You think Goree is giving you the business?"

"No. He probably hasn't put it together as it's so far back. He's a here-and-now man, as I suppose I should learn to be."

"Wes is still much around."

"That he is."

Kyle Richard, wheel shop foreman, was happy to get an experienced man and put me back on the bending machine. He'd done just ten years, but knew all about Wes and the escape attempt. "Hear it was up in front," he said my first day. "This it?" He pointed to a corner as we stood near the door.

"Other side," I corrected. The tunnel had long been filled and sealed with concrete. A machine I didn't know now stood over it. "Under that thing," I added.

"Well, I'll be damned," said Richard. "Everybody said it was yonder."

"Everybody is too new to know."

I liked not chopping wood and I liked running my machine, but I did not like being in a shop where so much had taken place. Wes was truly around, and, as I could do my work with little thought, I often drifted to that first sight of him, the notorious and grinning young man who wouldn't stay put. Such thoughts were both pleasure and pain and I finally saw my only way ahead was to push them away. This proved no easier a task than had been my failed attempt to push away the man himself.

To further occupy myself, I joined the library discussion group and orated a good deal when *The Life and Strange Surprising Adventures of Robinson Crusoe* was the subject. Dean Hawley said he was most impressed and asked me what book we should read next. I advised him to consider adventure stories as they would keep the men entertained. It pleased me that he took up several of my suggestions.

I also got back into playacting as I began to see even more how life is just that, me acting like a whole man when I felt but half. I went about my business on days when I thought my gut would burn me alive, such was the ache that would not depart. I thought about Wes leading a free life and tortured myself on who he might be fucking, finding I could handle the idea if it was a man, but if he'd gone back to his regular ways and put it to a woman, well, that I couldn't take. I kept an even keel most of the time, playacting so much that when I stepped onto the stage as leading man in a farce written by a prisoner, it came easy. In fact, I began to favor stepping outside myself to become another man entirely.

I didn't take up fucking until I got a new cellmate which was in August. Captain Goree left me alone a good while, I believe to honor my loss, but then came Tom Foley, just twenty-three, raw and brash, listening to nothing and nobody. He'd killed a man in a saloon fight and got fifteen years. Soon as he came in, I knew I'd give way.

"Hear your last cellmate was Hardin," he said right off.

"That it was. Nearly fourteen years together."

He went quiet and I could see he was wondering how much of Wes had rubbed off on me. He was as transparent as a man could be, or maybe I was just gaining the wisdom of age. Whatever, I knew him in an instant. And, as I'd once been somewhat the same, I liked him.

"You take the top bunk," I said. "Three buckets—water, wash, and slops. Don't mistake one for the other."

"Fine. Any other advice?"

"Not right now. You'll learn as you go. They'll have you chopping wood for a while as new men always get that."

"Where do you work?"

"Wheelwright, though I've done carpentry. Where do you hail from?"

"Mecca," he said.

"Don't know it."

"It's in Arizona. I came to Texas looking for cattle work and got in some trouble."

"Didn't we all."

He wasn't pretty, but I didn't need that. He was around six feet tall, slim of build, and had brown eyes. With his hair shorn away, I had no idea what color he had, but suspected it the common brown. He looked like a hundred cowpokes, sporting a tan he'd soon lose, and an attitude likely to go the same way.

"You got a girl?" I asked, deciding to get right to it.

"Nope. Which bucket is slops?" he asked.

I laughed. "One that stinks the most," I said, then added. "In that corner. Keep water and wash buckets opposite for obvious reasons."

He nodded, went to the pail, and got out his dick. As he pissed, I moved over to get a look at what he had and make it known I was interested. Funny how I'd not wanted to fuck until then. Maybe what I'd needed all along was a young buck to show me his cock.

When he'd finished and shook off the last, I said, "Fine piece of meat," and he turned with it still in hand. "You ever get up to things on the trail?" I asked.

"A time or two, yes." He began to pull his rod though it had already started to fill with just his hand upon it. I smiled in fond recall of younger days.

"Things in here, well, needs have to be met among ourselves," I instructed. "You get that?"

"Right."

He exhibited no surprise at such talk. In fact, he was much the opposite which led me to believe him not being straight with me. He'd done more than a time or two. He was just being cautious, not sure of me. "Two men in such a small space have to get along," I went on. "What do you think is the best way to do that?"

His prick was hard now, a good little piece of meat, fatter than what I'd expect for a man of his build. I wondered was his bottom broke in or, God forbid, was he a man who as yet hadn't taken a dick up there? As he answered my question, he wriggled and pushed down his pants and drawers. "You putting it to me, I reckon."

"We're going to get along fine," I said as I began to unbutton.

I leaned him over the table and parted his buttocks, aware the supper whistle would sound at any moment, but I didn't care. I was going to have a fuck for the first time in months and I began to wet my cock with spit. When I was ready, I shoved in at which he grabbed his prick and started to come. He cried out which got calls and hoots all down the row, calls I now welcomed as they spoke of things righted which included a fuck that lasted about thirty seconds before I let go a gusher. I clutched Tom's bottom as I unloaded, pumping with a fury, and when I was done and pulled out, I knew Wes Hardin had been chased further away. Tom then turned around, cock still in hand.

"Welcome to Huntsville," I said as I tucked away my dick and buttoned up.

Tom was still holding himself when the supper whistle blew.

After chopping wood for two weeks, Tom was assigned the shoe shop where he learned the cutting machine. "Wes Hardin did that work," I told him one night. "Never much liked it."

"You mean I could be working the machine he did?" asked Tom, wide eyed.

"Could be. I don't know that shop, but could be."

He giggled like a little kid and I found myself indulgent. He was becoming more likable by the minute.

After looking too long for a letter, I left off thinking I would hear from Wes. Why should he bother addressing the past when he had a good present working? I often pictured him in a courtroom, using his sway on a jury to set a guilty man free, and now and then I pictured him in a saloon, taking a drink and jawing as he so liked to do. Though I stopped hoping for his letter,

I couldn't entirely stop thinking of him. He was too present in me, the look of him and more, the feel of him. Sometimes when I put my cock to Tom, I thought of doing Wes and likewise, when Tom put it to me, I told myself on occasion it was Wes, never mind how different the men. Fucking was fucking, and long as Tom didn't know my thoughts, all was well.

Every now and then, when I got too wound up in recall, I saw myself as thinking too much. I still read adventures and spoke at length in our library discussion group, but for the life of me I couldn't exhaust thoughts of Wes. When I tried shutting my mind down, I started thinking on the shutting itself so it was no good trying not to think. Then, one night when I couldn't get to sleep, the weather hot, Tom and me both naked in our bunks, a new kind of stir came over me and I got up and took that spot below the window where not a hint of breeze could be felt. Noise on the row had long ceased, the men having worn themselves out and fallen asleep, so I stood in quiet consideration until I finally got my head around an idea that was new to me. The idea was that if thoughts presented themselves as words, why not capture them like I did the pictures for my mind book? Why not write down what I thought? I glanced at the table to recall Wes at work, pencil always busy. I had nothing to study, however, nothing but myself and prison life, but I could set that down or no, something else. Write on Wes. If ever there was a story, it was his, or rather ours.

I told nobody what I was doing and next day began this account which, by early the following year, 1895, neared completion. Though Wes had been gone fourteen months, it took but a few for me to write our story as words tended to pour out in a great flood that warmed rather than drowned me. They brought Wes alive and allowed me to enjoy him again while easing the ache that still troubled my heart. Only thing was, I had no ending. I refused to close it without Wes, but six years remained until I could meet up with him so I pondered on this a great deal with no resolution in sight. Then one day the answer arrived from Wes himself.

"Letter for you, Quick," came the call one Sunday.

"Me?"

Handed the envelope, I was stunned. It was on good paper and marked *El Paso, April 14, 1895*. My address was written in a hand I recognized. I opened it with great care to find a single page and a business card. The card read *John Wesley Hardin, Esq., Attorney at Law*. In the lower left corner it said *200 ½*

El Paso, Wells Fargo Bldg., and in the lower right *Practice In All Courts.* I then took up the letter and read.

"Dear Garland,

"I hope this letter finds you well. As you can see, I achieved my goal, having passed the state bar examination in July. Life has been full, what with family and obligations. I moved to El Paso recently as there is greater opportunity in a bigger place. I have a fine office on the second floor of the Wells Fargo building and look down onto the corner of El Paso and San Antonio streets. Though cases are not easily falling my way, I am doing fine, as are the children. I miss you, Garland. I miss nothing else of those fifteen years inside the walls, but I do miss you. What we had was good. Come to El Paso when you get out. I'll expect to see you.

"Yours, *Wes*"

Here was my ending. Wes was once again making an effort to give me all he could, and I saw in that the resurrected promise of himself. The loss of what I'd never had flew out the window. I would see him again and one day enjoy that promise. He said he expected to see me. Well, see me he would. I sat right down to answer him, which took some time.

"Dear Wes,

"I was very pleased to receive your letter and learn you are now Lawyer Hardin though I never had any doubt on that. All those nights with you hunched over your law books, no way to not become a lawyer. I admire you, Wes, for that and a lot of other things I'll tell you when we meet, as we surely will.

"Life goes here on as you'd expect. I have a new cellmate, Tom Foley, just twenty-three, nice fellow who, like us all, went wrong early on. We get on fine though it catches me off guard at times, hearing someone come in and finding it not you. Too many years together to make an easy switch, but I am working at it. I have acted in two plays and speak in the library discussion group so am well occupied. Goree put me back into the wheelwright shop which certainly took me back. The tunnel is long filled and covered by concrete on which stands a big machine of some new kind I know nothing about. Progress, I am told.

"Not much else going on. Johnny Rose and I remain good friends, Ned Lally died a few months back of heart failure and I do miss him going on as he did. New men come in all the time, some go out. Not bad, but still a grind.

"I have six years left, Wes, and when I am released my intent is to come to El Paso to see you. Wanting that has never left me. I don't stop missing you. I may have tucked you away as necessary to get through the days, but you remain with me always. So count on me in six and I'll buy you a drink. Maybe get up to some mischief together.

"Love, *Garland*"

EPILOGUE

John Wesley Hardin practiced law in El Paso, Texas until August 19, 1895, when he was shot in the back of the head as he stood rolling dice at the bar of the Acme Saloon. He died instantly, never knowing a disgruntled lawman got him. He had enjoyed just eighteen months of freedom and was forty-two years old when he died.

ACKNOWLEDGMENTS

The author wishes to thank Steve Berman for bringing this novel to print, as well as e-book. For all the hard work a novel requires, the physical book is the true reward, and it is refreshing to find a like-minded publisher. Thanks also go to Steve's supporting players who corralled me as needed. Lastly, warm regards as always to William Holden, who shares the journey pretty much by the minute, and Jerry L. Wheeler, who is such a strong and welcome presence in my writing life.

ABOUT THE AUTHOR

DALE CHASE has written male erotica for sixteen years, starting out with contemporary work in magazines and anthologies, and gradually slipping back into the old west where she is happiest among cowboys, lawmen, and outlaws. Her first novel, *Wyatt: Doc Holliday's Account of an Intimate Friendship*, was published in 2012 and has been followed by various e-works including *Crack Shot: Western Erotica*, *Lonely as God*, *The Man I Know*, and *Dime Novel*. Her lawman e-collection *Disturbing the Peace* is due in 2014. She is presently at work on various western novellas while pondering a cowboy detective novel.

CPSIA information can be obtained at www.ICGtesting.com
Printed in the USA
LVOW08s1952121213

365049LV00006B/612/P